They rattled over a ... o
the runway, half w...
prayed they had su... r
there was someone u... e
attempt before it w... was the tanned hijacker
handling the controls, or was it the co-pilot with a gun in
his ear?

The dirt and the slipstream burned his eye. The vibration reinforced the certainty that there was some terrible malfunction in the airframe. He already knew what was wrong. They all knew what was wrong and suffered the pain of it in their bones. They were trapping the pressure of their own slipstream and pounding the fuselage to pieces as they rolled. They were juddering full ahead with the power wide open and going for take-off, and almost certain disaster, with an open door.

Also by Michael Baldwin from Futura

EXIT WOUNDS

MICHAEL BALDWIN

Holofernes

Futura

A Futura Book

First published in Great Britain in 1989
by Macdonald & Co (Publishers) Ltd
London & Sydney

This edition published by
Futura Publications in 1990

*All characters in this publication are fictitious
and any resemblance to real persons, living or dead,
is purely coincidental.*

ISBN 0 7088 4442 1

Printed and bound in Great Britain by
Collins, Glasgow

Futura Publications
A Division of
Macdonald & Co (Publishers) Ltd
66–73 Shoe Lane
London EC4P 4AB

A member of Maxwell Pergamon Publishing Corporation plc

For Maureen Rissik

Holiphernes: (called English Henry in *Jerusalem Delivered*). One of the Christian Knights in the first crusade, slain by Dragutes (book IX).

Brewer: *The Dictionary of Phrase and Fable*

Holophernes: *Master Tubal Holophernes.* The great sophister-doctor who, in the course of five years and three months, taught Gargantua to say his ABC backward.....
Holofernes, in *Love's Labours Lost.* Shakespeare satirises in this character the literary affectations of the Lyly school. An anagram of Joh'nes Florio.

Ibid.

Holofernes: (i) Nebuchadnezzar's general, who was killed by Judith (*Judith*, iv, I etc.).

Harvey: *The Oxford Companion to English Literature*

ONE

1.

Matson had cheeky eyes. They all fell in love with his Irish eyes.

The Avaroc girl was watching his teeth.

They weren't the cleanest bits of plastic in Luton Airport that morning, so he ran his tongue over them carefully before asking, 'How long till boarding?'

'When I'm ready. Time for a drink, anyway.'

Tagging tickets was an unwelcome chore for a stewardess, but they had to do it as part of the security on these Forces' jobs. It gave them a chance to assess the passengers. Matson wondered if she was worth chatting up.

She tore a leaf from his ticket folder, then put a marker on the handle of his luggage. She still stared at his teeth.

'They're my own, you know. I didn't steal them.'

'I'm bound to credit you with some intelligence.'

She examined his eyebrows, his nose, his ears, his cheeks, his chin, as if none of them quite fitted. Then she returned to his teeth. 'A dentist never made anything so ugly,' she said. 'So I put them down to Genesis.'

'It's a long time since they've had any decent conversation. Can we give you dinner out there?'

'What rank are you?'

'I'm a civilian. Would it matter what rank?'

'It says Air Commodore on your warrant.'

He looked at it, surprised. 'So it does. My hosts must have done that at RAF Wildenrath – you know how it is. I'm flying out care of Her Majesty, so I have to have a status. Air Commodore is as low as a civilian can get. Dinner in Düsseldorf, say – or Gladbach, if you're in a hurry?'

A brush-haired queue of other ranks was forming behind him, and they were certainly in a hurry.

She touched her hand to her lapel. A yellow tin badge was pinned to the cloth.

'I've given dinner to lots of girls who wear those.'

It was painted in black: *How dare you presume I'm heterosexual*?

'Or we could find somewhere in Bruggen?'

'My lover wouldn't like it. Besides, I'm working two out and two back.'

The other ranks were breathing. He turned and walked past their unfriendly eyes, looking for the bar. He still felt a sad ache for his two women, one of them out of bounds, one of them dead.

Or he supposed it was for them. It might be his ceaseless hangover.

2.

The bar was packed with noisy people missing their mouths with drink. He was back among his own kind and hating it. All he could be grateful for was that the English didn't bring their buckets and spades anymore, except sometimes to eat with.

He jostled among a shop outing, or perhaps it was a club. The girls were wearing holiday vests with slogans on their tits, things like '*Hello, Myopic*!' or '*These last longer than ice-cream*!', even '*My shoulderblades are on the other side*!' He stopped at '*Home of the Whopper*!', then realised that this was lower, on a maternity fly. Thank God they were labelled for Ibiza, not Germany.

He read his way gravely among them, hesitated at one that said '*Try me in braille*!', and bought himself a pint. It was as full of bad air as the Camden sewers he lived above.

At this third gulp he bumped into the foot. One foot or the

other. Perhaps both of them. He trod backwards and somebody grunted, so he turned to say sorry.

One man was black, one merely tanned. They wore American Air Force uniforms, with flying insignias. Matson wasn't immediately sure about their ranks, even though it was his business to be sure. After all, he had just scraped a leg, trodden on a toe. All he noticed was their quick smiles. He concentrated on their smiles and tried to match them with apologies.

They both carried those little diddy-bags that U.S. aircrew carry, and like Matson they had been eyeing the girls with the labelled tits.

The labelled tits were jostling themselves two by two, or as some say, four by four, into a crocodile and getting ready to board an aircraft.

Matson thought he made an encouraging remark to this effect. The Americans kept right on with their smiling, and didn't say very much.

They had seen someone they knew – a young woman who waved and then joined them. She wore a smart uniform-tunic, and a pleated skirt that didn't seem quite right. Her peaked cap looked like something from an operetta – or did until Matson realised she was a cab driver from one of the jazzier hire firms, and then it appeared much more normal. It was only in a military context that it appalled.

Daft clothes or not, she was gorgeous. Matson felt a distinct perking up of the gonads just to look at her. They couldn't stay bereaved for ever.

She gave the black American a hug and he let her kiss him. 'You left these in the taxi, idiot.' She was holding a Woolworth bag full of cheapo toys. Matson noticed a denture-pink model tractor, and a water-pistol disguised as a spacegun in green see-through plastic.

'And I bet you're checked in,' she scolded. 'Anyway, give the little sods my love!'

Their smiles were their best answer. Someone had a wife and family, perhaps. This was the girlfriend.

The black didn't take the bag from her. His right hand was packaged with buff surgical tape, and he had his flight duffel to manage. His pal took it for him.

The girl left him to go back to her taxi. Her smiled stayed with Matson and he couldn't get rid of it. She was another one of those bits of luck that would never belong to him. There was something familiar about her good looks, too, as if he had already met her; but beauty is like that. You know it as soon as you see it.

The public address system cleared its throat and announced something that excited the other ranks into a gallop. Matson decided it must be his own flight number as well.

He was surprised to see the two Americans had got themselves to the head of the queue.

3.

The final security check was on either side of the electronic scanners. Several Britannia girls were watching the screens, and Matson realised it had always been Britannia Airways in the past whenever he had flown to the British Sector.

There were also some Avaroc uniforms, male and female, scattered about to reassure everyone the firm was properly in business. A pair of redcaps were in attendance as well, hovering near the little conveyor belt and the magnetic door-frames, with what looked like Sterling submachine-guns almost at the ready. It would take a lot of provocation to cause a soldier to open fire with an automatic weapon on a civilian airport, and Matson guessed everyone knew it. There were several thug-haired pseudo-civilians standing nearby in light grey easy-to-identify suits, all with swollen armpits. These would be the ones, using good old Browning pistols with hand-turned wad-cutters up the spout. He wondered whether they were Military Intelligence, the Sass, the Branch, or even some hairies from Ralph Dixon's little bunch. One day he would remember to ask, and Ralph would deal with the question as usual: he would change the subject.

Matson's stewardess had positioned herself between the two redcaps, and her gaze found Matson as soon as he joined the queue.

He was a sight for sore eyes among all this travelling informality, he would give her that. Soldiers on leave and military families in general are hardly the smartest people in the world. There were a lot of Americans, too – it must be party time in NATO – and Americans are American just as aircrew are aircrew. They are different.

Matson wasn't different. Matson was the same. There is no-one so smart as a reluctant member of the officer cast once he dresses up as a soldier dressed as a civilian. Matson was no longer a soldier, but he was going to see old friends at RAF Bruggen, and RAF Wildenrath, then go up to a Mess night with the Airborne Artillery at Gütersloh; and this made him smarter still. He was an ex-soldier dressed up as a soldier pretending to be a civilian, and the result gave the Avaroc girl plenty to grin about.

He examined the deep, blood-coloured shine of his hand-made shoes, the creased cavalry twill – and, by God! cavalry twill was a museum piece, if not a mummy cloth – and remembered his sergeant-major's dictum when he was a rookie in the Paras: 'a bandboy is a bumboy in brasso'. He amused himself briefly. He was smart all right, smart as a bandboy. Then he remembered the expression was 'smart as a bandbox'.

The alarm gong took the smile from his face. The black American had made the body-scanner play a tune, so the redcaps made him step back through the frame again. No-one seemed very alarmed. Apparently body-scanners play more tunes than one to those who have an ear for such things.

One of the Avaroc people went over the black with a manual searcher. He giggled, but didn't say anything. The searcher looked like a hair-dryer, or an elephant's vibrator.

The top pocket of his tunic had rung the alarm. It bristled with metal pens and propelling pencils, in the best U.S. tradition. If Matson had ever shown such a propensity for literacy in his rookie days, he would have been clapped in irons and charged. They did things differently in the States. A soldier was permitted his pen. Airmen could keep half a dozen.

This time the scanner passed their bodies for flight.

It also passed their duffel-bags and their haul of plastic toys. Water-pistols were allowed in passenger cabins this year – provided they were green and transparent, and didn't look real.

People began to laugh. There is nothing like a trifling embarrassment to make a Pongo laugh, especially when it happens to a foreigner. Then their brides began to laugh. Their brides started later and took even longer. So the two Americans laughed, and everybody joined them, especially the other Americans. It was a NATO ha-ha-ha. He was good at laughing, the black one. Even Matson's Avaroc lady laughed, so Matson did as well.

He had never laughed at a plastic water-pistol before. He never would again.

4.

Matson looked at the aircraft as he walked across the tarmac and concrete.

A Trident Three. One of those with not enough wing. He forced himself up the steps and aboard. No-one who's jumped likes flying without a parachute. And no-one who's used a military parachute enjoys getting on an aeroplane in any circumstances.

To distract himself, he wondered about giving the girl another come-on. An air-stewardess must have to cope with a hundred flourishes a day. Besides – how old was he? Too damned old to have a hoick at every woman who matched the fuzzy imprecision of his dreams. Soon his hump would run dry, and there would be no more North Sea oil.

There was no seat allocation by place-numbers, and Matson was last. He sat on the right, in the second row from the front. It was an aisle seat next to two women who spoke to one another as if they were married to senior officers or robots. Matson knew the language well. It matched his smile.

5.

The two Americans were one ahead of Matson and to his left in the front row on the boarding side. The row directly ahead of him was empty. His stewardess had prevented him from sitting there, so he assumed it was reserved for the cabin crew, or an absent Field Marshal. Or perhaps she was continuing to show him she was boss?

Two bits of khaki stooped into the vacant places, and he remembered. The flight guard. They wore khaki berets without insignias, ribbed mud-green pullovers with their shirt epaulettes pulled through the shoulder slots and buttoned over, and black webbing belts and gaiters. Their holsters were raw webbing from the stores, and stencilled with a number and date. These looked selfconsciously naked without either blanco or blacking to smarten them. A holster that means business is tailored to its make of gun; and since a soldier doesn't own a pistol, he doesn't own its holster, so he can't tart it up. He owns a holster, just as he owns a sling for his water-bottle: but water-bottles are standard issue and come in a standard size. Pistols suitable for close-quarter work on aircraft do not.

So far they hadn't come at all. The flight guards' holsters were crumpled and buckled – or as crumpled as webbing could get – and visibly empty. The two men made themselves comfortable in front of Matson, giving him an encouraging view of horizontal headbands, pink necks and close-fitting ears. He remembered the diktat of the Airline Pilots' Association. It had agreed, reluctantly, that trained and nominated personnel should be allowed to carry weapons on particularly sensitive flights – a Ministry of Defence British Sector charter being deemed to be such a one. But the weapons were the direct responsibility of the captain of the aircraft. The captain, and only the captain, would arrange for the issue of all the hardware, just as a skipper at sea makes himself responsible for doling out the cutlasses and grog.

The doors were closed and set at manual. The boarding ramps were pulled away. A Trident Three wasn't a hydraulic bridge job, not at Luton.

Matson took a tug at his seat-belt and received an encouraging smile from the senior ladies next to him. They'd already got themselves a gin from somewhere, presumably their handbags.

People began to buzz, and the buzz grew louder than the air-conditioning. There was a very discomforting smell. The smell of comfort. Space was becoming domestic, as it does on an Israeli bus. There were more women than men, more children than either, and almost more babies than children.

There was a damp note about everything, all bibs, nappies and sweeties. People were unusually relaxed and noisy for passengers waiting for take-off. This wasn't entirely due to the airport bar or the gin in the handbag. Matson knew that some of the wives came home every week – home or shopping or somewhere. It was a heavily subsidised trip, even on an open ticket; and there were plenty of ways of travelling free. They all knew one another, like people from the same village. In terms of their husbands' postings, most of them were.

Matson's air-hostess was in her element now. She stood by the front boarding door holding something that looked like a clock-key. No – not quite that. It was too self-important. It was one of those square- or hexagonal-nippled turn-locks with a T-brace for its handle, big as an old-fashioned bottle-opener. She held it like one and smiled encouragingly – not at the two Americans or the members of the flight guard who were all nearer – but at Matson. It was a heart-warming sign. They thought of bottles and they thought of him. He began to mouth one word – 'Di-n-ner!' – in her direction after all. At least, he thought he did.

He was aware he had a rival, two rivals: the smiling pair of Americans were watching her intently and mouthing at her too. But one of those fellows had a wife, at least one of those fellows; and they had a spare woman between them as well. They were behaving like stereotypes in a film.

He shrugged. They didn't have a chance, not now he'd laid his mind on her – and two fingers of Irish charm.

He watched her for a while and then looked elsewhere. What did he want her for? An evening of sharp talk? He'd found how barbed that could be.

She had a wit like a reamer, and she'd already offered him a sample of toffee-nose and gobology. Her extempore on his teeth had been very brisk, and she couldn't have been properly in gear at half-past nine in the morning. Wait till he'd got her in overdrive.

He looked at her again, and knew that the old psychic surge was flowing in spite of his hangover. There was no denying this pulse of sexual conviction. It never let him down. Something from the woman was calling it on, willing it to be there.

In spite of that silly bit of tin on her blouse she was going to be in bed with him soon. Not in Gütersloh, not in Düsseldorf, most probably not in Germany at all, but in some cosy woman-place in England when he was through with his booked-up military nights. He was going to be riffling her little body open, somewhere and sometime when he felt better than now, with no guilty leftovers from grief, and without his stupid cavalry-twill sensibility. Riffling it and rifling it, then calling up the field-guns for a sublunary stonk and total overrun, probably at tank-light. He grinned. The wolf is not worshipped for its teeth.

She was still smiling, smiling at someone, smiling at something, when the plane intercom rang its silly little bells and one of those educated South London voices began to display the usual Capital Radio confidence in its surgical replacement of all terminal consonants by a Pils-in-your-ear glottal-stop.

Matson began to translate and heard: '*Ten-twenty-three ... a couple of minutes to go while we wait to clear for take-off Luton – RAF Bruggen at ten-twenty-five ... weather at Bruggen reliably informed is hazy very hot clearing to sunshine very hotter ...*'

After the general applause, the intercom continued: '*Should have said I'm Captain Lyall speaking, Captain Finch is my first officer, and Sally Sherman who is now standing at the front of the aircraft is your chief steward.*'

Matson was grateful for her name. He watched her turn to unlock a cabinet panel on the bulkhead just beyond the passenger door.

'*This flight is, as you know, an MOD charter, and this plane will be in the in-flight command of Major Wellard-Browne, in uniform at the front right of the passenger cabin. Major Wellard-Browne will be assisted as flight guard by Sergeant-major Brownskill and by Sergeant Mulhearn. Sergeant Mulhearn is sitting with Major Wellard-Browne. Sergeant-major Brownskill is stationed at the rear of the aircraft.*'

Sally Sherman turned a reassuring smile on everyone but mostly, Matson swore, on Matson. She had the corner catches in the cabinet open now, and lowered its detachable front panel to the floor.

There were two submachine-guns in the cabinet, with their

butts folded. There were also three standard Browning automatic pistols.

The girl leant towards them, stretching out her hands for the pistols in a ritual display of arming the flight guard.

As she did so, the plane began to back and turn, before taxi-ing to take-off.

She hesitated. In the instant, she was swatted against the panel. A black indentation was chiselled into her blouse. Blood from her chest splashed between her forearms and hit the gun-rack, taking her tinny little badge with it.

Meanwhile the intercom explained: '*The flight guard will be armed* …'

Blood filled the hole in Sally Sherman's back, and something glowed among the wreckage of her shoulderblades like the tube of a spent firework. She slid down the bulkhead, and the tube cooled. It was the stump of a metal propelling pencil.

The detonation still throbbed in the ear. It echoed like a grenade, not like any gun that Matson knew. There was thick smoke at the front of the cabin, some dangerous-looking embers and a scattering of sparks.

The smell was not acrid enough for cordite. There was too much afterburn.

The black American at the front was standing up. Both Americans were standing up. The green plastic water-pistol had its barrel bound in deep swathes of surgical tape from the black's right hand. The muzzle was split wide open. It smoked excessively, darkly, as if it had been primed with old-fashioned black powder.

Old-fashioned black powder had just swatted the flight-girl's chest all over the cupboard.

The girl was sinking too sedately for the tanned American. He gestured her shattered thorax aside, and lifted the three Brownings from the rack, just as the intercom added: '*In the event of an attempted hijack please keep to your seats and sit low, as there will be a shoot-out.*'

The black American was bleeding. Or Sally Sherman had bled on him. His friend had hold of the cabin microphone now, also situated by the all-commanding front passenger-door. He used it to override the flight-deck announcement by saying: '*You hear what the man says, ladies and gentlemen. You've had your shoot-out. Now we're all going home. So keep to your seats and sit low.*'

His phrasing was American, but he spoke the kind of English you hear on the lips of an educated Gulf Arab. He sounded even more American and even less Arab, when he chuckled and added, for the benefit of someone unseen, '*Better get that jelly out of your pants before it blows your balls off!*'

He smiled again. He tossed a gun to his black companion and passed another to someone sitting further back. The third he kept for himself. He pointed it straight at Matson. Then he pulled the trigger.

6.

Matson knew that the gun was pointing at him just as certainly as he knew that Sally had smiled at him. Nobody mistakes a thing like that. He had no time to duck, no time to flinch, not even Matson who was used to guns.

He was wrong.

The soldier in front of him gave a tiny gasp of surprise, one of those phlegmy little tuts that stay in the throat. Then his head lolled towards the passenger aisle, and his shoulder followed in the dislocated fashion of those who are stunned or anaesthetised or abruptly dead. It was Major Wellard-Browne, of the threaded epaulettes. Sergeant Mulhearn did not stoop towards him or assist him in any way. The sergeant sat absolutely still and concentrated on problems of his own.

The gun had been pointing towards Matson but not aimed at him. The major was in the way. The major came first. What was surprising was that the bullet had stopped with him.

That suggested a reduced charge. The propellant had been doctored for use in a pressure cabin. The interesting question for someone as contemptuous of automatics as Matson was: would anything less than a full charge produce enough gas to recock the pistol and chamber another round? It didn't seem likely the armourers would make a mistake, but the thought nagged him. He kept his mind on it to stop giving way to shock. He tried to do the necessary sums as he watched the hijackers. For the minute, he had no will to act. Shock had got the better of him. He was part of the stunned silence of the aircraft.

His part of the silence reached a bleak conclusion. The Browning had to be fully charged or it wouldn't work, not in all circumstances. Wellard-Browne must be wearing a flak-vest under that pullover. He looked bulky enough. Otherwise the bullet would have gone through him and killed Matson too. A flak-vest wouldn't keep out a twelve-hundred-foot-per-second job point-blank. But it would keep it in.

A baby cried. Its mother hushed it, but the crying grew louder. The baby was howling for them all.

7.

Too much was happening. He was organising himself against the overall danger, not yet the details of it.

For example, he had seen the girl die, and looked to understand the manner of her death. Then he had watched the pistols being snatched down and distributed. Yet already, and unnoticed, the two submachine-guns had gone from the rack as well.

The tanned hijacker held one. He cocked it and went through to the flight cabin. The Browning was now stuffed into his cloth belt. That might give someone a chance.

The black still waved his Browning. He waved it with two hands covered in his own blood – though, God knows, there was plenty of Sally Sherman's everywhere. The damage was to his left palm. The improvised pistol had burst and cracked it open. It was a blast wound, not a cut. It would obey its own rules. It might close quickly, or never, or not until stitched. The immediate danger was in his temper. The smiles were all gone, were irrelevant now anyway. His wound hurt enough to make him rage. He was clenching and unclenching his fingers – not a good idea for someone with a gun in his hands.

The submachine-gun carried forward was an Ingram 10 or 11 with its long suppressor fitted – presumably to reduce its velocity. The extra length had made it look like a Sterling sitting in the rack; they both had. The tanned hijacker had cocked it, extravagantly, splaying his hand across the top of it like a concert-pianist. Matson hoped he had tapped the safety on by now – or at least stopped flourishing it.

The aircraft was standing still, only about five hundred yards from the terminal building. Matson hadn't noticed when they had ceased taxiing – not at once, certainly. The girl had been killed more or less as they had begun to back out. Presumably the flight crew had not heard the detonation. Was it the shot fired into Wellard-Browne that had halted them? Or had one of the cabin staff touched a signal button?

Now was the danger-time. The captain of the aircraft would seek instructions from the control-tower. The hijackers would refuse to let him obey them. Or they would make demands and the control-tower would reject them. Perhaps the control-tower would pretend to propose or impose some reasonable delay. He doubted it. There would be only one message, certainly only one overriding fact. The aircraft was not going to fly. It would never leave the airport. Luton was prepared for this above all else.

This was not an ordinary hijack, if there ever was such a thing: the flight did not carry a normal manifest. The plane was full of British servicemen and service families, and a few NATO guests. Vehicles would be moved to surround and isolate it on the concrete. The pagoda boys would already be on the way from Hereford, probably by air. So there would be an hour or two of sitting and waiting, then a lot of unavoidable sorrow.

It was then that the face appeared at the front of the aircraft. It had two chins and a painted diagonal crease-mark halfway up, just like a clown's. Matson's mind told him clown because the mouth was too big and too red and the nose was bulbed into a cherry. He took a second or two to realise that the cosmetics all flowed from the crease-mark, which was too bruised for bleeding, and that the nose and the mouth were broken, presumably from being hammered into by one of the square edges of the Ingram. The double chin might be the result of another weal, a broken jaw, or a generally flabby and evasive personality. Matson had these thoughts randomly, like a drunk trying to do his buttons up, before he noticed the face bled above an Avaroc uniform, with captain's piping round the sleeve. This must be Captain Lyall of the South London voice. He'd obviously had enough spunk to get in the hijacker's way.

The sight of him drove the black one into an unrehearsed frenzy. He pranced up and down, till the mess on the floor impeded his feet.

The captain stopped to identify the dead matter of his cabin-crew, and got the Browning rammed into his face for his trouble.

The black shouted. He shouted in Arabic, and jerked the door open. For a second or two, his gun was on nobody; but it waved at everybody. Matson sat tight. You don't bug a nutter when he's in a screaming whinny, particularly when you've got to detach yourself from an aircraft seat and turn a corner to get to him. Especially with two dead bodies and a damaged flight officer blocking the way. That was how it struck Matson, and it was clear that Sergeant Mulhearn didn't see the matter any differently.

There was that third member of the hijack team behind them, too, the one that had been passed the Browning. Perhaps there was a fourth. The other Ingram had gone somewhere.

An unpleasant smell slowly filled the cabin, the kind of smell a plane-load of people produces when a take-off aborts too far up the runway. It was this smell that made the black earn his first real hiss of protest. He kicked the body at his feet. A man shouted, but stopped when the gun pointed at the shout. Sally's body was being booted towards the door.

It didn't have far to go, but it was awkward to move. The limb-weight made it heavy, and the girl's legs had to travel furthest. The arms and the head must have draped quickly over the sill. She was beneath Matson's eyeline, but he supposed it was her legs that were difficult to move, particularly by stirring with the boot.

Captain Lyall crouched forward, to help or to hinder, but the girl went without him. She made a nasty sound on the concrete. The smell got better. The tiny rocket that had killed her hadn't been selective about the contents of her thorax and abdomen.

The black cheered up. He gestured towards the sergeant in

front of Matson, his fingers still twitching on the trigger, and said, 'On your feet, *mudíir*.'

Mulhearn stood slowly, his body hunched forward as if expecting a bullet.

'Pick him up, *walad*, and throw him out.'

Mulhearn straddled Wellard-Browne, and tried to extricate the Major's legs from the seat. He started by jamming his own. Captain Lyall stooped again and helped. Nobody else moved.

They carried the shot man to the door. He had been hit high in the chest, and the bullet had probably severed one of the big blood vessels above the heart. He was much too quiet for hope, too badly injured if alive to have made a decent job of feigning death.

The two men paused at the door, unhappy to drop him out.

The black cocked the Browning, so they dropped him.

'You too,' the black said.

Captain Lyall and Sergeant Mulhearn looked at him cautiously. Was 'you too' a command or a sentence of death?

He was telling them to jump. Mulhearn turned and jumped immediately. It was the liveliest thing Matson had seen him do and he fully applauded his decision. This might be the man's only chance. Besides, the black was daft to order a trained observer out of the plane, and he might change his mind.

He didn't change his mind. He gave Captain Lyall an even closer look at the pistol.

'The passengers are my responsibility,' the ruined mouth mumbled, as emphatically as it could. It started on something else, then gagged on the pistol. The pistol backed the plane's captain into the doorway. His poor bruised face gave him no option. He could be backed out or blown out, and everybody knew it.

He didn't jump. He anchored himself on the door frame to shout round the muzzle of the gun: 'You can see I have no choice, everyone. Do as you are asked and keep your courage up. This aircraft isn't going anywhere. Not until we come back to fly you home!' He began to lower himself down the door frame, then put his feet and legs out until he was hanging from the sill. Then, presumably, he dropped.

There was a little round of applause at this, a derisive

whistle or so at the hijackers. Matson gave the captain full marks, and hoped to live long enough to say so somewhere it would count. Captain Lyall was absolutely right in one particular. This aircraft wasn't going anywhere.

Someone on the flight-deck hadn't heard him. The Trident moved. Its turbines surged and it nosed forward and kept on going. It wasn't taxi-ing either. Without clearance, and before it was properly aligned on a runway, the thing was starting to roll. It was revving to full power and going for take-off, without even a preliminary run-up on the brakes.

Another tailplane moved beside them, veered towards them, crowded into the window and was left behind. They charged between stationary aircraft, outbuildings, fuel-bowsers, baggage-cars, guidance tractors and passed a relay-hut, its grid's strobing rotation emphasising the witlessness of their progress.

Somebody shouted. Somebody else yelled in panic, the voice rising to an asexual scream. Or perhaps Matson only imagined it, and the terror was a vibration filling his own head as he was hurtled into his most recurrent nightmare. He was trapped in a runaway plane that was also a train that was also a rollercoaster just about to dive off a cliff higher than the clouds, tall as the brain gets in the delirium of a fever. It was the way he always felt one second out from the Hastings' door, straining for the statischute to open. And the minute he recognised the fear he could wake from it.

The grass in the window was more grey than green, its colour fading with speed. They rattled over a lip of smooth tarmac, and yawed onto the runway, half weightless but nowhere near flight. He prayed they had sufficient concrete ahead to reach V2, or there was someone up front with enough clout to abort the attempt before it was too late. Was the tanned hijacker handling the controls, or was it the co-pilot with a gun in his ear?

The dirt and the slipstream burned his eye. The vibration reinforced the certainty that there was some terrible malfunction in the airframe. He already knew what was wrong. They all knew what was wrong and suffered the pain of it in their bones. They were trapping the pressure of their own slipstream and pounding the fuselage to pieces as they rolled. They were juddering full ahead with the power wide open and going for take-off, and almost certain disaster, with an open door.

TWO

1.

Three – no, four – stewardesses came forward and literally elbowed the black aside. There was only room for two of them, but they struggled with the door. These Avaroc ladies would all have to be killed one by one before they were dissuaded from the disciplines of the job.

There was nothing they could do in such a slipstream.

One of them fell to arguing with the black. She wanted to go through to the flight-deck. He let her go past him again.

If this didn't get her head blown off, nothing would.

The Trident juddered as it rolled. It was going to find it hard to build enough speed with the door dragging and with the spill of pumped-up air from the cabin.

Reverse thrust came on, fought their forward speed for what seemed forever, while stomachs churned sickly; the turbines almost turned themselves inside out till the brakes whined, smoked up and bit, and the aircraft sunk its nose as its weight hurried ahead of itself. The G-force was incredible, a sinus pain at the bottom of the skull as if the neck had been whipped with a pistol. The tanned hijacker had seen sense at last, or somebody else had shown him some sense – the flight stewardess or the co-pilot.

It was only a check, not a halt, not even a delay.

They weren't stopped yet.

They weren't stopped and they weren't going to stop.

The aircraft began to turn. As it did so, the three girls got the door closed.

Then screamed and flattened themselves down.

The turbines roared back to full thrust. The Trident slewed out of a 180° turn without checking on its brakes, and went for a full-throttle roll *downwind*.

Whoever was flying the plane – there was no doubt who was in charge – had eluded the attempts to block them off, and was now doing a roll the wrong way for the weather and totally against the other traffic.

The black braced himself against the weapons cabinet and everybody else sank to the floor, or to the staff fold-down seats.

The ladies beside Matson were hang-jawed, their faces white and gormless as clouds. Beyond them, a windsock whizzed past the window. It was pointing the wrong way, of course. It was pointing the way to ruin.

The strain underneath was massive, they were going some seventy knots too fast for this type of plane on this sort of concrete, but the vibration was already dying, they were beginning to drift on their own air-bounce, on a springboard of downthrust for take-off.

There was a bang as if they'd run something over, like a motorbike or small shed. Matson guessed it was a tyre blowing, but they didn't veer. They were already up in a flat climb to pass beneath a 747 that loomed out of nowhere. The giant body squatted on top of them, clung, then screamed away like a huge bird who'd been trying to mate.

They passed *among* the high-rises of Luton town, and none of those rises far. Matson watched the world flying past him in airborne towers. There were typists leaving their VDUs to look down on him with erased faces. The Trident printed out in a hundred windows. The windows shocked. The windows oscillated. The windows shattered. The typists glistened with awe.

There were housewives dropping cakemix ready to write to their local MP or weekly paper, or strafe the airport on the phone. But that would need sanity, and their world wasn't sane.

A tower zoomed close. Nose shock shook its panes out. Concrete uncladded. Stressed sheets scattered like confetti.

The Trident banked to starboard. It tickled a double-decker

bus with its wing, then with the right ear of Matson's second lady, who began to retch and vomit.

Vomit was an offering. The Great God of Aeroplanes already had his breakfast of blood. The tail dropped sickeningly and they started to climb. They climbed steeply.

They hung on the apex of their first lift, the woman's mouth choking on its panic. It was neat gin she was spilling, that and tomato skins – or perhaps her lungs were made of plastic. Together they made one of the wittier smells around. Then they powered again.

For the moment they were flying what Matson's sergeant-major once called 'a two-hundred-holer latrine'. It was full of bad air and steaming up at three hundred and fifty knots straight into the window of the sun.

2.

The first thought is: thank God for this moment. I am alive for now.

Matson was not exempt from such a feeling. He had learned many lessons from danger in his time. The best of them was to be selfish. Being timid came later, but he learned that too.

A softer face smiles over Catholics, however lapsed. That face had informed him during a rare moment of prayer that he'd seen enough action; he must kiss it goodbye. In return she might do him a favour.

He thought he was bleeding to death from a wound that defied tourniquet, so he agreed to her terms. He'd had his bellyful. He had the bullet holes to prove it. Mercifully not in the belly. The Mother of God in her mercy had left his appetite alone.

So he gave up the tough life.

He did so before it was ready to do as much for him. You can't crawl from Hell in a hurry, especially when the left calf-muscles are no longer attached to the ligaments of the knee. The mercury in the bullet had seen to that – mercury or a little Christian cross some Druse had carved in the nipple of a 7.6mm before sending it to Matson. Or perhaps the round had simply spun in off a stone.

He had been hospitalised in Beirut when there were hospitals in Beirut. The surgeons had told him the mercury, the splinters or the cross had entered his tibialis muscles and fragmented somewhere between them to rip out the end of the gastrocnemius and most of the short saphenous vein. You remember things like that. 'You'll never go varicose,' they said.

So he did a year as adjutant, and another year in a desk job at Defence. Then he'd gone to work with Leonard who reported direct to the Minister of State.

Thank God for this moment. I am alive for now. I shall thank you, Holy Mother, to remind me in due course to thank you again. I shall make you an offering of a candle. Not down in Camden where I live in your mercy, and where my smelly Irish pray. But up there in the little church in Hampstead where your light will burn clean.

He regretted this flight and this aircraft. But he thanked God because She had already granted three mercies.

The first was that he was alive and airborne, and not a contributory cinder in a molten furnace of alloy and putrid hyanogen somewhere on the Luton perimeter. The second was that the 747 had, by a ginger whisker, similarly failed to reduce them. The third was that the bullet had stayed with Major Wellard-Browne.

Beyond that he had little hope. He had almost exhausted adrenalin and prayer, so he let the truth depress him.

The killing had begun, and it had begun too early. There was no reason to suppose it was at an end. Two people were dead. At least one more had been brutally beaten. That one was the captain of the aircraft. In spite of the horrors of his voice, Captain Lyall had proved himself a captain and a half. So the hijackers had jettisoned him.

The aircraft was now being handled by the First Officer alone, assisted or impeded by the tanned hijacker. Or the hijacker himself was flying. Judging from the take-off, it might be the latter. Unless the First Officer was injured or under impossibly restrictive duress.

Wherever it was bound for, the aircraft was not necessarily fitted to get there, nor the First Officer qualified to land it there.

Then there were the abnormal factors in the passenger cabin. He had reminded himself of these more often than he had forgotten to commend himself to Mary Mother of God.

There were too many children. Children were trouble. They were noisy, untimid, undisciplined, hard to confine and likely to cause friction. They wanted the lavatory when lavatories were not allowed, and water when there was no water to be had. As a matter of record, whenever there was disaster through frustration on a long-running hijack, a child was the cause of it a – a child or its mother.

Too many children meant too many mothers. Mothers were even more trouble than their children. Mothers became shrill, were incautious and premature to act if they thought their offspring were threatened. They were likely to be thoroughly human in this totally inhuman situation.

Yet it was the male element in these families that worried Matson most.

Many of the men on the aircraft had been trained to violent action. They were young. They were aggressive. They were as fit as Matson had ever been, and their minds were alert to conflict, their reflexes fully programmed. And they would be defending their own. Luton to RAF Bruggen was a family bus.

There were also men without families, as well as a considerable number of NATO guests, mostly American: these would be like the single English, without the inhibition of blood.

Unless, like Matson, they had experienced enough mayhem to make them circumspect.

Otherwise, they would be weighing themselves against the three or possibly four hijackers, and the five automatic guns. Two of those guns, the Ingrams, had a devastating rate of fire.

And what had the tanned hijacker said about jelly?

Even if he were bluffing and there was no explosive on board, it was still a terrible equation: a large number of determined and trained men and women against a few fanatics with automatic weapons.

It was the old genetic recipe for self-destruct, as brewed by *Homo erectus habilis sapiens* since the dawn of Neanderthal time.

Self-destruct was the ugly, ungrammatic but expressive Americanism for the ugliness about to happen. You have to be brutal with language to describe brutal events.

3.

One thing was as sickeningly certain as the miasma of child puke that mixed itself with the sweat for action and joined the visceral fumes of death and fear already in the air-conditioning ducts: they were *not* bound for RAF Bruggen, or RAF or USAF Anywhere. Nor, surely, for any civilian airport in the Federal German Republic.

Rome was no more than a possibility. The Italians had a patchy record on extortion; but the hijackers must nevertheless assume the Italians would be forced to stop them. Italy was a member of NATO. The Italians would be bound to try. If they showed any tremors of indecision, the British would slap their wrists and the Americans set fire to their arses.

'*Dead children smell!*' The black hijacker had the intercom again. '*Keep your kids in their seats!*'

The aircraft was over bleak salt water, its waves grubby in spite of the sunshine. Children had been reacting to an aerial view of the seaside. Now their parents took care they stopped reacting.

The sun was on the left. This meant it was dirty English Channel water not dirty North Sea water. The hijackers were opting for the slower French reaction. The French would weigh everything up, they would be resolute and calm, and no-one would push them around. When they chose to act it would be in their best national interest and the aircraft would already be half an hour beyond French air-space.

'*Don't take no attention of what's out the window. Pay no notice. The people with the guns is in here.*'

The messages seemed chillier by the instant, and no-one thought to scoff at their misuse of English. Matson had a fit of Irish high-snob – the sort of spasm that anxiety often brings – and was just deciding that 'take no attention' and 'pay no notice' were pretty standard Pongo talk anyway – when his eye was taken by an RAF roundel, then the top-camouflage of a jet interceptor boring past the starboard window before settling back alongside with a shock-waving half-roll and a brief glimpse of underblue like a schoolgirl's knickers. A Phantom. This was what had been exciting the children.

Its twin was already on station on the other side, porpoising up and down beyond the port windows.

The mood inside the aircraft became distinctly buoyant, for a whole ten seconds. Then the black sucked blood from his left hand and gave them a Grendel grin with the red still dripping, while he showed them the gun in his right. He licked the slime from his teeth as if he'd been eating an orange, and they whitened back to a scowl. It was a neat enough conjuring-trick; but nothing like the transformation in his looks between Luton and now.

His hand hurt too much for their comfort. He shook it towards them, his red badge of courage. He printed it on the bulkhead for them, trying to ease its pain or simply to sign his intention. He was flaunting his pawmark, giving it space. He might live to regret such rashness later. So might they all, if he needed flame to erase it.

Meanwhile, the RAF jets were entirely superfluous, a gesture of solidarity at most. Matson guessed his fellow passengers felt much as the crew of a submarine feels when the divers tap on the hull. Their message was the same: There's no way we'll get you out, but we'll be as close as we can while you suffocate.

He did not know the drill in such cases. Perhaps there wasn't one. The interceptors must have been flown to put a pressure on the flight-deck, nothing more. They wouldn't be 'shadowing' the Avaroc Trident in any meaningful sense of the word: it was already being plotted by European air-traffic-control radar, by NATO radar, and presumably by satellite all over the world.

This flight was not going to get lost. Getting lost was the least of their worries.

He wondered if there was radio contact between Luton and the flight-deck, or between the RAF fighters and the flight-deck on the flick frequency, and if so how much. What details were known to the people on the ground? Were they in possession of the aircraft's destination, or the hijacker's motives and demands?

Much more important: when, if ever, would the distraction come? How would it be orchestrated?

For a moment they lacked a conductor. The roundels had changed. The mud was behind them, and so were the Phantoms. They were over France now, in a jumble of Mirages. Matson counted six. The French were laying their disapproval on the line in unnecessary numbers.

Meanwhile, he was at the front of the aircraft, the male who sat closest to one of the guns. He wondered when to start being a hero. He thought in about half an hour's time. Half an hour can last days.

4.

France took just long enough for Matson to remember something he had been taught when he first transferred from the Paras to the Thugs. He had learnt it in pain, and now he was forced to recall it in pain.

'Sooner or later,' the lecturer had said, while gently pricking at his cheek with a Stanley knife, 'sooner or later each of youse has got to learn and accept that his blood's not only piss, but stagnant piss.'

The lecturer was a sergeant and Matson was a full lieutenant, though neither of them were allowed marks of rank. Still, he was being held face down by the hair while he knelt at the other one's feet, and the liquid that was trickling down his cheek and into his mouth tasted like blood, so he thought his instructor was pushing things a bit too far.

'You've also got to learn and accept that your piss is overpriced as well. Or you have if you're going to be any good to us here.' The knife was being twisted now, and so was Matson's hair, so that twelve years later his face still bore the scar. 'The brave man ...' the instructor went on, 'the brave man is the man who ...'

It was then that Matson jerked from the knife, twisted the hand in his hair, and sent his right foot scything at the other's shin. Or it was then that he struck out on this multiple and carefully rehearsed adventure.

He was impeded by something like a pillar of reinforced concrete collapsing on his head.

Matson was good at unarmed combat. When he struck a blow it always went clean through and nothing stopped it, but the sergeant hadn't even flinched.

The block of concrete on his head had stopped it. The block of concrete was a third man's fist, a man whose existence Matson hadn't even guessed at.

Nobody laughed. There were twenty-three other men watching, but they all knew that their turn would come.

After a while Matson found he could concentrate again. As the instructor was saying, 'Some people have wax in their ears and some have weakness. Can you hear me, weakness? "The brave man," I was saying, "the brave man is not the man who refuses to eat shit. The brave man is the man who swallows it humbly and waits to kill the man who's fed it to him".' His instructor paused now, and removed the Stanley knife and let go of Matson's hair. 'When a man is feeding you shit, you can be sure he's waiting for you to protest about it. He's got his big guns waiting while he manipulates your anger. I can see you don't like shit. Well, I don't like your lack of intelligence, either. Sir.'

Matson remembered all this when the sergeant-major from the flight guard came down the centre aisle of the plane.

The sergeant-major had a little blood on his face. It didn't flow from his cheek, as it happened; but from his right eyebrow, the eyebrow nearest to Matson. The eyebrow was deeply disfigured, but the cut was irregular and did not produce much blood.

A lot can happen all unnoticed and unknown at the back of an aircraft when you are discouraged from turning your head.

The sergeant-major wore his neck-tie twice round the middle of his face, gagging open the mouth, crushing his nose. His hands were tied behind him with a little piece of wire round the thumbs. Someone at the back had done this to him. Alternatively, someone – a man or woman with the Ingram perhaps – had ordered someone else to do it.

Someone else had discovered that their blood was piss and

gone ahead and done what they were told.

Sergeant-major Brownskill did as he was instructed by the gun somewhere at his back – a gun that could be pointing into a child's ear – and came down the aisle with measured tread to stand a little way beyond Matson in front of and beside the black hijacker with the sore hand.

Who smashed him with the Browning, once, twice, thrice to the left side of the face, once certainly on the left temple.

Sergeant-major Brownskill stood until the third blow, then collapsed as if boneless, crumpling backwards at Matson's feet.

Matson was pretty sure he was dead. If he wasn't, he soon would be with that monstrous gag choking him. He stooped forward to pick at the necktie. He saw the American uniform coming closer, or the legs of the uniform, but he went on picking just the same. The knot wouldn't loosen. He was waiting for the first blow to fall, and wondering how to react to it.

He smelled milled steel and gun-oil, and the Browning was stroking his nose, then grating against his teeth.

Was he brave enough to eat shit and kill the man who fed it to him? No: his blood was piss. It always had been. Or it was with the Ingram there behind him.

'Better take that gag off,' the black said. 'You can use it to tie his feet.'

Matson did what he could, but none of this increased his opinion of himself – or of his own or anybody else's chances. They had killed three times, perhaps four times, within the hour. Normally, hijackers threaten before they kill; and their murders, when they commit them, constitute the beginning of the end.

With these, killing was their way of threatening. So far, the agenda had been all theirs.

Perhaps – bleak thought – the passengers weren't hostages, merely victims, a much less complicated consideration.

In which case, the hijackers had no need to strike a bargain, felt no necessity to wait. What they wanted was British servicemen dead. Or American servicemen dead. Or to strike a terrorist blow against NATO or the West.

Matson had pumped Brownskill's chest for several long minutes, but he couldn't detect a flutter.

He looked up to find mountains beyond his window, an angular saw of Alp. The aircraft was much too low.

5.

He did not claim to be knowledgeable about airports.

He identified Innsbruck with alarm.

He knew it was Innsbruck because he recognised the mountain. The aircraft had to nose up to clear the ridge. They shouldn't have been coming this way at all, but perhaps only Matson was aware of that.

The woman in the next seat was putting a brave but ginny face on things. Then a sunstruck crag, a mile-high crazy paving of ice, thrust itself into her window like Manhattan burning its lights, and a ski-lift pylon seemed to jump up this side of the wing.

The plane fell like a lift.

It dropped bowel-first, and if anyone screamed the noise was left behind in the sky. Nobody could move.

Nobody but the woman at his side.

She had been painting some lips on her face. She now closed her compact with a snap that could have got them shot, save no-one could shoot. The hijack was marooned in weightlessness, the black slumped against the bulkhead with his howl jammed open, just like Matson. His gun hand was steady, but his aim was unfocused, his grip catatonic.

Now was the time to stand the hijack on its head, but the plane was funneling down an airpocket, the world about to die; and nobody moves in a plummeting aircage.

The lady further over had a long-drawn-out moment beneath her tartan skirt. They would have to be very tolerant about it later; but there wasn't going to be a later. Besides, she had been sitting closer to the crag and pylon than he had.

The aircraft stopped falling and settled for a dive.

He knew it was Innsbruck's mountain because he had climbed here once. Then there had been that lousy winter holiday with a girl who wanted to ski instead of staying wrapped up with schnapps, and a mazagran and Matson.

It wasn't a ski-pylon they had nearly hit. It was a cable-run, and they bellied towards it again, lower down, stalling downhill like a bird in the crag air. Then they were parting branches of cloud and big lumps of valley-shadow to perch themselves into mist, drooping through nothing, the window all over wet as they went stinking down into rain.

He tried to remember the girl's name, to remember and stay alive. She was married by now, or divorced, and she had hair that had struck him as funny when clouding her face in bed, too curly, or was it too straight? Too dark or too palely transparent, and sexless under the shower just like this bloody mist.

Everything was throttled back. It was no good the black fella shouting into the public address system and waving his gun. Matson had gone quite deaf. The turbines had died. The world wasn't speaking anymore, except for his neighbour, who was mouthing dumb-talk. Her friend was waiting for death in her sleep.

His ears unblocked. They poppled into life. He heard all there was to hear: the silent aftermath of terror. The plane had blundered too near the vortices of the mountains and had nearly fallen from the sky as a result. Now its whole cargo of passengers was listening back at him, blinking its eye. One child whimpered, one child only. Anxiety was being reborn. It was gagged by a kiss or a hand, did a little gargle of protest. The air-conditioning fans seemed to be their only source of power. His fear became intellectual now, *real*. It did not belong to a coward any more. It was worse than the fear a coward feels. It was his mind saying quietly: this is one of the most difficult airport approaches in Europe, even when the meteor is clear. You fly a narrow valley with the Alps on either side. You fly a narrow valley that does a dog-leg turn. If you drift off by even a degree you collide with God.

An unprepared second pilot was flying them in and into an unprepared airport – an unprepared second pilot or an amateur. Matson remembered the second pilot's habitual moan in documentary after documentary: *I don't get to practise many landings. I do the take-offs*. He'd seen this one's take-off. What would his landing be like?

6.

The aircraft veered sharply to port. The pilot was taking them where there was no room to go, and then fighting shy and banking again. Matson felt pain in the jawbone, the pith of the teeth, and heard two hundred people clench on the tightness of the turn. His nose and eyes flooded, just as at the end of a long free-fall.

He prayed they were moving *towards* space, not just *away* from the huge wall of crag above them on the right – altering course on instruction from the ground or at least from a very clear image on the in-board radar. To the north there were those vertical kilometres of trouble – one of the great crag formations of Europe uplifted in a seemingly endless line; but the south had its mountains too, mere eight-to-ten-thousand-footers but still as high as Snowdonia stood on Cumbria planted on dear Ben Bulben's back.

It was south they were turning then, but inside these twin restraints; for the southern peaks were too close, and the storm was making from south; so a turn with the port wing down tightened till it seemed to Matson like a 'wing-over' – one of his least favourite manoeuvres, even in a light aircraft, with his own hand on the stick.

They were spiralling their height away, tangled in this sheep-gut cloud; and if ever there was a moment to get busy, that moment was now. The only hijacker he could see was the black, and the black was braced against the axis of the turn to keep himself in a posture of command. As it happened, he looked about as commanding as a gerbil in a spindle – though, like a gerbil's, his reflexes might be quick.

Yes, now was the moment for all good men to grow busy.

One gentleman in cavalry-twill trousers became very busy indeed. He couldn't see the Ingram behind him, but the Ingram might be sitting very comfortably on a seat and able to fire straight down the passenger cabin even if the passenger cabin was upside down.

He became busy with his fingers only. His fingers had long since found their way to his wallet pocket, but with such an overall air of apology that they were unlikely to be nailed by gunfire. Now, having scratched his wallet's heart, they had discovered the terrible object they craved and were stroking it until it rolled itself into a comfortable little cylinder.

This cylinder, palmed between the two middle fingers of his left hand – there were ladies on his right, and such people are unpredictable, hysterical, or – worse – think you are stroking them by the knee; they have ankles further down, just where your own ankles should be, past this uncomfortable clutter beneath the too-cramped aircraft seat – this cylinder was in his exposed left hand, which was stealing down his own calf to tickle his own ankle, there, just where something was fidgeting the pattern on his socks. A flea, perhaps?

The cylinder was at last snug inside his ox-blood hand-made shoe, and his whole intelligence felt better for it. That cylinder had been a tremendous kindness and honour intended him by his hosts at RAF Wildenrath. It would have ensured him VIP treatment wherever he went in the Sector. But the little word Commodore on his warrant in a hijack would single him out for whatever was special around here. A touch of the Wellard-Browne's, perhaps? And the major was only a major.

He now wore the honour where honours feel comfortable – under his sock.

7.

Matson felt oddly elated at his success in this spiritual exercise. He had managed to concentrate on his personal anxiety about the hijack while living through his imminent death in a plane-crash.

The feeling didn't last. He could now be consumed by the plane-crash.

So was everyone else. He had the local knowledge, but they all shared the feeling in the gut.

He had recognised the mountain. It was the Hafelekar Spitze or even the Rumer Spitze – one of twin crests in a rampart of ice. His identification had been immediately confirmed by the shocking closeness of the cable railway.

That meant that instead of groping their way along the valley approach, they had come in right on top of the town.

They had scraped over a three-kilometre-high crest ten kilometres at most from the airport. No wonder their dive had ended in this impossible turn.

Presumably they had opted out of the landing pattern in order to avoid a refusal: they would claim an overriding necessity – shortage of fuel, almost certainly – and try to drop straight down the chimney.

Unfortunately the cloud ceiling was at zero and the trick might be beyond the personnel on the flight deck.

Equally, Matson doubted if they had enough kerosene left to reverse their spiral and power out to another airport if this gamble went wrong.

Given all this, the gun seemed trivial. The black was unimportant. The Ingram a mere distraction. Matson wanted to pray, like a little child. He had wanted to have a good old weep and a pray for the last hour. He was good at prayer. He had learned prayer when the Druse had blown his leg off; and he hadn't practised since.

Looking at the gun, he knew it was irrelevant. It was going to kill no-one. He was going to die in an ordinary aircrash. She had promised him some such nonsense the first time he'd jumped with a parachute. It won't be this that'll kill you. You'll trip downstairs on your little black cat.

All this in the eternity of a second. They had swung for an age around an invisible point on an unseen earth. Now they came out of cloud and were almost on top of it, scraping their belly on the pinnacles of Innsbruck.

He saw brownstone and brick, trains on wet rails drowning among dumpling-coloured cobbles, then medieval roofs of lead, tiles, stone and the famous sheet of copper-gold.

He remembered the girl's name. He remembered it with a tremendous surge of interest in the thigh, just as their wheels hit the world with a bump, and they were making waves on a porridge of storm-soaked tarmac west of town, throwing up spray, but running dead straight and responding to reverse thrust with no trouble at all.

Her name was Lucinda – a fool's name only a fool could forget.

The ride on the big dipper was over, and he felt like a wimp. He'd not even tried to look brave for the women beside him.

The black had memories too. His hand kept his passions alive. Holding the cord of the public address system, he stepped a little to his left so he could overlook Sergeant-major Brownskill who still lay on the floor close to Matson and still seemed dead.

The black had it all rehearsed. He waited for the aircraft to come to a halt, then fired two rounds into the fallen man's thorax, and said into the microphone, '*This gun still works, ladies. It travels well. Now if anyone wants to make trouble, let them come up here and do it.*'

Nobody did.

8.

The intercom chimed. The Sergeant-major's body had made gruff noises like a sack being kicked, but now the intercom played its little bells just as if this were a Thomsons or Lunn-Poly tour: '*Captain Finch, your pilot speaking. I want to announce …*'

This was interrupted by the sound of meat being struck, followed by a crackle while the intercom cleared its throat. Its new voice said: '*We got no more news from here. Sod who fly the plane. We got people up here can fly any damn thing. You just listen to what's up back.*'

Presumably that was the tanned hijacker.

There was a young woman in front of them now, flourishing the second Ingram. Her skin was whiter than white, but dusky underneath, as if it had been locked in a box for years. Matson recognised her from among the passengers. He wondered how she'd got hold of a travel warrant.

She had unscrewed the suppressor from her Ingram. Noise was terror's main weapon, of course. Noise and noisy blood.

Without its barrel-length suppressor the Ingram looked like a video-camera. She handled it as if it was shortly to become a flash-gun, then moved backwards towards the flight-deck.

She only went as far as the galley. She wanted the first-aid box.

She passed the black some plaster and lint, but with an expression of supreme contempt on her face, as if he really shouldn't bleed just now. Matson had seen that look many times, mostly in his mirror: it was the aloofness of controlled fear.

The black bound himself savagely, keeping the bandage tense between gun-hand and teeth. The gun waved all about, but he didn't look any less prepared.

Even wrapping up a wound was an expression of menace. The puma had a sore paw.

The wriggle of the Browning, the histrionic flourishes of the Ingram, did nothing for Matson's general peace of mind.

'Excuse me!' Both muzzles became still, the black stopped bandaging, and the voice went on. 'Some of these people will need to use the lavatories.'

It was one of the Avaroc girls, coming forward and standing near Matson. He wished people wouldn't persist in being brave right where he was.

The female hijacker gestured for her to go back. She didn't move.

The two women had a tussle of wills, and for a second it looked as if the Ingram was going to be the referee. Then the black spoke up, with a mouthful of bandage.

His voice was gagged by the air-conditioning. The stewardess went on speaking, but her voice had shrivelled as well.

The black got the public address system and said: 'If people want to piss they can do it where they are. And when they have pissèd –' He shrugged, and went back to his bandage, the voiced past-participle leaving its suggestion of Classical rather than Gulf Arab in the air.

Only Matson could hear the flight-girl. She said, evenly: 'People want the toilets for all kinds of reasons. There are women with young children. There are nursing mothers. The passenger accommodation is becoming fouled enough already. And since we anticipate being on the ground here till this matter is resolved ...'

The female hijacker had the microphone now. She said, in an educated North American accent, 'Go and sit down, and I will comment on your demands.'

The Avaroc girl waited but the silence outlasted her. She moved away from Matson, affording him some relief.

'One more stop,' the young hijacker said after an interval. 'There will be one more stop and that will be all. We shall leave as soon as we have taken enough fuel on board.'

The bowser was already beside them. The Austrians were being over-brisk. Matson couldn't see enough of its bulk to tell what else it might conceal.

'Normally,' she went on, 'planes stay on the ground while politicians argue. Today there will be no argument, because the politics are self-evident. In a quarter of an hour we will fly. Normally Austria is very stubborn. Normally, I think, we should spend a long time on the ground – and be forced to kill *you* perhaps, and *you* ...' she indicated the people across the aisle from Matson '... and *you*, and even *you, you, you* ...' The rest of Matson's row, ending, disconcertingly out of sequence, with himself '... before we were given clearance to go. Today it will be different.'

She smiled at her own – or someone's – forethought. 'Austria is unaligned. The Eastern Bloc is just at the end of its road. You are NATO. I don't think little Austria will want to take sides in a matter so delicate.'

The black relieved her of the microphone. He had his nice white smile back at last. It matched his bright white bandage. His Browning sat easily in either hand, just like a harmonica.

'You hear the lady. Soon we'll be gone from this country. So piss where you are. When you are have pissèd, you may talk about it quietly like the cows in the field. But no-one – not a child, not a stewardess – no-one is ever to leave where they sit.'

Someone, sometime, would have to try to negotiate something better. The Avaroc girl had done all that could be expected for that moment.

The bowser moved away. Matson didn't get the feeling that it had left a twenty-man swat-squad crouching beneath the fuselage.

Everything had happened much too quickly; and now the plane was ready to fly.

Or people were going to die.

It looked as if he was already on a *de facto* short-list.

9.

They didn't move yet. Matson felt something on his knee, a pressure. It was a hand, a hand somewhat spatulate with drink, but a hand just the same, alive, comforting and human. He met the ginny eye of the woman next to him.

'I'm Anne Chambers,' she said. 'I'm a bit tiddly-pomp. I hope you don't mind. That's my sister. She's a bit tiddly-pomp as well.'

'Why not?' They'd been told they could talk. He bet it was Anne with an e.

'She's puked all down her cardie and she's wet her knickers.'

'She won't be the only one.'

'Nursery days. I'm the one called Chambers, too. Know my maiden name?' She nudged the sleeping ondinist at her elbow. 'What's your name, Becky? Tell him your bloody name.'

'Becky,' her sister said from a deep coma. 'My name's Becky. Rebecca for short.'

'Your surname, idiot. Remind the gentleman of our family bloody handle.'

Rebecca found a mite more sick in her mouth, smiled at the memory, thought better of it and kept it to herself.

'Tiddly-pomp,' her sister explained. 'Unutterably tiddly-pomp. Our name is Potts. So I was bound to marry a Chambers. It was writ large in Heaven. Know what he said when he proposed to me?'

Matson didn't know.

'At least you'll be upwardly mobile if you say yes,' he said. And he was bloody dead right, wasn't he?'

He began to feel sick in his turn, sick for her. 'You mean you're ...'

'That's it. I'm Solly Chambers' wife.'

Major-general Chambers was one of the three divisional commanders in the British Sector. Why his men called him Solly and why his wife called him similarly was a matter there might be a long time to discuss. The hijack could have netted two or three more useful prizes from the British Sector, Solly Chambers himself would be one of them, but a divisional commander's wife *and* her sister represented a good beginning. He hoped they didn't find out.

'You're an Air Commodore,' she said, a little too loudly.

'My name's Matson. Patrick Matson. I'm a civilian. I'm a guest of the RAF.'

'A pretty senior guest.'

'I think they wanted me to be able to get drunk with impunity, that's all.'

'So you must work for an embassy?'

'Something like that. Let's keep very quiet about ourselves, shall we?'

'Mum's the word. Totally hush is the translation. *Stumm* as our NATO interpreters will have it. What a pity old Irenson is on board.'

'I didn't see him.' Irenson was a Junior Minister of Defence.

'Five rows back with a rather pretty …'

'Shit.'

'It's a good job I'm tiddly-pomp,' she said, 'if you're going to use language like that. You mind sipping from the bottle?'

10.

Talk is a dangerous thing. It dulls all the other senses. When Matson turned to his front again it was to bang his face on the Ingram.

The Ingram had been thrust under his nose to attract his attention and it hadn't done. It was undergreased and unfired, so it had no smell.

The girl's hand did not smell either, nor the rest of her, not of scent, not of soap, not even of woman or cigarettes. She did not smell of fear or of anger. She didn't like the second or two he had kept her waiting, so she bloodied his nostrils on the foresight. 'Passport!' The snub inch of muzzle began chipping about inside his mouth.

He jerked his head away. 'Sorry,' he managed. 'Didn't realise you were collecting our travel documents.'

'Your life,' she said softly, 'is going to be just as long as my temper.' She relieved him of his wallet. 'So you're an

Irishman.' It didn't sound as if American was her second language.

'I'm a British citizen.'

'What else, Matson? Your passport tells me nothing. I wonder what your boot says. Before we landed I watched you hiding something in your boot.'

He let himself look very stupid. He felt stupid anyway, because now was when he was going to take hold of her gun. He was going to blind her with the first two fingers of his left hand, then kill the black with her Ingram. Then, if he was still alive, he would kill her as well. There was probably another hijacker behind him somewhere, but a long way behind, with a whole plane to cover, and a lot of people to get in the way.

He pretended to slip a finger in his shoe. He mustn't tense up, do anything to alarm her. He must work from the shoulders only, and keep his left arm then his right arm totally relaxed. Thinking of all this made him feel very stupid indeed.

She left him feeling worse than that. She stepped one pace backwards and cocked the Ingram. His aborted gesture – he hoped he'd smothered any suggestion of menace – left him overbalanced at her feet. 'Your left boot,' she hissed. 'Or do you call the thing a shoe? You put something in it.'

His face was ice-cold but it was running with moisture. He didn't think he would die any better if it was a woman who pulled the trigger. He lifted his left hand slowly from his sock and held out the little cylinder of paper.

He hadn't fooled her for a second. She looked into his wet face and she knew, she bloody knew. Knowing had made her take that step back. She gestured for him to put the paper on the top of the seat-back in front of him. He made to hand it to her, or to throw it. Either might give him a chance.

But she knew. So she made him put it on the seat.

The plane began to roll, to roll or at least to move.

'When we get there,' she said, 'I'm going to kill you.'

If she kept her distance, she undoubtedly would. Her eyes stayed on his face, her gun-arm tight to her body. She reached out and took the paper while the Ingram pondered his belly.

11.

They read the paper together. It was the black who spoke. Matson could not hear what was said, so the black tried again and the public-address told him: *'Air Commodore, Air Commodore Matson.'*

Joke. Perhaps it was the Browning persuaded him to come forward, perhaps the Ingram:

'So you're a senior officer.'

The girl had the mouthpiece now. This was a show trial, and hers was the swifter English.

'No.'

'*No*?' He heard a slightly relayed echo, his voice beside hers thin as tinsel.

'You deny it? So all these soldiers and airmen are to know their senior officers are liars and cowards?'

'I don't suppose ...' his voice sounded faint in the air, as if he were a ghost already. He reached out his hand for the microphone, but they weren't going to let him take it. *'I don't suppose any of them believe that for one minute.'*

'Remember you are talking to a machine-gun and answer everyone this. How would you advise the people on this aircraft to react towards American imperialism?'

Matson thought it over, but time was in short supply.

'Answer the question, man.' The black had the microphone again. His wound was troubling him. He was raging into his busted hand. *'A question has been squarely put.'*

The girl said, the sweet little Ingram with its pale face and dark hair: *'How would you advise the people on this aircraft to react towards American imperialism?'*

'Some of them are American. The rest are imperialists. I wouldn't presume to advise them in any direction. I'm Irish myself.'

The Ingram began to kiss the side of his head. *'So, you brave officer. If you ask these Americans and these imperialists to come up here and help you before you die, will they charge this little gun?'*

'I doubt it.'

'They're cowards?'

'They're not fools.'

'If you're insolent, we shall shoot you.'

'That's your privilege. Or, rather, it's the privilege conferred by your gun. The privilege of temporary power.'

He was in the super-league of death now. The major and the sergeant-major had managed far, far less.

'You don't think we will?' It was the black again, screaming into his bandage. *'You saw us execute these other pigs.'* He was, after all, a muslim.

'No.'

'The ruling cast are blind or merely stupid?'

'I don't think so.'

(Cute, muddleheaded little Ingram. At last he'd come across a woman he'd rather kill than fuck. Only here he was aging so fast he would never get to do either.)

'He asked me whether I saw him execute *Major Wellard-Browne or Sergeant-major Brownskill. I told him I didn't.'*

(Aging so fast and rushing upon death like a lover.)

'I saw him murder *them. Just as I saw him* murder *Sally Sherman, the stewardess.'*

The black didn't rage into his hand. The Ingram no longer smiled. The black said, 'We're flying now, pig. Maybe the bullets will stop with you, maybe they won't. So why take the chance? Go back to your seat. Maybe we'll wring your neck.'

He turned, and heard her say, 'When we land, the bullets will fly. When we land, like I promised you.'

He went back to his seat. He didn't move well. He doubted if anyone does, whether towards an execution or away from a reprieve.

His brain should have been pounding with righteousness, thumping with rage. It wasn't. It hadn't even felt itself rise up and fly, yet here were the big icy peaks turning their glass gaze upwards, and passing under the wing.

He doubted whether he would have registered the fact of being airborne if the black hadn't told him so. Even before he sat down he was nearly asleep. He knew what that was called. It was called shock. He wondered he hadn't slumped out earlier. There'd been too much shock in his life.

12.

He couldn't see everything that happened. In fact, sitting where he was, he couldn't see most things.

There was a fair amount of commotion behind him. Not the commotion of violence and certainly not of protest, and he didn't know what caused it.

He was allowed to talk but not encouraged to turn his head. If Matson had been one of a party of three, or at most four, hijackers he wouldn't have permitted talk either; so he thought it reasonable not to turn his head, unless he wanted talk to be forfeit as well.

The commotion, the sub-commotion, the bit-by-bit rumbling and mumbling, the stirring of bodies and feet was there all the same. What was wrong with it, if anything was wrong with it, was that it sounded so bloody normal where nothing else was normal at all.

A hijack should sound different, be noisier or quieter – he thought quieter. What he heard above the almost inaudible turbines and the all-too-audible air-conditioning that makes passenger flight seem an entirely private and personal matter conducted between left ear and right ear, right ear and left in endless suspension in the buzz that fills the gap, what he heard above and beyond his own Shakespearean progress on the broad back of the bumblebee was a normality that grew louder and louder and came nearer and nearer but never grew really loud and took an age to come absolutely close.

The woman hijacker stood beside him yet again, this time smelling of sweat just a little. He saw what it was that was happening.

Her sweat smelled gentle. It wasn't the sweat of fear.

Her bloody little Ingram was moving people about.

Her persuasive little Mark 11 was re-establishing the seating-plan. It didn't need to talk very much to do it, either. It was bloody convincing, the Ingram Mark 11.

When he'd had the thing in his mouth it had tasted just like a Mark 10, but his palate had always been coarse.

This was the one that dealt the .38 at eleven hundred rounds of cyclic fire per minute instead of tossing out the .45 at almost the same rate. For use on an aircraft, a .38 would be a trifle more appropriate. He didn't know how much of a trifle – a *soupçon*, say, or a smidgin?

There were two men to his left across the aisle, one regimental cook perhaps and one company clerk, with turmeric- or tobacco-stained fingers.

Two men with one mouse of a girl further over by the window. He had already taken stock of them all, the men not up to much, the girl whey-faced with terror.

The Ingram put the girl in the aisle-seat, just eighteen inches from Matson, and the two men by the window.

So that was the idea. Women and children by the access, toughies and roughies where they'd find it that much harder to make a move.

Matson got ready to move, not to make a move, not this time. He was a toughy and roughy so he got ready to do as the Ingram told him and replace one of the ladies by the window.

On, as it would happen, the damp seat.

The noose had already dropped past his neck and was firm around his chest and seatback before he was aware of it passing his face, or of there being anyone else behind him.

They weren't going to move him. They were tying him up.

The noose had been tricked over his head by a woman of about twenty-five. She had crudely lightened hair, to make her look like a Düsseldorf tart. There must be several of those on board.

She not only adjusted the noose round his thorax and upper arms, she bound the running end round his hands and tossed it forward to the black, who seized it like a love-gift.

Matson was a doggy on a lead. One of a line of doggies, because there was a tugging on the line behind him, a fidget of disapproval and discomfort.

So this was hijacker number four. Which meant there was a hijacker number five. This couldn't be the one with 'jelly in the pants'. Even though bred in Ireland, Matson knew that women don't have knackers to be 'blown off'.

He assumed the black was a literalist as well as a poet, and decided to lodge a protest with the Ingram. 'I'm Irish,' he said again. 'I'm entirely neutral.' He made sure his accent sounded as thick as a Provisional fertiliser-bomb.

The Ingram didn't answer. He noticed that the sweet little divided nut on the top of the casing had been pulled right back. The nut was back so the bolt was back so the action was back so he was one finger itch from oblivion.

He gazed at the dark-haired girl and he gazed at the nut.

The divided nut was, after all, integral to the bolt, was the cocking handle.

Called, because so elegantly formed and so cunningly divided, the pussy handle.

'We're seeing you stay neutral, Matson. On this flight there's neutral or dead.'

Pussy handle. You don't get explanations like that in a film script.

13.

Little whey-face on his right got a rope round her boobs as well. She obviously looked more dangerous than a regimental cook or a company clerk.

'Why are they tying me up?'

'They're tying everyone up. Everyone on the outside – the aisle seats – anyway.'

'They're going to rape me.'

'Sex is the least of your worries.'

'I'm going to be a nun.'

'It's no disqualification. Think of St Ursula.'

'I'm not a Catholic.'

This conversation was taking some time, what with the watchful pauses, the speaking through the side of the mouth, and the especially deliberate manner one uses when talking to an imbecile. He wondered why she had chosen to speak to him. They all wanted to call attention to Air Commodore Matson one way or another, by being defiant beside him or getting themselves shot right next to him, or bleeding to death round his boot – or simply opening their damned silly mouths.

'They're going to kill me,' she said.

'You're being very brave about it.'

'It's the least they'll do.'

'Silence is golden.'
'St Augustine. He's another Catholic.'
'And black, too. Who's that sitting beside you?'
'I hardly know anything about you.'
'The other side.'
'A person. My father's a regimental sergeant-major.'
'Fancy.'
'Regimental Sergeant-major Wilkinson. Mr Wilkinson. They call him mister in Daddy's regiment.'
'It's not your fault.'
'That's a rotten joke.'
'Use an abbreviated birth-certificate.'
'*And* I've heard it before.'
'It's not one they'll tell you in the convent.'
She began to cry. Another bloody way of attracting attention to him.
The black left his station by the boarding door and he took a step or two in their direction. He didn't look as if he was going to wipe anyone's eyes with a handkerchief.
He came and stood by them for a moment or two. Then he moved away again.
'He didn't rape you now, did he?' Matson said. The poor little nun woman was something to take his mind off things, his chance to behave like a man and do his bit. 'Nor make you recite the Roman mass.'
She sobbed like a frosty engine.
'In Latin. Which would be even worse.'
'You're poking fun at me.'
'Only the way the Snake poked fun at Eve. By paying her lots of attention.'
'That's not in the Bible.' She had got herself properly started now, with her tears all running smoothly.
'It's in mine.'
'You're a Catholic,' she wept.
'Only when danger is close at hand.'
The dark-haired woman with the Ingram came and watched them. The Ingram merely listened in. She watched them for some time. She approved of women weeping. Or she disapproved. She had some opinion or other.
'What's your name?' Matson asked, just to improve morale.

The little nun spoke and the hijacker spoke. Both women spoke.

That was a pity, social circumstances being what they were.

Matson didn't kill anyone this time, or even gouge out eyes. His hands were tied. If he had gone through with it earlier, before he knew about the extra hijackers, he would be dead now. Lots of people would be dead.

The General's Lady moved. Her sister snored.

The hijackers preferred people who wept.

14.

He puzzled over their final destination. Hijacks have a habit of switching from here to there and back again, like a broody bird seeking a nest.

Not this one. It was too precisely planned.

The terminal couldn't be in Europe. Even the few 'soft-option' countries in the West would quickly become dangerous for the gunmen. The Eastern Bloc would be trouble from the beginning. Spetzak, or one of the local equivalents, would storm the plane the moment it landed, and there would be a greater or lesser ration of mayhem.

Whatever the damage to the passengers, the hijackers would be killed on the spot. Any who survived – because injured, say – would end up in front of a firing squad. There were even nasty rumours circulating about the Iron Curtain garotte, or so Pomeroy said. And in Hungary they still broke your neck with the hook and stool. Eastern Europe was out.

So it had to be the Near East, Beirut and beyond. Or North Africa, with Revolutionary Libya or Marxist Tunisia the most likely.

The trouble with Tunisia, as the hijackers viewed it, was its overall accessibility. It was a country full of holiday-makers. Too easy to sneak in a planeload of special forces disguised as a package-tour.

Libya was not a good place for Matson. Nor, any longer, was Beirut. He pushed such thoughts aside. Frequent delinquencies in childhood had cured him of meeting trouble halfway.

It was like fearing the cane at school, or being caught nicking milk-bottles in the street: the Headmaster or the Old Constabulary Bill might just pass him by.

Hope springs eternal in the human vest, if not breast – especially one made of string and beating beneath a cavalry-twill waistcoat.

THREE

1.

He was no kind of warrior now, not with the cord round his wrists and chest, not now she'd marked him for death. Young men can be brave against this kind of odds; he couldn't remember being young enough for the necessary degree of optimism. Old men, too. They talk of bravery all the time. Matson wasn't old yet; and he didn't think he'd live long enough to find out what makes them so cocky.

Meanwhile the hijackers had the Minister, supposing they knew. They had the General's Lady beside him, if they ever found out. But these were the sort of people they would nurture to the last. They wouldn't coddle Matson. The woman with the Ingram had felt the gust of his violence. She had watched him in that second he nudged forward from his seat and known he was about to kill her. So, reasonably enough, she had sentenced him to death. The Düsseldorf Tart had trussed him up for her. When the time was right they would finish him with the minimum of fuss.

The rope that bound his chest was tight. The loop round his wrists was only as secure as the black wanted it to be. Matson worked at slackening it. He wondered about slipping out of a shoe, so he'd have something he could throw to cause a second's distraction. Then he thought: *they won't kill me in my seat. If they were going to do that they would have done it long ago*. It wasn't a matter of compunction, and certainly not of aesthetics. Terrorism was the Theatre of Blood. This lot had already spilt too much of it, and after three hours of cabin warmth it was beginning to smell. The black took surreptitious sniffs at his hand, as if checking that his wound wasn't the cause of it. It was getting up *his* nose as well.

2.

The sun was on the right. It would have to be. It was well past noon and they were flying south. South by what? Matson couldn't tell. To try anything clever with the dial of his watch would attract attention to himself. Anyway, Miss Potts' window was raw with light. The sun blinded the upper sky on that side of the aircraft, making a fix impossible.

Once more the sea was beneath them. Whatever their ultimate direction, they would have to run down the Adriatic. It was the nearest arm of the Mediterranean to Innsbruck. Coming this way saved flying over northern Italy to reach the Ligurian Sea, or flirting dangerously with the airforces of the Eastern Bloc and then the American air bases in Greece to reach the Aegean.

The Adriatic is like a drainpipe emptying itself on Libya. Once they were beyond the Gulf of Spezia the hijackers could change course in any direction south of due west and due east. They had 140 degrees to play with, and only the U.S. Sixth Fleet to worry about. The U.S. Sixth Fleet was going to be a lot more circumspect about disrupting their transit than Bulgaria or Rumania would be if they went further east. Blowing them out of the sky was not even a remote option for the Americans. The hijackers would know that with the Eastern Bloc it was at least a twenty-five percent chance at all times.

It was possible that one of the hijackers was still flying the plane – or bullying the co-pilot to follow an exact flight-path. In either case, the more rudimentary their course the better.

Nowhere in the Adriatic would they be further than fifty miles from a coast – Yugoslavia and Albania to port, Italy to starboard.

Today was clear enough for both shores to be visible from even a moderate altitude, giving four hundred nautical miles of navigational ease, all the way to Otranto and the Ionian Sea.

A little buzz of excitement bumbled among the passengers. One or two children stood up, to be hissed down by their mothers. The Düsseldorf Tart became shrill. She didn't shout in English. With a gun in her hand she didn't need to.

There was a coast – no, a coastal island – to the left of the aircraft, which was suddenly much too low – so low that Matson wondered if it was going to attempt to land. He put the thought out of his mind as soon as he had it. This must be the Dalmatian Coast. Yugoslavia would not be a good home for hijackers.

The islands, large or diminutive, continued to slip beneath the wing in a series of little frames of seaweed, mudflat or stone: tiny hills, scarps, red-topped buildings and olive-green vegetables. He was low enough to pick out tree from tree, if not quite leaf from leaf. He was looking from the side the sun struck, and their trunks were raw orange, ochre even, as rich as cork trees. The condemned man was going on a scenic tour.

The aircraft veered slightly to starboard and began to climb. Matson had guessed right. One of the hijackers had been piloting manually and navigating visually. He remembered his own efforts to learn to fly an Auster, years ago. It took him ages to get his wings, and his navigation had been one of the reasons. Asked, at eight thousand feet, to follow a railway line, he had done so, only to find himself down to eight hundred, scarcely ten minutes and fifteen miles later. Someone had been following the coast and it had led him down. Someone inexperienced had nearly drowned them. How the images of his past life flashed before him.

More shouting from the children. More screaming from the Düsseldorf Tart. Nothing changed. The coast was still there, but further. The islands, when he could glimpse them, were still slipping by, but looking smaller.

He saw the interceptor for the first time. There must have been a plane or planes before. It was the closeness of other aircraft that had excited the children.

They were Jastrebs of the Yugoslav Air Force. Matson was impressed they could keep up. One of them was the two-seater version, the Galeb, and from what he knew of its performance this was even less of a match for a Trident Three. For some reason the airliner was not achieving its maximum airspeed.

Even so, the Jastrebs lacked the pace to manage a force-down. Unless a slow plane, boring down gently, could be considered the best means to bluff a loss of altitude.

The passenger cabin bucked. There was an impact on top of the fuselage. Something detonated above them, below them, through them in a lightning of compressed images and sonic shock. It would be a lie to say he heard the scream of passing jets through the sound-proofing, above the air-conditioning, the Trident's own vortices, the roar of its turbines. But the ear imagined it. The brain suffered it.

Somebody screamed, and noise suggested noise. Here it was again and again, swatting them with sonic bounce and strobing shadow, pulverising the skull.

The Düsseldorf Tart and Little Curly Ingram took time to restore order, and before they did so the triple violence was repeated. They were too near to Yugoslavia for this to be Italy or NATO. They had just crossed another coastal island. This must be the Yugoslav Air Force's MiG 21s. They were trying to cow the Trident to earth. Or destabilise it into a tail-spin with Mach-2 passes.

3.

The MiGs had been much too close for Matson, who hadn't been able to see them coming, merely feel them when they arrived. The last one had been so approximate it had passed down the Trident inside the fuselage in a vibration of dismantled atoms. Its speed had beamed it through the skull the way unlit motorway bridges comb the brain at night – only this was at a rate of closure of two thousand miles an hour.

They were alone now, and going higher. Things must have been tense on the flight-deck. All of his airline training would have inclined Captain Finch to accept a talk-down or at least accede to a force-down. No pilot of a rear-thrust high-tail aircraft dare contemplate fighters buzzing him as close as the Yugoslav Air Force had done, nor at such a speed or rate of closure. Collision would have been the least of his worries.

When a top tailplane job like a Trident or a Boeing 727 gets into destabilised air it stalls. When it stalls, it spins. When it spins it cannot be returned to stable flight. At flying speed it can't stall – unless a pair of maniacs in Mach-2 airframes create artificial vacuums or negative vortices by wafting too close to it.

Now the Fishbeds were gone, leaving the cabin shimmering with puke and remembered electrons. The kids had enjoyed themselves, but only in retrospect. Gratifying to recall that the NATO code for MiG 21 is Fishbed – he thought Fishbed C in this case – and not Flogger or Mogul: it meant that death was concentrating his mind wonderfully. He was able to return it to the metaphysics of the hijack, and ponder some imponderables of St Augustine. Such as: if he had to be aloft on this causeway in the sky when it chose to collapse, would he rather be alone or, as now, among friends? Again: is it sweeter to die from a high-speed accident or a bullet in the ear?

Actually, he was coming to float above dissolution altogether. He was working out of this morning's hangover, acquired by sitting up all night with a girl who only wanted to drink Armagnac and talk poetry. Matson's talk is poetry at the best of times, but last night he'd ended up talking Armagnac; and the echoes had been loud and painful. He'd always nurtured a desire to die drunk. Last night he'd avoided this by leaving the driving to her (and her name was one he need do no other than forget). To die with a hangover was another matter. Now he was losing his hangover. His veins were feeling redder by the minute, and his brain was abuzz with quirks and quarks and neutrinos of sunshine in such a profusion of almost optimism that he saw no need to die at all.

Six miles high above a sunlit Mediterranean is an excellent place to exult, even with your hands tied. The Mediterranean had never been synonymous with holiday for him; and sitting in aircraft – especially latterly with that clandestine brute of a long-fall altichute on his back and a pressure-gauge strapped to his wrist – had nearly always left the Matson mind ajar on immortality. This time he wasn't constrained by orders. He was bound for wherever Fate took him, and he found it absurdly comforting.

One of the Avaroc stewardesses was beside him, tipping cold coffee into his mouth.

She leant her amazingly fresh body over him and did the

same for the catatonic drunk in the window seat. For the free hands of the General's Lady she had a polystyrene cup. She called the drunken Miss Potts 'Madam', and her sister, Lady Chambers, she addressed as 'dear'. To Matson she said, 'Have you had enough, Air Commodore? They said I was to give the Air Commodore a drink.'

It was a message brimming with hope. Surely dark-haired curly Ingram or the Düsseldorf Tart wouldn't bother to sweeten his breath if they were about to blow him away? Air Commodore might prove a useful title after all. He had concealed Air Commodore. He had rolled his fictitious rank into a cylinder and stuffed it into his boot. Since they'd caught him out they might just assume it was all he had to hide. Air Commodore might be reckoned too exalted for death.

'I'm afraid the answer's "no",' the stewardess was explaining to the little would-be nun-woman on his left, 'We're not allowed to bring a trolley. And we can only come one at a time – that's why this is taking so long. We've negotiated lavatories for the women and the children, but only the ones at the rear; and we're working from the rear forward.'

Lovely Avaroc ladies. He wanted to hug them all, to sing with them and weep and give them a medal. They reminded him of Beirut nurses, and of dear Miss Barr who had ministered to him so sweetly when he'd come as a little fatherless boy all the way from rural Ireland to a reception class in Camberwell, and an ILEA one at that, full of people even more evil than Protestants.

The Avaroc ladies had negotiated and their captors had acquiesced. The hijackers had proved beyond doubt that they were in charge, so perhaps, just perhaps, the bloodshed was over.

The Air Commodore permitted himself to sip another mouthful. He could be greedy with such a sweet piaculum.

4.

Where were the birds in the sky? Why weren't they being mobbed and deflected?

Their Trident would certainly be the most prominent dot

on every plot in the universe, yet so far only the Yugoslavs had made a major effort. They had tried, with horrifying persistence, to force them into a landing-pattern at Zadar, then Split, then Cavtat. Or even dump them on the karst in a box of fried cinders. But the Yugoslavs were scarcely friends. They were at best benevolent neutrals. Where were the Limassol Brits, the Yanks from the Sixth Fleet? Where were the bloody Italians?

Perhaps someone somewhere in NATO knew something he didn't. Perhaps the acronyms were buzzing out there, and SACEUR was asking SACLANT to liaise with CINCHAN ref this moment's *sitsum*. Some wunderkind must have envisaged the possibilities of a military hijack at some RPG or other, at an STC, NDC or an elsewhere so secret that even the angels dare not name its name. In which case there should be a well-documented STANAG waiting on file or on disc or in dump or dustbin, and the Trident would shortly become drenched in saliva, riddled with words.

Matson, with cords round his circulation, was growing dizzy.

Perhaps everyone outside knew what no-one inside knew – no-one inside the pressurised capsule of the passenger cabin anyway: flight-decks are ever wise.

Perhaps the wire-services, the press agencies and the TV reporters and the radio-companies already knew.

Perhaps they were bound for some benevolent kingdom, sheikhdom, empire or emirate where the Düsseldorf Tart and Curly Ingram, the white-handed blood-toothed and bilious black, the tan pilot with the tannoy tonsils and the ability to break bone even in the cockpit – not to mention the alleged body-bomb up back with the jockstrap full of jelly – would no longer wish, or be able, to present a problem.

Perhaps Britain, NATO, the West and their terminal host were already engaging in expediency-speak, swapping oil-wells, embassies, fighter-planes, dried figs, cultural visits by the Dagenham Girl Pipers – anything to set them free. Perhaps even now Marcus Pomeroy was on a direct line to Heaven. Perhaps, hours before touchdown, diplomacy had taken over.

Diplomacy was fine until you put a face to it. Diplomacy's

face was Marcus Pomeroy, who never bought a pint of shrimps without beaching a school of whales and selling a trawler-fleet right down the river. His shrimps, your trawler-fleet, God's whales, and the river invariably of blood.

Diplomacy and Marcus Pomeroy were powerless against hominids like this set of faces and fingers and teeth. This self-elected parliament of guns and blackjacks and bombs. They were the sexless clones of the Revolution. They had been culled from beneath the cloacal scale of the Serpent and cultured under hermetic seal in an equal suspension of conviction without reason and rhetoric without debate. Then they had been lifted from their jar and programmed to accelerate into disaster, their trajectory predetermined by an unknown co-ordinate in the grid of circumstance or the geography of the womb. They were already hurtling towards their own immolation – the only unknown factor was how many of the rest of the world they were destined to take with them.

No: diplomacy was for outside the aircraft, in a sunlight buzzing with theories and information. Inside it would be guns, not sputter.

Here was Matson's only circumstance, a scenario of non-event. The passenger cabin had been designed in an earlier dimension, before the universe was quite sorted out. It was as spacious as the draftsman's art could make it; but in flight it grew tighter by the second. Among its unfocused laminates, its astigmatic lushness, its lights growing blander, its airconditioning whirring hypnotically and huffing up the embarrassing odours of breath but not of death, for death gets into the cracks, he crouched in this shrinking hull with his legs stretching and bloating and all one hundred and fifty of his neighbours' pairs of knees rammed into his back. It was a time-capsule in which he was suspended for hours exactly as he was when he left, in the same socks and underpants, until it dumped him into what he would become, more dull than dead, more dead than alive, with every gulp of not-quite-air a premedication for death, if not death's anaesthetic, death's little nostrum of hemlock. Here, six miles above the brilliant Mediterranean, his brain was like an egg in isinglass, full of skulls and Sally Sherman, St Augustine and Donne.

There is no Now in an aeroplane. That was why this hijack was happening in a kind of unwaking. An aeroplane is designed solely for Was and Will Be. Matson, just like everybody else, normally progressed through Not Now towards Not Yet in a comforting haze of alcohol. The hijackers allowed no alcohol. Hijackers never do, for above the logistics of hate, sheer bloody-mindedness and undoubted religious conviction, hijackers permit no courage, whether Dutch or undiluted.

Ignorance capsule. Crap capsule. Compassion capsule.

It was now the Whispering Nun's turn to go to the bog. The Regimental Cook and the Company Clerk weren't allowed to move or to move themselves, because they were men.

5.

The Düsseldorf Tart was attentive to men. She raged above them, flapping them lower in their seat, like a buzzard over a pair of voles.

Lady Po and Sister Poo on his right couldn't go either. Although indubitably women, they had a roped-up Matson outside them.

One capsule was in impeccable shape – his obliging bladder. It was conditioned by diet and power-trained. Besides, dear old Armagnac evaporates through the listening places of the skin. You notice such things in a hijack.

The Whispering Nun came back with a plastic tray. The food was gelid. It had been kept long beyond its heat-storage time. Vol-au-vent, tomato, apricot and the obligatory roll, all laid out under perspex in a four-eyed airline lunch. God knows how long it had been there, or who it was for: Luton to Bruggen was only a bun-and-coffee flight. Trust a little nun to find something different.

Plastic trays and gelid food make excellent weapons. Airborne with a couple of satellite plates and a saturnine apricot unrolling its concentric syrup, it could divert a Browning in a damaged mitt for a whole second.

Someone with an Ingram might refuse to be distracted. Or simply close both eyes and inject the universe at random.

Well done, Air Commodore. You have won yourself a posthumous. What a pity all the young mums and widdy kids came too.

6.

Matson made himself relax. He set his mind afloat and let his body sag. He wanted time to blur onward before nervous exhaustion got the better of him.

Experience had taught him that the faculties combine more slickly when they've spent a few minutes being separate from each other. Soon he would need all he could summon – to seize life on the burst, or meet death head on.

He offered himself a coward's argument too. His instructor would have called it prudence. A limp man has no aura. He can't be picked out from the crowd.

With this mostly in mind, he drooped his attention floorward, practising invisibility.

The shouts came from behind, then the screams. Everything from behind, shots not yet included.

His nun choked, had ten seconds of silent hysteria, then choked again. Lady Chambers said 'Tut, tut, tut', like an old man sucking a pipe. Her sister's blue lips farted.

He woke up properly to hear the Düsseldorf Tart squirting orders through a mouthpiece or a megaphone in a language definitely not German. She was shrill in bleach-haired Arabic.

The oxygen cups had come down. Matson swung around to see two hundred dangling spirals of plastic, twisting their off-white latex. The little breathing masks had a life all of their own, each separate yet behaving in concert, like lugworms trying on condoms, or sex among the octopodes.

The Düsseldorf Tart should have been shrill in English. It is hard to shrill in English, true, but the Düsseldorf Tart would have managed. No-one could follow her Arabic, not even an Arab. She kept on shouting a word that was all glass-edges and gutturals – like the Spanish syllables for an orange.

His little blue nun had fainted. Matson hadn't previously

known she was blue, hadn't called her blue, hadn't seen so much blue before in what was a multicoloured place; but Miss Potts' lips were blue and the whole bloody murex was spreading.

Miss Potts herself was looking better, breathing great sea-slug gulps of the pure serene from her plastic lifeline, and recovering from alcohol hand-over-fist the way flight-crew do, by creeping into their cockpits and junking up on O_2. Lady Chambers, her true-blue sister, was even bluer as it happened, and growing bluer by the second. She sucked air calmly, as befitted the wife of a divisional commander. When you are a Lady and the wife of one of those, you learn to suck calmly.

Solly Chambers could be proud.

The Düsseldorf Tart ran out of spit. Matson's swivelled neck watched her – a man deprived of air watches without grammar, without syntax, with so much blueness in his eye that he senses light through the big vein in his neck and even the blood in his earlobes – Matson watched her cling to a condom and inflate it gratefully with impoverished lips. The Düsseldorf Tart grew invisible, though manifest and tangible, like a bollard in front of a drunken driver.

Matson felt incredibly drunk, but he knew he was not the driver.

Curly Ingram took over. She ran to Sally Sherman's microphone and spoke orders in a voice as loud as the Creator's – beautiful little Curly, the only sexy woman he would never learn to love.

'*We have depressurised*,' she said. '*You all know the drill. Remain calm and do not see the occasion as a chance to do anything silly*.'

The blue nun giggled a sweet little airless giggle, as if suckling on a teat of Liebfraumilch. Matson was so taken with his joke about her tipple that he nearly joined her in laughter, but he didn't think it prudent. Too many people had run out of spit and were blundering and lolling inebriated, all without leaving their seats.

The fantasy was now entirely blue. Everyone was drunk in a drunken disco party. The cabin lights were muffled in a smoke that was being wound on carmen rollers, then combed and carded through a vat of mauve rinse in the best South London fashion. The gelatine in the propeller spot was irretrievably jammed.

Curly was still speaking, but he could no longer hear her. He thought of grabbing her for a slow frenzy and soothing the Ingram 11 away from her once the intolerable slinkiness of the waltz had smooched her into a false sense of security, but there was going to be no more bopping tonight, boys and girls, because the floor tilted sharply, like the trap-door opening beneath a gallows, or a particularly violent case of the dry spins.

The cabin had depressurised. Therefore there was no oxygen. Therefore some people had shouted and were now experiencing symptoms of extreme drunkenness, he among them. After all, you can't stick your nose into the little plastic milking-machines, or whatever these glistening, damp-filled neon-lit danglers were called, if your hands were tied. Exactly one third of all the people in the plane – those in the aisle-seats – had their wrists corded up in an endless knot.

A suffocating man finds reason at the last, somewhere near the bottom of the whirlpool. Did I remember to switch off the gas? Did I pay the milkman? That silly little bitch – I bet she hasn't taken her pill.

It couldn't have been a big depressurisation. There had been no implosion or explosion, no cataclysmic holing of the Trident's hull, no peel-back of fabric. Perhaps it had been caused by the unnatural violence of manoeuvre – the evasion of the Yugoslav Jastrebs and MiGs, the wind-sheer at Innsbruck. Perhaps one of the black's bullets or a fragment of the sergeant-major's shoulderblade had made a tiny perforation on the far side of the baggage cabin somewhere beneath his feet. Perhaps the depressurisation was deliberate. Flight crew can arrange such things. They play around on long-distance overnight flights to help people sleep, but scarcely to this extent.

Meanwhile the trap-door or dance-floor had tilted because the plane was losing height.

If the depressurisation was deliberate, then it must be the prelude to something incisive and dramatic. Speaking for himself, he felt dramatically unincisive – not a phrase to say aloud after six pink gins or in his present state of the mumbles.

Others were in better shape.

The cook or the quartermaster's clerk did something terribly familiar to the nun, and she stopped her giggling. He knelt on her chest and dragged the smoking ceiling to his mouth. Lady Chambers meanwhile did Matson an enormous favour and became Anne, his dentist's nurse. Anne-with-an-e covered his face with a little swinging cup and sobriety blew back down the nozzle.

So this was what the Düsseldorf Tart had been telling them in Arabic.

Air is wonderful to breathe, and oxygen even better. It takes the blue out of things in about forty seconds. For a minute or so, he got too much red and then all his colours became adjusted. He could even see the pink bits in Miss Potts' face and the lovely black spots in the dice of her teeth.

The aircraft stayed low, at about five thousand feet. The outside atmosphere still couldn't come back in, but at this altitude the hull's pressure system was only marginally out of balance, so the air-conditioning slowly resurrected the oxygen supply.

The oxygen masks continued to dangle, but technically they were no longer necessary.

Always supposing there was no further need to climb.

The Düsseldorf Tart recovered enough breath to be shrill again.

Curly Ingram had no such need.

For the moment, there was a constriction in his chest, a pain in each lower arm. It wasn't his heart about to fail him. It was sweet little Curly, testing the cords and working towards him, always from behind. He let her do him up and fasten him more tightly without presuming to watch her. She didn't like the looseness he'd contrived for his wrists.

When she handed on their reins to the black, he saw the man's face was still grey with lack of air – crumpled like an old Chinese lantern.

Lack of air or loss of blood? The sharp lowering of atmospheric pressure would not have been good for his seeping wound.

The black hadn't read the necessary literature, so he didn't let himself become worried. He was intent on only one thing, to be steady with the pistol. It looked very steady indeed, as it covered the front of the cabin. It ignored Matson for the moment, but was perfectly able to find him, and likely to do so first.

7.

There were perhaps twenty minutes remaining for something to happen. After that, only bandit country awaited them – terrorist rule and gunman's law in the Levant; the confused politics of the rest of the Near East; and revolutionary North Africa.

In some of those places he would be in rather more danger off the aircraft than on it. His particular role in the Department saw to that. He was the one in charge of the B-list, the storeman who fumigated the rats and exported the riff-raff, and the whole wide world seemed to know and resent it. St Peter had a similar unenviable task in Heaven, and who was the Archangel at Time's Western Gate?

Miss Potts' face darkened. Not with a well-deserved spasm of sickness. With shadow.

The dark slot of a swing-wing's retraction cavity filled her window until it resembled a television close-up of someone's birth-canal – an elephant's, perhaps.

A U.S. star drifted past, then silver fuselage with water dots blowing off it in a savage unpeeling of freckles.

Before the tail-fin and stabiliser arrived, the image unzoomed to reveal all or most of an F1-11, the huge helmets of its pilot and navigator owling towards them. Then the fighter-bomber nudged its slimness back in, so it filled up the window once more, a stainless-steel signboard of stencilled numbers, check marks and Fleet hieroglyphics.

The hangover was half an hour gone. He didn't need six-five vision to read RESCUE – AXE HERE in a funeral black imprint as stark as the blood hole in Sally Sherman's back.

The world buckled, became a glistening pain in his nostrils, his eyelids drying as they peeled back from the whites of his eyes. The maniac Trident was throwing a wing-over, a right and left wing-over, swatting at the American plane or planes, cuffing off interception.

The hijacker was flying it. There was no way a regular flight-crew could be bullied into this.

Matson's eyes moistened and cleared. The window was still full of jazzy American star and insignia, a too-close jigsaw of stencil. The F1-11 was nailed into the hub of their manoeuvre. It couldn't break free. It had to conform or crash.

The window pulled back. Matson's brain unzoomed. He looked into the navigator's eyes, which were addressing the camera. They were empty of fear. They had no time for fear. They brimmed with dispassionate unbelief, their intelligence super-total, the way a rat can gaze point-blank down the barrel of a shot-gun.

The pilot was intent ahead. Pilots always keep their brain a mile in front of their nose.

The Americans had no time to give up on them. The Trident barrel-rolled all round them – or trapped them inside an illusion of shifting sea-horizon and cloud-skeins in the sky. More pain in the nose, and the F1-11 jerked upwards and out of existence as if the sun had snatched it up on a crane. The Trident was twisting and diving as it was never designed to dive, escalating downwards like a plunging lift in a mineshaft.

He looked past the drunken ladies at a green sea no longer pulsing, at a Sargasso of oil-slick and seaweed, then at ruler-straight bone-white sand. Then came a town in a jigsaw of suburbs, its pieces swarming towards him.

He knew what shoreline this was – if the aircraft managed to miss it. He had passed this way before.

8.

There was only one place where the sun, still high, could be on his right, the sea also on his right, the shoreline running south and ahead in an endless line.

A man comes to recognise towns, even from above and through a streaky window. He does when he has fallen into them, or onto them, or past them. Matson had once lain on the larded air in the free-fall position and gazed down on Benghazi by starlight from twenty-three thousand feet.

He had seen it through vaselined goggles – a feminine town, compact, but with sprawling limbs, breasted with gas-towers, neat domes of petro-chemical, its night eyes winking up at him.

He had hung over it in snaky space-skin and passed it by, losing height at man's terminal velocity of one hundred and eleven miles an hour. He had watched it drift past his chest, past his crotch, past his boots, his body powering ahead through the increasingly audible crackle of dewfall, the pre-dawn scolding of birds, till all around him, more intensive than the tempest in his ears and the pneumatic whirr and thump of old Saturn rolling, came the thin scream of frost on a million miles of sand.

Waiting in the aeroplane, five miles high with God, he had as usual nearly crapped himself. Outside in the wicked air, once his limbs were stabilised, he didn't give a toss.

In his two and three quarter minutes of absolute power he no longer thought of his altichute malfunctioning to plant him kneedeep in the rock. He could lay his gloved hands on the belt of Orion. No: he didn't give a toss.

He didn't give a toss about Libya either. He was coming to screw Libya. He was the Fallen Angel diving from beyond the primum mobile to seduce the silly woman and violate her garden.

That was then.

9.

Matson had more lives than one. Parachuting near Benghazi on the track to Beda-Fomm had been part of the existence he had tried to pray away from in the Levant when the sniper's bullet got him.

Libya could be deadly for him in at least two of his lives. Then so could this Trident. He must be like a cat, and defend his last life to the last.

A cat is more fortunate. He does not know when his last life has come. Nor his last minute until his last second.

He watched the sage-grey and olive strip of littoral run

down behind the wing. He listened to American voices. There would be no more company for them from the Sixth Fleet now, not in this land of bright green flags. He heard the Düsseldorf Tart tell them so.

She offered immediate proof: two Libyan Air Force swing-wings rollercoasting in stepped-up formation on either side of the aircraft – MiG 23s, from one of the Flogger squadrons. Matson had never seen any mark of this series before. From side-on they were not unlike the Yugoslav Fishbeds, but only from side-on. The earlier model was a delta-wing.

Over Al Magrun they peeled away, but drifted back to formate in distant parallel. Matson tried to tune his eye on their diminished roundels: black inside white inside red. The colours disappeared. The escort stayed. Ubiquitous Mikoyan Gurevich.

The Trident was flying oddly, and getting lower. The land rose to meet them in a gouged-out rockery of hills, shimmering in hazy sunshine. There was a sickness inside his pulse. His seat sagged on emptiness, then bumped as if they were scraping the ground. He knew the prosaic explanation – that this was thin-air turbulence. They had run into a steepening pressure graph, first sea, then olive grove, then scrub desert. And the desert south of Al Magrun was bad for daylight overflying, because it offered up all of its surfaces of *erg, reg* and *hammada* as well as these piling hills. That was why the MiGs had peeled away, and why he sensed this thinness underneath the heart.

Yes, he knew the prosaic explanation, but prose wasn't truthful enough. Something was expected of him; but he had no way of knowing what it was or where the expectation came from.

God expected nothing. Nor did man. God knew him too well and not enough men knew him well enough. Was it merely the conditioning of duty, or some odd idea he had of himself?

If they marked him down for death, was it his business to die quietly, so all the rest might live? Or to kill before being killed, because he of all the victims was probably the best trained, and seated to best advantage?

And what did the real choice come to: whether to curse or kiss the hangman?

Matson knew that whatever he decided he would have to act on it alone. He also knew that however right he was he would also be wrong. He was in a cruel situation where no man could be right enough.

10.

A few miles beyond Al Magrun the coast turned towards the sun. The Trident left it behind and pushed on. They were heading inland away from any possible landing ground.

He saw the first great spur of dunes that runs all the way from Tibesti and threatens to spill into the sea, the brown and then silver-yellow then umber Sahara that seeks to mop up the Mediterranean like a crust in a saucer of gravy. They were following it south between the jebel and the eastern gravel; but south as far as where? South as far as Chad? Or Niger? Or Darfur?

Somewhere along the route stood a steepening line of hills, the high jebel, and then the peaks of Tibesti – he forgot how high.

His brain was reeling with maps and mileages, the maps running out of places just as surely as the Trident would soon be out of fuel.

He listened again to the Düsseldorf Tart, stole a sly glance at little Dark and Curly, and then considered the black's bandages and its Browning from beneath lowered eyelids. They were all exactly on station: death was still in place.

They were all too far away, and he was disconcerted by the black's habit of holding the pistol in his damaged left hand. Was he ambidextrous? Matson was sure he had used his right, and only his right, to shoot Sergeant-major Brownskill. But what about Major Wellard-Browne? A Browning is steady enough one-handed; it's not a magnum revolver.

Yes, if anyone was going to act, it must be Matson. If anyone was to be violenced or shot as a further example, it would be him, and it would happen as soon as they landed. All he could do until then was wait.

Some men write notes before dying. Other men rage or sweat. Matson was no good at either, and he'd spent his quinquennial prayer.

He enlisted in the ranks of the Truly Resigned. He joined up with the others who had failed to beat the clock and stood alongside them all in the ghostly parade of the *morituri te salutant*. As the golden lions of sand came slinking past the wingtip, he closed his eyes and slept.

FOUR

1.

There was ice beneath his eyelids. He woke and saw they were over a Sahara of molten rock and little hills. The sea was a fan of sunlight behind towering dust. The jebel was burnished and glowed like a lamp.

He flexed himself muscle by muscle, retaining his posture and keeping his appearance relaxed. Aircraft seats are cramping at the best of times. After several hours with his limbs tied, and with the added tension of fear, he didn't think he was up to much.

Little Ingram wouldn't give him a second chance. But he might accomplish something with the Düsseldorf Tart. Or the black. He owed the black. He owed him for Wellard-Browne, for Brownskill, and for Sally Sherman most of all. The whole world owed the black.

Miss Potts and Lady Chambers were awake and not looking at all well. They gazed at him strangely, as if he had been talking in his sleep.

'You want to be grateful your father didn't include Gerry among your given names,' he said to Lady Chambers, to add to the lustre of the moment.

'My father did.'

It was obviously such a good family joke that it made her sister forget the consequences of her tiddly-pomp.

'But I damnwell changed it,' Lady Chambers added. '*And* I take jolly good care not to tell anyone, except *in extremis*. *In extremis* is where we're at, I suppose.'

'I suppose.' He couldn't think of anything even remotely cheerful. He turned towards the Little Nun. 'We seem to be landing,' he mouthed.

'You talk in your sleep,' she complained.
'Such as what?'
'Disgusting words. All blasphemy and body functions.'
Thank God for only that.

2.

At Camberwell he learned there were three kinds of desert. There was rock, there was boulder with stone, there was shifting dune: *erg, reg,* and *hammada*. He hadn't been taught which was which.

There were dunes on the left. On the right were rocky hills, running beyond the starboard wing in waves of silver shadow. The Trident was putting down between them – impossible to see on what.

The aircraft made a steep approach. The air was thin: it dropped in like a dehydrated moth. Dust billowed up to meet it. Then it slowed into grit, a tide of engine-fume and debris fouling the windows.

Then it squatted against its own retrothrust, and the perspex cleared. Matson saw they were running along a rectangular landing-strip scarred by neglect and over-use, but still compact enough to be workable.

The surface glowed with strange lights, like petrol in a puddle.

It had been fabricated from that amalgam of crude oil and loosened sand he'd seen elsewhere in North Africa, and all over the Near and Middle East; its smell was seeping into the cabin.

Expatriate Europeans used it to build putting-greens, soccer-stadia, and bowling alleys. Americans landscaped golf-courses with it, and baseball pitches. They all used it for roads, carparks and hardcore surrounds to their bungalows. This was the first time Matson had seen it laid out as an airstrip. It suggested, as in all other cases, a plentiful local supply of crude. The desert drank oil by the trainload, and drank it deep. You had to waste the oil where you found it. Play golf where the gushers had squandered the raw material before anyone could get a plug in, construct the gardens of your dream palace from dust and instant filth.

The aircraft turned to port and thumped slowly ahead, revealing a large compound of one-storey huts behind high concrete posts and steel-mesh. The concrete was brown from its iron tie-rods, the mesh was rusty; some of the hut windows were broken, as if from the pressure of idleness or decay.

The place looked like a penal settlement, or a barracks. Come to that, it might just have been a disused holiday camp: they all look the same.

Matson saw oil donkeys and a couple of ruined derricks, and remembered the runway. They were surely miles beyond Zeltan, but Libya had more oil-fields than one.

Either this place had been worked dry, or it had never got going. It had its landing strip and its accommodation, though. Once again, the hijack showed every sign of being meticulously planned as well as brilliantly executed. This time, of course, Libya would have to be at least covertly involved.

That was hardly much of a shock. The real surprise came next. As the Trident continued to move parallel to the line of buildings, another plane rolled into view, a stationary Jumbo, with its near landing-wheels ruptured, presumably as a result of thin air and the deplorable surface of the airstrip.

Surely the widebody had not been sent here to collect them. That kind of intergovernmental arrangement would have been premature, inflammatory even. Too many guns were being held on them. Besides, Benghazi International Airport was the natural place for a swap, and they had overflown Benghazi without a second thought to home in on the sinister privacy of a desert airstrip. This was clearly a multiple hijack, being conducted in a manner which suggested Libyan duplicity.

Three dull green flags, stirring above the perimeter buildings confirmed that they *were* in Libya. Matson's watch told him that they hadn't flown far enough for this to be part of the Libyan claim in Northern Chad. Then there were the soldiers, Libyan certainly, but far too listless and careless of their weapons to be near a front line, or anywhere else they considered dangerous.

A platoon of them, less rather than more, were lounging in small groups in the wing-shadow of the other aircraft. Their carbines were slung, or propped against the wheels of its undercarriage. Some of the guns lay in bits, or with their magazines stripped, on a pair of groundsheets strewn near a command-jeep with its bonnet off.

The soldiers were smoking, drawing on long white cigarettes with Arabic intensity. The cigarettes were smoked to the same length. They were the most uniform thing about the entire outfit, and clearly part of a recent issue – or gift. The soldiers smoked them energetically, working at them too hard with their hands and their heads and their lungs, as if smoking was a religious observance.

An elderly woman, in silvery-white elasticated stockings and a floral dress blooming with eyes as well as flowers in a quaint hypothesis of peacock tails, lay a little way away from them, perhaps an odour off. She was spreadeagled twenty-five feet beneath the Jumbo's front boarding door, from which she had evidently fallen. Blood fluttered from her ears and dabbled in the black sand, but otherwise she looked very neat and orderly, even to the mauve rinse of her hair. Perhaps the soldiers smoked in her honour.

There was a movement at this door of the Jumbo. A hand and naked forearm beckoned. The hand was sinewy and male, the wrist strong, but braceleted in a tiny gold watch. One of the soldiers tossed up a packet of cigarettes, or a packet of something. All very friendly. The hijackers defenestrate an old lady minus her watch, presumably to encourage the others, and receive smokes in return. Evidently the people in Matson's Trident were arriving to a suitably paranoid situation.

A hijack involving more than one aircraft suggested something very elaborate indeed.

There was one more fact for everyone to dwell on. Matson was neither colour-blind nor illiterate, but the body on the compacted sump and sand had briefly assumed a higher priority in the order of things.

What he was now looking at was the least mistakable logo of any airline in the world: four square letters in carmel white standing two by two up the Jumbo's fin.

EL AL.

Nobody hijacks an El Al flight. Terrorists have given up

trying. Everyone knows its aircraft are inviolate. There is an item by item luggage search before you board, a garment by garment body search, followed by an inflexible attitude towards extortion. Whatever the threat, El Al presses on – the hand-grenade does not deflect it: it goes down shooting. Everyone knows that.

Except for this lot. Their calculation and flair – plus an uncanny control of luck – had tricked every fail-safe to over-ride.

The idea that he might be in the middle of something really big was pushed from his mind by what came next.

3.

The Düsseldorf Tart stood beside him, her belly bulging over the top of her skirt. Her breasts hung unfashionably low, even though she was stretching upwards to the luggage lockers. Bathers who survive being savaged by sharks notice odd little blemishes about the snout, the tooth, the eye of their assailants and report them afterwards as if they were the most arresting facts in the whole encounter. What Matson was to recall whenever he thought of the Tart was damp cloth rippling in the sweat of her navel.

She took hold of a flight bag, Lady Chambers' or Miss Potts', and ripped it open.

Leaning over the back of the front seat she stuffed a pair of embroidered knickers into Anne Chambers' mouth, then bound her face with some tights.

'You talk too much,' she said. She liked using the pants and the tights. Perhaps they were emblems of decadence. 'And *you* smell,' she hissed at Miss Potts. She didn't squeal in Arabic now.

Matson did not witness her cure for Rebecca Potts. It was his turn.

A long line of men – and perhaps women – had been hitched up and strung out behind him. They had been patient, and unfidgeting, except when the cabin had depressurised and they had been unable to reach their emergency oxygen supply. But their presence had been there. He had felt the tug of their breathing, in the cord that bound his chest. They had hung themselves like the links of an anchor-chain to the thongs on his wrist.

Now, suddenly, he was sprawling. Not free, but released from their weight at his back. He fell onto his knees in the aisle.

He had been cut loose from behind. It wasn't the Tart's doing. Curly had done it. The black, in his turn, was pulling him upright and forward by jerking at the cord round his wrist.

It wasn't a slip-knot. It was a standing bowline, or once Curly had tested it after the depressurisation it was. It probably always had been. He should have recognised that such a knot singled him out from the rest. It meant he could be detached and drawn separate.

It took him a second or so to find his feet, and that was more than enough time for the black to grow impatient. Matson caught two quick loops in the cord to protect his wrists before the man tightened up on him.

The black did not like this at all. He cracked at the lead like a whip, trying to jar the loops from Matson's hands.

Matson hung on tight, retaining his yard of slack, but that was his only gesture. The black dragged him forward by tugging at the line, drawing him with fastened hands like a penitent, winding him in.

The cord was plastic-covered, perhaps plastic through and through. It slipped against itself, clenching up on the bowline, scoring his wrists.

It was probably a clothes-line, or clothes-line pulley. A whole file of men had been rendered immobile by an old-fashioned laundry aid. Matson gritted his teeth and left this odd little fact where it belonged – with the crater the Düsseldorf Tart kept her navel in.

The navel was behind him. The Ingram had never got ahead, not this time round. He heard one or the other of them being cocked.

Meanwhile there was the Browning. He had looked down the muzzle of a Browning High Power many times, but only to clean it. This one needed cleaning. It was in the black's damaged left hand and stank with smeared blood.

The cord was in the black's right hand, which punched up at him. The pistol swatted him in its turn, but only lightly, to soothe him on his way towards the door – the hand that held it was too damaged for anything heavy.

A pistol is hard-edged however it strikes.

Someone, probably Curly, kicked an expert toecap into the back of his knee, folding him down from behind into the approved prayer position.

It was where Sally had fallen. He crouched on slime and oxide and saw something like an owl's nest, a mat of hair or cloth, and tiny chips of bone. He glanced quickly away.

He looked towards the silver emptiness beyond the door and knew he had got it all wrong. He should have taken out the black a moment or two ago, while he could. He might even have finished Curly with the High Power, her or the Tart. Once his fastened hands had closed on the gun and squeezed a round off, all kinds of things might have happened. For the first time both Ingrams would have been pointing his way and not down the cabin. They might have checked their fire for a second for fear of hitting the black.

He had got it wrong. He was the one best placed to take the chance. He was probably the only one trained for it when it came. He had been waiting for it for hours. Now it had passed him by before he was ready. Just a lugging by the wrists, a kick from behind had been enough to distract him. Meanwhile, this kneeling at the door could only mean one thing. They were going to make an example of him. Every tiny notch in his tally of exemption was being cancelled and set aside.

Once he started blaming himself there was no end to it. Self-blame is too close to pity. Not only was he failing to keep himself alive, and perhaps others alive: he was going to die badly as well.

If now was to be the hour of his death, he wanted to bid life a proper farewell, as the condemned man can and should. He needed to find a tiny weeping place in his heart for his parents, his dead Brenda, his elusive Ginevra. Better, he wanted to speak out in the teeth of the gun, make a gesture like Captain Lyall's. He wanted to die like a man.

He remembered as so often in a crisis that silly poem

learned at school: 'I'd rather be a living mouse than dead as a man dies.' Crouching there, waiting for the bullet to come crashing in, he felt his nose and eyes flood with congestion. You don't expect catarrh in the desert.

Training took over.

If he tarried to make his peace with God, that was where he would be – at Peace, with God.

He wasn't ready for such a surrender. His hand touched a crushed piece of tin. It was Sally Sherman's silly badge. Whatever it had asked for, it certainly wasn't this.

The cord was tugged against his face, then over his head. His wrists went with it.

Kneeling is a difficult position from which to move quickly. If the hands are stretched back and up, then evasion is even more impossible.

He still gripped the loops of plastic. He had first grabbed them for comfort, then hung on to them as an act of defiance. Now their promise of a moment's slack was his only chance.

He let go of the double loop, unbalancing whoever tugged behind him, presumably the black. Then he dived forward a couple of feet to grab at the sill of the door with his bound hands, sending his legs following after in an untidy rabbit-hop.

Pain sliced into his wrists, but the black let go of the rope. Matson was free and falling.

4.

The world was not a great way beneath the Trident's door. The world was compacted sand.

Matson leapt forward and downward, diving beneath the line of reflex fire, but his wrists were snatched overhead by the rope, arching his body upright and over, causing him to crash heavily on his heels. This jarred his spine and spewed the air from his lungs.

He was already rolling just the same, tearing at the rope, trying to get back beneath the fuselage.

He was stopped by legs, feet, one of which was promptly placed on his face.

The Libyan Army had decided that the boarding door of the Trident offered more in the way of theatre than the current show inside the Jumbo. Matson had spoiled its fun.

His life was all smells just lately. There is a particularly nasty emanation from crude with sand, rather like offal and pig-shit. He noticed this entering one nostril from that part of the Western Desert which grated against his right cheekbone, and infiltrating the other one from a boot-sole only recently lifted from the same muck. Leather boots can be witty, too, especially if tanned in camel effluent – the fashion seemed to be for both sorts – and worn around a hot landscape by feet ignorant of socks. Not all the boots were like this, he noticed. Some were in rubber and plastic, like modern combat footwear the world over. Clearly he was being trodden on by an officer or senior NCO.

The boot withdrew itself and he sat up quickly, to look for its owner. Soldiers are disciplined people, reluctant to discharge guns at visiting civilians. He was in the right frame of mind to punch one for his forbearance.

The Libyan Army retreated fast. A second glance told him it wasn't so much retreating as stepping back to a respectful distance. He was going to be given some respect and some air. Not that the air so close to the ground was worth very much. In Cyrenaica even the rocks had *tinea pedis*.

Stunned, sitting upright in low sunshine, Matson realised that the soldiers were standing back so that someone in the Trident could take an unimpeded shot at him.

He lifted his eyes to the boarding door to see both Curly and the Düsseldorf Tart, each one-handed with an Ingram 11. They didn't shoot at once because the Tart was tossing a coin and slapping it down against her gun-wrist.

He climbed to his feet to find Curly had won. He supposed won.He didn't think she would think she had lost. She was already aiming down at him, and she had the doorway to herself.

This time there was nowhere to dive to. He could never beat the storm of fast-fire .38s.

He stood at the centre of the distant circle of soldiers, feeling terribly alone. He felt as the bull must feel as the blade slides in.

She wasn't even going to favour him with a grimace of triumph as she blew him away.

'Stop!' Someone shouted. It was a masculine voice, with a strangely familiar whinny to it. 'Stop!' Or perhaps it seemed familiar because it shouted in English. 'Stop that, please – I beg, and pray, and implore you!' The English voice did not come from inside the plane.

Curly stopped, but only for a moment.

Her moment was so curt that the voice shouted again, in Arabic.

A tall Arab pushed through and among the soldiers. He was dressed in burnous and sandals, but with his kaffiyeh worn in the Palestinian manner. He was evidently a man of importance, because he was accompanied, respectfully, by an infantry captain of the Libyan Army.

'You must not shoot Mr Mat*son*,' he told the landscape at large. 'Or certainly not yet.' He spoke to the soldiers once more in Arabic, and then to the captain, like a hunter soothing his dog. The woman in the doorway continued to look unsoothed, so he tried again in English. 'It would be quite improper to shoot Mat*son* yet, at least until I have had time to talk with him. Mat*son* is my friend.' He stepped forward as if to help Matson to his feet, smiling with that sickly green glitter of the teeth that had nauseated Matson several times in the past. 'My dear Mat*son*.'

Matson was already standing, but the largesse of the extended hand put him in mind of a biblical expression, as did the drafty benevolence of the gesture. He was being raised up.

5.

Dr Ibrahim Nuseibeh wore a dark green gem between his first and second upper front teeth. When Matson had first met him a few months ago, it was in a restaurant and they had been eating spinach, so he had assumed the man had food stuck round his face. He hadn't. He had precious stones instead. Dr Nuseibeh was full of surprises. Finding him here was one of them, and finding out why would doubtless provide another.

He led Matson towards the captain, and the captain and

some soldiers towards the nearest hut. Matson was glad to be among them. He didn't think Curly would go so far with her Ingram as to pick him out in a crowd.

Otherwise, as the captain motioned the sergeant with the boots to follow them, he didn't know what to expect of Nuseibeh. He had recommended the good doctor for deportation, quite recently, and the good doctor knew it. He had then reprieved him in return for a particularly nasty favour. The doctor did not think he had been reprieved long enough. Beyond Pomeroy's insistence that the man doubled between Mossad and the PLO when he wasn't wimping around London, there was the little problem of his proximity to a hijack which had settled down with its spoils in so outlandish a place.

The place itself didn't hold any clues, unless the oil-bonded runway was one. There was an oilfield at Zeltan, true, nationalised at the time of the Libyan Revolution but still in receipt of multinational funding. But Zeltan was off this lip of the jebel, perhaps fifty miles away. They must have overflown it.

There were oil-donkeys here, two of them – hence the runway – but they were old and unworking. The bores must have been deep. Could it have taken so many people to make them? There were enough huts here to house thousands – more than a battalion, anyway. Matson thought of the military establishments he had known. This was bigger than anything in Britain, of truly U.S. proportions, but weather-scarred, storm-penetrated, empty – a barracks for a brigade of ghosts.

Perhaps it was an old military establishment. There was no town to garrison, no strategic site to guard, but soldiers have to go somewhere to train. In fact, when it comes to training, governments generally prefer their armies to go nowhere; an excellent description of here. Even with the sun sinking low, Matson could see there was a great deal of nowhere lying round about. Some maps call it the Sahara Desert.

The captain had gone inside and his sergeant had followed him; but Dr Nuseibeh halted, so Matson found it prudent to stay with him and admire the scene.

The good doctor was once again surrounded by soldiers. Nuseibeh was no kind of militarist and no Pied Piper, but Pomeroy said he enjoyed what was young and daft and handsome, and some men have a way of conveying such things. In North Africa they are not always taken amiss.

Nuseibeh did not believe in hoarding his pleasures. He presented the dark-eyed circle of smiling faces to Matson lovingly and one by one. Then he introduced Matson to the faces.

'This man,' Dr Nuseibeh purred, 'this man is a Mr Patrick Mat*son*, formerly Captain Mat*son*. He is quite harmless. He is on the import side of the British Intelligence business, not the export. That, taken with the fact that he is of Irish extraction, should render him of absolutely no interest to you.'

'Bastard!'

The faces grew puzzled. Some even stopped smiling.

'A pity, Mr Mat*son*. You have just used what is still an offensive word in some cultures.' He smiled, and patted a head. 'This fool did not understand a syllable of what I said. Nor did this one. These gentlemen do not speak English. I assure myself of such matters, believe me. But they know when a man is being discourteous to an old friend, just as clearly as they can recognise a dog's intention by its bark. I shall now be obliged to translate what the dog has said, and explain just why he dared to say it.'

The doctor had stood in the open air long enough. He strode into the hut to confide his irritation to the captain and the sergeant.

Matson waited by the door, and listened without understanding. He could still hope. He heard no mention of his name.

There was no detectable change of mood inside the little room. Either Nuseibeh wasn't telling them, or he found nothing to say that they didn't already know.

After a minute or so he came out. His face was no longer bland and he did not smile towards his young men. To Matson he said, 'I expect your prayers to thank me. I saved you from being shot just now, and being shot is final. These Libyans will merely shave your knackers off.' He always did have a good grasp of English, Matson remembered.

Matson did not see where he went, or who with. Two words were shouted from the hut, and Matson was caught and jolted through the door. He didn't know how many hands had fallen on his back, but it felt like the whole platoon's.

FIVE

1.

It was hard to be absolutely certain about a colleague's leisure activities, but one tended to have an inkling. This one did, anyway. Leonard Fossit was pretty sure Matson's itinerary included Wildenrath, Gütersloh and Bruggen in the boring North German steppe, and since Avaroc could only service one of them at a time he decided to take alarm at the midday news and ask further.

He asked Miss Dalrymple, his secretary, on the office intercom. Miss Dalrymple sent in young Mrs Hyem. Leonard liked his ladies to have first names like Miss or Mrs, or even Ms. It made for harmony and order, and gave a chap a lot less to remember, and certainly less to think about.

'Miss Dalrymple asks me to tell you it's all on file,' young Mrs Hyem said. 'She said Mr Patrick is very good about things like that; so here's the file. She further asks me to remind you it was your idea and according to your directive.' She laid the file open on his desk. 'She is very particular I'm to tell you not to forget to enter your Canadian fishing holiday with as much detail as possible, in case of the minister, sir. She says Canada's a big country and we want to be able to find you.'

'People don't talk like that any more.'

'Hilda Dalrymple does.' Young Mrs Hyem dropped a person's pre-name in Leonard Fossit's presence.

'I'm going to be paddling a canoe up something called French River. Where do I file that?'

'She says under *Personnel Personal*; but not *Personnel Deep Personal*.'

'This stuff is all going on mainframe soon. How does Miss Dalrymple suggest we encode our holidays in that bit of wizardry?'

'She says she won't be here by then.'

2.

Fossit phoned Pomeroy at the Foreign Office.

Pomeroy was almost effusive, for Pomeroy. Just the same, he was, as always, ineffably languid about his affection. To define paradox was to define Marcus Pomeroy. It was not to define oxymoron, Fossit thought. Pomeroy didn't move fast enough. 'Why not bring yourself for lunch next week?' he suggested. 'We can't chat now. Some wog has just pinched an aeroplane with half the British Army on board. And a fair proportion of the American.'

'They got Paddy, I'm afraid.'

'What – half-inch the Kincora Lad? The thicky! Who, in his right mind, ever books a trip on a hijack? His jockstrap must swarm with fatal genes.'

'Marcus –'

'*Don't* try to make him *my* priority, much as I despise and adore him. Ironside Irenson's on board, did you know? Together with one of his muffins.'

'I don't understand "muffin".'

'Then you don't understand Irenson, dear thing. Something succulent for dunking. We'll keep her name from Lady Ironside, of course. Do you want my minister to know about Paddy? He won't be impressed. Well, say "Ta!", then.'

'Matson's worth a bottle of five-star to me.'

'You'll be coming to the meeting, I suppose.'

'What meeting?'

'The one the Idiots have called for half a minute's time. Just shows what a low number you rate in the interdepartmental peck. COBRA, CORK, CAC or CAMFLY – one of the subliminal ones. Quinlan's Lorna should have summoned you. Or Quinlan's Hattie. He's got two of the same person now.' Pomeroy made his desk-top amplifier sound as if it was tucked beneath his chin – a considerable feat, because the amplifier was huge and archaic, and he didn't have a chin. 'Here it is. CAC – you're down to attend, next under me on the list.'

'They can't call CAC for a hijack!'

'The hijack of the century, dear thing. You don't know the half of it yet. Somebody's been plucking aircraft from the sky like feathers from a stripper's bottom.'

3.

Matson was good at landings, could always find himself full of words in a crisis. He managed a 'Good afternoon' as he picked himself up. He held out his fastened wrists as if to shake hands.

The captain sat behind a table which was much too big for him and much too small for the room. The sergeant stood at its end, the way sergeants do, to see fair play.

'I'm afraid it's a bowline, not a slipknot. Who do I have the pleasure of addressing?'

The sergeant shouted something in Arabic. Matson didn't speak Arabic, but he understood Army. The sergeant was telling him to stand right where he was, be upright and exceedingly still.

Matson stood where he was. There were soldiers behind him, boys maybe, but the sergeant had reduced them to awe, or at least to breathlessness and no more cigarettes.

Attention shifted to a pile of paper at the end of the table furthest from the sergeant. The captain sighed and unscrewed an Osmiroid pen. He glanced towards the paper, then to the sergeant.

The sergeant was quieter this time, but he crunched camel-tanned boots, spoke a little word in the air, and one of the rookies stole forward on rubber feet and handed the captain one piece of this paper from its pile, which he straightened.

The paper looked blank, but the room was far from bright.

If it was British Army blank paper, or U.S. Army blank paper, or NATO blank paper in general, it would have a tiny serial number on it somewhere and an explanation printed in four-point pica to say it was blank and paper. Matson didn't know if they did things so well out here.

The captain paused, Osmiroid in hand, then wrote a line of spidery minutiae across the page, pondering his dots and little splashes, checking that his calligraphy was correct. He wrote the line backwards like an ape in a dream – no, a soldier in a mirror – so Matson wondered briefly if the hours of stress had blurred his perception.

He recalled that Arab script is semitic and runs that way, even to the dots and splashes. He chuckled quietly.

His chuckle wasn't approved of. The captain looked up at him, then back to his paper. He pocketed the Osmiroid and said, still gazing down, 'You're a spy, Mr Patrick.'

'My name is Matson. Captain Matson.'

'You're a spy, Captain Patrick Matson.' The man's English was good, unmistakeably Arab, but assured and incisive. He was obviously hand-picked to be in charge of the hijack's reception committee.

'I'm a soldier like yourself.'

'You've left the Army, I believe?'

Probably in Military Intelligence. He was looking up at Matson now and his gaze was bright. He had played these games before.

'To become a policeman, yes.'

'Captain is not, I think, a rank in the British police force?'

'Captain remains my courtesy title. To return to my point – in a general sense I'm a policeman. I use the word to make simple what I do.' Nuseibeh had shopped him. He must take care to set a limit on each lie.

'I am not a simpleton, Captain Patrick Matson.'

'I am a policeman. I sit at a desk, but I supervise policemen.'

'You're a spy. We shall hang you for it. You have spied against us, against the Libyan People's Bureau in London.'

So he *was* Intelligence. Nuseibeh hadn't had enough time for this.

'I cannot be a spy in my own country.'

'But you think you can be a spy in mine?'

'I didn't come here. I was brought here. It is my job to catch spies, not be a spy.'

'Set a thief to catch a thief, Captain Patrick? The Libyan peoples are spied on wherever they go, and we require retribution.'

'Generally by other Libyans. Libyans are of no interest to me.'

'No?' The captain stood up and walked round the desk to look very closely at Matson. Matson's ear and the corner of his chin seemed to take most of his attention. 'No? Well, now we will have a little time to begin to interest you.'

'Where did you learn your English? You still do not tell me your name.'

The man did not quite know how to deal with these questions. He decided to bear down on the questioner, like a nobleman being promised a knighthood by an urchin; but Matson was too assured an urchin. In the end he said, 'The South London Polytechnic.'

'Really? How very strange. I had a girlfriend ...'

The blow was hard and came from behind. The Captain had not struck it, but it fell midway between the ear and the angle of the jaw, right where he had been indicating for so long.

He watched Matson stagger, then said, 'There are no girlfriends here, Mr Patrick.'

'A pity.'

'Your girlfriend isn't going to like you when we're through with you. You'll smell when we send you back to her. Do you know what I mean?'

'I've brought my own soap,' Matson said. 'If only you'll let me get my hands on my luggage.'

Something hit him again, again from behind, but harder – a hand or a carbine or someone jumping their knees into his back.

Matson didn't fall. He tried to grin just as he had as a boy in Camberwell when the head had finished caning him.

'You will smell because you will be dead, Mr Captain Patrick. That is how we will send you back to her.'

'She won't mind my smell. She's already dead herself.' He heard his voice falter with too much smothered emotion, so he added very quickly, 'She's dead because some little bugger like you decided it was time he killed her.' He smashed out with a chinjab, chunking his left leg across his front and setting up and throwing the heel of his right hand with more speed and venom than he'd ever managed before, even though his left had to travel with it.

His cords burst open, and his wrists welled blood. The captain's face disintegrated in front of him. But only in surprise. Matson was already falling, chopped down from behind. His blow hadn't landed. He had shown his rage too early, and the sergeant had beaten him to the punch.

The captain's features were still intact and Matson was spent from hitting air. He found his whole attention had fractured. They dragged him up, bleeding and half conscious. Their fists had been enough. There was no need to kick the sand off their nice rubber boots.

They dumped him onto a chair, and someone brought some water, but only to drench his head.

When he managed to look up, the captain was behind his desk again. The sergeant was standing apart, as at the beginning. 'So, Mr Patrick. We shall punish you for that.'

'You'll cause a diplomatic incident.'

'So who else of interest have you brought with you on that aeroplane?'

'What did you study at the South Bank Polytechnic?'

'Who else is travelling on the aeroplane?'

'You still haven't told me your name.'

The sergeant moved noisily in his superior footwear. He took Matson's chin in his hands and began to brandish his head from side to side. Then he went and stood behind him, but only to gather his hands and lash them together again. Matson was glad of the pain. It was extensive, but quite remote – like the ache of an old wound. If they bashed his face any more, then his wrists would help him cope. He knew how to hang on to this much.

'Who were you sitting beside?'

'I really didn't ask. Shouldn't you be talking to the Italians? They're our diplomatic representatives in Tripoli, I believe.'

'Who were you sitting beside?'

'I didn't get introduced. I was reading a book.'

'During a hijack?'

'A most arresting book.' He had Anne Chambers to protect and hadn't she mentioned Irenson? Also like every professional, he had to spend time. 'But full of all kinds of rubbish. I couldn't follow the plot.' The sergeant was closer behind him. Try to distract your questioners into losing their temper. 'One of your fellows wrote it, I believe.'

'Who else is there on that plane? We know it's a military charter. Tell us the highest rank.'

'Now what was the fellow's name? ... Well, the book was called the *Qu'ran*, better known as *The Koran*. So he must have been –'

Professionally, the Captain disappointed him.

4.

Leonard Fossit had just been passed the memorandum that told him that the Minister had been tipped off about Matson. While he was waiting for CAC to begin, he tried to involve Pomeroy further.

Pomeroy was already launched on a diversion. He thought CAC was aptly named. 'Whenever our mandarins give us a new building, they always equip it with the same old dirt.' If Marcus Pomeroy wasn't a mandarin, what the hell was he? A shogun, perhaps. 'And their old dirt's dirty.'

'And how,' bleated Fossit, 'do they do that?' He wasn't too sure about CAC. He knew what it was, but not what it stood for. It only met at moments like this, and what it did was pass the buck. He adjusted his voice and said: 'I mean, where do they keep the stuff? We've got to work Paddy into the official chat somehow. You can bet he's not on the agenda.'

'Splendid expression, "work in". It's a plasterer's verb, fine and sweaty. Still, it fits the times. We're governed by a new breed of men – men who actually cultivate blackheads. On the backside, some can vouch for. In the nose, visibly. *And* wear them in public. Where, in the old days, did you ever see a blackhead? Or read about one in Hansard?'

'Disraeli's lot had them.'

'In Dizzy's time a man with blackheads would have used face-powder and kept his ears against the light. Look at that one. He was all right when he was yours.' Pomeroy smiled encouragingly towards Quinlan, who was chewing on a biscuit and being brought up to date by one of his senior ladies before calling the meeting to order. The biscuit so close to his ear, and the woman's urgent whispering, probably meant he was just out of hearing. 'Yes, we'll work young Matson in among the prattle, and sprinkle him around.'

' "Sprinkle" is pretty damned limp, as such things go!'

' "Sprinkle" is a fine stalactitic word, redolent of *frustrax* and flyblow. Not that it suits poor Paddy, who at least kept his nose clean. Until this morning, anyway.'

'The Libyans mayn't know what they've picked up.'

'They're Arabs, dear boy. They discovered algebra before the Greeks had even looked for it. They're not going to pass over a prime little number like Paddy. Let's hope he's genuinely indivisible.'

5.

Matson slumped in the chair at an odd angle and decided to stay there. The sergeant had been rough, the captain angry. Now it was his turn. He would treat himself to a few minutes' unconsciousness and see what they would do about it. Last time they used water. He could take any amount of water, unless they put a bag on his head first.

'Wake up, Captain Patrick. You're fit, and trained in such matters.'

The floor had been a dangerous place. But lopsided on a chair, for a man with his legs free? Matson lolled even further to his left and hoped to find someone's bones with his feet.

The Captain spoke quietly in Arabic, and Matson heard a match being struck. So it wasn't to be water this time. He said, still with his eyes closed, 'I apologise if I offended your religious sensibilities. My own have been rather disturbed in the last few hours.'

'You have no religion and no sensibilities. If you had, you would campaign to liberate your country from capitalist imperialism.'

'Of course.' The match was blown out. His nose bled, or

perhaps it was still this dusty catarrh. Even so, he could smell sour tobacco. He opened his eyes.

A young soldier was about to surprise his thumbnail with the hot end of the match. Matson smiled at him and said, 'The Socialist People's Libyan Arab Jamahiriya is aiding and abetting a hijack.'

The captain chuckled his appreciation of Matson's one word of Arabic, while the young soldier stopped in confusion. No-one told him to continue.

'Not true. The aircraft are delaying until we can decide an appropriate procedure.'

'You'll let the hijackers move them on?'

'Not necessarily.'

'You'll return them to their countries of origin?'

'Perhaps.'

'And you'll remove this private soldier from my line of sight? To do anything else would be contrary to International Law. I thought the Secretary General of the General Secretariat claimed to be attentive to International Law?'

'International Law is a complicated matter.' He had the sergeant move the soldier, just the same. 'Since you are so remarkably attentive to our ranks and titles, especially for a man who claims to be ignorant of us, what you must also understand is that the Revolutionary Republic is governed by its committees and its Congresses. It is they who observe the Laws. His Excellency is advised by them, and will consult them in relation to the situation we have here.'

'Won't that take a little time?' This conversation could last for ever as far as Matson was concerned.

'My answer is not His Excellency's answer. My answer is perhaps, but not necessarily.'

'We'll fly tonight?'

'You will not fly. As for the others, there is no illumination for the runway.'

'Tomorrow?'

'Hardly. We have no aviation fuel. There is fuel on the coast, but that will need to be brought here. Besides, we are not in control of the aircraft. Our concern must be for the safety of the passengers – once we have decided they are not an invasion force.'

'It's difficult to hijack an invasion force.'

'I speak of the safety of the British passengers, naturally.'

Matson decided to do nothing that might exacerbate the plight of the Israelis. He said, 'You're a soldier. I take it you regard the hijackers with disapproval?'

'If it is determined that they have done anything wrong, then they must look to be punished according to Islamic Law and Revolutionary Law.'

'What will that entail?'

'They could be beheaded or hanged. That is if they are to be regarded as criminals or terrorists.'

'They are, believe me.'

'The evidence is that they are freedom fighters and fellow revolutionaries – men and women without a country.'

'They're Europeans, some of them. Americans even. They have their own back yards.'

'They have chosen to deploy their destinies alongside the dispossessed.'

'My friend at the South London Poly would have enjoyed your command of her language.' So would Marcus Pomeroy.

'Your own case is simpler, Captain Patrick. Spies are merely hanged. By which I mean that decapitation is not an option.'

'You'll have to take me to Tripoli to sort that out.'

'Not necessarily. Up the road will do. The regional People's Congress will decide. We can hang you out here in the desert. Transporting you to Tripoli, or even to the capital of Cyrenaica, would be much too expensive for the local community.'

'You can't hang me, not here. I'm a foreigner. Who knows? I may hang, but it won't be down to you. I'm not a goat-boy caught stealing sheep.'

The captain stood up. It was hot, and the chairs were sticky. 'Why do you suppose *I* am here, Captain Patrick? I mean: *I*. Me above others?'

'How can I possibly tell? You don't give me your name.'

'You may take it that I am not without importance, not without influence in the world, *your* world especially.'

'I've already deduced you're a spook.'

'I mean I could arrange an accident for you, with a piece of rope, now, here in this room. Alternatively, my immediate superior, who will be here shortly, could have you processed on a public gallows.'

'Much to be preferred. No unpleasantness with the tongue.'

'Believe me, it would be otherwise. With an accident in this room I could contrive something quite humane. A public execution in Libya is a slow business. In some Arab countries, hangings are tardy because of incompetence or malpractice. In Libya, they are long drawn-out as a matter of policy.'

Was this the only deal that was being offered: a bad death or a worse one? 'We'd better come to some arrangement, then.'

'Indeed. So what will you tell me?'

'I need to go to the lavatory.'

The captain spoke something to the sergeant and the sergeant told the same something to the men. They all laughed. The captain was happy to be spiteful. He said to Matson, 'Al-Jamahiriyah Al-Arabiya Al-Libya Al-Shabiya Al-Ishtirakiya ordered this encampment to be constructed in order to bore for deep oil. Every hut in the encampment is furnished according to the highest standards of hygiene. Every hut is equipped with a water-closet. Each water-closet is plumbed in.'

'I am delighted to hear that.'

'In order that each room in each hut might be readily inspected and confirmed to be maintaining the intended standard, the contractors decided that there should only be one room in each hut.'

'So the lavatory is outside,' Matson said, and stood up decisively.

The captain moved. The lavatory was behind his chair. 'I should be careful how you remove your trousers in front of a group of Arabs, Captain Patrick. Especially if it is your misfortune to be one of the uncircumcised. Oh, and be very fastidious as to which hand you use.'

The joke was to be an ongoing one. The soldiers jostled Matson from behind and scoffed at him. They pushed with their hands and knees, and thumped him towards the foul-looking pedestal. They weren't torturers. They weren't even young thugs. They were going to have a party. They were waiting for him to lose his temper and barge them back. Then they were really going to have fun.

6.

When Quinlan had last been in office, everyone had spoken of him as the next prime minister. Now here he was, back again, as promised, persuasive and influential as ever, but demoted in corridor gossip to 'the next PM but one'. In other words, never. At fifty-seven, in an increasingly young administration, he knew his *Times* obituary was more or less finalised. Clearly he wasn't going to get his rump into any of the three major offices of state, let alone be the country's nominal boss.

What he was stuck with, sometimes like honey, mostly like tar, was the little world of secrets. Other men, and once another woman, had overall responsibility for the different hemispheres of that world, but they never touched it directly. Quinlan did. He did so himself only because he had to; and because he had to he did it well. He had started doing it at Defence. Fossit had first come into real contact with him as his direct political boss in the Home Office. Now here he was among the Foreigners, running Pomeroy, knowing that the cake-crumbs were already gummed round his cheeks but once more determined not to get his bottom glued with feathers.

The committee he presided over in all these places was peculiarly the same. Committees generally are, either in personnel or in appearance. A committee is a tub of frogs, and sometimes of frogspawn. This one, CAC, was only marginally unique: it had some toads – Pomeroy and Ralph Dixon to name but two.

Pomeroy and Dixon weren't really members of CAC, but they were always in attendance *vice* those who were. The committee was only convened when the shit hit the fan, and Pomeroy's boss among the Foreigners and Dixon's Number One at Home knew that this sort of unpleasantness could only happen as a result of someone dropping his trousers and lowering his backside over the ventilation shaft, and one didn't always know whose was the backside and which the shaft, nor how much more there was to come, did one?

This multiple hijack was a perfect example. They could only sit down quietly and hope that the hijack would stop. In case it didn't stop, there had to be a plan; with a prayer that events would overtake it before it could be tested. If the plan was ever needed, heads would be certain to roll.

7.

Quinlan began proceedings with a growl. He said, 'You know why we're here. Most of the broad details are public knowledge. If I miss any finer points, then the enlightened ones can bring them to the attention of the meeting.

'The morning radio flashes and the lunchtime television newscasts spoke of the hijack of an Avaroc flight – number AC303 from Luton. It was too late to stop some of those reports from including what we'd have preferred to keep under wraps – but it's information the hijackers probably already had anyway – namely that it was British Armed Forces charter. The passenger list includes Jack Irenson from Defence and one of his bits and pieces; a U.S. Air Force three-star general, Randall Mackie; and Lady Chambers, the wife of one of our divisional commanders in Germany. Plus her sister.'

Most people knew this, but they formed a dramatic group round the ministry table, and the recital of names made good theatre. Quinlan achieved his little murmur of awe if not surprise.

'We've gagged those facts. We've sat on the entire passenger manifest; there may be other NATO personnel of significance we've been slow to pick out from the list. There are also,' he glanced towards Fossit, 'one or two names we may need to take account of. If you want people kept quiet, then you can indicate by departments with a turn-down of thumbs. Or by passing up a fiche via Lorna here. Otherwise I want the whole matter in the open. Leonard?'

Fossit nodded his agreement while Pomeroy said in his ear, 'Lorna! He trots his principals around like bog-ladies and tea-women. They'll be bringing him the Andrex next!'

'That's the domestic bit. Some of you work in the afternoon, Marcus. It's even probable that some of you read the wires and know that three other aircraft were seized: one U.S. transatlantic 747, one Greek, and – incredibly – one

Israeli widebody. That's over a thousand people.'

They had that much from gossip, if nothing else.

'What you can't have got yet, what the world is just finding out, and what there's no point in stifling, is that all four aircraft have been flown to Libya. Libya declines to comment.

'Presumably it's the same operation, the one organisation. The hijackers have already shed blood. You won't know that. Two British nationals are dead. Nor that. At least two. Others have been injured. There were two other attempted hijacks, both on El Al flights. Whatever's cooking, Israel is an important part of the recipe. The Israelis also took casualties in the two they aborted. They don't yet say how many. So Israel is our first problem.

'The multiracial aspect is dangerous enough without them. It means we're into a very complex circumstance, even supposing *that* particular complexity forms no part of the hijackers' thinking. What is all too certain is that if Israeli blood, or Jewish blood, starts splashing down in Libya, then Israel will opt for direct action, and fast.

'If they go it alone they'll imperil everyone else. On the other hand there's no chance of getting anything concerted off the ground. Us and the Yanks maybe. All three of us and the Greeks? Not in a month of Sundays.'

'Not in a year of blue moons,' Pomeroy agreed. He glanced at Fossit's agenda.

Above the last C of CAC, Fossit had doodled 'Committee' in a rash inspirational fit. For the first C he had suggested 'Combined', 'Co-ordinated' and 'Concerted', each with a squared-off question-mark. His A was blank.

Pomeroy leant forward and obliged him. 'Arse-licking' was there for half the room to see, emblazoned in his frank schoolboy fist.

8.

The Spokesman for the Central Congress of the Libyan Arab People's Al Jamahiriyah had a message. An edited version would appear on the BBC *Six O'Clock News* and on *Channel Four at Seven*.

CAC watched the full transcription tape in silence. It took nineteen minutes, and was on several occasions interrupted by the Libyan national anthem and by martial music.

The Libyan People were pleased in principle to offer hospitality and protection to the passengers of four civil aircraft that had violated Libyan airspace by straying from the international airlanes and overflying without permission.

The flight-crews of these aircraft would naturally be questioned concerning the navigational deficiencies that had led them so far off course.

The Libyan People were delighted to welcome and support the representatives of various Arab and other people's revolutions who had accompanied these flights.

The Libyan Arab People's Al Jamahiriyah would deal justly with revolutionary fighter and passenger alike. All were equally welcome.

Particularly welcome were the passengers of the Greek airliner – the people of Greece being some of the Libyan People's nearest European neighbours.

The Libyan People currently had no diplomatic contact with the governments of the U.S.A. and the United Kingdom, though the rights of the citizens of those countries will always be upheld by the Libyan People, provided the citizens of those countries do not transgress international or Libyan law or offend Islam.

The Libyan People have never recognised the State of Israel, nor will they ever recognise it. The passengers of the Israeli aircraft may depend upon Justice and Mercy, but the crew must expect to be rigorously questioned.

A long silence followed Pomeroy's translation of this last edict.

'To Israeli ears that will sound ominously like the cocking of the starting pistol,' Quinlan said. 'The Foreign Secretary's already talking to them.'

9.

Matson kept his clothes on and kept them fastened. So far only one man had hit him really hard. Matson had kicked him in turn. Doubtless they would beat him for this, but it persuaded them to be cautious. For the moment, they simply jammed him down on top of the lavatory in his crumpled suit. The toilet bowl was filthy, but filthy with the dirt of ages, which was preferable to recent dirt.

The sergeant interrupted with a word of command and everyone stood to attention. Even the captain stood up.

It seemed as if he was to be the centre of a more elaborate charade, but the soldiers between Matson and the door shuffled away to left and right, with that silly little speed-step the military uses when trying to hurry itself into neater ranks.

They were inhibiting someone's eyeline from the doorway.

An enormous black man stood there, a mountain giant from Tibesti. His head scraped against the lintel, as he moved to control a ridiculous-looking dog, almost as high as his waist. It had the vacant expression and flopped-over ears of a mastiff or a Great Dane, but it was white with little brown freckles, like a cream and coffee-coloured Dalmatian.

The man was dressed in a tailor-made battledress tunic with its medals pinned on entire, instead of being worn as a ribbon. On his legs he wore flared silk trousers, in shop-girl red, and black boots with spurs.

He chuckled and stepped forward, the better to inspect Matson. He acknowledged the captain with a dismissive American-style salute, and boomed in fruity English, 'Ah, the cornucopia is full to overflowing. The stirrup cup runneth over.'

Matson stood up, but was waved down again.

'Stay where you are, Beloved. You would not expect to sit in Captain Khadduri's chair, especially for such a purpose.'

He led his dog in a little circle, making room for himself and his men, before saying, 'Observe the Englishman. What exquisite taste. Their women bath in their underclothes. Their men shit with their trousers on.' He waited for the captain to translate this for the benefit of the soldiers, and for the sergeant to embellish it further. 'Your Sergeant Modfai has a creative tongue, Khadduri.'

Matson suspected that Modfai had to work hard for his laughs. Not many of the lads would know any women, and the ones they did know would not have baths as part of their household equipment. He looked at the soldiers who had come with the giant. They wore battledress, but cut from superior cloth. Not quite khaki, not sage nor jungle-green, it was the kind of warm brown that stage-designers choose. They were pretty lads, too, toy soldiers the lot of them.

'My name is Dragout.' The black did not extend a hand. 'Lord Dragout.'

Matson had read enough history to be amused.

'It is what men call me, and what you will call me. Whether you continue to exercise that privilege, Beloved, will depend on how long you keep your tongue.'

Matson knew to be cautious. But he also knew about moral domination. Behave like a sacrificial lamb and expect to be slaughtered. 'I've already been shot at by one lot of thugs today. This lot have threatened me with hanging. Let's keep this third encounter a little more relevant to the plight of the hostages in that aircraft.'

'You live in London. London is full of tongue. It is all tongue. So you may be forgiven for your failure to understand. In Islam the tongue is an early forfeit. One meets many men without a tongue, many men and some women. And here, in the *hammada*, one can find many tongues without men. One can uncover them in the nests of birds or mating with lizards in the sand. I amuse you? A tongue is so easily removed with a hot spoon. I hope it may not come to this, you understand. So when you meet the public executioner, you may be able to bless him for his noose, forgive him his pliers.'

Matson stood up, and was forced down again. He had attended lectures about threat as an interrogation technique. He had also been in situations where interrogators had threatened him. He had never known the verbiage to be tossed about so early in an encounter. He tried a smile, but couldn't quite make it. His face set itself in a grin. A grin can be almost anything.

Dragout came closer to him, close enough to let the dog lick his face.

'The people on the aeroplane are safe. You, Beloved Matson, are an entirely different case. So what exactly do you propose to us?'

'That you should treat me according to International Law and let me go.'

'That we should return you alone to England, yes. And what do we get in return?'

'A certain *rapprochement*, a better understanding between our people.'

'And you will ensure this?'

'As far as it's in my power, certainly.'

'In return for your life? The trouble with this argument – and I have heard it many times – is that a man and his life are in the same place. If only we could send the man where he wants to go, but keep his life safely in our own hands, then we might believe a little more in his promises, Beloved. He could oblige us, and then we could send his life after him. Unfortunately, human beings are not made that way. We find they are worth more here, with or without their lives.'

How the man loved the sound of his own wisdom.

'Without my life, I am not going to be worth anything.'

'You would be surprised what some governments will pay for a body, Captain Matson – but, there! I'm not going to call you Captain, nor Matson, ever again. I shall devise a small pet name for you. You would be surprised what some governments will pay. The Israelis are one example, the Americans another. What about your own government?'

'If it was in the habit of paying out for all its dead Irishmen, it would have been bankrupt long ago.'

'I'm not particularly amused.' He motioned for one of his toy soldiers to handcuff Matson properly and to fit his legs with irons. 'I'm not particularly amused.'

Captain Khadduri's men regarded him with awe and his toy soldiers with amazement.

'It is against International Law for you to manacle me.'

'You are not in uniform. Besides, what law? Where is there any law between nations that you and America do not break? I shall keep you in these chains for as long as it suits me. Or I shall bind you in thorns or barbed wire. I may even strap you up in your own intestines. Believe me, such things have been done. Be grateful that the captain's men have rescued you from the aircraft.'

There had been several moments in the last twelve hours when Matson thought he was in a bad dream. There had been Sally Sherman's back, Captain Lyall's face. Now he was being drawn into a comic opera. No – he was joining the animals in the circus.

Dragout unfastened the collar from his white dog, and let it prowl about Matson on the floor. Then he fastened the collar around Matson's own neck as he squatted on the pedestal.

Matson did not like being ridiculed by an Arab, especially a black Arab, a Tibbu. Matson became very racist indeed. With a dog-collar round your neck, you can be anti nearly everybody. Especially when the collar stinks of Antimate.

Dragout smiled and clicked his fingers. 'Here, boy,' he said. A soldier translated for him with a prod from a hand-held bayonet. 'Here, boy.' He shortened the lead and tugged it. He did not bother with Polytechnic English. 'Here, boy. Come to heel.' He spoke perfect Oxbridge. 'I think I shall call you "Boy"!'

If Oxbridge is ever perfect.

10.

'The Prime Minister's view is a simple one,' Terence Quinlan said. 'It is that this is a hijack, not a war. So it will be dealt with not by Cabinet but by a senior committee in the Foreign Office. Since it is a multiple hijack, the Foreign Office is double predicated. But a hijack is an indisciplinary matter, so it's bound also to include Ralph and Leonard, the police and the military. Such a committee already exists, and I know it well, having already chaired you on numerous occasions with a number of different hats on. Since I am now in the Foreign Office, it makes perfect sense for us to do the job again. You may call it musical chairs. You may be grateful – as I always am – at having a seat to sit on!' He roused them to weary amusement: Quinlan was one of those plain men who have so much energy for the obvious that people who do not know him well think they're in the presence of a great wit. 'Nonetheless, gentlemen, and this time ladies, I think we're all going to find the chairs at this particular party are damned hot.'

The committee began to buzz. It was forming itself into sub-groups behind the backs of hands.

Pomeroy disdained the side of his mouth. Like all of the truly sly, he was not made for whispers. He was talking to one of the women from his own department by addressing his blotter in a dictatorial boom. The woman listened.

The ladies in general were being very well-behaved, so Quinlan wanted their attention to himself.

'Gentlemen, there is one more thing. The last time a Prime Minister asked me to activate this committee' – he shot a smile at the ladies: there were no ladies then – 'on that occasion Leonard was very ably supported by a member of his department called' – his pad didn't help him, but he knew the name well enough – 'Patrick Matson. He might even have been sitting among us this evening. Yes, I think we can take it his presence would have been indicated in a matter like this.'

Leonard Fossit nodded and Pomeroy's blotter could be heard to say, 'Well below the salt, old dear – *nonetheless*.'

'Unfortunately for us, Leonard tells me that Captain Matson was on this morning's Avaroc Airways flight from Luton intended for Bruggen. Which means the Libyans have got him.'

'Poor old Paddy.' Dixon spoke for them all.

'I am told by Leonard that he was not on duty. In any event he is a member of the Security Services, and not –'

'The world knows what he does, and it hates him for it,' Pomeroy put in. 'Leonard's little crowd mayn't cost much in Heaven; but they operate the B-list, and that's worth blood anywhere.'

'Captain Matson oversees all diplomatic exclusions,' Fossit explained.

'Or so does wickedness think,' Pomeroy corrected, 'and award him the larger blame. In Libya, there is much ill-informed wickedness.'

'Let's not bicker till the gravy's been spilt,' Quinlan said mildly. He took a piece of paper from his Lorna, or was it his Hattie? 'Here's some more highly relevant information. The Greek – it's Hellenic Air, flight number not important – is grounded at Tripoli International. As is the American TWA widebody – flight numbers again going on the board if anybody wants them.

'Our own case looks rougher. They've got us, and the Israeli

Jumbo, at a place called Sifr WaaHid – God knows where *that* is.'

The Navy looked smug. Fisher, from the R.A.F., acknowledged by lifting his eyes towards the altostratus that he knew he should be able to answer such matters but couldn't. The military, bless them, had their map-cases and their map-cases held maps, but maps take space and time and –

'It's south of Zeltan, Zoltan or Zaltan, according to which little atlas you've got,' Pomeroy remembered.

'How do you know that?'

'It's what I'm not paid for, Minister. Background to what I am. About a hundred kilometres south, perhaps by a little east. The same line north will find Benghazi in another two hundred.'

He sipped at a coffee-cup which held a particularly florid coffee, and waited while they identified an unmarked area of perspex.

'I'm not expecting you'll find much,' he said grandly. 'As a matter of absolute fact, I didn't even know there was an air-strip. Believe me, it won't be more,' he informed Fisher. 'Probably just a lucky configuration of sand.'

'So the aircraft could be bellied in?'

'Exactly. I know the place as an oil exploration that came to very little. Its name tells me that. It has been awarded neither a revolutionary nor an Islamic title. Sifr WaaHid means Zero One. It's a site number that never got itself promoted further.'

'Anything else?' Quinlan looked around. 'Well, it tells us a deal about the Libyan involvement if they've already got troops there. They don't have many in the first place.'

'Limp little army,' Pomeroy agreed. 'Five or six brigades, some lorries and some guns.' Then he shut up. Even Pomeroy recognised the military should be allowed a tiny incursion into fact.

'Tells us even more about the hijackers, I fancy. Particularly if we fit it to the stuff Israel has just passed on.' Quinlan consulted his other piece of flimsy: ' "A combination of methods were employed in an attempt to secure at least one El Al flight, judging from the two thwarted attempts. Acid was sprayed from a child's feeding bottle, temporarily incapacitating the flight-guard. Potassium cyanide pellets were dissolved in sulphuric whatsname – again in a baby's feeder – and the attempt was made against the distraction of fatal clouds of hydrocyanic gas. Newspapers were set on fire to prevent the cabin being depressurised and the oxygen seat-masks deployed". Seemingly gas was used for the successful hijack, because the pilot radio'd that he had prussic-acid poisoning cases on board. How many, and whether passengers were fatally affected, remains unknown.'

Whatever Quinlan intended to say next was interrupted by the Committee Room transcription set. It cackled, hummed, crackled, then grew itself an enlarging star which broke into fracturing diagonals like the lances that gave Utrillo his celebrated headache.

'We have a direct line to God,' Quinlan growled. 'Let us listen and hope to hear him.'

11.

The Libyan Queen lit himself up in a dozen ministry portholes and said, 'The Libyan People are taking a stern view of the presence of the British airliner on Libyan soil at Sifr WaaHid. This aircraft contains many soldiers, including American soldiers. Many of the women passengers are also soldiers. This aircraft – like the Israeli airliner also at Sifr WaaHid – carries automatic weapons. These weapons are not the property of the freedom fighters. The passengers of these aircraft together constitute an invasion force of battalion strength and their presence on Libyan soil is not lightly to be tolerated. The presence of Americans in both of these armed aircraft at Sifr WaaHid must call into question the status of the four hundred Americans on the seemingly unarmed aircraft at Tripoli.'

'No sooner do I mark your little maps,' Pomeroy said, 'than the Tartars call you all to battle.' Then he remembered to translate for them, and they grew unamused in their turn.

The spokesman for the Central Congress of the Libyan Arab People's Al Jamahiriyah was well-known both in Whitehall and the State Department. The experts had listened to him before. He always dressed elaborately for the cameras, and spoke from voluminous notes; so Quinlan called him 'the African Queen', corrected to 'the Libyan Queen' by Pomeroy, who preferred 'Philactery Pete' anyway, and knew his own invention was nowhere nearly as funny. Others, on both sides of the Atlantic, knew him as 'Ali', 'Ali Baba' or 'the Sheikh'.

'I shall need to talk about this upstairs,' Quinlan said. 'However autonomous the hijack – and let us not overlook what is intrinsically dangerous and nasty about *that*! – however autonomous, the fact is the Libyans go on muscling up on us. At lunchtime, the Yanks simply spoke of toughing it out. I wonder what they'll think now? Candidly, I don't think toughing it out is either quick enough or any longer very clever.'

Terence Quinlan examined the knuckle of his left thumb, the knuckle of his right. The meeting was nearly over. He only had one more thing to ask of them. 'Cabinet will want me to broaden this,' he confessed. 'When it comes to the Yanks, we'll hope for someone good, and possibly we'll even get someone *they* think is good; but we'll get who they give us. The Greeks – I dunno. They never do anything right. They'll probably send us a Turk. But it's the Israelis I keep on coming back to. We'll need to know who to ask for.'

'Zefat,' Pomeroy yawned. 'General Yigael Zefat, without one shadow of doubt.'

'But Zefat's in charge of –'

'He's in charge all right, I agree with you there, Minister.'

'Isn't he persona non grata?'

'He needn't set foot in London. Cyprus is nearer.'

Quinlan wasn't done yet. 'His people include' – He struggled for names; he'd been changing offices since then – 'certain chaps some of us can't work with. Ralph?'

'We'd have to pull them in if they came back to the U.K.,' Dixon agreed. 'Otherwise –'

'There's only one of us who can't work with them,' Fossit said.

'And he'll be away for the duration of this little lot,' Pomeroy reminded.

'Squabbles between security services must not be allowed to affect international relations.'

'Is that a quote, Minister?' Seeing Quinlan colour, Pomeroy

added hastily, 'I mean: it's the sort of statement one might need to go public on.'

'I'll go public,' Quinlan said. 'You'll go carefully.'

Pomeroy watched the ministerial backside all the way to the door, then added, for Fossit's benefit, 'Talking of dirt, dirt grows crystals. You see what I was on about at the beginning? Zefat was always going to be here, and your lad was always going to be away. If Paddy hadn't been on leave, God would have sent him there.'

The screen lit up for another starburst of hysteria. There was no Hattie or Lorna to pop it in focus for them, so they missed its time of origin.

They heard the Libyan Queen ventriloquise Pomeroy to say: 'The Libyan People's displeasure has acquired a further dimension. The aircraft at Sifr WaaHid not only brought armaments and a possible invasion force inspired by the Cain of America and its British satellite. It has sought to abuse the hospitality of the Libyan People by attempting to infiltrate a notorious English spy into Northern Cyrenaica during the confused circumstances that always accompany a hijack.

'The spy has been arrested, thanks to the unremitting vigilance of the Security Police and the Armed Forces. The spy must expect to be punished according to the enormity of his intended crimes.'

'So what do we say to that, Marcus?'

'We say that we need a drink, dear boy. Paddy is not going to get one.'

SIX

1.

It was dark outside. The compound lights were on, but these were patchy.

The two aircraft were illumined by some narrow-gauge searchlights mounted on vehicles. Earlier, Matson had only noticed jeeps. Perhaps the searchlights were on the jeeps: the light source was too intense for him to tell. Still, the presence of the beams and the necessary generator units underscored his notion of Libyan preparedness.

There were now no soldiers surrounding the planes, though the searchlights must have had operators somewhere. This meant slackness or increasing complicity. Captain Khadduri did not appear slack. Nor did Sergeant Modfai.

An aluminium step-ladder rested against the door of the Trident. There was no way of getting into the Israeli Jumbo, or out of it, short of falling. The ladder was too short. Both lots of cabin lights were on. A woman with a gun stood at the door of the Jumbo. Matson couldn't tell whether the British flight was full or empty.

His professional self was walking much too slowly for his captors. The toy soldiers trod on his heels. At one point, Dragout tugged him so violently forward on his chain that the dog, which slunk beside Matson, whined and then decided to bark. Its yelp was undersized for so big an animal. Its puny domestic panic echoed around the cantonment as if someone had just kicked over a dustbin.

'Hurry, boy!'

Perhaps the dog spoke English.

The huts were not as uniform as they had first appeared. Some were built in brick, some in a rough kind of cinderblock, and some were in adobe. These were smaller and perhaps of earlier construction. They were not always squared off, or even aligned with the rest of the buildings, but the alley-lights showed they all had the same tack-and-turn roofs, God knows in what fabric.

One or two were built from those hollowed-out tile-bricks he'd seen all round the Mediterranean. He wouldn't have thought they'd be much good here: too much creeping dust.

They stopped at one of these just the same. There was a long wait at the door while Dragout searched himself for keys, and Matson was able to examine how the tiles had been used. If he wanted to break out, he'd better understand the architecture. Each was a cluster of open-work ceramic tubes. These had been plugged with quick trowelfuls of cement. A section could be left unplugged to let in light and air.

Dragout got the door open at last. It was a stout one.

Inside, Matson found there was no light and air. There were no windows. Everything had been filled in.

A lamp was switched on. The interior was all stark white cement and very clean. The entire ceramic surface had been plastered over and limewashed. The sloping roof was concealed by a flat ceiling, though this was above the crossbeams. There were three of these, but no ropes or chains. Matson took no comfort from uncovered rafters just now. Nor from the floor constructed of sealed tiles. He tried to remember the captain's hut. That floor was different, he couldn't think how.

At the centre of the room stood an iron bedstead of the sort beloved of armies and contractors the world over: it was mattressed in military 'biscuit', presumably of similar pedigree. A wooden table, two folding chairs, and an upright frame chair completed the furniture. There was the usual publicly-placed WC, of course. Maston did not dwell on this. The last one had threatened to be as dangerous as an electric chair, and it was certainly less comfortable. Beyond the pedestal there was a wall-tap, and near that on the floor a ewer and basin. The basin, incredibly, held cut flowers. The Dragout was an original.

Three of Dragout's artificial soldiers had followed Matson into the room. So had the dog.

'That's an excellent collar,' Dragout said. 'And an unbreakable leash. The collar suits you. And as for the lead' – he chuckled heavenwards – 'I hanged a man in it once. I think a man. Someone, anyway.' He added something in Arabic, and the dog, still whining, licked at Matson's crotch.

The Arabic had not been addressed to the dog, just the same. One of the pretty boys stepped up to his master and took the leash from his fingers. Another of them unfastened the studs from Matson's neck and handed the collar to the first one, who secured the dog with it and led the animal outside. It began to howl again.

'Death makes them do that,' Dragout said. 'Death and their intimations of dying. Have you read George Orwell, Beloved?'

Matson was through with answering to 'Beloved'. His throat felt too sore.

The dog-handler came back in again. With Dragout that made four.

2.

'Take your clothes off, all of them, and hand them to these young gentlemen.'

The young gentlemen slouched in elegant echelon. 'Toy soldiers' was too robust a comparison. They resembled a chorus-line.

'What are they going to do – dice for them?'

Dragout's hand flicked Matson's mouth, a ring chipping along his teeth. 'The Nazarene is a prophet according to Islam. You have just blasphemed.'

Encouraged by self-righteousness he struck Matson several times more. When he had finished, he said, 'No, Beloved. They have instructions to incinerate them. You have no further need of them.'

'We'll get to you,' Matson said. 'If you harm me. You know what my service is like. You must be aware of its reputation.'

'If I were ever foolish enough to walk across St James's Park in my pyjamas, I dare say someone might get to me. If they ever find out I exist.'

'They'll find out – if they haven't already.'

'What they know, you'll tell me. Certainly you are not going to be around much longer to tell them. Your clothes, please. Starting with your shoes and tie.'

'Let me propose an agenda,' Matson said.

' "An agenda"? You will tell me everything. What Her Majesty has for tea. Who mates with her dogs and horses. Every little secret of your great British system, including the name of each and every one of Her Majesty's agents in this part of the world.'

'I don't have that kind of knowledge.'

'I'm glad you know so little. In that case, I shan't be hurting you for any other motive than the sheer enjoyment of so doing.'

'Boo!'

'It will soon be "Boo hoo!", believe me. "Boo hoo" was what I learned at Harrow, Little One. There – you've discovered my last secret.' He flopped his huge body modestly onto a folding chair, but it creaked. He winced and stood up again. Life was euphony for Lord Dragout. 'There are men who enjoy women, and some who love boys. Others delight in placing bets on a camel. I do all of these things, but they are ephemeral. Pain is my only enduring pleasure. Pain lasts almost for ever. Other people's pain is a wonderful source of inspiration to me.' He examined Matson's thickened lip and bloodied nose, and added: 'It's rather like *couscous*. A man either has the stomach for it or he doesn't. I find my appetite inexhaustible.'

'So you reject my agenda?'

'No agenda. What I find in my business' – he went towards the back of the room, skirting the lavatory pedestal, and ran some water into the ewer which he carried back towards Matson – 'what I find is that I do better with a recipe – no, recipe is too rigid.' He began to splash water on the tiles, then stopped, indecisively. He had tripped his tongue, and it threw him in a fury. Matson realised that this unlikely giant of a man, so expert in English, couldn't find a word. He'd mislaid it. He had spoken the language since childhood but he lived where he couldn't practise it. He could *perform* it, and probably performed it to himself, but he couldn't *talk* it. Now, with Matson's tired and belligerent eyes on him, he was thrown.

Dragout set the ewer down on the desk. He went to the back of the room again, while his three minions fidgeted uneasily. The wait was intolerable. He came back holding some of the flowers, then dropped them on the desk with a grimace of triumph. '*Menu*. It's French, you see. I love the French almost as much as I love you, Sugar Bones.'

His entourage relaxed.

For the moment, Matson had won. An interrogator should be dominant, should always enforce his will. Dragout had told him to hand over his clothes, and he hadn't.

The huge man shuffled the blooms on his desk, and went on with his soliloquy: 'Menu: *you* choose. There's the whip, there are boot-studs, there are hot irons – do you have a preference?'

Matson decided not to answer.

'So you don't like to talk? You'll talk *your* agenda, but not *my* menu. Well, talk! Talk interests me very much in these cases. Talk, you will concede, talk is the foreplay.'

Matson tried to grin.

'Or I can simply call in some of Khadduri's soldiers. They are not so gentle as this lot. They slap you, they spin you, and then – eventually – you will go down. Even you, my little Pebble Skin. You, of all people, will know how uncomfortable it is once a crowd has you at its feet.'

'Do I get my hands free?'

The dark face considered and chuckled. 'If I call the soldiers in, yes, you may have your hands. You'll try to damage some, no doubt. I'll place a little wager on you.'

'You're a gambler?'

'No: I bet. You're the gambler. I only lay my money on certainties.'

3.

Do you watch your gaolers? Do you let them so intimidate you that you circle with them until your head spins and your neck aches? Or are you more self-confident?

The giant was behind him. They were all behind him. Dragout breathed. The others were silent. Dragout breathed more and more loudly, importantly, like a fat man changing into his bathing costume before plunging into the Serpentine.

Lungs echo everywhere. Dragout's were universal. Matson needed to keep track of him, to locate him by talk. He said, 'I suppose this place is wired for sound?'

'No, dear boy. For silence. It's a torture chamber. You can scream here without inhibition.' He stopped his wheezing. 'I say that because you're an apparently brave and considerate man who will not wish to alarm the ladies on the aircraft. Their turn will come. For the moment, have no fear. You have my full and freely granted permission to yell away. No-one will hear you, and I've already told you how much I enjoy it.'

Dragout reappeared. He had changed some of his garments. Perhaps he had changed them all. This accounted for the wheezing. The result looked distinctly odd, even to tired eyes. He was wearing what could only be described as a designer burnous hitched up to show Western trousers.

The black face glowed and dripped, the personality purred. Dragout meant to be odd, or did not think this was odd. Whatever he thought or meant, he intended to be exactly like this. This was what got him down to the business.

Business was not brisk.

He was missing something. He needed a sunshade or a hubble-bubble.

He lurched across to the desk and picked up a pen and a flower. 'Your name is Patrick Matson, my Tiny Fountain of Starlight?'

'My name is Patrick Matson.'

'I'll find you a pet name later. I promise you something later.' He left the pen and the desk, but kept hold of the silly flower.

Matson knew what the flower was for. It was to persuade Matson to snigger. Then when he committed such a flagrant indiscretion, dear old Dragout would lose his temper and hammer him into a pulp – either to repair his self-esteem or to uphold the dignity of the Revolution.

'How old are you?' He gave Matson's chin a whack with the flower. The bloom was neither coastal nor hothouse. It was a finger-creation in wire and plastic, and as springy as a whip. 'I asked how old are you?'

'Too damned old for this nonsense.'

'Or too damned old for me?' He took another turn. 'I wonder.' He stopped and smirked for Matson's benefit, before directing his attention inwards, towards some memory or other. He licked his lips with a thick tongue, tasting the beauty of his own recollections. 'You see, the way I question a man is so *intense* that even a fifteen-year-old ages beyond recognition or redemption. To be interrogated by Lord Dragout, you might say, is to be conducted rapidly through the Seven Ages of Man. So, in reality, a subject's starting age is of comparatively little consequence to me. Beauty is a bonus, I suppose, but only that. You are not beautiful, of course. You are English.'

'Irish.'

Dragout hacked at Matson with his outrageous lupin, or whatever it was, until the lupin disintegrated and Matson bled. Then he lurched round behind Matson to adjust his dress.

The bandboys helped him. Lord Dragout encouraged them to snigger.

Matson saw no reason to alarm the ladies on the aircraft. This time he wasn't even frightened. He was angry. He drew strength from that.

He let his emotions seethe away at a puzzling conundrum. Dragout, like Khadduri before him, was prepared to waste an awful lot of time on talk.

4.

Dragout had managed another quick change. A gold watch, a kind of grandfather of the sternum, was part of it. Were his men bringing in props from outside? Was he a conjuror? He was now even less a product of the Arab Revolution, still less of the Libyan Revolution. True, he wore a battle-dress top under his now opened-up dressing-gown, and he wore it 1945 (or denim casual) style; but it had been lovingly cut from an exquisite cloth – the sort of material Matson had seen NCOs give five weeks' pay for to a bespoke tailor, only to have the Regimental Sergeant-major refuse to let them wear it on parade. It was even better than the lads wore. The robe itself was odd. It had balloon sleeves and was gussetted like an academic gown.

On his legs and much more evident under the parted robe, he sported a pair of morning-dress trousers, jazzy with intricate silver weave. It was a design stockbrokers had taped up in Savile Row to wear with their short coats in 1930, or pox-doctors' clerks bought from the peg in Messrs Burton's circa 1950 – both good years for left-hand dressers.

The gold watch hung on a chain especially cut from a lavatory designed for short gentlemen.

Matson couldn't see whether his gaoler wore a tin hat or a bowler under his burnous hood. He was more interested in assessing the man's intentions. It was time he started to sing. He knew the tune.

'I want to see someone from an independent consulate. I know there is no direct British representation in this country. But you're abetting a hijack and holding me illegally here. The Italians or French are representing the United Kingdom, I believe.'

Dragout busied himself with lighting a large cigar.

'I demand to see the French consul.'

'Darling, there ain't a French consul for miles. America is even further. You may as well lay yourself back and accept that I'm going to interrogate you.' His speech was suddenly a grotesque parody of what an English public schoolboy thinks is a Bronx accent. He was, after all, an English public schoolboy.

'I claim –'

'Bullshit, man. I got no more time to waste on you, darling.' He was deeper South now, or perhaps New York black. He produced something from the labyrinth of his clothing. It looked like a small vulcanised truncheon, or a fisherman's priest. As he flourished it, Matson smelled disinfectant. 'Now you be a good gentleman and get your fucking clothes off. Like I told you half my life ago.'

'Certainly not. I know my –'

'You ain't got no rights. You're a spook. We all know that.

Just lower your bloody pants, man. Or I'll ask these gentlemen to help you.'

'Why don't you try and do it yourself?'

'I'm not doing *that*, man. I'll just do the rest.' He spoke briefly in Arabic and there came a patter of little feet.

The leg-shanks had been wide enough to walk in, so perhaps he could dance. Matson turned his left side towards the chocolate-box Arabs, peeled the nearest man's shin with a toe-stamp and grind, lifted the next one's jaw off its hinges with a two handed chin jab, then swung round to look for Dragout. At last he was getting it right. He'd garotte the bastard in his handcuffs.

Dragout retreated. He was already behind Matson, but he wasn't hiding. Matson felt a splintering blow next to his lower vertebrae, as if his back had given birth to a kidney. The pain merged into the thump of his knees and cheek hitting the floor.

More feet. Feet that were bare. Feet that wore boots. Matson struck out, missed, woke to find himself back on his bed.

The room was full of Captain Khadduri's soldiers. Some of them looked at him curiously. A couple of them helped the shin case and the dislocated jaw from the room.

As far as Matson could make out, Dragout was smoking an even larger cigar. He smiled at Matson briefly, like a nurse to her patient as he wakes from the anaesthetic. Then he gave an order to the troops.

Three of them pounced on Matson, spread him face up and tied his wrists to the iron frame of the bedstead. They pulled his trousers down to his ankles, then smashed him in the stomach, each in turn. He was ready for this, but their fists pumped the breath from him. He retched and tried to twist away. He nearly passed out, recovered himself to find his trousers gone, his ankles handcuffed, not bound, to the bed-foot.

The soldiers bowed to Dragout and left. Bowed rather than saluted.

Still smoking his cigar, the giant knelt over Matson and tore his shirt to shreds. He stood up and watched Matson contentedly, puffing down at him. Then he went into the corner and found the wash basin and ewer. He carried them close to the bed and soused Matson all over, then dried him carefully with a rough towel.

Matson's head throbbed and he still found it painful to breathe. The cold water and slow towelling brought him slowly back to himself.

Dragout leant nearer, puffed once more on his cigar, then dropped it into the water jug.

After watching Matson for perhaps a whole minute, he produced his rubber truncheon.

Matson waited for the first blow.

Instead, the big black man stooped all the way down and put his mouth close to Matson's right ear. 'Now, Sweetmilk,' he whispered, this time in camped-up coon-talk, 'You and me is going to have a *very* long chat. And in that chat you're going to tell Uncle Dragout everything you know. Everything.'

Matson squirmed as if a leech had bitten him. Uncle Dragout's mouth had fastened on to the side of his neck in a long ecstatic kiss, where it sucked and blew hungrily.

5.

Pomeroy tugged at the phone-cord, winding it in slowly across his desk. He lit a cigarette.

He was about to be honest and open and direct. He was going to keep his promise to Leonard Fossit and that hirsute hetero Dixon: the job must be getting on top of him. To hold to a bargain struck with an enemy was one thing, but to be bound by every piece of prattle he dropped in front of his friends …

He did not smoke his cigarette. He shredded it, still smouldering, onto a tin and copper ashtray, and wrinkled his nose at the smell. If it became really nauseous, he intended to sniff it as a cure.

He felt inside his waistcoat and consulted a small piece of card one of his tame ones had given him a couple of months ago. On one side it said, in the spidery English hand of an Arab: *£5000.00 (sterling) this time*. On the other, was printed a Tel Aviv phone number. The same person had written: *I* *observed this – you know when. It will not form part of their operational net, but I heard it ring in the building.*

Pomeroy tried to remember whether he had parted with any cash or simply promised to pay by results. He couldn't stand the odour of oxidising metal any longer. He threw his cigarette, his packet, his box of matches and ashtray into the bin, and poured three fingers of brandy-substitute into a whisky glass. It wasn't cognac, armagnac or even *eau de vie*. On the bottle its birth-certificate simply said Brandy. It sported an unheard-of four stars, meaning it was distilled in Limbo. It also bore the name Napoleon, which was a lie. A man who drinks brandy all day long from breakfast time learns to be tolerant of cheap things. He asked for an outside line and dialled his expensive number in Tel Aviv.

A woman's voice answered in Hebrew. She told him she was the Chaim Azriel Weizman Marine Library and Sub-Aquatic Collection. This too was a lie.

He said in English, 'Connect me to Major Barel, please. If that's not your Director's name just connect me to Shlomo Barel.'

'I'm afraid –'

'Tell him it's about Patrick Matson, Paddy Matson.'

'There is no –'

'See he gets the name Matson. Say Matson's calling him, if you like. Just ensure that someone in authority hears the word Matson. Only hurry. I'm in a London phone-box and running out of pennies.'

'Is Matson the name of a book or –'

'It's a specimen. The Matson. A cold-water silted-foreshore bivalve: *Matsonius Patricius Hiberniae*. Shlomo Barel will respond simply to Matson.'

A male voice, sounding much nearer, spoke inside his ear. 'How was it in the sand?'

'I don't know, Major. I was merely using the name as a –'

'*Carnet de voyage*? Perhaps there are many Matsons. Perhaps you are all called Matson in Whitehall? You have certainly been a Matson before, haven't you? A tape of your voice is among my favourite late-night listening.'

'My name is Marcus Pomeroy.'

'Ah – *that* Matson. How important must he be, if Marcus

Pomeroy condescends to play him? When the Queen dresses up as a coachman, who is the less deceived?'

'Presumably you already know where he is?'

'I can't think of anywhere I'd prefer him to be – except downstairs here in the formaldehyde. You must know he's being looked after by some appreciative fellow professionals of Libyan Military Intelligence. They're making him very welcome because they're so delighted to see him. However, I have a man there, and – alas – he tells me Matson is finding it difficult to adjust to the climate.'

'Flies and things?'

'That certainly. I wonder who gave you this number?'

'I confess to having a man as well.'

'I suspect it is the same man, Mr Pomeroy. He is highly reliable when it comes to phone-numbers, clearly. So what do you have for me?'

'Simply that David Ben-Yosof has arranged clearance for my minister to deal with your General Zefat direct.'

'It's a beginning,' Barel said. 'But a slow one, and Israel can't wait for long. It would be political suicide for Ben-Yosof and career-suicide for Yigael Zefat to seek anything to the contrary.'

'Our view must be –'

'There isn't time for a view. You'll know us well enough to assume we have a snatch-squad practising jumping in and out of aeroplanes and doing push-ups. I know nothing directly, of course, but I have this as an item of faith. And my religion tells me we are not going to let them grow stale. Your minister must talk to my minister at once. And my general.'

'Meanwhile there's Matson. We'd pay money –'

'If you know my man as well as I think, then agree he can do nothing. Just the same, I do hope they won't kill Matson all at once.'

SEVEN

1.

Single-room huts seemed a splendid innovation to the State as contractor. They were an excellent simplicity within which to keep a workforce tidy and hygienic.

The Europeans objected. So did the Libyan engineers, surveyors, doctors – and anyone else who craved a room to sit in and another to sleep in, a kitchen to cook in and a lavatory within which to be entirely private.

So the first week's prospecting for oil was spent nailing up partitions. At the end of that week, some hundred engineers, surveyors and doctors – and of course the Europeans – had a four-room bungalow hut each; while a workforce of five thousand men shared the remaining ninety sheds.

Captain Khadduri had found himself one of the bungalow huts. It was grubby, and there was a grey rat to share it; its damp interior shadow allowed sage-coloured vegetation to thrive in the bedroom. But it would do for tonight. Tomorrow his men would weed it and scrub it and perhaps kill the rat; Captain Khadduri was not the kind of officer who is indiscriminate in the use of his pistol.

Dragout did not have a bungalow. He had found himself a private dwelling tucked away in the hills: a stone and cement building belonging to the oil-company's former chief engineer. It had water-plants and a well, and together with Matson it made him entirely happy.

He prowled about Khadduri's bungalow and favoured the officer with a smile. 'You have told this riff-raff on the plane that they will control the situation much more easily if they release the crew of the British aeroplane into our hands?'

'The Freedom Fighters have already promised them to us.'

'Good. See they do this at once. Then put the women in one place, the men in another. Under secure guard, you understand? We cannot be sure what these people are.' He arranged his smile again. Khadduri's hut had glass in the windows, and lamplit glass after dark is an excellent mirror. He crinkled his face some more, and admired the effect beyond Khadduri's much lower head. Then he peered into the blindness of the night, as if practising ominiscience.

'That woman's corpse is a great untidiness, M'med Khadduri – I speak both as a soldier and a landscape gardener.' His gloved hand used his other hand's discarded glove to brush first his khaki tunic then his strangely garbed legs. 'Also, there are cameras that can see for miles and television lenses that go even further. A Jewish corpse is an embarrassment to me just now. You don't have any ice, do you, Khadduri – I mean, not even for your sherbert?'

The Captain shook his head in amazement.

'Then you had better wrap her in a rug and drop her down a hole. Have the scoundrels who killed her dig the hole, but be very careful to mark it yourself.'

'The Freedom Fighters –'

'Gunmen, Khadduri. They are not all Moslems and they are not all Arabs.'

'They will not like this.'

'Tell them to dig it. Tell them I said so. Then tell them to spit in it.' He smiled at the soldier guarding Khadduri's door. '*You* don't want to dig a hole, do you?' He rounded on Khadduri. 'Talking of riff-raff, have their reinforcements arrived?'

'Seven of them.'

'I do not want them to board the aircraft until some of the others have disembarked. I intend to stay in charge, Khadduri.'

'Of course.'

'It is tiresome to have to remind people who is in charge.'

Dragout's smile was intended to promote serious thought, and then to dismiss it. 'You have been very good, Captain. So have your men.'

He padded into the little kitchen, opening mesh doors,

inspecting scraps of filth too old to be repulsive, and finally the refrigerator which was still as clean inside as a newly drilled tooth, even though its gas-bottle was empty. He indicated the plastic boxes of German margarine, the still sealed can of corn-oil. 'You should offer them some sweeties.'

Khadduri was reluctant to understand. But once he understood he sent for Sergeant Modfai.

2.

'I have been thinking with the Lord Dragout, Sergeant Modfai. We came to the conclusion that the men needed some reward for being out here. They have had their cigarettes. Now they are to have their sweeties.'

Sergeants are men of great experience whose opinion of the world is never allowed out to embarrass their superiors.

'European sweeties are extremely rich, Sergeant Modfai. It is best if they are sucked gently, and then there will be no indigestion. And, in case we have to put any back in their box, they should be very carefully unwrapped, and their wrappings kept. And the men, too, sergeant. They must be unwrapped and without their labels. You know what I think about even such a trivial matter as smoking while the men are in uniform.'

'And yet, sir, you like the men to smoke.' The Sergeant knew when it was his turn to speak. It was always last.

The Captain was not yet finished. He showed him the happy inspiration in the refrigerator. Neither knew that Dragout had put it there.

3.

Matson had been held captive twice before in his life; held captive and interrogated.

Yet a cage for prisoners-of-war is not like a prison. Nor, come to that, is a torture room. He was now in a kind of prison, being watched by a pair of Dragout's ornate little thugs. He was still manacled, or he would have tried to escape.

He had quite recently spent an hour in Wormwood Scrubs.

It was during his Albany Street days, and he'd been asked to lecture on Special Forces. The lecture had gone all right – prisoners will listen to anyone, do anything, or pretend to, rather than drone on by themselves for more of the same intolerable boredom, particularly if they are banged up two, three and four to a cell. Yes – the lecture had gone all right, even though it had been a poor piece of work for an Irishman. Matson found it best to forget it.

What had stayed in his mind was the walk to and from the Education Block. Wherever he went, he was watched. Men weeding gardens or up ladders mending roofs would stop whatever they were doing and eye him up and down with a most particular interest.

The two who were guarding him were watching him in exactly the same way: somebody new, somebody to screw.

Dragout had told him the place was soundproof. That was a lie, for certain. Matson could hear all kinds of noises. There were people being shifted around in the neighbouring huts – the hostages, perhaps? Certainly there were some of Khadduri's soldiers.

There was quietness again. Then he heard an English woman's voice. It was protesting, shouting not screaming. It became muffled very quickly among male laughter, male giggles, some of them eerily pubertic. There were similar sounds elsewhere about the compound, or he fancied so. Repeated blows to his head made him notice everything as if through quadrophones.

He listened, nursing himself in his handcuffs. Yes, it was protest, not screaming, he heard; and the sound of a bottom being spanked with an open hand. Of all human sounds, it is the most unmistakable but one. He heard that sound, too. There were a number of women's voices. Perhaps an hour of little silences, exclamations, but always the glimpse of voices. He only recognised one. It belonged to the cabin stewardess who had stood up to Curly Ingram. A long time later he heard someone sobbing. He didn't know whether or not it was her. It certainly wasn't Curly Ingram.

4.

Three iron bedsteads had been lashed side by side with string, and then piled with mattresses. A man, older than the rest of the soldiers, sat on the furthest bed with his back against the wall. He might have been an officer or a sergeant. The girl couldn't tell. He wore only his boots and trousers, barechested – and soldiers do not have any badges of rank on their bare flesh.

She stood looking at him as he sprawled on his makeshift throne, a coffee-skinned hard-muscled Buddha, the beds' heads and feet running rail-like towards him on either side. There were sounds behind her, but he was clearly in charge, and she knew she could best keep hold of her dignity by not turning round.

He held out his hand for her to join him on the bed. He had a huge can of drink beside him. Mohammedans don't drink. She looked at it again. It was corn-oil.

She moved backwards and knocked against bare flesh, which tangled her from behind. She struggled, briefly, among the arms and fingers not of soldiers, not of boy soldiers, but naked men and boys, perhaps half a dozen, the arms holding her, the fingers unfastening her clothes.

Her skirt was first as it dropped from her waist to the floor. Then her blouse and then, kicking, her underslip. When she pushed them off, still in her tights and bra, she saw, in the way one records such things in shock, that her shoes had been placed side by side on a box; her skirt lay folded beside it. A naked boy of perhaps fifteen was folding and patting her underslip, while a slightly older youth held up her uniformed blouse by the collar and the two sleeves, preparatory to folding it away.

Again the man on the bed summoned her. She was nudged from behind and tripped forward with her outstretched hands on his legs. He reached and caught her by the armpits and drew her head down between his knees, crushing it hard between them and holding her squeezed and muffled face just above the dry mustiness of the mattress while he undid the clip of her bra. She couldn't breathe and she wanted to sneeze.

Someone pulled her tights and pants and dragged them clear of her feet, someone who gave a boyish shrill of delight. She heard them chuckle and giggle together, discussing her in soft voices.

The man who was holding her lugged her face further towards his crotch, but only so he could pin her more tightly. She tried to shout out, to bite the soft flesh between his legs, but he changed from fondling her breasts to being cruel with her nipples, then stopped and she stopped. She felt his hand reach down underneath her, forcing itself between her legs until his wrist was between her crotch and the palm of his hand could lift itself over her buttocks, its fingers spread in a fan. His other hand reached round her back and began to strike her bottom, but gently, and so far away from her unbreathing head that she scarcely felt it. What she did feel was liquid being poured over the base of her spine, being massaged over and into her rump with those spreadeagled fingers, her thighs being moved more apart by the wriggling of his wet wrist.

5.

The Crown in Kingsway offered canned music and real ale in about equal measure. Fossit bought himself a pint of Old Dorset Spectacular in a jug and went over to the juke-box. He was in favour of loud music and juke-boxes. Nobody could eavesdrop, and bugging would be impossible without the most elaborate preparation. He felt for a tenpenny piece and eyed the chart with scrupulous disinterest, waiting for Dixon to leave off simpering at the barmaid and recognise he was here and make tracks to join him. At last Dixon stood up and folded his paper, tearing himself away with the studied urgency of a man preparing to catch a slow-moving urinal. Fossit selected *Synchronization Two* and *Roxanne*, then punched a number at random for his third choice.

'*The Police*,' he explained. 'That lad's father was a good spy for an American.'

'Good spies don't write books,' Dixon said. He was drinking from a straight.

Fossit wondered what was indicated by their choice of glasses. 'Where's Pomeroy?' he asked.

'What do we want Pomeroy for, anyway?'

'Because he comes up with the occasional creative thought. I regard him as our best chance of bringing Paddy out alive.'

A bowler hat came upstairs, with Pomeroy's head fitting very beautifully inside it. His body was clothed in something so impeccably unnoticeable it might have been woven from shadows.

Fossit congratulated him on his bowler. 'Beautiful aerodynamics,' he said.

'And I bet his underpants are tied at the ankle,' Dixon added. 'I didn't see you come in.'

'I've been here for some time.'

'What, stuck in that bloody loo? You want to oil your fly.'

Pomeroy beamed and said, 'I have a reluctant bowel. Slow as the Northern Line.'

'I know all about *them*. What'll you have to ease it?'

'Nothing, thanks.'

'You'll stand out like a sore thumb.'

'Do we have to meet near this thing?'

The box began to give them *Roxanne*.

'No,' said Fossit. 'We can sit down by it.'

'Sounds like a newt being fried,' Pomeroy said. His breath smelled sweet with brandy, in spite of his reluctance to drink. 'Sorry it has to be me,' he said. 'I have overall sight of the Arab desks as you know, but I concentrate on the Gulf and the Levant. Young Whatsit is the Libyan chappy. Such a pity he's taken his expertise to Washington.'

'What's he doing over there? Leaking?'

Pomeroy considered Dixon's question as if it deserved an answer. He was only programmed for his own humour. 'No,' he said at length. 'He's promoting Perrier. He's got some shares or something. I believe it's Perrier. I say, do you suppose they'll do me a Perrier here?'

'Doubt it.'

'Then perhaps I'll take a tomato juice.'

He watched Dixon amble off to get it and mouthed abruptly, 'Do we have to talk to such an oik?'

'Fraid so. There's the home security. Nothing'll come from

Quinlan's meeting, as far as Paddy's concerned. We're the spooks, after all, and Dixon's the domestic exorcist. If the hijackers have any pressure-points in the UK, then he's the man to find them for us and dig in the horny thumbs.'

Dixon came back with a long glass full of muddy liquid. 'Lots of Worcester sauce,' he explained. 'It'll make the old colon a bit more slippy.'

'You sure there's no vodka in this?'

'Moderately sure.'

'There *is* vodka in this. What did you ask for?'

'Something to improve the Northern Line. What do you think the chances are of digging old Paddy out of the Revolution's evil clutches?'

'Nil.'

'By diplomatic means?'

'Nil.'

'What would your Whatsit think if he weren't in Washington?'

'He'd think what I tell him. I say,' Pomeroy said to Fossit, 'that was jolly good. Do you think I might have another swig?'

Fossit picked up the glass with considerable disdain. It looked as if its insides had been rinsed in molten lipstick.

'Just ask for Northern Line,' Dixon called after him.

Pomeroy leant forward and tapped Dixon's knee to gain his attention. 'Do we have to talk to such an oik? I sat next to him back there.'

'Fraid so. He's Paddy's boss.' He started to explain Fossit at length, but the jukebox began its random choice. It was *Uptown Girl*.

'I'm afraid he is, too,' Pomeroy agreed.

Pomeroy waited for Fossit to return with another pink and brown glass, then said, 'This chap of yours, young Muscles Matson – does he know anything?'

'What about?'

'Anything.'

'Why on earth should he?'

Pomeroy pursed his lips and said, 'There's an old saying among interrogators: "The less a man has in him the longer it takes to get at it".'

'I never knew why that chap's security-rating's so high.'

'Like hot manure, you mean? I fancy it's 'cos he's been privy to the Cabinet Office.'

'And now that sod Gadaffi's got him by the monkeys.'

'I doubt it. Matson wore his balls out years ago.'

'Not riding a horse, I bet.'

'No. Not a horse.' Fossit paused. 'Paddy's a good lad, you know. A *very* good lad. I'm going to miss him.'

'You don't give him much chance?'

'I don't give him any.'

6.

Modfai waited as patiently as he could for his young men to finish with her; then he shoo'd them away. He gave her a friendly pat on the bum, and unclenched his knees. His legs were weak with cramp and exhaustion but he managed to rub some circulation back into them while he watched her squat naked and retching on the dirty little lavatory in the corner of the storehouse. He had seen no harm had come to this sweet, or its wrappings, just as the captain had ordered. He hoped his junior NCOs had been as circumspect with their own great good fortune. Now it was his for the rest of the night.

One thing about not sharing a language is you don't have to waste time with words. She had managed well enough so far without any explanation from him or from anybody else.

Modfai hated that Dragout, big fat Tibbu that he was. Still, the giant had come up with one good idea. It was this. Who would have supposed he had such an inspiration anywhere about him, touching on women as it did, and on this one in particular, to Sergeant Modfai's mounting delight?

7.

Dixon looked at Fossit, then glared at Pomeroy. 'Leonard here tells me you're a clever fella. Well, we're not coming up with anything.'

'I am clever. So what's the procedure on those flights? I

mean, how could some Yank impostor cop the lot with a zip gun?'

'Broadly speaking – they arm the escorts just before take-off. It's a sloppy business, but we're talking about a charter, not a flight under our direct control. The Airports Authority had to have a say, so did the Airline Pilots' Association; also the unions that represent the crew and the baggage-handlers. We've all been on one of those trips – I take it you have at some time or other?

A nodding of heads.

'I've always thought it's a dodgy one, that handing out of the hardware. The military hate it.'

'Who's in charge?'

'The Sass ultimately, the Sass most of the time. But it depends on other commitments – I mean, the Special Air Service ain't a constabulary, so occasionally they bow to pressure of work and pass the job on. Sometimes it's the RMP. Sometimes it's some poor sod of a travelling quartermaster, I shouldn't wonder – anyone other than a medical officer or padre, I daresay.'

'So we ask the Thugs about their exact procedure?'

'They say it varies. They say they reserve the right to hold an ace or two up their sleeve.'

'If it varies, it must vary on somebody's say-so.'

'The officer in charge of the escort selects what little act they're going to pull. But he has to clear it with the captain of the aircraft first. Whatever anyone pretends, there aren't in reality too many options. Obviously, if they were expecting trouble, they'd have some back-up, they'd be mob-handed. They might even smuggle the odd extra sharp-shooter aboard in mufti, but not willingly. I mean it's meant to be a deterrent. You want it to deter. But if it don't and you reach a shoot-out, well, a shoot-out on a plane has got to be kept simple. Uniforms against the rest, sort of thing. You don't want one of your own side picking a shooter out of her handbag in case you brass her by mistake.'

'We'll have to wait and ask Matson, then.'

'Ha bloody ha.'

'I still think it's an inside job,' Pomeroy said. 'No recce, an expert leak. Have a look at the flight crew and the cabin staff.'

'No-one would duff their own flight.'

Fossit knew the answer to this one. 'Try explaining to a bank clerk that by gossiping in the pub about procedures in his own branch he might be setting a thumbprint on his own death warrant. Try it. The banks have. Their employees won't listen to them. A counter-clerk I bump into in my local from time to time has given me information about every little wheeze they operate down at the local Barclays. I didn't pump him. He offered it. How does he know I won't gossip in turn to some other tippler with a yen to try his luck with a shotgun and plastic sack?'

'This is aircrew, Leonard.'

'They get used to talking. People think they've got a glamorous job. *They* think they haven't. They talk. I agree that it probably won't be someone on that flight, but that particular charter company only operates some half a dozen planes – I mean, it's a largish company, but the charter end of the business is meagre enough. Six planes and how many crew? Probably only a dozen crews for short-haul operations. They don't serve food on that run, only coffee. There's no in-flight shop. We're probably talking about a hundred people. Get some of your chaps to look into their backgrounds. They must have needed to blab to a friend, or a member of the family.'

'It's a thought,' Dixon said. He preferred thinking thoughts of his own, so he soaked up Old Peculiar and threw in some instant wisdom. 'I've *studied* every hijack our flights have ever been involved in. I keep abreast of any information I can pull, worldwide. I've even got the whole problem computerised, in case I feel a need to accelerate into dementia. There's *never* been anything so sharp, so ruthless, so inventive. Nor with such an odd mix of nationality. We don't know who they are. We don't have a clue about who planned for them.'

'We need more from the Libyan end,' Pomeroy said.

'We don't know if these people are terrorists, criminals, or some of Gadaffi's idiots inviting their multilingual friends for a joy-ride.'

'It's still a question of completing the Libyan jigsaw.'

'Basically I'm a policeman,' Dixon insisted. 'That's what the Security Services are – right, Leonard? – policemen with knobs on. I've *got* to believe I can find out the truth by backtracking as well as thinking forward or, worse, waiting on event.'

'Tell us about the Greeks and the Yanks,' Fossit said quickly.

'Method? The Greeks never know, so there's no need to enquire. Anyone can skimble-rig a flight from Athens. Ask the Pilots' Association. Kennedy International is another matter, of course. Security tight as a nut. That said, they've no Captain Lyall or sergeant from the flight guard to tell them how it was done. No flight guard on a civil aircraft anyway. The Americans are inclined to suspect a sleeper.'

'In the crew, you mean?'

'Got to be, they think. It's a slim chance, and it needs help outside. All of the Americans I spoke to think the weapons came in with the stores – in the food, say – and that there was someone with the cabin staff who knew just how and where to collect them. It's a viable option, just, for a hijacker who knows all of the ropes and who is totally trusted. So it's got to be a genuine old-fashioned sleeper.'

'So what are *your* thoughts, dear thing? I mean your *real* thoughts?'

Dixon was not entirely alone in detesting Pomeroy, but he was here to oblige. 'Concentrate on what we know. It just so happens that what we know is the bullseye. It's our own flight – God tell us why – it's our own flight that's the significant one.'

'How do you come to that?'

'Two reasons. First, it was a Forces' Charter. They knew it was a Forces' Charter. They planned for a Forces' Charter. But why pick something so tough? When we know why, we may well know it all.

'Second. Why eject people from the aircraft so early? Why provide us with the two best-trained observers there were? I mean, they didn't know about Matson or that U.S. General Mackie, or we assume they didn't. So they sent us the visible pair. They either intended to give us some kind of clue, or to feed us a lie. Think about it.'

Pomeroy didn't want to. Pomeroy wanted to change the subject.

Pomeroy yawned. 'The cabin girl who was shot,' he said. 'Sorry, but she's got a good old Maronite name, hasn't she? Some papers spell her Sherman with an e and an a. Most call her Shirmin with two i's. I wonder if she was born in the Lebanon? Or if any of her family were? And just where they are?'

'All the evening papers say she was shot,' Dixon said. 'Even the London Arab press on sale at the Aldwych mentions her by name. If any one of her family has a guilty secret, I bet we're going to hear about it pretty soon.'

Pomeroy stood up. 'Go for the cabin girl's background. Look at all the staff, but sift the chief stewards in particular. She was a chief steward, was little Sherman or little Shirmin.'

'That's what I'm about to do,' Dixon growled, again showing signs of too much Old Peculiar. 'Leonard's going to go home, light a candle and bite his fingernails. So what about you?'

'I've already done it. I almost always have. I spoke to Tel Aviv. They tell me they've a man in place. I don't even have a camel.'

'So what does that man say?'

'Paddy's down the latrine.'

'So what will their man do?'

'Refrain from pulling the plug.'

EIGHT

1.

Nuseibeh watched the soldiers pick up stones. Their energy was beautiful, so exaggerated, so sullen – in English, so *pert* – that he felt he could sit and study it for ever. They stooped their tobacco-coloured hands to the dust of Dragout's garden and, each time they did so, their trousers would lift above sockless ankles to reveal shins as pale as the outside of a European cigarette. The men loaded the lumpy bits of desert into their hods and their baskets, or quite simply tossed them over the wall; while the doctor was so overcome by heat he unwrapped too many sugar-lumps, and flooded his tiny cup of coffee.

Khadduri had brought just the one platoon. Ten of them were in Dragout's garden, and ten more were inside making ready his house. The doctor was very exact in his sums.

'Ten remain to guard the aircraft. No – more than ten.' It was as if the giant could read his mind. 'Plus the excellent Khadduri himself, and his very capable sergeant. Meanwhile, my soil must be tidy; and the land is empty of women.'

'Why not work your own men?'

Dragout crossed his pyjama-clad legs in a very English gesture, and smoothed the Marks and Spencer cloth he had taken from Matson's luggage. He tucked it carefully back into the tops of his riding boots. 'My own fellows are much too grand for this sort of thing. For a start, I keep them in very expensive uniforms. But then, I also provide their wages. The Revolution pays for this lot.'

'You could have taken women from the aircraft.'

'You lived in London longer than I did. Whenever did you see an English woman content with her dusting and cleaning, let alone picking stones? They'd prefer to stay where they are and be shot. Those two aircraft are full of Jewish grandmothers and British soldiers' wives – between them the most surly and quarrelsome females in the world. Except for the Americans. I praise God we do not have the American plane here.' The dark face was forever inscrutable until it chose an expression for itself. Now it chuckled and said, 'Have *passengers* leave their cabins? I do not believe you are taking this hijack at all seriously, Nuseibeh.'

'It is not right that men should do this work.'

Dragout shifted. Matson's pyjamas were becoming transparent with heat. 'Is it not correct for me to have my house in order, so Dragout may live in style?' He knew what was coming next. Arabs always talk in circles or, in Nuseibeh's case, spirals. It was as if Euclid had not existed. He chuckled again, as a warning.

'There are women on both aircraft who are employed to do domestic work on the aircraft.'

'Are you suggesting that the air-stewardesses might have been induced to dig my garden?'

'If they had been well-used, they might have been induced to stretch their legs.'

'Khadduri's men used them very well. You might even go so far as to say that their use of them was exemplary. They were indeed induced to stretch their legs.' It was worth paying attention to this last chuckle, an angry blur of the tongue like a snake's tail in the shadow. 'Come, you do not suggest this little adventure was anything to do with me? I have already rebuked the good captain for letting his fellows go over the top. He is now permitting me to correct them with my dusters and stones.'

'How much of this is for Tel Aviv?'

'Holofernes requires you to inform Tel Aviv of everything.'

'I do not understand this Holofernes.'

'Holofernes requires simply that you tell what you do understand.'

'And say no more than that?'

'Say that more than that you do not understand.'

'I am being made use of, Dragout. Even calling you by this ridiculous "Dragout" when I know you by –'

A hand reached from the sweating sky and lifted the good doctor up. Dragout towered above Nuseibeh, and Dragout on his feet beside the seated man was huge, blotting out daylight like a tumbling Babel. He held him by the bone behind his neck and shook him in a torrent of words Nuseibeh failed to understand in spite of his many tongues. Dragout in his stolen pyjamas, his exquisite boots, his skin embroidered by the mountain sun, was possessed not by rage but by the ice-calm soft-syllabling frenzy of the Dervish. He shook Nuseibeh for so long that to the doctor's strangled eye it seemed that Dragout, not himself, fell apart in a kaleidoscope of blood-drops and pain, so witless was he. Nuseibeh had only seen such a thing once, and that was in Iran when the Sufi danced, striking off heads, arms, genitals and legs with their ritual blades to the beating of a drum; and the severed limbs had danced, the genitals with the eyelids and the brains until the old Ayatollah who kept every miracle alert inside his skull gathered up the fragments of his dream like so many dice or cards so the whirring scattered limbs came together and were healed, all to the music of the drum. And that drum still beat while their blood slunk back inside the tubes of their bones.

That drum was in Nuseibeh's blood, and it continued to beat aloud long after Dragout set him down among an embarrassed ring of soldiers too timid to watch.

Dragout was no longer a blur of blebs in the dance. Nuseibeh's oxygen-starved eyes reassembled him into two muscled metres of meat which spoke to him so gently that Nuseibeh couldn't hear.

They spoke again: 'Tell Tel Aviv what seems natural to tell. Tell it what you want. But know that *if* what you want is not what Holofernes requires, then I will squeeze your slippery neck again – this time until your brain splashes out between your teeth.' Dragout pushed a finger between Nuseibeh's lips and dragged at an incisor. 'First I would pluck out this gem so your treachery does not dirty it.'

He stepped back and watched the doctor lick his gums and his lips where his hand had been. 'Salt of my finger, salt of your own blood.' He relaxed, as if the exchange made them brothers, as in a sense it did. 'Now I must make Matson ready for Holofernes.'

'He is here?' The doctor was startled as well as afraid.

'I have him downstairs, where everything is quiet.'

Nuseibeh grew bold. 'You must not forget in your reward that it was I who found him for you. I pointed him out among all the men on the flight as the most suitable instrument for Holofernes.'

Dragout had Matson fully on his mind, so he neither cursed Nuseibeh nor kissed him. He simply said, 'You *found* him, yes. You gestured with your hand when Providence dropped him at your feet through an aeroplane door. A man who earned his fee would have identified the flight that had Matson on it.'

'I did find the flight. I found you the flight that held such a man.'

'You found me the Forces' Charter. That was the extent of Nuseibeh's calculation. The rest was Lord Dragout's luck.'

2.

A boxer would be feeling worse, far worse, after a fifteen round heavyweight fight – even a fight he had won. Matson checked his lips with his tongue, and diagnosed occasional mild damage. A little sour probing and sucking confirmed his teeth were in place and still much as described by Sally Sherman.

His hands were cuffed, his legs fettered to one of the contractor's universal frames: otherwise he was no more discomforted than a hard-scrumming lock-forward on an average Saturday afternoon. He had suffered far worse knocks when training with the Thugs, once in the Hebrides in particular.

His long-ago injured leg felt a touch tender above the ankle, and decidedly numb beneath the iron. He must be mindful of his missing saphenous vein, but not brood about it. He had been left here to brood.

A pity they had shifted him from the hut, but the move was

inevitable. A man can run from a one-room single-door building and vanish into darkest night. Or there's always the fear he can. He had even contemplated using Dragout as a battering ram and erupting through the wall.

Here was different.

Here was in a cellar. The cellar to what? His eyes had been bandaged when they brought him. Now they were blinkered with dark. To his right there was the door, and the seeping of air from that direction suggested it was at least partially open. He had been bundled downstairs – slipping on cuts of rock or compacted earth – then across two other spaces, through the squeeze of several doorways. The sun must be up outside, well up, but no light reached in. His eye could just detect a thinness in the darkness, a tremble of locked-away light in the direction of the nearest door, but this might simply be a malfunctioning retina. To look towards the fancied light he had to stare into the draught, and this and tiredness could be playing havoc with his optic nerve.

They had blindfolded him to bring him here, but the cloth round his eyes could only have been meant to intimidate. The truck had made three flat-surface turns, to cross the compound and perhaps the air-strip, then climbed for ten minutes at little more than walking pace up a twisty hill-road popping with loose stones.

He was only a couple of miles from where he had started, perhaps less than one as the crow flies.

This was the problem. There always had been a problem since Modfai's first little slap to the angle of his jaw. If one Patrick Matson was what they claimed he was, then why was he not in Tripoli or at least Benghazi being interrogated by hordes of the State Police's very best?

Khadduri's claim to be eminent, and his insistence that Dragout was exalted even above the angels, might just be true; but they would not be exempt from orders, normal Intelligence procedures, nor plain common sense. So what they were doing was official, however maverick it might seem. Matson was being kept close to the hijack because he was still part of the hijack's purpose.

That purpose must be pretty damned important for a security-conscious spy-obsessed nation to pass up the chance of milking him dry, with or without coercion.

Doubtless Dragout still had time for the latter. In the calendar of the torture chamber these were early days. But the signs were that the giant would spoil him as a source of information. He had been threatened too early and roughed up too soon.

'Softened up' would be the term. You don't soften a man up for an immediate cough. You soften him up to make him receptive to a programme.

He must cling to that thought and remember to spit back what they fed him.

3.

His trance shattered. Someone had switched the light on.

There was just the one bulb overhead but its wattage exploded towards his bruised face like so many arrows of glass.

He twisted away from his discomfort, registering what his intelligence already told him: that there was another room beyond the one outside: a box beyond a box beyond a box, all three of them equally and simultaneously lit, a tunnel of receding door-frames imprinting rectangle within flaring rectangle inside the pain of switch-on sight.

He jerked his gaze towards the opposite wall. It was whitewashed. Everything glistened with salty lime. The aching parallelograms of frame swung with his head and burned there, griddled inside his brain by retinal retension.

The geography of the place might be accidental. The simultaneous switching on of this honeycomb of lights certainly was not. He mustn't forget that Dragout was a professional, with this blinding light out of sightless dark playing the oldest professional trick of all.

Light bounced back from an endless whitewash of featureless walls, from a cloudy inconstancy of ceiling.

The whole effect had been designed by this black-faced and glittering Lucifer, whose white teeth in their ebony oasis among this desert of light made his smile seem like a bore-hole into infinity.

Dragout had smuggled his head on a glittering platter into

the room and let it float here quietly, savouring his prisoner's presence, snuffling and truffling his air, until, at some secret signal, *hey presto*: this napalm had sprayed down from all of its filaments.

Dragout's smile floated disembodied because the rest of him was concealed in a bone-white mackintosh of opaque plastic such as butchers wear in the slaughterhouse.

Matson's brain awarded him a body and his eyes found it, just as the giant stepped towards the bedframe.

'Wounds, lovely wounds,' he said, pointing to the manacled swelling. 'Let me touch the holes in your leg.' It was the first time he'd asked permission for anything. 'What's it like being shot, at that exact moment the bullet enters you?'

'I intend you to find out.'

'Viperish tongue. And for a member of Her Royal Majesty's whatever-you're-a-member-of. I must have you whipped for it, most deliciously spanked, dearest wildblood lad.'

'Anything to get your face out of here.'

'Face'll stay a little. Face'll stay and watch you whinge and squirm. Do you like my raincoat?'

'Not terribly.'

'It's functional, though.'

'I daresay it's spit-proof.'

Dragout performed a pirouette or two for Matson's benefit, while one of his brown-cloth soldiers arrived with a whip.

'Whores always like to show-off their party frocks.'

Dragout examined the whip, tested its leather on thin air, then darted into a corner and swished it again. 'Look,' he said, holding out a small piece of excitement before dropping it on Matson's stomach. 'It's killed you a scorpion. Or I think killed.'

'Damned somnolent scorpion for you to catch it.'

Dragout soothed his hands on his plastic. 'In Islam, the executioner, like the butcher, serves a religious function. Here his dress is purest white.'

'Red would be appropriate.'

'The condemned is robed in red, for obvious reasons.' He brought the whip down hard across Matson's stomach.

'Isn't that scorpion dead yet?'

'I'm not going to give you the last word, Sucklemilk. Not even the last squeak.'

4.

Dragout sprinkled liquid in the corner of the room, and then crossed the floor to sprinkle it again, from a stone bottle he hoarded like a miser.

Matson thought it would be something appalling, some slow release of toxicity that a free man could walk away from, but a bound man would have to stay and confront. Even ether or chloroform would be terrible in this confined space.

A cloying stench twisted his nostrils. He tried not to breathe in, but he had to; and now Dragout was sprinkling the stuff on him. 'Perfume,' he explained. 'What your effete shopgirls call scent.' He beamed and gave Matson a big squeeze. 'Torture is such a smelly business. There's the blood, always. There's the shit, often. And sometimes my boys become over-excited as well. So, even, does the prisoner.' He tousled Matson's clogged hair. 'Sometimes, as you know, a man's cup runneth over.'

He placed the stone jar carefully on the floor.

His raised his smooth hand skyward and eyed Matson carefully from ankle to chin. His hand fell edge downward, like a scimitar, just beneath the diaphragm.

'You do not answer me, Little One.'

Matson took a long time to speak. He spat a little pain from his mouth, but the rest stayed inside, on the battered ends of his floating ribs. 'Don't overdo it,' he said at last. 'I'd hate you to tax yourself.'

5.

Dragout wore a swimming costume now – not trunks, but an old-fashioned male one-piece, such as lifesavers wear. The costume was black, and its effect on his black skin was to make his appearance seem nude – an illusion enhanced by his silver bathing cap and beach-pumps. The eye saw only silver. Silver was all he wore.

He was arranging flowers. Someone had brought in two white jugs full of flowers. The jugs were invisible in the white radiance, the flowers blanched. Everything disappeared beside the black giant in the white room.

'Flowers – in the desert. Isn't that remarkable?' He struck Matson's mouth with a flower to show him it was a real one this time, not a whip of wire and plastic; then left it on his face for him to smell. 'But then, you see, I am a man of means, a man of power – a great magician, a mage even.' He beamed. 'I am also, you will have observed, something of a hot-house plant. I am a creature of the oasis; my life is all art, believe me. And what are you, Beloved, but a tiny grain of sand?'

Matson was too battered to answer. He had done his fifteen rounds. His brain told him he was not hurt worse than a boxer can be hurt; but he had been unable to strike back, so his pride suffered. Also there was the possibility that Dragout was more than an eccentric professional. He could be a maniac whose madness was about to take over. There was no apparent purpose in anything he had done: he might simply be working himself up to some final obliterating rage.

Matson drifted, then woke to Dragout heaping ice on his stomach.

'Were you a woman – and thank the Great God of Goatherdsmen you are not – were you a woman I should arrange these flowers in you.' He patted Matson affectionately. 'But you're not a woman. Not even a girl. No longer a boy. So I shall have to cut holes in you. Then we shall plant them.'

6.

The Thug's lecture room was white. Fletcher's eyes were bloodshot, like so many flowers. The lecture room was full of Fletcher's eyes and amazing bloodshot flowers.

'Fletch' did not wear uniform. In this little trip down memory-lane he wore a dazzling white coat. 'Fletch' Fletcher was the psychiatrist the Home Office leant to the Thugs.

He knew exactly what he was talking about. He had been a Thug himself. He had been in places where a Thug can become badly unstuck. He had come unstuck.

He lectured without notes. He lectured with his eyes shut. Even with his eyes shut, there were lots of flowers in the room: 'What they are going to do is hurt *you – hurt you in short, sharp spells. These spells may be repetitive, they may be repeated over hours, but they will try to avoid constant intense pain. This will merely make the body retreat into unconsciousness. In other words, you will faint. Or the mind will retreat into …*

'Of course, some pain will be a constant. When the dentist finishes with your mouth it does not necessarily stop aching. When the boxing or rugger match is over, the pain does not go away. Often it will increase. But it is your *pain.* You *are in charge of it.* You *can welcome it or otherwise.* You *can bless it or curse it. Ultimately,* you *are the person who can seize it by the scruff and send it out of doors.*

'When the pain is intense, breathe deeply like a woman in natural labour. Try to hyperventilate, even. If they know their job, they may try to stop you doing this by striking your abdomen or the base of the ribs above the diaphragm … you will discover why these ribs are said to float.

'Try to concentrate on something or someone pleasant …

Matson thought of Brenda, but then there was her wreckage, dying faceless in his arms … He thought of Ginevra, as he'd known her once, on a green settee that the moment made squalid for both of them.

He conjugated a succession of girls about the office. He recited a heavenly declension of necks and ankles, bums and tits. And beautiful eyes: blue ones, green ones, grey ones … stay away from flowers.

Sally Sherman: how many hours ago? She had a smile, but then she was a wreckage too, her ribcage splintered by a little charge in a propelling pencil blasted into her back.

Only one face came on strong. It was a smiling face, a face in a silly hat. Women ought not to wear hats even in places they are supposed to wear them, like weddings or funerals, or Ascot, or Palace garden parties. This girl was a kind of doppelgänger for one of his inner dreams … she could support his pain for him, the little unknown so-familiar face …

'There, Beloved,' Dragout whispered. 'You see how I do what I can for you? Now what have you got to say?' (Dragout now dressed as a Tuareg or a full-blown Bedouin sheikh.)

Sometimes she had her own face and sometimes it was – no, not Brenda's – it was Sally Sherman's …

'I wonder, can you take any more just now?'

No, not Sally Sherman's either. It was undoubtedly ...

'There is one more thing I must ask you to bear in mind. Really, you may well argue we are back at the beginning. Indeed, it is a kind of circle. But first off, at your arrest or detention, at the moment you are blown, you are likely to receive very rough treatment, as a matter of policy. They will karate-chop your breasts if you're a woman, knee your groin if not, all as a matter of instruction and policy. And for why? You all know why. To impress upon you the unpleasant fact that you have come to a rough place without hope. To soften you up.

'But then they may do sophisticated things to you, use structured techniques, including starvation, or dietary interference or drugs ... and then the rough time may come again, I mean another unbridled and seemingly wild and witless time; you may be subjected to more abuse, even more sexual abuse ... or it may have been like this from the very beginning, until you conclude: I'm here with a set of sadistic monsters who have been given no other instruction than to kill me ...

It is then you must think, then you must remember ...

The pause was so long that fat and perspiring, and once hideously over-tortured, Fletcher seemed lost in his own memory like a dreaming puppy-dog ... he shrugged, smiled, and looked about him at them all ... 'Ah, but what is it exactly you must remember? You must remember to stay on your guard until the executioner's bullet hits you.

'They may be softening you up for something you cannot glimpse or guess at. Lots of people have been kicked as far as the gallows.' He smiled properly. 'Even Dostoevsky. And what was he being prepared for? To believe his existence was a gift not of God nor of the Devil, but of the Czar of Russia?

'Or perhaps he was being prepared for the gambler's purse and his secretary's thighs.' Fletcher was finished at last. And Fletcher who would never know sex again was once more talking the language of sex.

So was Dragout. He washed a little blood from Matson's lips and whispered, 'Is there anything else, my Beloved?'

7.

Dragout was back again, looking cool in prison pyjamas that were not quite prison pyjamas. As with his earlier attire, the smock and trousers seemed constructed of some superior material. He was sucking an orange, nibbling at it and whistling it through his gums like a baby milking a nipple. Matson remembered the long intimacy of the kiss that still ached on his neck. He did not feel soiled, nor did he expect to live long enough to feel soiled. Not live free of pain, anyhow.

Dragout had thick lips, and stubbly hair on his face. Matson looked up at him and experienced his first pang of self-pity. He was reminded of his father, that bearded alternative Irishman, and of being hugged by him long after he felt too old to be embraced by a grown man.

Dragout finished with his orange, bowed, and wiped his fingers on some scraps of Matson's shirt, and then again on his own pyjamas, as if he had begun by committing a dreadful indiscretion. He sat on the bed and displayed the little truncheon again.

'Well, Beloved,' he smiled.

'You know what my name is. You have my papers. Nuseibeh told them my name.'

'Let me call you something different. I shall call you Ming. It will be something personal between us. Let me tell you why, my little Paddy Ming. I am a man of – what shall I say, my dear? – a man of a pronounced susceptibility to Art. You are familiar with Chinese jars?'

'Not exactly, no.'

'Then I am afraid you have wasted your life. The Ming dynasty is, after all, very well known.'

'True. I know the name, but not the crockery.'

'The name is yours now. The crockery, as you call it, can never be. Let me explain further. I think of a certain coloration in a certain vase that some observers call blue, and others green. That is precisely the hue of this little vein just here in your neck.' He touched his truncheon below Matson's ear and it throbbed. 'A blood vessel towards which I permitted myself a certain affection. In Anglo-American they are called "love bites", I believe. But they are not bites at all. They are little sucks, little embroiderings. In Arabic they are called *bashi*, adornments, not *bites*. Believe me, Ming, if I bite you – and it may well come to that – it will be to kill you.'

Matson licked his lips and said, 'I can't wait.'

'For death, you mean?' He smacked his hand deftly across Matson's nakedness, and Matson seared with pain. 'You mustn't be cheeky you know.' He kissed him hard on the mouth, while Matson tried to shake his head to one side, at last holding him by the ears and blowing and emptying breath from his lips as if he were a schoolgirl being unreasonably reluctant on a first date with the big boys. The giant watched Matson gasp and retch, before asking gently, 'Has your lover not done that to you?'

'I don't have a lover.'

'A woman, then?'

'She's dead.'

'Well, we are making progress, Little Ming. I said you were going to tell me everything, and I promise I am going to enjoy listening to you. Have you yourself ever used violent forms of persuasion?'

'I've thumped people about a bit.'

'With your fist?'

'Yes.'

'Like this? How unsavoury. I have made it a rule never to employ any form of persuasion that I do not deeply enjoy myself. In the inflicting, of course. That limits me, but it makes life more agreeable. Torture is a messy concept. Blood stains. A man would have to be a sadist to commit the bestialities that some people use.' He leant himself closer to Matson's stone-white face and whispered: 'We have such people here, Little Ming, among my own men, among my *brown* shirts. I would prefer not to have to turn you over to them.'

Matson understood his technique at last. It was to be the carrot before the stick, standard police-procedure stood on its head.

He felt Dragout moon over him again, and flinched from the mouth clamp of yet more kissing, on his forehead, his neck, his shoulders, his arms.

'You are not talking to me, Poppleskin!'

'I thought I was supposed to be enjoying this.' He decided to be cheeky, perhaps mistakenly.

Dragout broke off to whisper confidingly, 'What I use is this.' He showed Matson the little rubber priest.

'You said you were not a man of violence.'

'Ah, my love, you mistake yourself. This is not a cosh, not a truncheon. I *thought* you hadn't understood. Surely, as an ally of the American Imperialist you have read the literature –'

Matson recognised the threat too late, and felt the sweat run on his forearms, behind his knees, in spite of the cold cellar.

'A little town in Oregon – or is it Utah? – earns its living by manufacturing these things and exporting them to certain Central and South American police forces. They are much in demand, and it is a self-perpetuating piece of business because the motors burn out very quickly – they are very worthwhile, however. I have never had to use more than one on any single prisoner.' He smiled, self-deprecatingly. 'Or, indeed, needed to treat anyone to a second session, save for my own pleasure.'

Matson turned his head away. It had looked insignificant as a truncheon. Now that he recognised it –

'Where do you obtain yours, Dogface? From the Kremlin?'

'Certainly not. I get them mail order. I won't say by the gross, but I'm a good client. This little model has several refinements that are particularly attractive to the male. Of course, I'm prepared to use them on women, naturally I am, but the ladies do not have anything so deliciously susceptible as the prostate gland, the right attention to which – without the least element of real pain – seems to drive some people out of their mind with acute depression.'

'I've read the literature.'

'Good. I'll give you a little time, to think things over, and then we'll see what sort of an arrangement we can come to.'

Matson knew better than to ask him what he wanted to find out. The lies might just sound better if they were spontaneous.

8.

Fletcher had something else to say.

'Only an amateur will rough you up indiscriminately, an amateur or a sadist who is being employed by someone who has no further use for you. You must never overlook the unpleasant fact that in many places, and among many régimes into whose hands you may fall, torture is to be regarded as no more than a form of execution.

'Anthony Farrer-Hockley wrote a few words that have become standard ... remember when he was talking of his torture by the Chinese, he said that only by accepting the possibility of death can a man or woman survive.'

9.

Dragout wore his snow-white coat, his face drenching with sweat.

Several of the others eyed him with contempt. All six of them sat in his sealed-off hut on the edge of the compound: the hut built of ceramic brick, the hut with tiles on the floor, the hut with the plastic flowers, the hut whose three beams ran under the ceiling.

There was the black with the bandaged hand, accompanied by the Düsseldorf Tart. There was the woman in charge of the El Al hijack. These three all showed their disapproval. Not so certain was the dark-skinned Palestinian with a small gold watch on his wrist. Among them, deeply uneasy, sat Dr Ibrahim Nuseibeh.

Red-brown uniforms lined the walls; not Modfai, and none of Khadurri's men; nearly a platoon in all. Who would have thought there could be so many of Dragout's private army, hidden in the house in the hills?

It was too hot to be dressed in plastic. The hut took the full roast of the sun, although sealed from the outside air and painted refrigerator white.

The sweat broke out on the crown of Dragout's head and trickled all the way to his ankle. So three of them watched him with disdain, for to sweat so much was weakness. And only a fool would choose circus clothes.

Dragout said, 'There is no comfort here. This place is a wilderness. For generations, prophets, madmen and priests have come to places like this to discover the truth of things.

'Such places belong only to God, and God has lent this one to me.'

The red-brown uniforms on one side of the room flicked the safeties from their carbines. The other three sides remained entirely still.

'I do not like people to meet me wearing guns,' Dragout said. 'So unsheath your weapons very gently and lay them on the table.'

'You're sitting very close to me,' said the black.

'A carbine is a most selective device,' Dragout smiled. 'You'll find my men are excellent shots.'

The hand-guns were taken from their holsters and laid on the table. There were some slightly tense moments when the Ingram was taken from the knees of the Düsseldorf Tart and added to the rest, and one of the El Al two picked an Uzi submachine-gun from the floor.

'Rest assured you shall have them back,' Dragout promised.

The men on the facing wall stepped forward and collected them from the table.

'All of you but one.'

The men could be heard removing magazines, and ejecting cartridges from their clips. When the guns were handed back they would be temporarily without teeth.

Dragout had so far spoken to them in Arabic, so his words could prompt his men. Now he switched to English. 'Let me rehearse my arrangements with you. You were, you remember, to seize these aircraft at whatever cost in blood. I, for my part, provided these facilities. I provided the plan. I provided the logistics. I provided, where appropriate, the weapons.

'The Israelis are logical people. They would have had their revenge for the blood you spilled during the hijack. They would have taken their toll, directly or indirectly; but they would have bided their time. Some of you would have died later in the year, perhaps. Somebody might have died instead of you a year or two after. They are, as I say, a logical people. You may dislike this logic, but it's there.

'You went beyond my plan. An Israeli woman was killed *on the ground*. Some of you wanted to kill the Englishman *on the ground*. If you start to kill English on the ground, then they'll send a rescue. It may come slowly, they may give you time to kill some more just to check your intentions, but that rescue will come within a day or two. If you start to kill Israelis on the ground that rescue will come at once.

'In either case, the rescues may succeed or they may fail – that is beyond the point. I do not want the complication of a shoot-out in this place.'

The black wanted to speak, the Düsseldorf Tart to shrill. Dragout waved them aside.

'At some moment, I estimate today, television cameras will arrive. So far they have contented themselves with the American and the Greek airliners in Tripolitania. The International Airport is easy. That's why we'll have to move the planes. Now they're curious about here. Our story is getting bigger. We're only half a day's drive from Benghazi, after all.

'Our security is very tight, most extremely tight. But I cannot guarantee that some busybody of a journalist will not find out something. All of Khadduri's soldiers saw the woman's body on the tarmac. Many of his soldiers saw her shot from the doorway. Soldiers are always poor men. Television companies are very rich – do I make myself clear?'

'I've a feeling you're about to get clearer,' the black scoffed.

'So far the news of that old woman's death has not reached Israel.'

'How could it?' asked the black.

'Ask Doctor Nuseibeh.'

Nuseibeh let his mouth hang ajar.

'Nuseibeh tells them everything except what we tell him not to. He will tell them of the old woman's death and give her name tonight. He will tell them before someone digs it out.' He changed back to Arabic. 'But by then the murderer will have been apprehended and executed.' His men removed their safeties again. 'The Freedom Fighters will have acknowledged his mistake and surrendered him.'

The Palestinian was siezed, his golden wrist twisted to meet his other wrist high between his shoulderblades.

'He will have been punished according to Islamic Law. His hand will have been severed for his theft of the watch. He will have been hanged as a common murderer. The Israelis are a hard people. They will approve of that. They will see that the Libyan people, in spite of the emnity between states, in spite of our sympathy to the causes of freedom, they will see we are protecting their people.'

Dragout's men were prompt in these matters. One of them tossed a noose over the beam. Three of them held its free end by means of wooden ratchets spliced through the divided rope like spade-handles.

Two more seized and handcuffed the lad with the stolen watch, then dropped a red sleeveless gown over his head and shoulders.

The black, the Düsseldorf Tart and the woman from the El Al flight grew briefly noisy.

'Sit down and keep quiet,' Dragout admonished. 'This is a delicate operation that must *not* be interrupted. It can, if you insist, be repeated.'

They were quiet.

The handcuffed lad was lifted till his head was in the noose, then lowered so the rope tightened round his neck. His feet were settled on a folding chair, its back against his knees. The slack of the rope was taken up on the spade-handles and then slackened off by the length of a man's forearm.

Dragout, sweating even more with concentration, mounted an upturned bucket and stood beside the condemned man, whom he blindfolded.

'Take comfort that you will die among friends,' he whispered. 'Also that I have done this many times.'

He kicked away the folding chair, simultaneously jerking the youth's head backward by means of a blow with the palm of his hand to his forehead.

The robed figure fell so his feet were just clear of the floor, his neck snapping aloud like a wet branch.

Nuseibeh was immediately very ill.

'He is not a doctor of medicine,' Dragout apologised. 'You will notice that it is part of the clemency of my Court not to cut off the hand till after death. But his is a thief's hand, living or dead, and it is forfeit. So it will be cut.'

His men were ushering the hijackers towards the door. Dragout detained the black with a gesture. 'Thank you for surrendering this man to justice. Justice is a corporate affair. You may take the condemned and bury him. His hand is yours to cut.'

He opened the table drawer and unwrapped the ritual knife.

The black would not take it up. He said, '*Your* court?'

'Yes. I have power in many courts. Yet I was perhaps being presumptuous. For this is not my court, although I preside here. This is Holofernes' court, as I think you know.'

'Indeed.'

'And in this court, the hand is still yours to cut.' He tapped the black with the flat of the blade. 'Take it, and cut it now.'

10.

'You mustn't be anxious, Sleepless One. Nor shocked that I've had to change for you. There was a dead man's blood on my sleeve, and I thought its smell might frighten you.'

Matson opened his eyes. He felt comatose in spite of fear and discomfort – the airlessness of the cellar saw to that. Also he ached from the thongs at his wrists and the handcuffs round his ankles, and suspected he had been close to fainting.

'Well, my little Houri of delight?'

Dragout stood looking for approval. He was wearing a dark blue gown – or perhaps Matson was hallucinating.

He drifted into a sort of darkness, and wondered whether he was recoiling from a deeper sexual-shock, whose disorientation he was not prepared to face up to, but which was a deliberate part of his dilemma. He had only once been to bed with a girl he didn't fancy, and remembered how impossible it had all been. Perhaps women were always getting into this sort of situation with men. Perhaps. What a pity he hadn't trained with the K.G.B. According to the Sunday papers, they give their heterosexual agents crash-courses in homosexual manners.

Dragout's hand shook him gently by the shoulders.

'I can offer you a graded application, Little One. Tell me, for example, if there are any interesting people on your aeroplane.'

'I have already told you I know no-one. Told Khadduri, anyway.'

'Ah, your debutant gesture! Your first refusal to cooperate! However, I owe it to your stay here to proceed with compassion.' He moved his left hand between Matson's spread legs and lifted his penis, which was clammy with perspiration.

Matson lay bathed in moisture, and felt his body chill after the sudden rush of warmth to skin.

'This has a little cup, you see.'

Matson felt something touch him beyond Dragout's imperious hand.

'When I switch on the motor it take about six seconds.'

'Nonsense.' There was a slight fluttering of vibration. He knew it wouldn't work, not on him.

'*Oops, that's me*!

Just like guava jell-y!'

Dragout sang, cleaned his hand, and smiled. 'Do you know that calypso? I can do this to you again and again.'

He did.

Matson noticed that the giant was sexually excited, then stopped being able to notice.

'The male is not designed for this sort of repetition, is he? And yet what have I offered you? No more than a warning. You feel a trifle sore, perhaps and – well, yes, we have left you receptive to suggestion.'

He was at the bed-foot suddenly, beyond kicking distance and deftly unfastening one end of the cuff that secured Matson's left ankle to the bed. Before Matson realised what was happening, Dragout had locked back the foot in a wrestler's grip, then swung it across to the right-hand side of the bed-frame, securing it so both of his legs lay to one side and his body half turned over.

He leant his weight against Matson from behind and wriggled himself onto the bed. 'Now, my little Cinnamon Stick!' Matson felt himself being entered by something blunt and plastic and much too big. 'There's a lot of juice in the motor, but next to nothing in you.'

'What do you want to know?'

'Everything about every aspect of English Counter-intelligence you can think to tell me.' Dragout snuggled closer, intruding his rough-coated piece of American technology to painful depths. 'You know,' he whispered in Matson's ear, 'Heads of Departments, responsibilities, how much is known over there about Libyan agents, particularly in London. Also –'

'I know nothing about that sort of thing.'

Dragout permitted himself a few disgusting endearments which Matson shut away from his mind. His body was totally numb and his spirit was in another place.

Trussed up and twisted like this, the left side of Matson's neck was uppermost. The black man from Tibesti settled his lips against it and began to croon.

Matson felt a dark vibration growing through him, a shudder of voltage boring deeper than bone. He heard his face make a noise, as the sensation rose higher and higher, and turned in a second into an enormous sadness as if God and then breath had forsaken him and he had to live an eternity without them. There was no reason in it, no scale of comparison. It was neither sex nor pain, but a pinnacle of disembodied anguish that enlarged and grew larger until with everything clear in his mind he went quite mad.

He woke without limb or sensation. Dragout's lips were still at his ear and he knew from the man's thickening breath that use was being made of his body, but Matson felt nothing at all. His spine had been inflated with emptiness, and he lay without bones or strings.

He woke again to water. It took him an age to realise he was being washed.

'Well, Silken Bones?'

He did not really hear, or think he could speak.

Again Dragout settled closer. Something, his body or the infernal machine, was starting it all again, but not to him, not to Paddy Matson or even little Ming, but to quite another person in quite another place.

11.

The angel was a woman and beautiful. He knew he must concentrate on this angel – Fletcher had said so. He must remember his angel was a woman.

If not, he would be forced to accept the Brute who was torturing him.

Sally Sherman had a slim, ballet-dancer's neck and exquisite ankles. These were old-fashioned things to notice about a woman, but he noticed them. He watched her neck on and off, for several minutes, and he glimpsed her ankles whenever she moved from the door to the gangway. There were plenty of reasons for noticing them, the chief one being that his Old Mum had told him to. 'Look at a girl's neck and ankles,' she said, 'and if you find you can't drag your eyes away from these, be warned about the rest of her. It means she'll spell deep trouble for you.'

His Old Mum – his young mum then – had gone away for the first time when he was thirteen. He was so upset about her leaving him that he had fallen in love. The girl was two or three years older than he was, in the Fifth Year at Camberwell. He used to follow her from school. Although he was taller than she was he was also much more stupid, so she and her friends used to laugh at him. They would have laughed at him anyway. She had ankles, too, and a neck, always seen from behind, under too much hair. He told his Grandmother about her.

'To make a woman love you,' she crooned, as if she was still living on the farm in Ireland and distilling the poteen she called mountain dew, not existing south of the London River and halfway up a brick tree, 'to make a woman love you, take the darkest hair of her head, a thimble of her blood, and her little toenail.'

He had not thought this girl through as far as her toenails; so he told his Granny she was either pulling his leg or being impracticable. 'She'd be in love with me already, Nan, or out of her mind, if she gave me any of those.'

'Smart boy. Clever boy. What the lads do back home, and sometimes the colleens too, is invite the person they love into their dreams. If you can invite that girl into your dreams she'll love you. And leave you a lock of her hair in her sleep. All you have to do is

fall asleep thinking about her every night.'

'I do, Nan. Every night. I dream of her laughing at me.'

'You can soon change all that. Before you invite her into your dream, invite her into your imagination. It's an old Irish trick. The imagination is like a light-switch. You can turn it off. Then you can forget her. It's an old Galway trick.'

'You mustn't forget *me*, baby! What's all this inelegant woman rubbish you're babbling?'

He neither woke nor slept. He changed focus, turned a tiny corner in his mind, to notice his favourite Tibbu from Tibesti black-faced at his ear.

Dragout, the puppet-master, said, 'Do not die on me, Patrick Matson. Do not die on me, Captain Matson,' not calling his name by code or any other linguistic Charlie William, but speaking out loud and clear, 'Do not die on me, Ming. My needs have a use for you. My uses have their need.'

He resumed on Ginevra, then Brenda now refusing to be dead.

Sally Sherman could not refuse to be dead.

He had seen her heart drop out. He had knelt for his death among her leavings. He had knelt at death's door.

Dragout said, 'Listen closely, Matson. There's just one thing you've simply got to remember!' Dragout was splashing water and carbolic and perfume, then the hot blood of flowers. Dragout was not, alas, a nurse nor even dressed as a nurse. The inspiration must have left him.

Dragout was shouting. It was silent thunder. Matson could no longer hear. He returned to Sally Sherman.

He must be near death himself, to cling to the dead like this.

Dragout was still shouting. Death is like virginity. It heals in your sleep.

'How do I make a dead woman love me, Nan?'

'You must die yourself, my son. Or look for her double. If she's a witch, she'll be bound to have her double, and every worthwhile woman is a witch. You can make her live in her double.'

'Fuck you, Matson. You've broke my little battery. I'm going to wring your neck!' The Tibbu always sounded loudest when he whispered.

Men do not dream like this. Only the fever of death can make such dreams. He must stay with Fletcher's lecture and return to his angel.

To his mother or his angel. To his angels and his mums.

The angel wasn't Brenda or Ginevra – he was returning over ground already established. The woman had Sally Sherman's face, Sally Sherman in a silly hat.

Sally Sherman was dead. He had to believe his angel was still alive.

Something was alive in his hands. There was blood in his hands. He had cut himself on blood. Now, even now, even here, he twisted his face to his hands. He was holding Sally Sherman's silly piece of tin and plastic. He must have picked it up as he'd tumbled through the aircraft door. Sally Sherman's message had cut to the bone.

Yes, he'd stolen it at the door and kept it in his pocket while they'd left him with a pocket to keep it in.

Silly hat silly hat silly hat. A face like Sally Sherman, silly hat. He'd forgotten the taxi-girl. He must remember the beauty of the taxi-girl not only for now but as a clue – a palpable professional clue.

How dare you presume I'm a heterosexual?

12.

The giant was back again, stooping his Tibbu head through the doorframe, hunching his shoulders. He was carrying something that maddened his dog and made it leap round the Captain's office, yelping and whining.

Khadduri dragged the silly brute to the door by its collar and shut it out. He wished he could have done the same with Dragout himself. This was his office.

'You shouldn't have done that. Kick my slaves and you kick me.' Dragout retreated into himself, breathing soundlessly, as if his whole presence was an illusion.

'I am very far from happy, Dragout.'

'Eternity moves in a great circle, Khadduri. You may be so far from your joy at this moment that just one further step away from it will let you fall into its arms. Let me make you laugh.' He threw something like a Benghazi cuttlefish on the captain's table, a squid bleached from rubbing on the sand, with its split end raw from the grit. It was a man's hand and forearm, a gold watch still ticking round its wrist. 'A little present for you, my friend. Something to cheer you up.' Together they watched the flies cluster to it like fruit on a sticky cake. 'It will look very well at home in a pickle jar. You could make a lamp. No need to thank me. I've too many of the things. The watch is what makes the experience unique.'

'Who –'

'Someone who is not at all happy with life, Khadduri. Far less happy even than yourself. No – he is not one of yours. Nor is he a passenger, so do not be alarmed. That is a Jewish watch. What sort of believer would steal a Jewish watch? Now let me feed you some other sweetmeats.'

For the moment he seemed forgetful of what they were, and stood picking at the fly-marks on his neck as if they were memory beads.

'Yes – how shall I put it? Nuseibeh is being obedient. And Matson – Matson is as stubborn as a herd of stones.' He liked what he had said about Matson, and spoke it again in English, perhaps as a charm to keep him alive.

He held Khadduri to his chest, and waited patiently for him to struggle free. 'The Second Phase,' he said. 'We have fed them the riddle, so now we can begin. Come *in*, Ibrahim!'

The dog had become quiet outside, and that was a warning.

When Nuseibeh shuffled in he looked ill and uncertain, his face sicker than sick. He reminded Khadduri of a malingerer who chews cordite.

'Nuseibeh has just helped me hang a man, Colonel – the other end of this one, in fact.' Dragout pointed to the hand in its bandage of flies, and watched Nuseibeh grow even more uncomfortable. 'In an hour or so he will tell the world all about it. But first he is to join us to play cards.'

'Cards?'

'Yes, or dice. Or even toss stones or draw straws – anything so we may wager a little. Believe me, Khadduri, I hide little from you. In the space of a game or two, perhaps tonight or tomorrow night, everything will become clear. Why not send for Modfai to make up four?'

NINE

1.

'Last evening,' Quinlan said, 'the Prime Minister put me in sole charge.'

Fossit's note-pad asked: '*A write-off?*'

Pomeroy wrote: '*Not necessarily.*' He added, after some thought, '*Damage limitation. Boss Cat has intervened, to demonstrate commitment at the highest level. BUT!*'

'We already have our diplomats and our information-gatherers, including the military. Now, in consequence of the PM's instructions, I've asked field to step in. I'll introduce you all later.

'What it means is this committee is totally executive. CAC is where it's at. If we decide to send in a commando or bomb the colonel, then of course I'll ask higher. But we, and we alone, are to lay the plan. And we, subject to that caveat, will give the order. Our command centre is here.' He banged the table with his carpenter's thumb. 'Here is my command.

'We have the necessary channels. We have the land-lines. I want a twenty-four hour signals staff specific to all echelons, and I insist that up at Northwood, and across the road or wherever, these requirements are matched. I'm asking for immediate implementation at all levels. Which means people with the necessary clout being available not only at the other end but at every other end. Hereford and Plymouth give me no worries. I want the same thing on the Rock and in Cyprus. Full listening watch. All commanders on hand. Universal

Sunray One!'

Quinlan was going to be his usual arrogant, imprecise, ambiguous self, and be it so forcibly that he left no-one in doubt as to his intentions. 'Got it? I don't want a dink up because an admiral's off yachting, a group captain's sieving soup, or soap, a general's stuck in a bunker.

'Ship and squadron movements to begin. Exercises to be cancelled. Aircraft fuelled and armed. Jump planes on station. Air-landing planes ditto. Command support ships and beach assaults boats ready ready ready. Etcetera. Etcetera. Etcetera. We don't have much, so whatever we do have let's have on war-footing. When we decide to go, we must be ready to go.'

'*A lot of "we",*' scrawled Pomeroy, '*not to say widdle. Do you suppose he's a closet socialist?*'

'If compasses, range-computers, triluxes, battle-sights need to be calibrated, do it *now*, if not yesterday. Run your gyros, straighten your bloody fins, powder everything's bottom. Check all your spares, and check you've got spares to check.

'I do not care if that means an extra billion or two on defence budgets. I'll dock you all later. I will not have action frustrated because some erk has mislaid a cotter pin – is that understood? Cotter pins will be inspected, blancoed and laid-out now.'

Yesterday there had been enthusiasm, laughter. Today there was none. The civil servants were wary of having Quinlan's greatness thrust upon them, and anyway they felt sorry for the military.

They were wasting their time. The action-people had been hearing tunes like this since their induction and indoctrination. They had heard them so often that they no longer listened to them. Quinlan might feel he was showing them he was at heart one of their own kind, but they did not see him that way. He was louting about like some sergeant-major from an inferior regiment. None of them came from such a regiment. Hardly any of them had spoken to a sergeant-major recently, let alone listened to one.

'*All* leave will be cancelled: weddings, funerals, evening passes, the lot. No sick parades, no pox inspections, no excused boots. *No* local OC's discretion. Nothing nothing

nothing. Nothing. Everything and all for effort. Do I make myself clear? You've had your bloody increment, so let's have the tanks where they belong – out of their kennels and sitting on the mat as a visible instrument of government.'

'What about security?' One of the cream-faced sailors was growing tired.

'No point. He knows that if he doesn't disgorge those aircraft someone will slap his wrist. Us going to evident and massive alert – and it's what the Yanks are already doing – us beating drums may exert sufficient pressure to make him glimpse reason. If not, drums are far from being all we are going to beat.' He beamed at the Navy. At last someone had spoken to him. 'Get on with it, then. Let your people know, set up your nets, and reconvene in fifteen minutes.'

'Sprung-rhyme and pig-metaphor,' Pomeroy muttered. He looked at his '*BUT*' on Fossit's jotter, underlined it and added: '*the blame will stop with the blarney, with poor old whinnying Quinny!*'

They could sit and talk now. The fifteen minutes' recess was for the military phone-ins and for Terence Quinlan's bladder. The intelligence-gatherers were already at work. All there was for the likes of Fossit and Pomeroy was to make their reports.

'So,' said Fossit, 'Quinny for the next PM after all?'

'Nerx. There's going to be gore all over the Persian carpet. All over the Berber rug, anyway. Gore as thick as dromedary droppings. Old Pustular is going to plant a hoof in at least some of it. Blood sticks, and stinks and congeals, and is anyway not kosher.'

'Aren't you being defeatist?'

'Soldiers are defeatist. I'm a realist. The Foreign Office is staffed exclusively by realists. Consider the scenario – you don't have to play War Games to get the score:

'This hijack has already killed people. So the *Guardian* sits on the fence. *The Times* calls for clear heads. Soon the hijack will make demands or do something dirty and kill some more. Egg on Quinny's chin. *The Times* calls for clear heads. Quinny stalls for time. Death and then more deaths. The *Guardian* alights from the fence. *The Times* calls for clear heads. The *Sun* – same owner – uses two-letter words and manages a three-word sentence. Quinny goes in. The *Express* banners "Gungho!" The *Sun* girl has red white and blue nipples. *The Times* exports her to the States, and the egg on Quinny's chin begins to trickle down the pustular dicky. Quinny loses some more hostages. We all lose assault troops. We waste the airliners, fifteen helicopters, several Libyan soldiers together with a million Libyan bystanders and the Secretary General of the U.N.'

'Come on, Marcus. Hyperbole excluded, that's the worst case!'

'That's the best case. The worst case is total military penis-entanglement: vectors upside down, screwed-up ADTs, lates on Romeo Victor – what's the plural of Romeo Victor, by the way? – all hostages dead and mutilated and sold for spare-part surgery, Benghazi blown up, Tripoli burned down, the *Sun* girl not only fully frontally *dressed* but attired in widow's weeds, and the *Guardian* hopping right over the fence – and I do mean *right* over! – and *The Times* calling for Terence's unclear head before he can even dust the crumbs from his chops!'

Pomeroy stiffened his coffee with some varnishy liquid he carried in a hip-flask before adding gloomily, 'And that's only *our* problem. What do you think a cock-up like this will do for the Yanks? For alliances? Administrations will crumble, and everyone sitting round this table and every similar table in Anglo-Judaic Christendom will be pensioned off.'

'Not necessarily a bad thing, at that.'

'You're talking about *me*, Leonard. Not the moody mug in the moon. You're talking about important people.'

'Important people top up their friends' coffee,' Fossit grumbled. 'We're not important.'

People are important because of the size of their mouth, like Quinlan, or the size of their brief-case, like Quinlan's Hattie. Then there are people who achieve greatness because of the size of their function, like Quinlan's Lorna.

Quinlan's Lorna was in charge of the transcription screen or the video-link, whichever honour she chose on the morning to call it by. She rushed in this moment to switch it on.

'They've just named Captain Matson by name,' she squeaked.

'Dear child,' Pomeroy said. 'You do not know Matson in Arabic.'

2.

'You are from the big city, Khadduri. Your sergeant here is different. Modfai is a country boy just like me.'

The two country boys, giant athletic black, and pear-shaped pyknyk white, eyed each other with total unaffection. Dragout's gaze passed over Sergeant Modfai. Dragout's lips smiled. They said, 'Sergeants must never be handsome. Whoever heard of a pretty sergeant, eh, Modfai? Modfai is like a milch-goat – lean about the head and fat around the basket. And hairy. You're not entirely Arab, Modfai. Look at the whiskers on his hands. His mother was a Turk.' He turned for applause. Instead he glimpsed a shadow bat away from Khadduri's open door, and called, 'Come back, Ibrahim! Come here, Nuseibeh! Modfai, fetch the doctor home, there's an ugly sergeant!'

Nuseibeh was in a fever to be gone; but Modfai caught him by the shoulder-cloth. Nuseibeh stepped back into the room and salaamed as soldiers never do, like a bit part in *Kismet*. Like a London Arab trying to stoop to his roots.

'Nuseibeh's a country boy, eh, Ibrahim? And sly with it. Ya, Ibrahim? Ibrahim minds his flocks on Hampstead Heath. That's not a joke for sergeants, but the captain understands.'

He dropped a hand on Modfai's shoulder, and for Nuseibeh's he had an arm. The arm and the hand led them to the window. They saw the concrete wall of a hut and the porthole of an aircraft; beyond them to the East a huge wave of dune, still gold against the light.

'What we country-boys understand is that space is never empty, eh, Ibrahim? Ya, Modfai? I have seen some six or seven of these hutments, deserted in the *reg*, standing empty by the *chotts*, like an abandoned column of tortoise-shells; and so has Modfai. And in each of those deserted hutments there are people, squatting impoverished people, people who don't belong – not perhaps in the first shack, not even in the second, but somewhere before the hundredth.

'If you pick up a shell I don't expect you to find the tortoise. Not out here in the sun. But after a shell or two there's bound to be something – a lizard, a scorpion, a rat. Go and find them for me, Khadduri. Better – send Modfai with some men to round them up. Modfai has the nose of a Turk. I want some old women for my garden, young men for my house. When you've found me those people, you can take back your soldiers from my thornbush and my stones.' He lifted his hand from Modfai, who knew better than to move.

Nuseibeh he rewarded with a squeeze. Nuseibeh had planted the idea in the first place. 'Cards,' the giant said. 'Cards and a game of dice.'

Nuseibeh was suspicious of both. This time he said he would leave, and to his surprise he left.

3.

The brown tailored uniforms seemed normal down here. When the light was shining brightly the brown looked like khaki. The light, after all, was as brilliant as a stage-set.

Two of them bumped about Matson, obtrusive as moths. They dizzied between his face and the naked light-bulb. They unfastened his wrists from the bedframe, and clipped them to each other. They unclamped his legs from the legs of the bed, then hobbled chain to chain to give him the freedom of a fetter.

They jabbered.

Matson, even at his fittest, was not fluent in Jabber.

They rolled him off the bed onto a distant bruise of earth. The earth was dusty rock.

He was numb now, and feverish. He felt nauseous, he thought with hunger. He felt like an undoctored hangover. The beating had filled him with sleep.

Jabber. More bloody Jabber. He'd buy a Berlitz in Jabber. They kicked him to his knees. They knee'd him to his feet. He understood their boots. They had expressive knees. He could talk boots and knees. He must work harder at Jabber.

He fell across a shoulder and was sick. His sick was neater than Becky Potts' sick – how *were* Lady Chambers and poor

Miss Potts? – because he had the advantage of a nice brown brushed denim back to be sick down, and his vomit looked good on a brushed brown denim back. It looked better still on the brown denim front when he sought to apologise. It dropped about the pockets like a silken lanyard and a golden sash.

He couldn't apologise in Jabber, so the brown thing punched his head.

Nurses, in Matson's experience, are very tolerant about sick, even all over their uniform, even all under their hair. In Beirut he'd been sick almost into an ear.

The brown thing wasn't a nurse. It raged and hit him. And then it went hurrying out, taking all of his vomit with it, just like a two-legged mop.

The remaining brown thing kept a safe distance – say half a leg off. It called out for reinforcements while booting Matson towards the door.

They were going to shoot him? Or hang him in that hut with the beams? Or simply change his address to a deeper hole?

In the next room there was a kitchen sink. It was huge, square and dirty, on crude brackets of iron. There was also a terracotta urn.

Matson savoured the sink. It had a tap with a green brack of water. God knows what fed it. It was damp rather than wet, slimy as a sun-blown eel, but it tasted sweet on the lip.

Hands took charge of him again. A fresh supply of browns were in. They pressed him down on the urn. Their jabber was measured and grave. Shit, before being shot? If they were granting this, they were clearly going to hang him. Executioners wear white and prefer an empty sky.

This time nobody mocked. A man so accurate with vomit could be how much more dangerous with his pot?

They carried him back to his room. He realised he was almost naked, dressed only in genitals and socks. The genitals needed changing. His socks were good for another day.

They didn't oblige him with laundry, just shackled his feet to the bed, one foot now dangerously swollen.

4.

Some men collect stamps. Some collect people.

When the shot rang out, Dragout knew his people-collection was going well. He picked up his dice and his winnings, then chuckled for much too long.

Khadduri was not so sanguine. 'I have the aircraft to consider,' he scolded. 'I have a hut full of women – *those* women.'

'The British stewardesses? How many?'

'Six.'

'Keep the door locked, Captain. Then there'll be no need to shoot them, unless for practice or pleasure.'

'Shots are an unnecessary alarm, just the same.' Khadduri was not soothed by Dragout's little joke. He seemed worried about the women.

Modfai returned with even more for him to worry about. His file of soldiers marched in smartly. The sergeant was still sore from the giant's tongue: men always march smartly for a sore sergeant.

They brought some twenty people with them – old and young men and women, children, three families in all. And a seven-year-old boy with a bullet through his arm.

This was because a file of soldiers cannot bring anyone with them as such, especially when their sergeant is forcing them to march smartly. It's their guns that have to fetch for them. The boy's father had to carry.

The three families and the ten soldiers stood apart from each other in the captain's command hut. There was no love between them, and little from Modfai.

The child lay on the captain's table with his eyes half shut.

'Who fired?' Khadduri was angry.

After hesitation, Modfai prompted a name from the side of his mouth, and a young soldier shuffled forward.

'Excellent marksmanship,' Dragout congratulated. 'Slap through the flesh of the arm. Missed the bone, didn't strip muscle. Look at the exit. Absolutely no enlargement, eh, Modfai?' He penetrated both holes with his propelling pencil.

The arm fluttered like a frog on a pin. The boy was deeply in shock.

Khadduri was appalled at Dragout's disregard of sepsis. He sent quickly to his jeep for a first-aid kit, and poured aquaflavin through the wound.

The boy screamed awake. He howled worse than Dragout's dog. The dog didn't compete. It growled, then barked instead.

The giant cuffed both of them. 'Lock him in the hut with the English women,' he instructed. 'That will keep this lot in place. I want *her, her* and *that* one' – he indicated three old women, the grannies from each family – 'to pick up stones from my garden. And those three mature men for tasks about my house. The children I'll consider later. They'll be paid. You'll all be paid if I need you. This boy's father will be recompensed, but he must forfeit some monies to the Revolution to provide for his child's food and medicine and the expensive waste of a bullet.'

Dragout shoo'd them out. They stooped their necks to Dragout, but the giant did not respond. He was in a thoughtful mood, and when he grew thoughtful he lacked the manners even of a squatter Arab.

5.

'You cannot leave that child with those women. For a start he is a boy and the women are not of the faith. Then, as I continually indicate, the women are complaining.'

'Let them nurse this child. He will put paid to their unrest.'

'These women are airline women, *haroor* Dragout. Their complaints go deep.'

'You and that Nuseibeh! Airline women are no different from other women. Women always complain, often when they are most in joy. Supposing your wife complains, supposing she has no cause, how will you pay her?'

'I have no wife, Dragout.'

'You will beat her. The scripture says that you will protect all women and guard them, your wife and the old women of your family even above other women, but if having been well treated they continue to complain you will beat them. Or if one continues to complain you will beat her. Or if one continues above the rest you will beat her above the rest. You will not beat her every day, hence the prophets say "*continues* ... continues to complain". Abu-Bekr says once a month, according to the moon but not the woman's moon. Prophet Abraham in the Abesta says once in seven days – but perhaps he lived among unruly women!' Dragout guffawed, as if the unruliness of women was something appropriate to Prophet Abraham.

'Lord, I was thinking of the political consequences.'

'Call me Dragout, only Dragout, even though you honour me in private.' Again Dragout laughed. 'We have, after all, governed among ourselves and by ourselves –'

'Yes, Lord. But –'

'And we now live in the Revolutionary Republic.'

'Yes, Lord. But these women from the aircraft –'

'These women from the aircraft *continue* to complain? You will notice the use of the prophet's word "continue", Khadduri? Clearly we must beat them if they continue. You used the oil I found you?'

'My men used the oil.'

'Even though a woman is not as pleasing as a boy, as slender, as frenzied, as sinewy –' Dragout shuddered, remembering his pleasures. 'Even though a woman is not a boy, and even though – I speak to you man to man – even though these women are *infidels*, you gave them this honour, with the gentleness of oil. So how did they thank you?'

'They sat on the lavatory and they cried.'

'It is an immodest thing, that lavatory, for a woman. You should not have let them sit on it. You should have sent them into the sand.'

The captain began to say it at last. 'They are complaining that *my* soldiers have abused them. They may complain later to –'

'To whom, my little Khadduri?'

'To everyone, Dragout. To the world.'

'Listen, *little* Captain. You will excuse me calling you that, but I am making that Matson listen as well as you, and I sometimes call him so. Listen, little Captain. If they should ever be alive to complain to the world, the world will not heed them. Oh, America will heed; the Beast will always listen. So will Cain in Europe. But Islam will not listen, for it *knows* the servants of the Beast and the Children of Cain, it knows they feed on lies.'

The captain struggled politely to free himself, and Dragout released him with reluctant affection. 'So how did you learn that these women complained?'

'We *heard* them complain.'

'What? You yourself watched them perch on an immodest Western lavatory and point towards their arse? Of course not. Your men did, perhaps. *You* speak English, Captain Khadduri, but your men speak *no* English.' He was once more the intelligence-gatherer, again the interrogator, his antennae never more alert than when he trembled with love. 'Who among these women of the aircraft speak Arabic? You did not dare to set them among the Jews?'

'There are those on the aircraft speak Arabic.'

'An English speak Arabic? An English has no tongue. When God struck at Babel, English was the first fool he struck, and God's first bite was fiercest, like the viper's in the *hammada*.'

'The hijackers talk Arabic. The hijackers *are* Arabs. The women complained among the women.'

'So they spoke to the Freedom Fighters, and Freedom is always Arabic?' He drooled and squeezed again. 'I am not a prophet, but I do not think these Fighters will have much freedom to tell their tale.' He led Captain Khadduri to the desk, and sat him on his knee. Dragout's legs were long but the desk was tall, so consequently the captain was forever slipping off, but was returned to obedience by the strength of Dragout's hand.

'Now listen, little Khadduri. Pay attention, Captain mine.'

The captain protested, but politely.

'I require you to sit still with me and listen. I shall not undo any buttons. I have the white-bottomed Matson for that, and I thank you for him. All I want to be sure of is your ear.'

'Yes, Lord Dragout.'

'Though I am sure you could be an excellent boy to unbutton, if somewhat old.'

'Thank you, Dragout.'

'Now tell me truthfully. Those stewardesses on the Israeli aircraft. How many?'

'Ten – no, twelve women, and eight men.'

'Have your brave lads done them honour?'

'No, Dragout.' Captain Khadduri shuddered even more violently than at the black giant's mawling and pawing. 'They are Jews.'

'Because they are Jews your men would not have them as the English, that is true. But there will come a night when they will perhaps go into the fire. Not the passengers – we have a need for the passengers –'

' "Holofernes", Lord Dragout?'

'Yes, but never say that name except to me. Holofernes has need of the passengers, but wants the uniformed ones in the fire. It is honourable to enjoy a dishonourable woman before she goes into the fire, Khadduri.' Again the squeeze. 'Or a dishonourable boy. A man owes this courtesy to his enemy before killing him, even his most *loathed* enemy, his enemy's *virgins* especially.' He embraced Captain Khadduri only briefly, before setting him on his feet. *Virgins* was a word that always transported him into a delirium.

The captain straightened his tunic and sat behind the desk. Dragout was only just beginning. Khadduri sensed him warming to his theme.

6.

Half-hearted brutality, sloppy familiarity. Was this the technique, and could this be all? Matson was eating his first meal for twenty-four hours, and to break bread helped introspection.

He hunched on his bedframe and waited for Dragout. The man was either indolent or had other matters to attend to. Had he found out about Irenson and Anne Chambers? Was he busy securing the aircraft? Were the planes still here?

Were the planes still *there*? Here was a hole in the ground. The toad was too far down the well to know what the world was doing.

A succession of princesses had already left him.

A tear formed among the bruises of his forehead and wept a tiny bleb of clearest lymph to roll down his face to find his eye. He did not brush it away. He knew his inertia was a bad sign, but he sat and admired his grief through the lens of it.

Meanwhile he ate his bread like a watchmaker repairing watches, very close to. Save there was no time here, except what dripped from his face or crawled about the floor.

There were weevils in the bread. They were a sort of time. He pulled his food apart, then reassembled it carefully like a man who repairs weevils. The bread was much too dry. It was badly engineered. Only the weevils worked. The loaf was running slow.

'I'm bloody going under. I will not go under.'

Bootsteps overhead. He was under.

The boots were coming downstairs. He dried his broken face. He clenched his teeth alert.

7.

These were not Dragout's brownjobs. These were Khadduri's lads. They were gazing on naked Matson and evidently finding him good.

One was squat and tubby. One was elevated and lean. One had known dorsorectal distortion as an embyro. The other was anteroposterior.

'Cor,' said Matson. 'A pair of sodding look-alikes!'

They couldn't understand him, so they lacked the satisfaction of his wit. They contented themselves with unfastening their trousers.

'Did you think of this yourselves, or does Dragout charge a fee?'

Matson was too weak to defend himself. A strong man can be virtuous for hours. He laid aside his crusts and his weevils, and peered into the tin plate he had eaten them from, like a woman fixing her make-up.

This time he must remember he was hobbled by the ankles. On the other hand, the bedframe was a pretty unsurmountable chastity-belt, unless they had borrowed a key.

He gave them a moment in case; he could make good use of

a key. His smile was just an arrangement of teeth at the epicentre of a limp morale.

Alas, they had no key, and no little place to put one.

Their army provided no underpants, and in consequence no trouser-pockets.

Matson was kindest to the short one, who chose the right side of the bed. He chopped him hard on the Adam's apple, where his neck was a-wobble with hope.

His friend on the left was the tall one, too tall for a seated man. But a warrior in such a condition should beware of the edge of tin plates.

'Will you take it with you?' asked Matson. 'Or do you want it wrapped?'

They weren't official visitors. They didn't come back.

8.

'You are hiding from me again, Khadduri. You are sitting behind your table. Know that when I give a man his orders I like to be able to touch him, to feel his brain at work.'

The captain rolled his Osmiroid on his blotter. The Osmiroid was his dignity.

Dragout leaned across it to deliver his instructions. 'Take the El Al stewardesses from their aircraft. Soon, I think, you will separate all the women passengers and take them from the aircraft as well, but wait for the ordering of Holofernes. Meanwhile, put the Israeli stewardesses with the English stewardesses. Then tonight, and with oil, you may honour the English again. They will squeal or perhaps they will like it and merely cry. The Israeli women will comfort them. Then you will give them all wine from both aircraft. Both aircraft are infidel and full of the fruit of the grape. Both will carry a large jar of the grape named Rum, for what they call an emergency. Judging by these silly women's complaints, there can be no greater emergency than this. So you will pay the English fresh honour, again with the oil, and given them all sweet tea and rum. This time, withhold the English their clothes. You will take a photograph. It is disgusting for a woman to be without clothes, and for her to partake of the grape in that condition is unthinkable. You will give back their clothes after the photograph. You will then take them all, Christian and Jew, to Al Wahah or even Daf. You will send your sergeant, according to your own discretion, to show the People's Revolutionary Committee at either Al Wahah or Daf these women's naked photographs and these jars of rum.'

Dragout swung his legs from the desk and walked to the door. He stood there adjusting his dress, considering Holofernes, and wondering how much more Holofernes would require of Matson.

'When they see the rum, the People's Revolutionary Committee will have these women flogged in the market place. When they complain of being abused, remind the Committee of the photograph. If the women persist, and the Committee calls for further opinions – well, there are doctors at Al Wahah, are there not?'

'There is a clinic at Daf.'

'Send some of the Israeli women as a sample. Show their bottoms to the clinic. Let the doctors of the Faith examine the eyes of as many Jewish camels as they are curious for.'

Captain Khadduri began to speak his praise of such an intelligence, but Dragout's shoulders were shaking with mirth. The dark giant was chuckling in admiration of his own cunning.

'You will ask why was this all necessary – why did we do it in the first place? As a smokescreen, Khadduri. When a woman wails aloud, the noise travels far, especially when the woman is Cain's or the Beast's. But steam also rises from her mouth, and that steam and that noise obscure many things.'

'Even the breaking of the Laws?'

'Holofernes is our Law. If we have broken a law, they have broken a bigger one. The Revolutionary Council will thank us for that.'

9.

Captain Khadduri was not a child of the Revolution. He wished he had been. He was too old.

Anyone who has lived through a revolution, even as an

infant, knows that what the Revolution does is set a man completely free within the Law to do as the Revolution tells him. Khadduri could deal with this. He knew that a sweet-smelling semolina in its basket above the stew is worth more than any amount of intellectual certainty – is perhaps the only intellectual certainty worth pursuing. But he also sensed that the seed sown in pre-revolutionary doubt will grow in doubt and wither in doubt. Adam, the First Prophet, knew this, and the True Prophet certainly did. They were both revolutionaries of a fundamentalist kind, but they had done absolutely nothing to remove the everlasting anxiety, though the latter had gone a very long way towards tidying it up.

The People's Revolution had made it tidier still. It had said, There is the Truth the Prophet tells you and the Truths the Revolution brings you. Obey this Truth and these Truths. Do not choose one before the other, because they are both yours and by their nature they are never in conflict. This was so. After the Revolution they were never in conflict, except once or twice on a noisy gallows, where the man would be visibly in conflict and the crowd audibly in complete agreement. In general this policy led to less and less conflict. Khadduri was in no doubt about this. It was just that as time went on, with the truths never in conflict, there seemed less and less truth around. Then he was not a child of the new age. His was not a seed sown in light.

Even so, it was reassuring to be on the side that placed dissent on the gallows – on everybody's side that is, but in a uniform that made him a somebody.

He wished he knew more of the Prophets. He wished he knew more Prophets. He was, he thought, a learned man. Certainly he had met nothing in London, at the Polytechnic of the South Bank, to make him feel unduly ignorant.

He was learned enough to know everything that had ever been written concerning the Prophets. Unfortunately – doubly unfortunately for a religion whose Book was called 'The Reading' – there seemed to be many more truths than were ever written, many more truths and many more Prophets. Some men had access to those truths and could cite those Prophets. Dragout was such a man, and his Holofernes was such a Prophet.

He knew that what Dragout's Holofernes had instructed him to order his men to do was wrong. He would have liked to have done it for himself, for a woman would have been comforting among all the suspicion. He could not do it because the True Prophet said 'no', and because he was an officer. He was also fairly certain the Revolution said 'no'. The Revolution valued women even as the Holy One valued the daughter of Abu Bekr. Yet he had ordered his men to do this thing because Dragout had said so, and there was the suspicion.

He was an Intelligence Officer, however well-trained in infantry. He knew this hijack was not as it seemed, and that something universally terrible would come from it; but what it might be he could not tell.

Until he met Dragout he had not heard of his Holofernes. But he had heard of Abu Jahia, as who of the Faith had not? Abu Jahia also named Azrael, the glittering Angel of Death. He feared very much that Abu Jahia might be impersonating Dragout's False Prophet or that Holofernes might prove to be one of Death's masks.

TEN

1.

CAC had enlarged, as Quinlan had promised. CAC, thought Fossit, had engorged. He glanced at the military representatives and found nothing to interest him. He saw the usual cream-skinned sailors and strawberry-faced soldiers. Airmen, as always, were blue.

'Look at them,' he whispered, foul in memory if not of tongue. 'Know what Paddy puts the three types down to?'

' "Gin, sheep-shagging and prayer",' Dixon quoted with approval.

Fossit didn't like it now he'd heard it aloud, not even in honour of the dead.

Pomeroy sank into himself so far and in such a disgust he nearly grew a chin. 'You ought to go and examine the rear end of a baa-lamb, Ralph, before you pass that kind of filth as fit for human consumption.' Then he rounded on Fossit. 'I wish you wouldn't go on quoting that lost little boy of yours. Think of him as a dead soldier, not as an absent friend.'

Brigadier Barkworth snorted. Brigadier Barkworth was one of the newer members of the committee and he did not approve of death. He approved of Pomeroy even less, and less again of his immodest guzzling of brandy from a coffee cup and calling it 'O.K. Soup'.

Several of them had been sipping 'O.K. Soup' all morning, and Brigadier Barkworth was looking for a way to snitch on them.

It was then that Quinlan's Lorna rushed in to tune up the Libyan Queen.

'Terence says we don't know what he's saying, but he's dressed up for important.'

2.

The spokesman for the Central Congress of the Libyan Arab People's Al Jamahiriyah spoke always from the wrong place. He spoke from Tripoli. When he talked of the American airliner or the Greek airliner he told of the Beast before his eye. But when he spoke of the Israeli passengers or the British passengers and aircrew at Sifr WaaHid he castigated the unknown Cain. He had no film to give. A spy satellite could show them more; and the spy satellites showed them nothing.

The spokesman was not helped by living permanently in a box on Quinlan's desk, another box on Pomeroy's personal filing cabinet where the drinks were kept – no Moslem would be – and in a huge fake mahogany cube on wheels in the CAC committee room. He was seen an awful lot of times in the committee-room cube. When the meetings were over, people used to tiptoe in to play him again, from the highest in the ministry to the lowest, from secretaries right down to typists, and from philosophers to the merest doctors of philosophy.

It was unfortunate that he prophesied not to the winds but to a system that used only 450 lines and which – like the American – seemed to give strong men jaundice and make all women Chinese. Unlike the American, it offered an image that collapsed from the edges as if built from a burning abacus, or just a lousy frame of little beads.

Not for nothing did Pomeroy refer to him as Philactery Pete.

He appeared with many faces and he disappeared with even more, but most he was to be remembered for his two distinct voices – a phenomenon so mysterious and magnetic that housewives and other people of treacherous disposition were said by *The Sun* to be in love with him.

He barked his English in a bass masculine huff like a New England disc-jockey. He grizzled his Arabic with a click of the tongue, a fancy-nancy whine of Chaucerian quinnible, and a truly mesmeric and Messianic vibration of the Adam's apple.

He was not helped when he spoke with thyroid a-blur in the tongue Pomeroy called 'Turkey's Goitre' in having the said Pomeroy translate him. A translation by Marcus Pomeroy would make even the Gettysburg Address seem peculiar: he had been known to send a roomful of Foreign Office typists into hysterics by performing *La Marseillaise* in spoken English prose.

The message generally was in Turkey's goitre. Very little of it came via the BBC, or the European or American commercial services, although they were offered it by the yard. He came with few pictures, except of himself, so was only of indirect value to a newsgatherer. Normally he came via Cyprus dish, or Egyptian landline.

'So what does the monkey say?' Barkworth barked. Quinlan wasn't here, so he felt he could bark things like that, particularly at Pomeroy, who was the ape who had to translate for him.

3.

'It's an odd language, Arabic,' Pomeroy reflected. 'Only one hundred million people speak it in the world.'

'So what do they say?'

'And when you come to think about it, people who speak Arabic pull nine-tenths of all our hijacks. So it's strange that CAC can't run to a proper interpreter.'

'Is it important, man?'

'Still, I suppose Terence is always looking out for something suitable for me to do. Yes, I suppose you might think it important, Brigadier, if you were an air-stewardess on the Forces' Charter.'

Pomeroy looked at his notes, and Quinlan's arrival put paid to the brigadier.

'The Libyans are complaining formally,' Pomeroy explained. 'They have been subjected to – I quote – "an invasion of alcohol-crazed libidinous British women" who "threw themselves upon our young Libyan conscripts, making amorous importunings to the very great embarrassment of themselves and their officers".'

'What does that mean, Marcus?'

'It means the Libyans raped them.'

'You don't seem very surprised.'

'I had heard a whisper, Minister.'

'But you didn't think it important enough to pass on?'

'I thought it might prove a distraction to chaps like the brigadier. The fact is, Minister, I had the information last night from Tel Aviv. Tel Aviv is a good source, of course. But neither of us trusts the originator. I thought it best to wait upon event.'

'Isn't that the sort of thought I should be allowed to have?'

'Meanwhile, man, what do you propose to do about it?'

'I am but one of a team, Brigadier. And that team will continue to pursue diplomatic ends through the normal channels.'

4.

'Diplomacy in these cases operates in the following stages,' Pomeroy said. 'I have to detail them for the sake of the Action People, Minister.' He beamed above the assembled military heads, then lowered his gaze carefully to encounter their wrath at pineal eye level. 'Otherwise they accuse us of unzipping their camouflage. *One*: we say to the corrupt, incompetent, or plain contumacious host-nation: "Our aeroplane has been snaffled, together with its passengers, payload and crew. We know we can rely upon you as a trusted friend and responsible member of the world community" –'

Somebody snorted. Somebody else guffawed.

'I prefer to arrange for my own punctuation, please, Minister.' Pomeroy continued to admire the military lobes and eyebrows.

'We can't possibly say that to a country like Libya,' Brigadier Barkworth put in.

'I can say absolutely anything to absolutely anyone,' Pomeroy said. 'Even to you. That's what diplomacy is about. *Two*: while repeating its former protestations, diplomacy says, "Since your own gallant soldiers are such cowardly idiots who don't know the backside of a carbine from the breach of a camel, would you like us to lend you some of our expert help, unworthy though it is?" That's when we post them your jolly self, Brigadier. *Three*: while the Brigadier –'

'I won't actually be directly involved,' Barkworth confessed.

'I speak in parables. I do but take your name as an example. While the Brigadier is parachuting into the desert, armed to the teeth, and tumbling in heroic free-fall at the head of his Brownie pack augmented by an entire muster of the Dagenham Girl Pipers, diplomacy says, "Although you spurned our offer of help, we know you didn't mean to, so here it is and welcome to it, and we hope it doesn't trample on your cucumber frames. If it does, there'll be restitution, reparation, running repairs and a quick rub down in the shower." *Four* –'

'*Thank* you, Marcus.'

Pomeroy didn't hear Quinlan. He was brisking to his theme. '*Four*: when the Brigadier is lying bleeding in the desert with his kilt shot off, and raped like those poor unfortunate women –'

'Never talk of defeat to the military, Marcus.'

5.

Dragout preferred not to talk to the military at all. A soldier's dress was a pretty one, no doubt; but so was a party frock; and he had known goat-boys, naked under a single mohair, who were sweeter than either.

Besides, he was a wandering man with a wandering mind, and a soldier spends his life thinking one thought only.

If a man is to change that thought and riddle it through with another, then it is best to wander in and out of it, in and out – in and out of rooms, in and out of heads, like a bird eating holes in a tree.

So it had been with Matson. So it was now with Captain Khadduri.

Dragout was wearing his coat of blood again, for he knew blood earns great respect from a soldier.

He went into Khadduri's ugly little hut and made the man

stand to attention for him. He said, 'You think of me as a black-faced nomad, Captain, because my people live in tents and folding shelters. Well, my people are not nomads; they are migrants. They shuttle to and fro, as I with you. But the land they rest on belongs to me, as you belong to me. They are giants and I feed them bread. You are not a giant, so I offer you sweetmeats.'

Khadduri felt annoyed. He was too down-to-earth for this sort of nonsense. He flopped back down on his chair. The moment he sat, he shuddered. 'Sweetmeats' was a dangerous word on the Tibbu's lips. Those women were supposed to be sweetmeats. None had been for him, and they had all been trouble.

'I wish you'd pay attention, Captain.'

'I pay attention all the time. I pay you –'

'That is why I bring you sweetmeats. Now listen for what I tell you. Elements of two battalions of infantry will be moving in tonight. There will also be an anti-aircraft regiment. That is not for you to play with. It is to shoot down low-flying Israelis, should we be so lucky. Its commanding officer will report directly to me.' He groped for an envelope inside his white coat's plastic pocket. It was smeared with somebody's blood. 'In this envelope you will find a piece of paper ordering you, as now, to report directly to me.' He tossed it onto Khadduri's table and allowed himself a generous pause before adding: 'You also find that you have been promoted Major, acting Lieutenant-colonel. As I say, the artillery commander is to report directly to me, but you are to take precedence over him. The elements of the two infantry battalions are yours to play with. I promised you sweetmeats. Are you in the arms of your joy, Khadduri?'

Khadduri stood up and saluted. It was an excessive, unmilitary gesture, but it seemed the best way to avoid being in Dragout's arms as well.

Dragout watched him benignly, 'I shall have some detailed orders for you in a minute. Intelligence is a dirty business, Khadduri. A man walks too closely to the dark eye of the camel. Do this job tidily and you will never have to walk that way again.'

6.

A colonel of infantry is a man of infinite resource. He is not so minutely powerful as a well-established lieutenant, say, and nowhere so rooted in the subsoil as a good sergeant, but he can have coffee made for him and insist that it is hot. Khadduri called for coffee and iced water. Ice had been made in the refrigerator Dragout had found for him. The coffee, when it came, was served European fashion – no, *soldiers'* fashion – in a large metal pot.

Dragout contented himself with water – he felt responsible for the ice. He said, 'I think we ought to find a way to make that Modfai up a bit. Or at least to whisper in his ear. I daresay the Revolution could promote him Lieutenant.

'He has no intellectual credentials.'

'He is very very cunning. Let us promise ourselves we'll make him Regimental Sergeant-major, then. When you think of God, Khadduri, do you think of Him as a general or as regimental sergeant-major?'

'I think of Him as God.'

'God must have His power. I always think of God as a regimental sergeant-major. Sip on your coffee and listen to my orders.'

The dog screamed behind the door, but Dragout swore softly, and at God's name the dog became silent – at God's or Sergeant Modfai's.

'Now here are my instructions. I want the passengers moved from the planes at once, the Israelis to be separated from the British, the men from the women; the children to go with the women in every case. This suggests at least four huts, but we have a widebody there, so we could need more than that, Khadduri.'

'Supposing the hijackers will not release their prisoners?'

'They will. I have already told them to. Besides, they know some aspects of my plans that I have not yet discussed with you, Colonel. They know that they will be given their passengers back again.' Dragout enjoyed watching the rage and frustration on the captain-recently-promoted-major's face being chased away by a timely reminder of his temporary rank of colonel. He added, simply, 'They also know I will kill them if they go against my wishes.

'Your soldiers are visibly and openly to unload the baggage holds of both aircraft, Colonel Khadduri. They are to leave the luggage in tall piles beside each aircraft. That is paramount. I have experts coming here tonight who will be making certain installations in those holds during the next three days. I want the holds in a fit state to receive them. I want the baggage left where the world can see it and deduce that something is afoot.

'Your new command is to be used to keep the world at a distance, just the same. Television cameras – *if* they arrive – are to be halted three kilometres down the road. No-one is to get into the command.

'That is one of the reasons I had those squatters rounded up, so we could look at them and know them. They are not to leave the compound except to go to the runway for reasons I shall give you. I do not want them to talk to anyone or to be impersonated by anyone.

'Let us talk about those squatters: I have taken the old women and the senior men. I have disinfected them and burned their clothes. They will work, as I say, about my house where they can cause no trouble. The young people and the children you are to have. You are to disinfect them likewise, then give them some dungarees. They are to clean the passenger cabins of the two aircraft. Have you ever seen an aeroplane after a hijack? It is worse than that lorry driver's camp on the road that used to run to Chad –'

Khadduri shuddered, as if agreeing such things are not soldierly.

'Otherwise, let these so-called Freedom Fighters live in the aircraft. Let them help guard the passengers by day and let them guard the aircraft by night. Do not let your men near the aircraft at night, Colonel. Let them guard the perimeter and the encampment. It is not inconceivable that someone will try a rescue – give some thought to how you will deploy your men. I do not think the Israelis will try yet. I predict that the Americans will make them wait and wait a very long time, provided no further harm comes to their passengers. If harm comes, then the Americans will not be able to restrain the Israelis. Well, harm *has* come. It came yesterday. That is why

I have cut off the life and its hand.'

'Dragout, I must *insist* my men guard the aircraft.'

'By day, yes. By night they have a greater responsibility.' He walked towards Khadduri and slapped him on the chest, then leant with his arm about his neck. 'There, Colonel – there. Let me tell you quite frankly, let me confess to you freely as between brothers, that I have *never* cuddled a colonel of infantry. Never. You see what honour we do one another?' He moved away from Khadduri and from the desk. '*Yes*, Khadduri, your military instincts are impeccable. Your men *should* guard those aircraft at night. But they will not.'

'You will be playing a dangerous game, Dragout, if you mean what I think you mean.'

'A precarious game. A gambler's game. But not, I assure you, a dangerous one. Holofernes requires it of us. And, because it is a gambler's game, we shall continue to perfect ourselves at dice and cards. So that we may learn to play with elegance even when we lose.'

'And what do we propose to lose?'

'Our honour, Khadduri.'

7.

It was distressingly clear to Pomeroy that there was little to be had from CAC. He shredded another unsmoked cigarette and allowed the languid brow to crease in imagined pain while he pondered just how much CAC had a right to expect from him.

The internal rang. It was the exchange that processed the secure traffic. 'We've got an Outsider with a high negative rating bulling through from Tel Aviv on our own embassy signal.'

'I'll take it. Ask me at message-ends for a procedure voucher. I want him cleared, but keep his rating smudgy, please.'

It had to be Shlomo Barel.

'Hallo, Matson Pomeroy. I'm enjoying the fruits of our new found amity. I'm using your embassy scrambler. What a mean and nicotiny little place your signals room is!'

'You should have popped over to Cyprus. All the Tel Aviv

silver was pinched long ago. What can we do for you?'

'I want to share my desert songbird.'

'We've heard his latest song. That's what Cyprus is for.'

'Bugging your friends?'

'Bugging whatever use is made of that old bugger with the green tooth.'

'Nonetheless, I think we have something to discuss.'

'Little green tooth himself. I've been losing sleep over his warbling from among the dunes.'

'We must have very similar dreams. So what did you conclude?'

'I merely questioned how clever you really are, Shlomo. I know you're bright, you and your den of post-doctoral neck shredders – *but*!'

'Excellent. We should share our worries more often.'

The scrambler decided to interrupt communion. It unserialised into a rash of static, and began to fry eggs in Pomeroy's skull. He heard albumin crackle and shell being broken in every celestial pan between Whitehall and Tel Aviv, before the pulse strobed back to pre-signal and strained to come through.

'It's your embassy tea,' Barel said. 'They just brought me some. You're right, of course. We didn't put Nuseibeh in place. He put himself in place. To be frank, I thought he was in London. He told us an attempt was going to be made on a flight to Lod, but definitely not an El Al flight, and certainly not yet. I did not infer he was privy to any plot, still less a part of it.'

'So, like every sneaky Janus the wide world over he contacted one of us in order to protect his back?'

'I wonder. Did he warn *you*?'

'Of course not. Well, yes, Shlomo: he did, to be frank. He said nothing about our flight or the other two. Only yours. And leagues away in the future. I laughed at him. I did nothing to process the information. I didn't believe it. He didn't even ask for payment, or set up a bargaining position for a precise contingency. I took that to be the give away! I doubt if our Embassy would have passed on such a low-grade morsel of unintelligence. If they had done, your people wouldn't have been impressed.'

'So! you tip him for piece-work! My General insists I place

all such vermin on the pay-roll. How we exchange secrets.'

'My real thought is this, Shlomo. Neither of us trust him, merely accept him as useful. We're bright fellas, but so are these hijackers. I don't believe anyone in the world would really trust Nuseibeh.

'Conspirators are, by nature, downright paranoid. And yet they let him sit in an office there – or what? trundle down the road in a truck? – and pick up a telephone? Don't they ask to whom? They wouldn't let one of their own number call their widowed mother, say, or consult the vet about a sick donkey.'

'We're not certain who is doing the allowing, of course – Libya or the hijackers, or even that madman Ahmed Khalil Dragout going solo.'

'Everything suggests they're in it together.'

'That means that I, or my unit, or Israel at large, is baited to adopt a false position.'

'And me, Shlomo. And the Yanks. Anything Cyprus catches we pass on.'

'How did you know he used a telephone, by the by?'

'It had to be landline as far as Benghazi. Or Cyprus would have intercepted it back in the desert. Besides, he made some reference to the quality of the link. Something about a hollow phone, according to the transcript.'

'Get them to uncover a tape if they can. He has several stabs at a word he doesn't know and can't pronounce –'

'Nuseibeh?'

'Even Nuseibeh. *Hollow fern*, it sounds like. Or *Holly fern*. Then *Hollow phoney*. *That's* what your operator picked up.'

'He ignored the rest.'

'Teach him to do a better job.'

'Did Nuseibeh speak Arabic to you at any time?'

'I prefer him not to know how good my Arabic is. We always use English. It's our *lingua franca*. He won't condescend to Hebrew. Another bad mark for your monitor.'

'Some little aircraftsman or other. Do you have any news of Matson?'

'Only what you and your aircraftsmen already know. Nuseibeh is worried for his survival. I'm not.'

Pomeroy almost told Barel the truth about Matson, but he didn't want to spoil a new relationship.

8.

'I'm coming to you directly. There are some things so portentous I don't propose to waste CAC's time with them.'

Quinlan gazed at Pomeroy with early morning caution, while Pomeroy outlined the newest information he had from Tel Aviv, then added the strangely hysterical conversation between Nuseibeh and his Israeli control that had been picked up by radiophone interceptors on Cyprus.

'Portentous but not important enough for CAC?'

'No. Because no-one can put any meaning to it.'

'I wonder,' Quinlan mused. 'Then politicians are paid to. We instal all these grids and dishes and gubbins costing billions of pounds of the tax-payers' money, and what do we get served up? They either don't work or we don't use them properly. Cyprus works, as it happens. It's even better than Meccano, better than Lego even – and that's high praise from me. We can listen to the Colonel's bedsprings and count how many times Arafat brushes his tooth or picks his nose in the lavatory. So we get *this* – we get an incorrect transcript, and when we ask for the tape it's already erased. So how do we find out the truth of it? We'll have to ask the bloke we're eavesdropping on for a fuller account – or so you'll tell me next.'

'I have,' said Pomeroy. 'That is – I've asked his Israeli control.'

'So what's the desert saying?'

' "Holofernes", almost certainly.'

'And what does that mean?'

'I'll read to you from *Brewer's Dictionary of Phrase and Fable*. Do you want the Shakespeare next? It's a bit early in the morning for Rabelais.'

Quinlan listened and said, 'You still haven't told me what it means.'

'It means we've got a code word. Outside of Jules Verne it's my contention that code words don't mean a thing.'

'Stuff. It's the name of a plan.'

'We always assumed the hijackers had one of those.'

'Don't you see what this means, though – hearing it now, at

this time?' Quinlan wasn't done with winning. 'If the desert is still using codewords it implies the desert still has its plan. It's a tiny enough point, but significant. I think you must tell CAC. Most of them will have concluded, like me, that the intention was to snaffle those aircraft, dump them in Libya, then ride out the storm. An ongoing codeword means an ongoing plan. Ask the military. *They shred yesterday's codes* before they sit down to breakfast.'

Pomeroy was already on the way to sip some breakfast of his own.

Quinlan stopped him. 'I need that plan, Marcus. Put someone in or get Matson out.'

'Impossible. Impossible the one. Impossible-minus the other.'

'Then tell Cyprus to rinse out its earwax and burn no more tapes.'

9.

Evidence of a code word was evidence of a plot. Granted such a morsel CAC became electric. It used its Quinlan to wheedle America and its Pomeroy to harangue the Eastern Mediterranean. It wrote down HOLOFERNES in its file and HOLOFERNES HOLOFERNES HOLOFERNES on a new foldex and time-chart. It fed the word and its every imaginable assonance, metathesis and paronamasia into the Home Office's terrorist programme, into the Yard's criminal computer, into the Interpol net; and it processed it written forwards as in Shakespeare and Rabelais and backwards as in Hebrew and Arabic, and phonetically as in goo-talk into the Foreign Office code-breaker. It employed Arab-speaking confidants and every ministerial crossword player who had signed an updated official secrets declaration to devise an infinity of acronyms feasible, fanciful and farcical for each of HOLOFERNES' ten letters in sequence. It gave the word to Military Intelligence who promptly gave it back again, to Air Force Intelligence who said it was nearly a bombing range in Queensland, and to Naval Intelligence who said it had been rejected as the name of a Dreadnought in 1898. CAC emended all files including computer files so that the hijackers were no longer called the plotters but the enemy then finally the Enemy and accorded a fitting respect. Then CAC sat back and waited for the world to end or rebegin.

Cabinet were impressed, no doubt, and the Americans grew busy. HOLOFERNES, if such it was, was new and exciting. Nonetheless, CAC hadn't invented the wheel; it had merely discovered the circle, and no-one rides to work on a circle.

ELEVEN

1.

How long had he been here?

His watch had been snaffled by Khadduri's men. If it hadn't been, then Dragout would have insisted on its removal anyway.

He had been underground something less than a week, something more than a day. He guessed three days, because it felt like five. So it was probably two – a clear day after landing and then another day. He was suffering that other day now, or perhaps its night.

Matson had only eaten one meal, had drunk little. If there was 'an hourglass in his bowels' – another instructor, not Fletcher this time – it ran with slow sand, what with no exercise and one thing and another.

Without the surrealistic components in his interrogation, he could have done better with his estimate of time. Dragout always did the main work himself. He deployed his assistants only the way a stage-conjuror makes use of the girl in the bathing costume: to fetch and carry, to rearrange the props – in this case the chains on the bedstead – or as a distraction. Yes, Dragout was all distraction. Time was the second joker in his pack. The first was illusion.

Yet even Dragout must sleep. A day is the interval between your gaoler's sleeps.

A man pursuing his fantasies could perhaps resist exhaustion that much longer. But Dragout was a professional. His 'fantasies' must have a purpose. They were deliberate acts of will. Matson was not central to a single genuine fantasy; still less could he be his fancy. Surely that was a pretence? Pretending tires a man.

Even so, the giant might not need sleep. He could be high on drugs or simple adrenalin. Matson dared not let himself lose sight of the larger picture, the hijack and what it might mean. Perhaps that was so enormously important or exciting that it allowed Dragout no rest.

So perhaps he had been here for a hundred days. Or for how much more than a hundred minutes? There was a metronome in his pulse and it beat loudly. He began to drift towards sleep.

He knew where this sleep came from. It came from his torturer. It was called fatigue.

2.

It was then that the man with the turban came in. He was a middle-aged anorexic, one of Modfai's rounded-up squatters. He had to wear the cloth in a knot because it was too small for him. His clothes had been burnt. He had been given prison fatigues for his limbs and this demeaning cloth for his forehead.

He had been given it by the men in brown who do nothing except burn clothes and tell him what to do. They had burned his clothes and told him to burn his wife's clothes as well. This was an outrage. They had offered him something quite ridiculous for her to cover her back, then they had set her to pick up rocks in the garden. The garden was all rock. The hill was built of rock. There would only be no rock in the garden when his wife and the other women had picked it into a great hole that reached to the bottom of the world. Perhaps these women were not making a garden. Perhaps they were digging a well.

Still, it was proper work for a woman, and there was to be food for it. He was just squatting down in the shade with the men in brown to supervise his wife's industry when they gave him a broom and a bucket of white disinfectant water the colour of goats' milk, and told him to clean the cellar. They said the cellar was a prison of many cells. If he did not clean it properly they would chain him up in one of them and feed him with rats and scorpions.

He had eaten rats, but he needed a fire to cook them by and a woman to cook them. He had never heard of a cell with either fire or women in it, so he took up the broom and picked up the bucket of scented goats' milk.

They had not lied to him. The cellar held a great number of rooms. He counted three. In the first there was nothing, except the stairs that led down to it. In the second there were two of the men in brown with their guns. There was also a sink where they said he could empty his bucket, and another sink low to the floor, the sort men in big houses use for shitting in; men in big houses, like the men in brown and their master, are too mean to give even this to the soil.

In the third room he saw a man tied by his wrists to a kind of bench covered in wire, a bench like the empty beds in the huts. The man had skin whiter than holy, with curious little brown spots on his back, and red hair on his head and his body, even at his armpits.

The squatter examined him closely and saw that he might just be of the faith and that his camel's eye wept old blood.

He thought he would have a game with him, and reached forward with his broomhandle to poke the camel's eye.

Something smashed against his nose, leaving odour and pain. It was a peeling, unhardened, unwashed white foot.

The squatter stepped back and reversed the broom and began to thrash the man with it.

The man roared in a language he wouldn't understand. He twisted and he writhed and he kicked.

The two men in brown came in, but they did not hurry. And then the giant came in, the man he had seen when the soldiers had caught them.

This giant was taller than the doorframes of those European huts and wider than the doors that fit them. His face was black as the blackest goat, yet he caught up the wretch on the bed and took him in his arms and began to sob.

'Luminous One,' he cried. 'Little White Bones – who has been doing this unspeakable thing to you?'

The squatter thought the giant would kill him for ill-treating his pet. Instead, he called to the two men in brown to put chains on the white man's foot. Then he gave the squatter money.

3.

'Right,' said Quinlan. 'You'll have heard the buzz. Northwood has a plan, and we're going with it. Brigadier.'

Barkworth left the table and strode towards the data-link where Philactery Pete normally stood on his trolley. The link-screen was obscured by a six-foot by eight rectangle of smoky perspex on a vertical easel. The perspex came in a chromium frame, or perhaps it was stainless steel; and its right-hand or teacher's side edge was set with a bewilderment of buttons and an importance of lights.

The brigadier pressed one of those or one of these, and the perspex showed them a brilliant blue sky sitting on two humps of sand.

'I know,' whispered Fossit. 'It's a map of Libya.'

Pomeroy tapped his watch.

Barkworth illuminated Sifr WaaHid with a fiery red star and gave Tripoli International Airport a far less enigmatic blue rectangle, all no-handed.

Pomeroy continued to resonate his wrist.

'What we are going to do,' said Barkworth, 'is take the long chukka round in the desert and steal out our people and our planes.' The star became green and neutral. 'Meanwhile –' Tripoli now wore an apoplectic flush. 'Meanwhile, we'll drop straight down his little chimney *here*, and snooker him up the arse.' Tripoli returned to its blue benevolence and then exercised a second option for green and benign.

Pomeroy hovered above his chair without quite standing up.

'Oh, very well,' Quinlan scolded, 'Yes, yes, Marcus. I suppose so. I'm sorry.' The wrist-tapping had got to him at last. 'Someone had better keep an eye on the Libyan Queen,' he explained, and watched Pomeroy sneak from the room like a schoolchild on the way to the lavatory. 'Sorry, Brigadier.'

It was all right by Barkworth. The more times Pomeroy left the room the better as far as he was concerned. 'The desert will be easy,' he said. 'We'll do the desert as always – a Special Air Service core in a Second Para apple. We'll hope to get at least one aircraft out – in which case we'll take everybody in one hop, using that aircraft and our delivery vehicles, which'll be Hastings. *If* neither aircraft flies, we'll leave Two Para in, and come back from Cyprus to fetch them. Hastings double flight and turn-round time RAF Akrotiri – Sifr WaaHid is three hours.'

'Flak?' a voice asked from the door. Whether Pomeroy was still going out or already coming back was unclear.

'We can accept aircraft casualty. We can wear fifty per cent loss and still be viable.

'As I said, we'll take the long chukka round, so there's a chance they won't rumble us. We'll air-strike the phone-line between WaaHid and Zoltan, again between Zoltan and the coast. The Libyan units at WaaHid will be on battalion-link sets at most, so we'll probably succeed in blacking them out if we cut that wire. We can't provide air-cover for the whole operation, but we can give the ground commander an air-strike option if he wants to knock out anti-aircraft guns. And have it overhead for –'

'Sixteen minutes,' Fisher put in.

'I'm obliged. Now, Tripoli is going to be the funny one. And what happens at Tripoli should distract attention from the desert end in a very satisfactory manner and to a very satisfactory degree.'

Barkworth paused and considered the door. Pomeroy was still present or again present, but Barkworth was calm, the strawberries in his face all frosted away. Standing made him happy. It was sitting and listening that left him fruity with frustration. On his feet he was bone-white.

'We're going to befuddle Tripoli's reaction-time with a hijack,' he said. 'The People's Republic is amenable to receiving hijacked aircraft, so let's give 'em another one. Our TV intelligence of Tripoli International is good and bang-up-to-date, so we'll drop our little hijack right next to the other two and steal them both away.'

The explanation was enough for Barkworth, but it wasn't for most people, Fossit included.

'We're going to fly a widebody from Paris to Rome,

Barkworth said. 'I mean, it'll start in the U.K., but no-one'll notice it till the hijack's announced five minutes out of Rome, when it'll be a Paris-Rome flight diverted at gun-point towards Beirut. It'll have enough kerosene on board for a transatlantic crossing, and somewhere about Athens or Cyprus it'll divert yet again, this time for Tripoli. Get the scenario.'

'Who'll be on board?' Dixon asked.

'The Pagoda Troop only and a lot of spare room.'

'You can't do that,' Pomeroy said, still at the door.

'It's a sound plan.' Quinlan was irritated with him beyond irritation.

'You can't do it to the U.S.'

'The U.S.'ll thank us, even for a cock-up.'

'The State Department?'

'No. The Pentagon. They can't get the political clearance. By the time they do, it'll be too late for them. They'd prefer the egg to be on our chin anyway. But it won't be – eh, Brigadier?'

'True,' agreed Pomeroy. 'Because we won't be going.' A squeaky shoe would have helped his progress to the table, but Pomeroy never squeaked, unless by design. 'We won't be going because they've just moved the aircraft from Tripoli.'

He brought bad news, and Quinlan hated him for it.

'Well – I never did like Sifr WaaHid,' Fisher reflected.

'Ours are still at WaaHid.' Pomeroy enjoyed his moment. 'It's the other two have been moved – west along the coast from Tripoli International to Az Zawiyah.'

'That's a military airfield.'

'Bang goes half your plan, then.'

'We can still go with the other half,' Quinlan insisted. 'We can fix it with the Yanks.'

'Depends whether they'd prefer us to kill them with our kindness, or leave them alive in the lurch.'

4.

'I'm all for the Duke of Wellington's little bits of string,' Dixon muttered. 'But we're looking either at deceit or a total reluctance to face reality.'

'It's a two-headed beast and its name is Quinlan.'

As soon as the meeting was adjourned, they went in to confront him in his private office, barging aside the Dacres who kept his appointment book, and hauling a confused Leonard Fossit behind them to balance their argument.

Quinlan did not enjoy deputations. If you sat on his committee you spoke to him in committee. Otherwise you shut up. He said so sharply. He decided to rub in some salt. 'You're literate chaps. You've got oodles of hired help to work to dictation. My office would appreciate a memorandum, say – or at least the forewarning courtesy of a succinct little note.'

'We're here,' said Pomeroy, 'because we need to tell you things.'

'Gentlemen, what *are* you saying? I keep an open table.'

'Well, I don't, Minister. Besides, you don't preside over an open table. You operate a circus ring.'

'Complete with clowns and elephants,' Dixon said, before halting in self-awe.

'There are things we have to know, that the military don't,' Pomeroy went on. 'Things we have to impart, but certainly not to them.'

'Indeed? Leonard?'

'Like you, I'm all for open management, Minister. If not for open government.'

'The Barkworth plan will fail,' Pomeroy said.

'I've backed that plan, Marcus.'

'It's a gesture merely. You want the plan to exist, but you don't expect it to happen. You said so yourself. You professed so as an article of political faith. Well, the clock moves. The plan is pre-Holofernes anyway.'

'Ah,' mused Quinlan, 'Holofernes.'

'Your cabinet colleagues expect that plan to fly just the same, Terence.' Pomeroy was being absolute. 'They're probably placing bets on it at this minute. I mean, they know the day and the hour it's going to start flapping its wings. They know all the things that are being kept from me. What I do know is that the plan has Barkworth and Fisher playing four-legs in a horse. It isn't Pegasus, but it's got more than just your shirt on it. It's carrying your reputation.'

'You're being unusually frank.'

'Loutishly frank. Why don't you beat your colleagues' drum for them, but let me buy off the Libyans?'

'Impossible.' Quinlan was wondering how much to give away. 'Cabinet has already discussed it. The PM's against a buy-off.'

'Let Mad Eyes keep the aircraft, Minister. They won't be good for much now. It needn't be announced in public. Chuck in something else for luck.'

'No arms.'

'I was thinking of Concorde, Terence. No-one else wants it.'

They could see that Quinlan thought parts of the suggestion had merit. But he clearly knew something that made it too late for him. Why else should he continue to look like the castrato who has just inherited a harem?

'I'm surprised at some of the things you chaps come up with. Still, you don't have to pay the political price.'

'Just carry the can.' Fossit was tired.

Quinlan stood up. 'You fellows have got a man in baulk. One of your own kind. Out there, in what you call my circus ring, people are trying to rescue him. Don't you think you ought to join them – you especially, Leonard?'

Quinlan was like all bullies. He picked on the weakest. And if no-one was weak, he turned on a friend.

5.

To keep the spirit intact in the torture-chamber depended on acceptance. He must understand that his enemies could do anything to him, and that he might die as a result of it.

Fletcher had suggested religion. He spoke about Faith rather as if it were a child's climbing frame. When the body is straitened, when the brain is *in extremis*, religion is a natural option, he had said. God is not necessarily there, but the chemistry of torment produces an extra presence in the room. That presence is a projection of oneself, he had said. The mind throws its own image on the wall and invites one to pray to it, or at least talk to it. Matson had seen this image many times in the last day, and he did not think it was himself or his own. It was too calm, too benign, and the face lacked freckles. He did not pray to it.

It wasn't that he mistrusted Fletcher's God. Fletcher was a Thug and a good bloke. It was simply that he was not yet ready for religion. He had St Augustine as an example. Religion was the beginning of old age.

The body ages quickly under torture. Dragout had promised him that. The mind, too, fractures on paradox. But acceptance was not Matson's way. Not now. Not yet. Not until the last midnight.

He kept a hold on himself by measuring his wit against Dragout's rhetoric, and he went beyond this by finding hope in vituperation. He cursed Dragout systematically and aloud, in his absence as well as his presence, shouting curses when alone, and greeting him with curses before he entered the cell. Dragout hated being cursed. He took curses very seriously – so much so that he threatened to cut Matson's tongue out. But he needed Matson's tongue.

Matson also prepared his death for him. He killed him many times. He did not kill him elaborately or painstakingly – that would have been its own form of madness. Matson's pain might cause him to turn aside from God and look towards the Devil, but it was always the same Devil, and not any other from among the canon of demons in the Catholic arcana. Dragout was going to die at his hands, in an explosive cancelling second. It would not be revenge enough, but that was how it would be. Dragout would die as a man dies, or as the men Matson had killed had died – not necessarily cleanly, but quickly. Yes, Dragout would die as Matson's men died, just like a mouse or a dog.

6.

The man in the cavalry-twill suit propped himself against a straight-edge of illusion just inside the door. He did not own a shooting-stick, so he rested his elegance against a convenient shaft of light. It was a column of light, columnar electric light, a directed beam of torturer's neon, and consequently not quite stiff enough to prop him up. He lent both against it and through it. The light and himself shone on each other, interpenetrated each other, were each other. He looked upon the light and it upon him. The light and himself were one flesh. They melded.

Melded was the word the dreamer searched for. Too many consonants for the expanded tongue.

His eye had sunk lower, down among the ox-blood shoes. The cavalry-twill trousers drooled their way into its orbit several seconds later. So did the matching jacket with double slit on the backside, the hairy tie, the suede waistcoat once so fashionable in officers' messes up and down the land and throughout the world's imagined corners, the buttons of woven leather each as big as a badger's testicles, if not a terrier's.

It was himself Matson witnessed. Or himself as transubstantiated onlooker saw corporeal Matson when alive and at Luton. Non-Matson, as ghost Matson, looked upon Matson of the starchy footfall, the dry-cleaned armpit, the comedy crotch and if not jewels in the countersunk sphincter, at least an aquascutum bath-salt. Matson, the action man, had been warned about this in lectures. When a man comes to see himself he may truly be said to be entering the fire. He will soon faint away and, if lucky, die.

One should only give torture a reluctant best if it produces two of oneself, a separate two, making three. Matson could not see a third Matson. Matson RIP was here, watching Matson model the garb that made a dead girl smile.

'I had my chaps sponge it and press it,' he said. 'And you needed a new shirt from your luggage. But don't you think it's me to a Tee?' Matson simpered, and did a pirouette, then finished in the Number Two ballet position beneath the pulsing light, umbrella a-dangle. 'I see you've scissored all the labels,' he said, 'so it's hardly a bespoke tailor, still less your Saville Row?'

Matson was now Dragout, who came boldly forward in his millionth quick change of the day, this time in his captive's suiting. 'I don't complain about your Marks and Spencer underwear, just the same. Do you have any spares on the Trident?'

'I thought you were going to have them burnt?'

'Laundered, really. They fit me rather well, don't you think? Except round the pinnacles of exploitation and centres of appetite.'

Matson's clothes were in ruin. They had been razored down the stitching and taped to the bigger man's body like cut-outs on a cardboard doll.

'You're a bit skinny about the intelligence, Beloved.' Dragout lit and smoked a cigarette, using Matson's chest as an ashtray. 'Lean about the intelligence and mean about the crotch – Pah, you smell like a cooking pig.'

'It's hair.'

'And some of your crackling, porker. An Arab doesn't have hair there.'

'I'm not an Arab, thank Christ.'

'Blaspheming again. I omit to mention the racism. Perhaps I'll shave you.' He stubbed out his cigarette. 'I may even skin you. It's been done here before, you know. Here in this cellar.' He picked up Matson's face by the hair and grimaced. 'You want the Little Girls' Room, Eagle Bones. Bloodshot eyeballs and bloodshot teeth. You look like Count Dracula after an all-night visit to the convent dormitory.'

'You black bastard.'

' "Dramatically apprehended, Othello and Iago are the twin natures of the one protagonist." '

' "Ere Babylon was dust",' his prisoner conceded.

'Again the duality. We transport a Cockney deep into the desert, and he immediately understands the essence of Zoroastrianism. How well we relate to each other. Mazda and Ahriman would be lost without their ritual dance, their eternal rivalry. I could fall in love with you, Patrick, if my lust to destroy you were not so overwhelming.'

'At least you're wearing something decent at last.'

The giant looked more outlandish than ever. His brown body glittered through the seams of Matson's trousers like a chestnut bursting its husk. 'This suits my purposes,' he said. 'I have to dress like a gambler. I'm going to play cards.'

'So what's the stake?'

'I had an intuition you'd ask. About six hundred lives, dear thing.'

7.

Matson did not ask him if he had won. When he returned he was holding the little vulcanised truncheon again.

'A beautiful little object. Certainly it must be designed by the angels, don't you think? The ones that fell with the Great Lord Lucifer.'

He flourished it like a relay baton. He was wearing running shoes and the green strip of the Libyan athletics team. His victim had no time to see if he wore spikes. Spikes might have been preferable.

Matson bled. His eyes were bloodshot, his lips bitten. But he bled in ways he thought that only the dying would bleed.

'Women can apparently resist this, *some* women at least. Though, of course, it disturbs them in other ways. But even if a woman cannot resist it, well – her physiology is adapted to such matters. This does not involve her pride any more than it is already involved.' He dribbled. That is, he half-spat with delight onto his lower lip and chin. 'But it drives men mad. The sons of Adam are not designed to cope with so much good fortune. What did you say?'

'You're beginning to repeat yourself. You are becoming boring.'

'Odd it should be manufactured in America, in a bible town. No true follower of the Prophet would do such a thing, even to his worst enemy. Seemingly a Christian would. No, no, no – I'm not your enemy. I'm quite unspeakably fond of you.'

8.

Ordinary pain is a bonus. A man can cling to the pain God gives. Fletcher was right.

Matson was alone. He began to howl.

It was only recently dark. The guards in the outer room sounded much too comfortable. So he decided to take charge of their smug little rhythm. He howled as the drunk sometimes howl, like an owl.

The swelling of his clamped leg was causing such a pain as God gives. If any ordinary leg is shackled too tightly, or ligatured, the surface blood finds outlet through the deep veins. Matson's leg lacked a saphenous, and much besides. His blood was already deep, latticed between surface and bone by a complex system of vascular evolution. To bind that limb too tightly was to cause him more than discomfort: it was to threaten him with an aneurism or deep clotting, with a rapid progress to atrophy or gangrene.

He had progressed far enough. It was time to put his situation to the test. He howled.

The guards were silent. They thought he was merely in pain. They could listen to a lovelorn donkey for hours, or a tethered camel being savaged by a pack of dogs. So why not Matson?

He persisted. It was good to find himself in such good voice. He lifted his muzzle towards the distant stars. He owled. He searched through the floor for Dragout's sleep.

The giant arrived, ridiculous in a white bed-shirt and cheap ornamental slippers from the souk.

It's always hard to know whether to complain to an inquisitor. 'You'll have to loosen my right leg,' Matson growled.

'What, the pretty one? It's swelling like a goat's bladder.'

'If you don't, then it'll die on you.'

'On you, I think. I shall merely cut it off.'

'I don't think you will, and I doubt if you'll be able to put up with the stink of gangrene, either. You're a fastidious bastard.'

'Gangrene is beautiful, Beloved. In fact, gangrene is one of the most gorgeous things in God's Creation. It doesn't always stink, either.'

He signalled to one of his brownjobs for Matson's leg to be unshackled, just the same, before saying, 'You use "fastidious" as a term of abuse. Well, I am fastidious, Sweetheart. But not about sawing off limbs, believe me. Yesterday I cut off a man's forearm, for instance. Ask Khadduri, if you ever get to see him again. He's keeping it for me.'

9.

Matson's leg felt better. The pressure had been making his head ache.

There were no more gains. Dragout, wide awake, sent for his American toy.

His midnight made him even more surreal.

'It's said that Prince Charles is in charge of Western Intelligence.'

'I've heard rumours.'

'But you cannot confirm it?'

'I'm reaching certain conclusions. But I'm not quite ready to share them with you.'

'Are there any political prisoners in Great Britain?'

'Only in the Labour Party.'

The pain became intense, but Matson had won. The giant merely hit him. He should have realised that all this madness was leading him somewhere.

10.

Dragout was in his true colours. He wore the woollen caftan of the high goatland beyond the mountains. This was surely a clue. He was near to his biggest truth or his heart's lie. He said, 'Beloved, let me tell you of certain savage peoples.'

'Boasting again!'

Only a fist. Such things no longer hurt. Matson did not know whether his body's analgesia was good or bad.

'When a man is about to die among them, when his life is forfeit – you are not paying attention.'

'Correct. I am not paying attention.'

'They allow a last request.'

Matson neither grinned nor groaned.

'You will not think it such a cliché, not when I elaborate it for you. Such a man, you see, in such a situation – a man in your situation, for instance – does not have the wit to formulate a *really intelligent* request. So they tell him what his last wish will be.'

'These certain savage peoples?'

While Dragout was talking his lunacy became still. Matson hoped to keep him talking for some time.

'His last request is always the same. He lives a poor life without the luxury of mirrors. He lives in a dry place without pools of water.'

He began to croon to himself. Now he would think of causing pain.

Matson lifted himself quickly. 'What *then*?'

' "Then"?'

'What is the last request?'

'To see the small of his back, of course. A man must not die deficient in self-knowledge.' He drew a fingernail across Matson's back. 'So we cut it off and show it to him.'

11.

Matson found it almost impossible to stay awake; but he knew deep interrogation could be like that. He didn't need Fletcher to tell him.

Perhaps he heard the next words in a dream:

'I am going to blow up Berlin, and lay waste Constantinople –'

'It's been done before.' His face burned – no: he wasn't dreaming.

'Sorry to slap your face, my poor one, but – *will* – *you* – LISTEN: I am also going to annihilate New York and Jerusalem.'

'When you were at Harrow, did you ever get to see the *Eagle* or *Chums* or the *Boy's Own Comic*?'

'Of course not. I'm much too young. Very well, I confess to boasting a little. Constantinople, Berlin and Jerusalem will certainly perish, and so, incidentally, will Tel Aviv. I'm not so confident of New York.'

'A becoming modesty.'

'It might be Boston instead, or Washington, or Philadelphia – we're very bad at geography, we *coons* from the Third World – but I'll *hit* their East Coast somewhere, Beloved' – he smacked Matson again – 'and it'll be louder than this when my Wrath strikes.'

'It had better be. That scarcely woke me up.'

Dragout enlarged with rage. Dragout tore Matson's clothes, and began to squeeze his neck. Matson's clothes were on Dragout, but his neck was underneath his own chin and Dragout tore at it as if he were breaking bread. Matson's neck was already sore; he first shouted aloud, then his eyes darkened, pressurised and popping from the violence of those dark thumbs.

When he came to, Dragout was bathing his temples and crooning to himself. When he saw Matson was fully awake he stopped singing abruptly.

'Why do I tell you this? Truths my father taught me?' He took Matson's bloodshot face in his hands. 'Do you know what my father taught me about truth, my old friend? He told me a wise man discusses nothing, save with – do you know who?' He patted Matson gently. 'His secure prisoner. His special woman. A man about to die.' He hung above Matson's fever. 'You see, my friend? You see why I tell you so much? You are all of these things to me.'

'You really are a most disgusting tick, Dragout.' Matson was proud of 'tick': he'd read it in a book, and it seemed more appropriate to all this fluff than anything he'd picked up round Camberwell.

'You're likely to get yourself did, if you carry on like that.'

'Dead is a better pronunciation.'

'I went to Harrow, Brittle Face.' He ruffled what was left of Matson's hair. 'So don't make fun of my English.'

'I was merely seeking clarification.'

'Good boy. Did means dead, anyway.'

'Did will do.'

'You're really getting quite scabby. I must ask someone in to give you a wash before I sign your warrant.' He regarded Matson sadly, like a child mourning a broken toy. 'Otherwise I don't know what I'm going to do with you, Little Ming – the Revolution won't let me keep you for my pleasure. The problem is – do I wring your neck, or salt you down and pack you off in a coffin with the other sweety-pies?'

'What coffin will that be?'

Dragout wept. Then he spoke for a long time in Arabic, before smiling his last words: 'There – I've said too much. Death's Angel tells me I have said too much.'

'I don't understand Arabic.'

'I believe you, little one. But there's no time for you to learn.'

'So what is to happen to us?' After a pause, 'When will I die?'

'So you've guessed. Soon, soon, soon. You will all die soon. In your case, perhaps when I have made you truly my own I shall strangle you in our lovemaking.'

'You're not even a decent pansy, black man. You're a slob. Do I have a last request?'

'Assuredly you shall have a last request.'

'I should like you to bring me a woman.' The hyperbole was in the thought rather than the expression, but even soldiers read Pepys.

'I do not think you will be much good for that. On the other hand, it would be pleasing to suppose your last gasp might get me a boy child – someone like you, but born in the Faith, somebody I could keep here for ever.'

Dragout went away. He walked from the cellar as if finally, but perhaps that was not his intention. Maston was too weak to tell, weak from self-disgust mainly, that and lack of sleep.

Besides, Dragout always left something of himself behind. In this case it was his smell. He smelled very sweetly – not with the grassy odours of Arab body oils, but of cinnamon, nutmeg, clove. So much spice was left floating in the air it was hard to believe the genie was at last back in his bottle.

12.

Bodies are laid out in much the same manner the whole world over. The male cadaver has certain unique requirements, and the meeting of them can either dignify it or degrade it. Except among the tribes who buy their deaths in shops, and a few other fee-paying professional cultures, this laying out is generally performed by the old women of the village, so the male corpse has a bad time.

The three squatter women were ancient enough to be mature in irreverence. They had seen many corpses, and given birth to not a few. For the moment, laying out a body was going to be much more agreeable than picking up stones.

The black ugly giant had told them there was a death in the cellar and given them money to treat it properly.

They came hissing and giggling in. Normally they wouldn't be so noisy, but this death was a foreign one, so it couldn't understand them.

The corpse was already naked and lying on wire. This meant there was very little heavy work to do. The body was dirty, of course. So one went for water to wash it, and to see if there was any oil.

There was some oil and some spice upstairs. Now they knew their skills would be properly employed, one busied herself by wearing a small piece of ornamental string. One cut a few inches from the end of a coil of rope, and soaked it in disinfectant and then in scented oils. She bound this ropes' end with crude cotton and soothed it with some more of the same oils.

While she was inserting it, the corpse woke up. The women hissed. The one who had been tying off his thing finished what she was doing, then clamped a hand across his mouth.

He tried to swear through her fingers, but her hand was too strong. She also pinched his nose.

His legs thrashed about, but only his legs. His wrists were tied.

They tutted at this, tittered and hissed, then clucked and not quite giggled. Sometimes, as now, a corpse comes to life when it is being laid out; and if so, as now, it has to be rebuked and sent back where it belongs with the Angel of the Dead. This is necessary in order to keep peace with him and stop him growing greedy. It is also important to spare the feelings of the family.

Meanwhile the corpse kicked and thrashed, while they coaxed it back deathwards. It had fine legs, so they teased as well as tutted, fine white legs with copper brown hair. If one of them had it to herself, she might have kept it, but no Lazarus is to be encouraged. A man must not damage his heirs and his women by bereaving them twice.

The corpse was not so ill as it looked. It was taking a long time to die.

13.

'Mister Mat*son*.'

When he opened his eyes again, the old women were cowering against the wall.

Much nearer, all green tooth and snuff, was Dr Ibrahim Nuseibeh. He left Matson's bedside and shooed the old women until they stopped their hissing and wailing.

'Come to gloat, have you?'

'No time for that, my dear.' The good doctor came close and chuckled. 'Amusing, in all the circumstances of his preference, to discover His Excellency is also a gambling man. A man who enjoys his cards, but favours the dice. He honoured me at dice.' He shook a bundle of keys.

Matson still didn't understand. All he knew was the man was very close indeed now, whisperingly close.

'What I mean is that I've just won you, Mat*son*.'

Dr Nuseibeh began to unfasten him, not all of him, but some of him.

TWELVE

1.

'I'm afraid all our hard work's come to nought,' Quinlan muttered. 'In the light of recent events, that is.' He liked to slip them the bad news before the meeting was properly to order – it made his life easier – but he needn't have bothered. CAC was already stagnant, its members doing absolutely nothing to advance circumstance or retard their careers. Sometimes it seemed to Fossit that their agenda was being written for them on the box and the wires by the Al Jamahiriyah's spokesman. They met several times a day, and frequently at night; but only so Quinlan could set his thumb on them: and it did not escape anyone that timings were arranged to coincide with the arrival of videotape from the transcription services or moments when the Libyan Queen's pronouncements could be tapped direct by satellite dish.

'The place is being run like a newsroom,' he grumbled.

'Like an editorial conference,' Pomeroy agreed. 'Minister,' he said with upraised hand, 'Perhaps it's the lateness of the hour. I've quite forgotten what our second C stands for – but it *sounds* too operatic to my ears. I'd like to propose that CAC becomes CAT' – he rode over Barkworth's hiss of contempt – 'with a T as for Team, and that we actually function as one.'

Quinlan had been a chairman for a long time. He had a joke ready about Marcus not wanting to pussyfoot. Then he said, 'Cabinet has changed its mind about a solus operation. I mean – we knew it would, once those planes were moved to Az Zawiyah. Now it's official. I thought you'd like to know.'

'So we've been forced to drop the intact half of an inept plan,' Pomeroy said. 'I'd like to develop a point, if we're all through with reporting.'

He got the ministerial nod, if not the wink.

'The people most at risk are the Israeli passengers. By the same token, the Israeli rescue team is the one most likely to jump the gun. They promise me as much on the hotline by the hour. So why don't we improve our intact morsel by jumping it with them? That way, we might cook the duff. Militarily, as distinct from logistically, the Sifr WaaHid location must be the easier one for us to operate at –'

Brigadier Barkworth contrived a neat little vocable, without uttering so much as a whisper.

'This morning your heart was bleeding for the Americans.'

'No-one can seriously believe the Americans are in real danger. Neither are the Greeks. From anyone save the hijackers themselves, that is. And the hijackers will be in charge only for as long as Libya tolerates their presence.'

The brigadier looked like a man trying to spit with his mouth closed. People began to feel uncomfortable for him.

'The Libyans'll make a bad fist of storming those aircraft,' he said at last. 'There'll be some dead passengers as a result, and then where will all your windbagging have got us?'

' "Windbagging" is your word for diplomacy, I take it?'

Brigadier Barkworth was triumphant.

'I like it.' Pomeroy made a note of it on his pad. 'I shall use it in my next lecture to the W.I. Windbagging, as you call it, will lead to the Libyans deleting the hijackers, at an incalculable but probably acceptable cost in passenger casualties. Action-manning will lead to your chaps killing Libyans, and Libyans killing your chaps while the hijackers slaughter passengers at their leisure. Hurrah for windbagging, I say. If we can achieve it, a deal with Libya offers not only the best result, it actually represents the best likely result – *at Tripoli*. But only at Tripoli, where the military risks are great, and where the diplomatic odds are good. The diplomatic odds are good because the Libyans know, from experience, that they mustn't push America too far.

'At Sifr WaaHid there is the opposite balance of factors. Therefore I would urge this committee to reconsider the option it has passed over. Namely that – in concert with Israel, rather than by ourselves – we should contemplate an immediate rescue there in the desert, and leave diplomacy to bandage the damage in the short term and rescue the passengers of the American and Greek aircraft in the long term.'

'You keep on, don't you?' Brigadier Barkworth muttered. 'But you make your point.'

'Why he's here,' Quinlan said.

'I did my sums with the navy and the RAF,' the brigadier said. 'Our view is, and was, before we heard Mr Pomeroy on the subject, that we could stage a feasible solus rescue *if* it could be done tomorrow, when we had planned to do it. But it can't be. Our political masters didn't just put us on hold: they stood us down. It would take days to get going again. Tomorrow it would have been a Special Air Service type operation – you had the details. Any later, we'll need a whole commando. The SAS are still ready, of course. Unfortunately we can't offer more than a one in four chance of being able to fly those aircraft out. If we can't mobilise the aircraft, then we cannot, in these countermanded circumstances, assemble the means within twenty-four hours *both* to ferry in a strong raiding party and its equipment, *and then* retrieve it together with some five hundred passengers and flight crew.'

'Move some more aircraft.' Pomeroy appealed to Fisher.

'I moved my first half squadron round ways about, and singly. If I move more planes all at once, I'll tip off the Libyans. Obviously we'll need to move more squadrons at some point, but that will be better if it is seen as part of our overall threat – and perhaps disguised among the mass of U.S. activity as well.'

'Why can't you shift the Trident and the Jumbo?' Pomeroy asked.

'We'd have to fly in some fuel. Fuelling up on the ground, with the level of equipment that's available for airlift, is likely to be a very lengthy job. The Trident Three will need all of its capacity. The 747 is big and therefore thirsty.

'Over and above all this, though –' he caught Quinlan's eye – 'May I, sir? Over and above this there are the additional problems of that desert landing strip to consider. We'd have to fly off by day: day's a bad time for the SAS. They'd prefer to do the rescue in the dark, naturally. They won't want to hold ground while their clocks wait for stars and planets. Desert airstrips are short. They have heat affected surfaces. Day air is thin. We'll be lifting huge loads, particularly if we have to stow all of the passengers in the Jumbo, or – in the event of the Jumbo being incapacitated – share its passengers between the Trident and the raid aircraft.'

'Why won't the planes fly?' Dixon put in.

'Any number of reasons. In a case like this, I'd say universal Sod's law, stepped up to the power of ten for each day they wait on the ground. In real order of magnitude: no electrics, therefore no engine-start and no avionics. Sun-softened tyres – that's if the landing gear isn't already damaged as a result of the inevitably rough let-down. Sand driven into the turbines – well, that'll do, sir. Sand, wind and heat are three dice we can't even guess at.'

'So, you've developed your point, Marcus.' Quinlan was dismissive, but not discourteous. He had a nice little digest for Cabinet as a result of the last ten minutes' chat – quite the best, in fact. His jotter was full of hard facts that added up to absolutely nothing, and his smile said he was thankful for them. Cabinet had wanted him to go on a plan that time had overtaken. That was his favourite sort of plan. Now here he was with another alibi for yet another twenty-four hours of frantic inaction. If that was what CAC could provide by becoming CAT, or perhaps having CAT as a working party, or as a nice little subcommittee, then *floreat* CAT. '*Floreat* CAC!' he said to them all as he gathered his papers.

Barkworth put his foot in it. You don't get a brigadier to fall out just by rattling your ball-point pens – and doing eyebrow semaphore to a couple of junior principals like Lorna and Hattie.

'I'll give Mr Pomeroy this much,' the brigadier said. 'If any of those passengers get themselves dispersed round that desert encampment then we'll be too damned late for a rescue.'

'What are we saying, Brigadier? What *are* we saying?'

'I'm saying that Mr Pomeroy has told you exactly what we must do, and that the RAF has just proved conclusively that we can't do it.'

Quinlan raised his hand, but not to strike God in the face. He was ensuring that Lorna had halted her minutes before he huffed out.

Fossit wrote: 'Eyebrow semaphore or eyebrow morse?'

Pomeroy took the Action People, including Barkworth, to his office for a nightcap of OK soup.

Quinlan was already waiting for them, and that was a pity. Two cups of brandy only faintly diluted by coffee opened him up. Or perhaps he was afflicted with one of those whiffs of elation that management so often catches when it mixes with the workers. 'Get Matson out,' he said. 'Why can't he be got out? Once upon a time a chap like that was trained to get himself out.'

2.

'I thought you preferred little lads.'

'One hand will remain fastened, Mr Mat*son*. Until I am absolutely certain that you're one little lad who has no desire to break my neck.'

'They were trying to kill me.'

'They were washing your corpse. To do that, they needed a corpse to wash. It's logical enough, and common practice.' He spat, to show his respect for it. 'When we have a grouchy old man who tyrannises his children and keeps to his bed, we send in the women. The whole thing was Dragout's doing. Dragout arranged it. He's a bad loser.'

' "His Excellency"?'

Nuseibeh turned his attention to the old ladies. Their whimpering was becoming orchestrated, so he kicked the most senior, the one who had been smothering Matson. Her upper lip was toothless, and arthritis glimmered chalky at her wrists, so he kicked only gently, with the inside of his slipper. Something he hissed while he did this made them shut their noise and take themselves quietly from the room, like old cobwebs in a storm.

'Not a title, Mr Mat*son*. A politeness. There are only a hundred million of us. Yet we are the custodians of all the courtesy in the world.'

'So you won me at cards?'

'Dice. Men wager many things. Dragout was obliged to wager his prisoner. Not because he wished to forgo you. But because he coveted this.' He touched the green gem in its tooth. 'Valueless, I know. But complete with its mounting and its roots? Shall we say such ivory attracts him?'

'We may say what we like, so long as no-one has to believe it.'

'Modfai's prize was an air-stewardess, wagered by Khadduri.'

'The captain is too much of a soldier to part with a prisoner.'

'The captain is a colonel now, and colonels do not think of themselves as soldiers. But you are quite right. He bought her back. He bartered a hand in a jar of oil. I saw a man hanged yesterday, Mr Mat*son*. And his forearm severed – just to lend wit to a worthless timepiece! Bad things have been happening here – especially to the stewardesses on your English aeroplane. What do you say to that?'

'I say it's time you undo my wrist. I won't harm you. Anyway, I'm too weak.'

'We need all your strength now, Pat*rick*. And we do not have much time. There's not much more than an hour till midnight.'

'My name's not Cinderella.'

'At midnight, Patrick Mat*son*, I have to give you back.'

3.

Once off the bed, he fell. His leg was too big for its neighbour.

Nuseibeh clapped his hands.

'What's that?' Matson whispered from the floor. Had it all been in whispers?

'He out there. He will think I am beating you. The guard, I mean.' Nuseibeh giggled, deliberately and unnaturally, very aloud.

'So what are you giggling for?' Matson was on his feet now.

Nuseibeh merely giggled.

Matson caught his shoulder, hard. 'I've served my purpose

here. You arrange my escape for them. I collect a bullet in the back. It's an ancient scenario.'

'What purpose do you think you have served? I have seen the transcripts. As an interrogation it was a nonsense. You were magnificent, no doubt. All we have is that idiot drooling about pain, and power, and privilege.'

'And sodomy, Nuseibeh.' Matson's leg was a touch better. Nothing else was. 'Don't forget that.'

'Sodomy's a commonplace out here. It's like chips in England. Universal as sherbert.'

'Thanks for the absolution.' He was sitting on the bed again, naked and shivering. 'What else can you give me?'

'I can summon you a uniform. I can bring you cognac.'

' "Summon"?'

'The guard will be wearing it. He's a big lad tonight. I'll even provide a weapon.'

'What weapon?'

Nuseibeh pulled a flat bundle from beneath his caftan, and unwrapped it reverently. 'It's as far as I dare go.'

'That's a toy.'

'It belonged to my –'

'Spare me.'

'It killed a man in 1964. It featured in a famous murder enquiry. Look at the date the police scratched on it.'

'Every ornamental dagger in the Kasbah killed a man in 1964. 1964 was a vintage year for killing.' He took the knife and tested it. The handle was much too light, but the blade was agreeably solid. Blunt, perhaps. But solid. Even a propelling pencil would do. 'Yes,' he said. 'A very good year. This year is going to be better, though.'

His leg felt like pumice. He touched it, and his fingers sank in as if he was testing Brie. Still sitting, he was growing colder. 'I want that cognac,' he said. 'Not the guard. Not yet.'

4.

Nuseibeh had to go outside for the cognac. He had to go outside and giggle for it. When he came back he was carrying a bundle as big as a laundry basket. Whatever was at the middle of it was a long way in, and took an age to unwrap.

It was an opaque green bottle, handled so tenderly it might be the Grail.

Or nitroglycerine. The faithful do not drink.

The cognac was fierce and tasted medicinal, like something made from carbolic and wood alcohol for old country dentists in County Mayo to keep their syringes in.

It was furry in the brain and made him feel sick. He needed to be sick. However sad sick is, it is always preferable to death.

He obliged the floor. His stomach was empty at the beginning and emptier now. He was flushing his weakness with alcohol, filling and flushing, like a clinic cleaning its drains.

Strange, strange people. They're denied the fruits of the vine and yet they make some of the best wines in the world, and write all of the best poems to the grape.

You think such thoughts when you're psyching up to kill.

'This stuff is awful.'

'It's Courvoisier Five Star.'

'It's filth.'

He wasn't a man. He was a wolf-child, rinsing his teeth, sharpening his claws.

'Water,' he croaked. 'I must have lots of water.

Nuseibeh was gone for a long time. Matson heard him talking outside, and again the giggle. His shame flared at the giggle. But it was his brain that hurt most. He didn't like Nuseibeh talking out there. He pushed the doubts away, then filed them carefully. Even a rat in an electric trap gives himself time to consider.

Nuseibeh's slippers slap-slapped on the stone floor. They went further away. They came back after due interval.

Dr Ibrahim's teeth came in first, then the jug of water. His teeth were smiling. His tongue examined its green gem, while Matson took the jug, filled his mouth and stomach, and was sick again.

'How did you explain this?'

'I told him I was going to wash you, for obvious reasons.'

'Pah!'

He watched Matson pick rag from the corner and dry his

face carefully. He watched Matson clean his crotch and armpits. He watched Matson drink more water, without being sick.

'And what did you tell him on the way back?' Matson asked. 'To have soldiers wait to kill me as soon as I was outside?'

'I told him how pretty he was. You mustn't be jealous. He's younger than you, but not so talented.' He waited until Matson had finished drying himself before saying, 'If you were intended to be killed, why would I endanger the guard for it? There are plenty of other stratagems. You may be killed, Patrick Mat*son*. I may be killed with you.' He shuddered at the thought of it, in ways no drama school could teach. 'If so, it will be the product of misfortune. An Arab would have washed his feet,' he said.

'Not enough water.' Once he allowed his body to acknowledge pain, the sensation spread all over him. He hoped his back did not open again. He hoped nothing bled. Blood would make him stink like bad meat. A stinking man cannot kill close in the dark. 'Besides, I do not wash to be clean.'

5.

'Why else would a man wash, if not to be clean?'

'To kill.' He stood very close to Nuseibeh now.

'Oh, my Pat*rick*. I have heard of *dressing* to kill, but that is what women say, my dear boy!'

The jesting stopped. Matson might be weak, and agreeably naked, but his hands were on Nuseibeh's neck. Nuseibeh's neck had been felt many times, but these weren't lover's fingers.

'A cat does not wash to be clean. It washes so it does not smell. The little mouse's whiskers may twitch, its nostrils may quiver' – he squeezed Nuseibeh, feeling for sore spots, not the killing points – 'but it doesn't sniff the cat.' He watched Nuseibeh wince, but went on testing his fingers for strength before letting go of him and saying, 'I was taught to kill, Ibrahim. I did not like the man who taught me, but he taught me very well. That is why you have to consider what you do when you set me free.' He wondered whether to kill the bastard now, but the guard was near, and would listen for the murmur of voices. 'He taught me I mustn't smell of alcohol, or of sick, or of sex, or of sweat. I needed that brandy, but I needed to be rid of it. So I was sick. Then I needed to be rid of the sick.' He knew he was talking too much, but he needed to gossip himself back to some kind of manhood. Killing Nuseibeh could come later. If he himself were to die soon, killing the doctor now would be a waste of moral force.

Nuseibeh nodded, without further speech.

'Say something,' Matson whispered. 'He needs to hear your voice.'

How he would love whispers!

'What shall we do about the guard?' Nuseibeh asked.

'Didn't you plan that far?' Matson hissed.

It was the doctor's turn to look a little sick.

'Call him in here to share in the giggle. There's been a lot of that.'

Nuseibeh seemed relieved. He went for the guard.

The soldier came in by himself. Nuseibeh followed half a minute later.

'He's not dead,' Matson grimaced. 'What are you a doctor of, anyway? Medicine?'

'Philosophy.'

'I'll tie the knots myself, then.' Matson made a gag and a toe-and-thumb tie with some twisted shreds of the rag he had washed himself with. He didn't tension it back round the man's neck. He was unconscious and might strangle himself. If any strangling had been necessary, Matson would have killed the lad outright.

Besides, he was in ordinary khaki denim. He was one of Khadduri's men. Matson was troubled by the likely significance of this, but the lad was a soldier. He had nothing against soldiers.

'We must hurry.'

'Not yet, Nuseibeh.' He had flexed his muscles and was growing insolent with the return of power. 'First I shall need to hear many things.'

If the doctor grew agitated at the delay, it would tend to

confirm he was indeed on Matson's side. And an impatient man finds it harder and harder to string his lies together.

6.

'I was here on business, Mr Mat*son*. Funny business, you will say. Perhaps. I am an Arab. I have an interest in Arab causes. I would be lying to you and – worse – a traitor to myself, if I attempted to deny this.

'Certain intelligence formations in the West require titbits, for which they pay money. When possible I oblige them. Sometimes the money is good. Sometimes it is merely adequate. Again whenever possible, I pass a little of that money on – hence my welcome in places where other diplomats dare not tread.'

'If you are a diplomat, Nuseibeh, then diplomacy has changed its frontiers.'

'I am a realist, Mr Mat*son*, and I wish we could hurry from here. I do not deny I knew there would be a hijack. I did not know it would involve a British plane, a Service charter, and still less you. I saved your life nonetheless.'

'You shopped me.'

The soldier moved on the floor, but only the way a drunk moves to reorganise sleep.

'I delivered you into the hands of the highest simply in order to rescue you from the lowest. When I spoke out, you had two – not one, but *two* – machine-guns pointing at your head. I saved your life then. I am risking my own to give you your freedom now.'

'Why?'

'This fellow is likely to be relieved soon.'

'Believe me, he is not.' Matson's hand whipped against the doctor's face, playfully, painfully, loose-knuckled. 'That's in case he listens in his sleep. He will hear how I bully and coerce you.' His leg was in need of exercise, but he didn't use its toe on the man yet. He would wait till it had some boots on. 'I asked you why.'

'London is an attractive city, Mr Mat*son*. So are the great metropoles of North America. I should hate never to walk there again.'

'So that's why you're setting me free?' Matson picked up the ornamental cloth that had wrapped the dagger and sliced it into five pieces. He used one to improve the soldier's gag. Then he worked on, letting the doctor's words spill over him, concentrating on the lad's boots, his trousers, his denim blouse, and finally leaving him lashed outspread on the bedframe, naked as he himself had been, face downwards in case he should be sick or otherwise choke himself.

The doctor approved of the activity, the abrupt surge of urgency. He even helped with it, with the trousers and boots at least, but he was shut out by it. He spoke against the side of Matson's bowed and busy head, talking more and more quickly, desperate to persuade him. 'No, Mat*son*. No, Pat*rick*. That is not why I am setting you free. Your freedom, taken by itself, will be a bonus to me. But not essential to my cause – providing I could find an equal good.' Matson at last had a shirt on, and he caught it by the arm. 'Something has come up here I dare not, cannot, sit on. Not and be allowed into the West again.'

He had all of Matson's unattention now.

'That madman, His Excellency, is constructing atomic bombs.'

'Bullshit.'

'You say. It requires much technology to build a battlefield nuclear device – much technology and a supply of high-grade fissionable material. You need much less technology and *no* high-grade material to improvise a *really large* bomb. A bomb as big as a house, say. You will doubtless have learned this at school.'

'Doubtless.'

'What stops it from being done – moral considerations aside – is the impossibility of entering an enemy's country with the necessary medium-grade material and erecting your device at the heart of his cities –' Matson shuddered, this time not from cold or the long exposure to violence ' – or the improbability of building your house in your own back yard, then devising a flying crane or some such nonsense to transport it above your enemy's head. In either case, Mr Mat*son*, your enemy would be likely to notice.'

What Matson was likely to notice was that the soldier had worn sockless boots and trousers without underpants, and that these or the soldier – no, these and the soldier – smelled. The soldier smelled so much that the doctor's wit escaped him entirely.

'An aeroplane is a convenient casing for a bomb, Mat*son*. A Trident Three has quite as much space in its baggage hold as I daresay you have in your house.'

Once more he had Matson's arm, this time with Matson's fullest attention.

'He has two other aircraft – you will not have heard the extent of this hijack, perhaps – two other aircraft including another widebody. He intends to send one bomb to Berlin, one to New York, and of course one to Israel. And one to – I don't know where the Greek one is going.'

'We'll shoot them down.'

'The passengers will fly with them.'

'The Israelis will shoot down anything that violates their airspace.'

'With four hundred passengers on board? Especially if they know about the passengers but not about the bomb? That is why we have to get you out.'

'All right, Nuseibeh. You'll get me out.' He used a little more brandy, then rinsed his mouth with water.

He felt half-convinced by the doctor's story, but his brain was still numb from Dragout and the resulting chemistry of doubt. One thing he did know. When such a story exists, someone must get it out. That someone was himself. Not because he had the will, but because he was on the move. He was already committed, however sluggishly. He had to step out or die. Or at least bear the consequence of savaging this soldier. 'How will I go?' He didn't want to hear.

7.

'You're going to hijack the Trident. It's got to be the Trident because –'

'Don't be bloody silly.'

' – they're awaiting new tyres for the 747.'

'Why don't I go to the oilmen at Zoltan?' Zoltan seemed near. Zoltan and its oilmen would not involve violence. 'Or find a camera crew? There must be a camera crew. There always is at a hijack.'

The cognac was his totem now. He held it between still naked knees, a gutless manifestation of the inferior faith, and crouched beside the soldier on a corner of the bedframe.

'There was talk of a camera crew, Pat*rick*. It is either being kept a long way away, or it hasn't arrived yet. I told you there was another hijack. The world is getting its pictures from the other hijack.'

Camera crews were good guys. They were shifty, ambiguous, just like himself, but above all resourceful, unlike himself.

He had to get this story out. It tasted better with brandy. He did not have to believe it. He wasn't at his desk now. An intelligence-gatherer gathers. He does not evaluate. The brandy gave him dragon's breath. He must remember to rinse his mouth. 'Drive me to that camera crew. Or take me as far as Zoltan.'

'A camera crew will film you. Whatever they promise, they will turn you into news the instant they find out what you are. Then the cause will be lost, and you will be lost. How do you suppose anyone – camera-crew or oil company – could possibly get you out, even if they'd a mind to?

'Even I could not get you out directly. If I could drive you to the coast, and find a boat at the coast, don't you think I would?' His own sense of delay made him tremble with fear. 'We would be hanged in the same string, Mr Mat*son*. If they give us back to Dragout, it would be the same thorn of barbed wire. Listen to me –' He looked towards the soldier and his voice sank. The man was waking up.

He woke to the pain of Matson's fingers, one behind each ear. Matson listened to his breath stop then grow noisy, go slowly again. Five seconds more would kill the man. Matson unwrapped his brain to sleep.

'*Matson* – a Libyan flight crew comes aboard both aircraft at midnight. They run up the engines and check the electronics, the hydraulics. You need to find a gun. The pilot will be bound to go if you show him a gun. The plane has been refuelled, so he can offer you no excuses.'

'Except that he can't take off in darkness.'

'The strip runs beside the compound. The perimeter lights are on. There is, believe me, a moon.'

Matson confronted the boots, the disgusting trousers. Dirty laundry was no kind of excuse. 'How will you explain your own part in this?'

'You will be kind enough to – how does TV put it? – to *mark* me, perhaps.' He chuckled, glad to find the moment so near. 'Otherwise it is merely an extension of winning you at cards, my dear Mr Mat*son*. Or was it only dice? Why do you suppose I took so much trouble with my bids?' He held out the soldier's boots, folding back their tongues. 'Sexual desire. A man is allowed to make a very great fool of himself here for sexual desire. Providing it is not for a woman, who is not allowed in heaven.' His chuckle became a giggle. The good doctor's social graces were returning. 'No-one supposes you are a woman who is not allowed in heaven, Mr Mat*son*.'

8.

When the sun beat down, Matson had a simple recipe concerning dress: if it doesn't smell, wear it. If it does smell, wear it with conviction.

At the moment there was only the rumoured moon. He could not wear this man's uniform with conviction. 'I can't wear this. I'll never get within a mile of a sentry. It stinks like a stagnant ferret.'

'So does this desert. Down there you can only smell the crude in the sand, believe me. Besides, Pat*rick*, are you so far from military civilisation you have forgotten the smell of new denim? On a hot body, it stinks like a sacking store.'

'I don't want new. I want clean.'

'Out here new is the only clean.'

Matson dressed in the trousers and wished they could have belonged to one of the cleaner pansy brownjobs. In the absence of underpants he splashed their crotch with Nuseibeh's cognac. What with soap and sweat and

Courvoisier, he began to niff like a date-palm at sunset. He knew what the poet said. No man is an oasis.

9.

'My jeep is at the top of the cellar steps. The back is rolled up. Get in quietly and lie flat. There is a guard in the courtyard, by the gate. The gate is to the left. I parked as close as I could.'

The jeep had been there to proclaim his sleazier purposes. Matson limped up quietly.

It wasn't a jeep. It was an ill-considered attempt to customise a Land-Rover, presumably to provide camping space. The blankets and cushions in the back smelled like ancient buggery or Portuguese catarrh. Matson was all nose tonight, but he did his best to stay alive.

There was a thin-air chill, but the diesel started easily and noisily.

Noseibeh rolled the vehicle down and then stopped to joke with someone, presumably the sentry at the gate. He chatted through the window for some time, flirted even.

When he drove on he spoke without moving his head. 'It's only two miles to drive, but on a very slow track.'

Matson remembered the track. However slowly they went, everything was too fast. He wondered whether to jump out and lose himself in the jebel. His news would stay with him, but he could be a good man in the jebel.

The vehicle skidded and grated on a slither of stones. Nuseibeh was reading his mind. 'What an enormous snake,' he said. 'We've just run over a snake.'

Snakes were all right till the moon set.

10.

He fondled Nuseibeh's ridiculous knife. He moved it from hand to hand, with no sort of approval.

His biggest doubt about the doctor was that he had failed to provide a gun. Guns are accountable, of course. Soldiers do not leave them lying around. Surely the old sod had a pistol somewhere, just the same?

Matson would have commuted half his pension just to get his mitts on an Ingram with suppressor, or any other muffled automatic that could be as silent and deadly as a choirboy's fart. He'd have blown away Mr Dragout with such a benefaction, and half a dozen brownjobs as well. It would have been a very satisfactory step towards self-improvement.

That was why the cunning old doctor hadn't let him take it. To kill Dragout now would be an unnecessary luxury. They couldn't afford the complication. He wanted to. He needed to badly. He daren't accept the risks attendant upon such a piece of indulgence. He hadn't killed the Druse who'd ruined his leg. He hadn't squared Shlomo Barel who'd shredded his girl – yet.

He spent the remaining moments of the drive pondering the back of Nuseibeh's neck. He decided the multi-faceted plurifaced doctor was probably more use with his throat uncut, though he gave himself permission to return to it later.

If the news he was carrying was correct, it would be worth a lot of death to deliver it safely.

The little truck turned off the side of the hill, and ran out of shadow, smearing its screen with unsatisfactory moonlight. Visibility was poor. At ground-level there was a kind of haze, a hover of dust. The moon was low and clinging. It hunched like a grey squirrel, not like a desert moon at all.

Then they were skirting the compound, but up at the end closest to the jebel, away from the lights.

Nuseibeh swung into the shadow of a darkened hut, and parked. Matson realised he had been driving without lights.

Then he took charge. The doctor was experiencing a bad bout of terror, hunching his indecision over an unlit dashboard. Matson lifted him out and held his slippers half an inch above the muck-drenched sand. ' "Don't give up on me, baby." ' He set him very gently down onto muffled feet.

11.

The walk was good for his leg. His footfall no longer felt like an elephant hobbling beside a gazelle, but he was in bad shape all the way from the brainbox down, and he mustn't forget it.

'Sentries?'

'Guards. I mean' – the doctor licked an enormous dribble of moonlight and returned his top lip to shadow – 'the hijackers have – the aircraft are under the control of the Freedom Fighters.' Arabic is a language that trains a man to pronounce his capital letters.

'Indeed.'

Why did he think there was something not quite right about this? He told himself it was because he had been tortured and humiliated. He had the use of his muscles, just, but not of his mind. He only had as much of his willpower as had not been thrashed out of him.

Was he left with any of the finely-honed will that led him to be selected for the Thugs in the first place, the determination to push on to the end, any end? Or was this merely the will to survive? A man left with only his will to survive is no better than a rat in a maze. Matson was in a maze, all right, and Mr bloody Dragout had designed it; but he felt, consciously, a little better than ratlike, if only a little.

He felt like a practised drunk who had taken more than was usual, even for him. He would try to find his way home. He was programmed for home and for bed. He would select a way, and that would become the only way, no matter how many dustbins he knocked over.

Nuseibeh was sobbing under his breath. The shadows that night were full of dustbins, footloose drink-cans at least. History had drunk a lot of lager in its search for oil, even if religion had censored it to cola and root-beer.

Matson stubbed another can, just as a banshee howl burst from the silence to smother it. An aircraft was running up its turbines, making the landscape shake then settle to a tremble of rusty tins. He moved on.

Nuseibeh held out an arm. Matson's eyes were still raw

from three nights of neon. He did not notice the guard. Nuseibeh stopped him.

Matson was in no mood to be stopped. The engine noise was too good to waste. He crouched beneath sight level, sank into nothingness and thought his way forward.

Sentries are easy. Sentries are soldiers. They have webbing to distract them, carbines to impede them. They stand in their own noise. You can easily get close to their pressure points. You can use your fingers on them. You can use your knife.

With a knife it is easy. With a knife the problems can be ironed out in training. Matson had been trained in the knife by the Thugs. He had used his knife on a dog. He had used it on a sheep. He had cut and severed several bellyfuls of sickeners. He had used it on men in the Lebanon.

Matson's knife had been laserlike. Matson's knife had been double-edged and razor-sharp. It had been sweet with science.

Matson had Nuseibeh's knife. Nuseibeh's knife was single-edged, plump and damascened. Nuseibeh's knife was notched along the return. Its blade was blunt and its point unsharp. But Nuseibeh's knife was justice, and since hijackers were minding the aircraft Matson saw no need to temper it with mercy.

Guards are never as easy as sentries. They are nonce-people, here for the one-time only, high on adrenalin and nervous as cats, even of the dust on their shadow, the thickness of moonlight.

This one had a Heckler submachine-gun, with the butt unscrewed and no trigger-guard.

Matson encircled the waist with his left hand and got a finger underneath the trigger, before he realised he was killing a woman.

She smashed backhanded at his crotch, but he was too close against her. Then she dug for his eyes, but his face was burrowing into her shoulders.

She was confident, for a second much too aggressive to shout.

He needed to muffle her trigger and her mouth, so he couldn't use the knife. He dislocated her jaw. He dislocated her neck. Something wasn't enough. She began to rictus violently, flailing about.

He daren't risk the sound of a bone snapping, nor the way her heels were pounding the sand. He threw her forward and stamped on her head.

No-one he knew.

He rose beside the doctor and dried both his hands on him.

The Heckler was a dolly.

12.

The aircraft agitation was reduced to a simmer.

'The Trident, Mr Mat*son*.'

The shedding of blood resurrects all titles. 'I may take the Jumbo. I've always wanted to pinch a 747.'

'*Please*, Mr Mat*son*.' Nuseibeh's shadow began to whistle in fear. His mouth was invisible, but his processes were a-grumble from larynx to colon like a leaky bagpipe. It was his ramshakle metabolism that finally convinced Matson of his essential trustworthiness.

'Where will the device be carried – in the passenger cabin?'

'Yes. No, of course not. The passengers are too important a component of the plot. In the baggage holds. The entire stowage will become a primitive bomb.'

'Are they still working on the Trident? There are vehicles out there.'

'I think they may have finished the Trident tonight. They plan something more sophisticated for the widebody. Something much more powerful. Or perhaps a "dirty bomb".'

'Why?'

'It's the one that's destined for the U.S.A.'

Matson savoured the doctor's fear. He wasn't done yet. 'Where are the passengers?'

'Please ... please ... please.'

'Show me.'

'Please, Mr Mat*son*.'

'You are beginning to talk in circles.'

'They're in all those huts with the lights burning.'

'I can see about forty huts with their lights burning.'

'The second row.'

'Why the second row? Show me.' His leg was feeling better now. His leg matched his leg.

'The second row, believe me. In case there's a rescue. Khadduri has a company of infantry in those first huts there.'

'A platoon to a hut?'

'No, less. He has spread them out and made them fortify the huts, some of them with sandbags. *Please*.'

'How are the passengers dispersed?'

'The flight crews of both planes are here.'

'That's the front row.'

'The flight crews and the cabin crews are where the soldiers can keep an eye on them. The English women and their children are in that second-row hut there. Their men next to them. The Israelis from the widebody are in the next four huts, men on the far end, I think.'

'Show me.'

'Look – look hard, Mat*son*. You can see men at the windows.'

'I can see dots before the eyes, Nuseibeh. Dots with beards. I believe you. Which way round are the airline personnel?'

'The flight crews from both aircraft are in one hut, the cabin crews in the other.'

'So which way?'

'I don't know. So the women can be near Sergeant Modfai.'

13.

Matson checked the submachine-gun. 'I'd better steal a Trident,' he said.

'First you must make me look good.'

'I don't suppose you'll want me to run to a broken nose?' Matson jerked Nuseibeh's face with the heel of his hand and heard the nasal cartilage sever, rubbing ends like slate under water.

The doctor fainted in a most authentic and visible Niagara of blood, to lie on his back with his naked left knee folded upwards and glimmering from his caftan in the moonlight like a cauliflower under frost.

Matson straightened the leg, not out of kindness but simply because a bent knee is protected from lateral displacement.

When the leg was flat, he kicked it sideways on, lifting the kneecap.

The doctor groaned, too deeply unconscious to perform with any feeling.

Matson had made him look good.

Dr Ibrahim Nuseibeh wouldn't disgrace himself in comparison with the messily adjacent corpse.

14.

The doctor had been his training bag. His juices were now aglow.

Between himself and the Trident there were the vehicles noticed earlier: two flat-backed trucks.

He could see no-one, but surely there were other guards?

The area between himself and the trucks was lit by the spill of light from the compound, and by the moon. The nearside of the trucks were in moon-shadow, the far side was shaded from the compound by the back of the truck, and hopefully from the moon by the aircraft. Matson couldn't really tell.

He would draw breath when he got there. He wasn't fast. His leg was good enough, but it still lacked spring for running. He reached the far side of the truck in a silent, crouched hobble, drew breath quietly, and plunged into deep shadow.

Both of the vehicles were multi-wheeled tractor-trailer combinations. They each held a single crate tensioned amidships with steel pulleys. These crates looked huge in the dark, but objects always appear bigger than they do in the precise light of day. Matson thought they were probably eight feet each way, or a bit less: say two-metre cubes. Whatever their size, they must hold clues to the truth or otherwise of the doctor's assertions.

He crept along the side of the truck and tripped forward, almost stumbling against the person who stood there.

The shadow bulked like a woman, was a woman. Left no trace on the air save sour cigarettes and long-ago chypre.

Again a woman. Wasn't he the hero?

He tore her chin over quickly from behind, the jaw

snapping first, then the neck. He was killing the same way, but properly this time.

The ground still trembled from the idle of the jets.

He had killed scented men in his time. They all made the same smell when dying: the bowels, the hot piss, a strange gust of heat from throat and armpit and groin. The woman smelled just the same. Animals do it better.

Meanwhile he held her gun, the ubiquitous Kalashnikov. It was the one with the wooden stock but the plastic overstrapping, its banana heavy with ammunition.

He slid it up onto the sled of the truck, and pulled the corpse behind the wheel. It was flabby, its hair white and sticky as lard. The whole package bore an agreeable resemblance to the Düsseldorf Tart, but how could he be sure?

Matson had been tripped by stepping into a rut. The rear tyres of the truck had broken through the makeshift tarmac of crude and sand.

He lifted his hands from her body to the hardness of the crate. It wasn't wood or polystyrene. It was uniblock concrete: the sort of fero-cement compress that is used to transport fissionable material, all grades of atomic waste and any kind of godalmighty bluff.

He examined the Trident. There was an aluminium ladder up against the open boarding door. There wasn't a crew ladder. The luggage ports were closed. There were cases everywhere, in a looted scatter.

He was a man with a useless knife and two good guns. The Heckler could be best for a climb up the ladder, especially on a springless leg.

On the other hand, the Heckler had tumbled in the sand. Automatics with grit in the vent or the ejection are very prone to jam. He decided on the AK47.

Never mind the Thug's armourer who claimed that Kalashnikovs are popular not because they are any good but because there are a lot of them.

The turbines were purling like a vacuum-cleaner.

It was time to go aboard.

THIRTEEN

1.

Matson knelt into the aircraft, placed the Kalashnikov to hand, and pulled up the ladder.

Someone in the vicinity of the rear toilets spoke to someone who replied, also to his right.

A Trident Three boarding door is only a jump and a heave from the ground. It takes a good jump and an overhand heave, but he daren't risk anyone attempting it behind him. He swung the door closed on its counterbalance and secured it.

He regained the Kalashnikov and released the safety, flicking the forward trip to automatic, not repetition.

The ladder lay across the aircraft, exactly where he needed to step. He straddled a foot on either side of it and immediately gouted blood into his Libyan Army trousers. His morale began to drip.

He still couldn't locate the voices on his right: one man, at least, and a woman.

The forward aisle was halfway up the ladder to his left.

It was full of the tan hijacker. The man hadn't unslung his Ingram. He was amazed by the ladder at his feet.

Matson's bowels were in radiant sunburst. He was in no mood for violent murder. He shot the man once through the sternum. If he had to pull the trigger in a Trident, this was the place to do it, among the urns and jugs, the racked-up serving trolleys. He hoped the bullet stopped.

The detonation racketed and rattled. Muzzle-shock to the thorax imploded the Tan's lungs with a huff like the death of contemporary fiction.

He sank in a froth, and Matson trod him under. He glanced quickly backwards for strangers, unclipped the Ingram from its sling, and dunked it into the towel-steamer. He hadn't the time to check it for action; so there it had better stay out of reach and unusable.

His bowel continued to drip.

As all his instructors said, if a soldier goes on haemorrhaging he'll be in a lot of bloody trouble.

2.

There was only one man on the flight-deck, occupying the left-hand seat. His grimace of alarm at the shot changed to a smile when he saw Matson's uniform, then choked against the Kalashnikov's foresight.

'All you need do is fly.'

'I'm not the pilot.' Arabs have no particular reason to speak English. Flight crew do.

'What's this, then?' Matson's gun poked at his uniform, scorched a lapel with its heat. 'Fancy dress?'

'If you shoot me you'll be shot yourself – like a dog in a box.'

'Don't worry about me. Worry about you.' He knew he daren't shoot, and he knew the man knew it. Not in a pressure hull. It wasn't pressurised now, of course; but it would need to pressure again.

The Ingram would have been better. The Heckler better again.

'Besides,' the man said, exuding advantage, 'if you shoot me, who will fly your plane?'

'No-one,' Matson agreed.

The compound lights went out. Someone had rumbled him somewhere – presumably Dragout back in the house.

'So you'd better do it yourself, and you'll have to do it on headlights. Get the bloody thing rolling.' The fellow's last remark was an admission he was a pilot. 'You can use the moon as a beacon.'

'I'll nose her in,' the man said, still evenly. 'I'll nose her in after take-off. Aircraft nose in without runway markers. The eye becomes disorientated. It's called –'

'The accelerating train effect.' Matson was amazed at himself. It was like being drunk enough to be visionary. He felt drunk. He'd had enough cognac. And he was visionary. He had been subjected to a long midnight of fantasy, and now his red oxygen dripped.

'I haven't got a second officer – a co-pilot.'

'I know. I just shot him. You're better off without him. I suffered him on the flight out.'

Terror picked at the man's face. He was brave enough, but his situation was desperate. A gun-muzzle is a nasty crater to look into for long, especially when there's a deranged finger on the trigger – Matson counted on that. A rational man may bluff and counter-bluff a rational man, but Matson did not feel rational, and guessed he did not look that way, either. He was the red-eyed weeping camel-boy, bewitched and buggered from the storm: weaker than a child and yet murdering mad.

He blinked. They licked dry mouths at each other.

Chance will do it. The Kalashnikov wheezed. A vent must have been clogged with soot, so it fuffed a little gas from behind the piston and the pilot winced away from it. He thought the action was running back before smearing his head.

At the same time a whisp of greasy smoke gusted from the muzzle.

His eyes closed. The lids stiffened. He turned forward in his seat and lifted the palm of his right hand against the throttle lever. The plane began to roll.

Matson was too done up to care whether the man got his eyes back open or not. At least he seemed to have stopped bleeding. He was discovering what his mother's half of the world could already tell him: life is sometimes better with your legs closed.

3.

A searchlight came on at the end of the strip, but only half-exposed, possibly while the crew adjusted carbons.

Operated like that it was no kind of hindrance. Its red lens acted as a useful marker.

There was no slap of small-arms fire, no attempt to block

them off with vehicles. They powered straight at the searchlight hub, its flat-bed jeep now visible on a transverse track of stones, then lifted over it.

The Trident's beams bounced the desert with a dizzy sequence of rock-shadows, before they lifted skyward.

'What heading?' The pilot's face was all alone with the instrument lights and developing a strange wet shine.

'North – three sixty dead.'

'We've only got twenty minutes' fuel.'

'Leave the lies to me.'

4.

Matson waited till the dials stopped climbing then let him feel a little more gun against the brain. 'I don't know whether you're being considerate or naughty. Either way, switch off the headbeams.'

'I can't fly with this much stress.'

'Do you want me to sing to you? I'll sing to you. Who's up back?'

'Cleaners. Riff-raff squatters from the encampment.'

'Arabs?'

The man didn't answer.

'What's your name?'

'Anwar.'

'I didn't want to kill you before learning your name. How many of them?'

'I'm flight crew. I don't take an inventory of people like that.'

'Who's the woman?'

'Riff-raff.'

Matson did what a wise man does sooner. He leant very gently across the pilot and patted him for weapons, then relieved him of his wallet. The wallet woke up his faculties.

'This Libyan stuff – what's it worth?'

'Roughly fifteen dollars.'

'If anyone will accept it. I'm going to take one step beyond the door. Don't touch the WT and don't try any wing-overs.'

He examined the forward passenger cabin. No hijackers.

No cabin crew. No sign of his pilot's so-called riff-raff cleaners. They were skulking somewhere at the rear. Poor little casualties of peace. They'd probably never seen any aeroplane in their life, and now they were sky-high in one and soon they were going to die in one. Only Matson knew that this was a one-survivor flight. One survivor maximum. One survivor if this survivor survived.

He knelt in the galley where he could look either way, at the pilot's back or to the rear of the plane. He began to frisk the Tan.

A pity about the blood, especially from an exit wound which was all spine and shoulderblade. Matson had a fancy for the clean American uniform.

The preparation had been thorough. The man's pocket book held a U.S. leave-pass, a U.S. travel warrant, an Avaroc boarding card, a British Northern Sector courtesy-ticket, a U.S.A.F. identification that looked good enough to Matson, a few nostalgic dollars, a sizable wad of five-pound notes and half-a-dozen Deutschmark tens for absolute verisimilitude. Matson halved all of the money, keeping enough for Sicilian travel and bribes, then wrapped the book and the rest of its contents, including the rest of the notes, in a plastic mini-bin-liner. He pushed his own half of the notes and the Libyan's money inside another one, rolled them up tightly, and pushed the both of them deeply into his own tunic pockets.

Until now he'd been so concerned with the take-off that he'd not considered the economics of landing.

Back in the flight cabin, he found further signs of the hijackers' purity of motive. A tunic lay behind the right-hand seat, folded neatly on the floor. It was blue with royal silver piping. Inside was the Second Officer's ID card from Avarel, Avaroc's parent airline. Captain Finch had obviously discarded the tunic while he sat it out alone with the Tan's gun in the blistering desert heat. The inside pocket contained an unstolen wallet with three English twenties and a ten.

Lucky Matson. Luck always comes in threes. He'd found three guns and now three wallets. In the last half an hour he'd caused three deaths. The Nine Muses and Triple Hecate could content themselves for now.

Only for now.

For the moment he was rich in an abundance of currencies. He added the pounds to his personal waterproof roll.

Pilot Anwar raised an eyebrow at all this.

'I may need to take a taxi.'

'So might I.'

Cheek was going to get Mr Anwar nowhere.

5.

There were lights ahead. The plane's heading was perhaps two degrees east of north.

'Do you want me to put down at Benghazi International?'

'I'm not hungry yet. Are you?'

'I'm bound to point out –'

'Just concentrate on staying alive.'

The Benghazi lights passed beneath them to starboard.

'Where?'

'Sicily. Catania to be precise.'

'There isn't enough fuel for Catania.'

'We'll take turns to push.'

They didn't dip a wing. He was cool as well as surly, was Anwar; and he believed in stretching his luck. Just the same, Matson watched the heading swing slowly to three hundred and fifteen degrees gyroscopic. Catania. They weren't going to fly this one by computer.

They had lost the moon. They had lost Cassiopeia. Ahead was Mars, a red pinhead close to Aldebaran in the grouchy Bull.

They flew a long time in silence.

'I need to call –'

'Forget air-traffic control. Just concentrate on the mother of your children. In a few minutes' time I want you to circle, so we can burn off some of this fuel we don't have.'

'They have passable night-landing facilities at Catania. Better at Palermo. At Reggia on the mainland things are excellent.'

'What's the time?'

'Three and some seconds.'

'I make it forty miles south-east of the Cape Pasero beacon.'
'Twenty.'
'Circle now. We're going to hold station till the sun comes up. When we've got enough light we'll put down here in the sea.'

6.

They found Cassiopeia. They circled clockwise between Altair and Procyon, Arcturus and Betelgeuse.
'You're mad.'
After a little while the sun floated up from a steamy cloud that might have been lying on the horizon's water. The cockpit took dazzle, filled with petals of fire, but the sea was still dark, six miles below.
'You're insane.'
'I'm partially from bonkers, part Camberwell Irish.'
'So why don't you tell me your name? In all the circumstances it would be good to know your name.'
'Start to let down.'
'Ten minutes. Why here?'
'There's a bomb on board.'
'In which case I'd like to put down at an international airport with an ambulance standing by and a fire tender.'
'It may be set to blow.'
'The military can defuse it.'
'It's an atom bomb.' Matson gave him time to digest this little fact. 'Or allegedly an atom bomb. Your lot are such liars. Don't you know what you're carrying?'
'The plane feels empty.'
'It's lost its passengers. Perhaps it's designed to blow when we land. Perhaps it'll blow anyway, bombs being what they are.'
The pilot looked as worried as Matson felt, both of them persuaded by Matson's rhetoric.
Madness took over. 'I must have a fire tender!'
'The sea's very tender. So now you know the problem. A nice soft landing, a very soft landing, on the enchafèd flood.'
How much English poetry should a foreigner know?

Anwar gazed into the gun, then began to let down into lunacy.

'When did a passenger aircraft last manage a successful ditch?'

'So long ago it was never.'

One of them asked it and one of them answered.

7.

'Here will do.' Matson wanted empty water, but not too far from a boat heading north. 'That fisherman will have seen us. Now let's give him some room.'

Matson braced himself behind the captain's seat, head well down, the gun on safety.

The plane stalled a fraction high, but only a fraction, and that was good luck.

It hit tail low, but with its wings level, the flaps spraying debris like slates in a hurricane.

Then the nose dipped in, drenched with spray and dived deeper, gluing itself under until it had smothered all forward motion.

The flight deck was still dim and submarine when Matson picked himself out from behind the seat.

Anwar was undoing his harness, cursing, self-congratulating, numb with fear and with his upturned face bruised from the deceleration.

Matson struck him a heavy blow with the wooden stock of the Kalashnikov.

Anwar sprawled on the floor, and Matson finished him with his feet, kicking head and epigastrium, stomping on his thorax. When you die in a plane-crash you have plane-crash wounds.

Anwar spoke once in English, pleaded in Arabic. He was dead when the cockpit surfaced.

The squatters hadn't been warned. Matson hadn't wanted them warned. He had an unreasoned impulse that, with so much unexplained and no time to lose, dead would be tidiest.

There were two of them slumped up against the forward bulkhead, right where Sally Sherman had died. One man and one boy – explaining the woman's voice. They might or might not be dead; they were damaged beyond any need for him to kill them.

He threw open the right-hand forward passenger escape, and the water lapped over the sill of the hatch.

The plane was riding high, but that lap of water was comforting. It had to sink.

He opened the boarding door. The weather was making against that side, and the sea splashed in more strongly. One of the squatters stirred, flapping an arm as a wave picked him, stirred then floundered. Matson was compassionate with his rifle-butt.

Then he realised the centre starboard escape was open.

He was weak from blood-loss, or weak from something. He lunged down the slope of the passenger aisle as far as the middle bulkhead. The water wasn't spilling in there yet. The door had been torn off. It had simply disappeared – presumably on impact.

The aircraft was clearly about to sink.

The whole sea to starboard was bobbing with rafts, six yellow, one red, with others inflating.

He daren't risk there being a survivor somewhere with hysterical news to sell.

He levelled the Kalashnikov and fired from the shoulder, starting with the flight-crew boat, the red, shooting till the firing block thumped back empty.

The rafts sank slowly, or at least began to contour the water line, all except the near one. The near one was yards too far.

By this time the wing was awash. He jumped into the sea.

Getting aboard the float was the trouble, but he managed in the end. It was as comfortable as his Old Mum's bathtub and nearly as full of water.

It was all of ten minutes before the Trident disappeared. It had behaved really well. Its escapes had all functioned. Even the water in the float was the wet he'd brought with him.

He basked for a time, slept for no more than a minute, then woke to feel his raft bumping something.

It was another raft, presumably from the other side of the aircraft. He gazed all about. He saw no others.

He noticed the bullet hole in the top, the partially collapsed freeboard of plastic. This must be one he had fired on after all. Then he saw the red splash-marks and lifted his head a little further.

She recognised him with hope if not affection. His bullets had made an incredible mess. There was abdominal slime on the plastic, green among splintered bone. The flotation coil had only one puncture but was collapsing slowly.

There were two of them: an Arab lad he didn't recognise, perhaps another cleaner, and Curly Ingram. He strained to push the float away.

The girl opened her eyes again and looked at him. She had taken it all in body shots. If she'd ever had a gun it was in the aeroplane somewhere.

She tried to tell him something. She couldn't shape the words. Her syllables had no end and no beginning.

He asked her why she hadn't come forward during the flight, then began to explain that he wished he had known he was shooting at her, that he was only firing to deflate the raft, and that if only he had known she was in it he would have done it anyway, but with accurate relish.

She was already closing her mind to him and dragging under. Her hair was still curly. He was good at killing boys and women.

Then a wave unwrapped and he saw the boat. He supposed it was the same one.

A single waterline bullet hole. Nuseibeh's ridiculous dagger had to be good for something. He enlarged the hole. He knew now why Anwar was dead and why the little Arabs were dead, and why a lot more people were going to be dead. He knew it as surely as he knew why Curly was dead at this time. It was because he'd passed up the chance to kill her three days ago, properly, when he was a man.

FOURTEEN

1.

CAC was tremulous with imminent session. The Action Men had spread out plastic map-cases and huge files of teleprinted, phone-linked and faxed messages that traced back the Ministry of Defence's computer involvement to a distant point in history, perhaps as long ago as yesterday so awesome was the weight of printout. The Action Women had done the same. Now they sat sweet and still, faces serene as varnished dog-biscuits, and greeted one another with lumographed smiles and horrendous intercostal consonants.

Quinlan was attempting to get his mouth in front of his jowls while listening to Lorna and Hattie and another Principal who between them earned more than the entire Inner Cabinet.

'He's funked doing business with the Israelis,' Pomeroy said. 'You can see it all over his frog.'

Dixon sulked.

Fossit laid his hands, which were clean, on his agenda, which was cleaner.

Pomeroy had lined himself up three – no four – cups of coffee:

'When old Spotty Chops convenes his committees for ten in the morning, you know where he's tending? You see what all this is paving the way towards? He's going to hand over to the Yanks. All-night sittings and pos beneath the table'll be next in the rule book.'

Fossit thought he heard 'Snotty Chops'. He didn't like that

sort of thing, as he thought he'd made clear, still less the rest of it.

He was about to make himself clear again, when Quinlan reached his chair. He owled at Fossit. 'There's a phone growing cold in Hattie's office,' he said. 'It's for you and supposedly more urgent even than this.'

Fossit went out and he added, 'I don't like phones, not in committee time, not in private rooms. If your wife's having babies give her our love and tell her to put them back again.'

Magnanimous bad taste settled over everything like Pomeroy's famous dust. His blotting pad voice could be heard explaining: 'Both parties elect them now.'

Dixon said, 'I don't think Leonard is married, Minister.'

'A joke,' Quinlan muttered. 'It was a joke.' It wasn't, so he added, 'He must be married. He lives in Surbiton.'

This was incomprehensible enough to be rewarded with a laugh – an English phenomenon that does not translate.

Quinlan beamed. He called the meeting together with a scrape and a thump.

2.

He was interrupted by the door banging open, and a muttering outside. A very young woman was propelled in – too young for anyone present to acknowledge. She 'blushed white', as Pomeroy called it, because Quinlan's scowl blotted her previous blush to the bone. She pressed ahead, ignoring Quinlan, and walked with chilly-looking knees up to Lorna. She began to whisper.

Lorna leant forward and conveyed her whisper to Quinlan.

'You let the ladies in,' Pomeroy explained, 'and you get drama out of a burnt sausage.'

Quinlan slapped his hand down and said, 'Apparently we've got the Libyan Queen on the cube. It's early for him, so we'll take him live – he's coming by satellite or wire or –'

Lorna and Hattie did not allow the new girl to do anything as exalted as approach the committee-room display link, but here, in his little box, stood Philactery Pete once again, remarkably free of interference.

Libyan State Television had kitted him out in the uniform of an Air Force colonel, as befitted the gravity of what was clearly a portentous occasion. His medals were many, but liberally awarded by the property wardrobe; for among them, doing well on the largely yellow screen, was the unmistakeable purple of a British VC.

He was reading from his usual clip-board, at the counter-tenor and click end of his register, so Pomeroy downed a quick cognac soup and began to translate:

'The Libyan People is about to declare War upon a nation or nations to be named. It will declare War within the next hour upon a number of its enemies. These countries, all of them members of the U.S. hegemony – and not necessarily excluding the United States of America itself – may expect the justice they deserve at the hands of the Libyan People. The Libyan People intend to punish them. They should be warned. The Ruling Committee of the Central Congress of the Libyan People is now in session. Its decision will be known immediately.

'Friends and Allies of the Libyan People will be shocked to learn that a powerful and well-equipped military raiding party has infringed the rights of the Libyan People by violating Libyan territorial frontiers and launching an unprovoked and murderous assault without warning upon the Freedom Fighters at Sifr WaaHid. These Freedom Fighters enjoy the protection of the Army of the Libyan People. The attack was consequently repulsed, with heavy casualties.

'My God,' Barkworth muttered, 'the Izzies have beaten us to the punch. They've done as Pomeroy said they would, and they've cocked the whole thing up.'

'If the raiding party's intention was to abduct the passengers of the two aircraft brought to Sifr WaaHid by the Freedom Fighters, then it was unsuccessful in this attempt. The passengers of the two aircraft are at present the guests of the Libyan People. They enjoy the hospitality of the Libyan People. This means that they too may expect the protection of the Army of the Libyan People. Our Army is always victorious. Our Army will never experience defeat. Our Army will punish the enemies of the Libyan People, if the committees and congresses of the Revolution shortly so decree.'

Philactery Pete came to attention in a jingle of international medals, and placed his clipboard under his arm. He saluted. The cube began to play the Libyan national anthem.

'So what does this mean?' Quinlan demanded. 'Have the Israelis really jumped the gun?'

'It means that a soldier has shot himself through the foot with an empty carbine,' Pomeroy explained. 'That at the most. You know the way these hot-weather hominids tend to exaggerate.'

Fossit came back in. '*Our man's broken out*!' he blurted, quite out of turn and regardless of protocol. Some news is like that. 'Matson has broken out.'

'That's what it means.' Pomeroy congratulated himself aloud. 'Matson's shot the Sahara in the foot.'

3.

The strings of action were with NATO, but the risk was to human beings. If Matson seriously believed there were a number of atomic devices about to be hurried to unknown destinations across Mediterranean airspace, his first priority on being lugged ashore at Syracuse should have been to contact the Yanks or even the Italians, and his second to shout a warning to as many human beings as possible.

Matson's world was growing short of human beings. He had just killed eight of them. In any event, duty did not work like that. Humanity might be saved, but Matson would have been out of a job. He cobbled up a code that might evade computer recall for an hour, but would not fool a halfwit in a listening post for more than a minute, and dialled Fossit direct on an open line.

He had to wait in his phone-box while Miss Dalrymple negotiated with half the exchanges in Italy to reverse the charges. He had just bought himself an inexhaustible supply of change with Anwar's money and Captain Finch's money and the Tan's money, and had them convert it in his madness to telephone-sized coins in a cambio, so she was wasting everyone's time.

Eventually she traced Fossit as far as Quinlan.

4.

The man with the plastic shower-coat and the rolled *La Stampa* came across the square in a rapid saunter and sat hard against him.

'Matson?'

He was too European. Americans look that way after a long dunking in the alternative culture.

'My colonel wants to see you. You spoke to Leonard Fossit in London, right?'

'And you all listened in?'

'No. Mr Quinlan called direct. Seem a likely scenario? I've got a gun on you if it doesn't.'

'You could take me with your wet newspaper right now.'

'The hijack's still the lead story. We don't hop a car. We walk three blocks by the side alley. I haven't brought an umbrella. This is only the water-cart.'

The rain was falling quite steadily from a high white sky. Matson decided that he wasn't the only one who was mad – unless they had tall water-carts.

Matson could scarcely keep up with the plastic mack, so the gun was merely rhetoric. They elbowed through throngs of people, who held Matson back. He could not bear to be jostled.

The building was brand new, with an antique bas-relief of Apollo indecently renovated. A brass plate promised the U.S. consulate on the third floor. *La Stampa* finished melting into *papier-mâché* as they steamed up in the lift.

Salt water and now rain had not improved the Libyan crotch. Nor had the foetid blood.

They had to ring a bell to be released from the lift. They were disgorged into a high, roofed cage of gilt metal lattice. The lattice was surrounded by deep carpet and three walls panelled in bleached sycamore or some similar expensive coffin-wood.

A redcap G.I. unlatched the cage and took a hygienic hold on the *papier-mâché*. He pointed towards a small grill in the facing wall. The grill was about a foot square and guarded as if it were a rare and expensive painting by two Italian civil police with white belts, truncheons and sub-machine-guns.

The redcap identified the plastic mack at the grill. This caused the opening of a section of panels about as wide as two coffins. This was bandit country. If you wanted a U.S. visa, your business was done at the grill.

Inside, there was the usual bureaucratic mausoleum. Everything was numbingly modern: white slatted blinds being cruel with the sunlight, an oatmeal-carpeted floor, black and grey surfaces, lots of very new tubular steel.

Several people surrounded Matson. He could have been surrounded by one. He was handed an effervescent glass which tasted largely of vitamin C. Then he was given a beaker of lukewarm black coffee – presumably so as not to waste the world's time – and one slug of Scotch. The effervescence nearly blew everything back up again. He hoped he didn't feel sick for any more prosaic reason, such as good old-fashioned inability to cope.

They were looking at him. One of them said, 'An Irishman, Mr Matson? Come – you speak with a London accent.'

'To American ears, perhaps.' Matson hadn't spoken at all.

'To trained ears.'

'Maybe. To English ears, even. No Irishman would think I speak with a London accent. Nor, for that matter, would a Londoner.'

There was a long silence.

Matson said, 'Where's the bloody colonel?'

A tall man said, 'I'm Grant. You'll do.' They were all tall. They all wore civilian suits. This one had a bright face, as if he had been at sea in the sun, or had obsessive shaver's acne. He shook Matson's hand and said, 'We'll talk when I've spoken to Washington. In here, please.' He opened a door, or someone opened a door.

Colonel Grant helped him quickly towards it.

5.

'What for?'

'Ten minutes with the doc. Sorry – eight minutes with the doc.'

The doctor was old for an American, old for anyone connected with the U.S. Forces, anyway. He was pink cheeked and his thick white hair gave off the faintest suggestion of a blue rinse – or perhaps the white caught the hue of his suit, which was petrol-coloured giant cord, the way white will. He might have been Embassy rather than military, of course. He said, 'Undo the front of your tunic, please, Mr Matson.'

'No, thanks.' That was the first step.

'Very well. I've got one of those electronic collars for your blood-pressure. Got any objection to slipping out of that tunic? Or I can just about manage with your tunic on.'

They managed with his tunic on. The doctor didn't wrinkle his nose at Matson's smell. Matson watched the light come on for systolic and again for diastolic, and heard the fast rhythmic buzz in between, but his eyes refused to focus on the gauge.

'Blood pressure a trifle low. Your interval is poor. Your pulse is fast, too. Can you read English?'

In Scotland, before a man was hanged, the law required he be asked his name. Speaking it always made him dissolve in tears.

'For instance, can you read the label on this bottle?'

'Two,' Matson faltered.

'Two capsules, right. That's for any pain. They won't junk your mind, or not worse than it's junked already. You don't need me to tell you you're in shock. I don't mean physical shock, in the usual clinical sense. I mean battle-ground trauma. I've seen a lot of that.'

Matson did something inarticulate with his lower jaw. Kindness he couldn't cope with. If it were business as usual, with people like the colonel or Dragout, he could cope. Kindness was like strychnine.

The doctor was holding out another bottle.

'Three,' Matson read, before realising he wasn't being tested this time.

'Three will bring eight hours' sleep. Take only one if you're using alcohol.' The doctor shuddered at the thought. 'I suspect you've got a powerful motivation towards life? A strong current responsibility, anyway, from all I hear of your circumstance?'

Matson agreed, his jaw still numb.

'Many more than three would kill you. Three with alcohol just might. Dilates the capillaries in the brain, you see.'

Matson was marooned among his low blood-pressure and his dilated capillaries when the door opened.

'Eight minutes, Matson.'

It was the colonel again. Enter a bleeding sergeant.

6.

'What now?'

'Five minutes with Nurse Willoughby.'

Nurse Willoughby was waiting for him in a bathroom full of steam. A shower-room, actually. Nurse Willoughby did not steam. She behaved as if most of her body simply did not exist, and as if what did exist had been washed in distilled water a thousand years ago, then shut in a cool drawer lined with lavender and pages torn from the Bible. Her smell was restful and old-fashioned. Close to, she gave off a slight aroma of wood-alcohol, as if she sipped early morning vodka with the doctor. Psychiatric nurses have to behave that way, and some women can look like psychiatric nurses even when they're twenty-one – American and Swedish women particularly. Nurse Willoughby was beautiful and all-American. She was going to do a bath for him, but not scrub his back. She was not going to touch his body or even notice he had one. She was not even going to touch or notice the body he did not have, either, or remark upon anything he did not have. She had seen agents come in from the far side of the field, had Nurse Willoughby, so she washed him and got some white cream onto his back, and covered his chest and shoulders with a free-hanging tabard of lint. Then she found him a shirt, a loose summer jacket, some underpants, some socks, some trousers, some used shoes, and a tie so he would feel American and decent. Nurse Willoughby did not know what nice American standard suiting he had left in the desert, nor what else he had left. She was trained not to touch. She was trained not to ask. That was beautiful. All of Matson's Irish aunts had been like Nurse Willoughby, and they were not American or Swedish.

One thing bothered Matson. Just before his five minutes with Nurse Willoughby were up he noticed she had breasts he was unable to register, a teeny backside that was continuing to escape his attention, and really wonderful eyes he could not bear to look into. Of course it would have been no more than rhetoric, because God and Colonel Grant had refused him the time, but it came as a terrible shock to realise he had not asked her out to dinner, not just for now but for ever.

7.

Nurse Willoughby's shoes did not quite fit him, but her underpants did and were suitably hygienic. He watched Colonel Grant study him, aided by the man who no longer had his plastic mack – presumably because it was being dry-cleaned by Nurse Willoughby.

Plastic Mack did not smile. He either spoke or he laughed. He did a lot of both. He was the kind of man who uses laughter as a punctuation mark. Matson preferred longer sentences.

Grant's acne brimmed over with lava. 'Better take that pill, Matson.'

Matson blushed or whatever it is schoolgirls do when they're unlucky enough not to be camouflaged in spots, and took his pill. One only. He remembered the whisky. He realised that he had not bothered to remember or even find out Plastic's name, or taken in a single word he had said.

Bad sign. Good pill.

Grant tapped Matson on the knee and stood up. Matson stood up, and Plastic left the room.

Grant said, 'Don't sit down again. We haven't time. We're taping this. Your people insisted you be told. I don't know why. Paul will listen in on the circuit.'

'I always assume there's a bug somewhere.' His lot were used to it. Even CAC was bugged – allegedly so Quinlan's or the PM's speechwriters could crib Pomeroy.

Grant was peering at him oddly again. His brain was still taking little rambles in the elsewhere and otherwise.

'We've only got time for two questions from my people.

The tape will go to your people as well.'

'Virginia?'

'Pentagon. Question One. Fossit understood you to mean that all four aircraft were being turned into thermonuclear devices – on what evidence?'

'My interrogator boasted he was going to destroy a U.S. West Coast city, as well as Israel and Berlin. And somewhere else he couldn't be bothered to remember. My rescuer, Ibrahim Nuseibeh, told me of the atomic plan itself; and identified the same targets.'

'You believed him?'

'I believe he believed himself.'

'So you ditched the aircraft. Question Two. The details of your actual escape.'

The Colonel listened and said, 'The first bit is very low grade –' he flushed – 'sorry, but it's not a story that really rings true, is it?'

'The substance makes sense: it's only the setting that's bizarre. The substance is that Nuseibeh wants to come and go in the West. Facts are his ticket. I believe him. I'll also believe that he found the story too big to sit on. After all, if the plot went ahead, and the world leapt to some likely conclusions, there might be no West to return to.'

'I won't follow up. It's a thought for your debriefing. Tell me about your hijacking that plane again.'

Again Grant listened closely, this time with his eyes shut. With them still shut, he said, 'There's another conclusion, and it goes with that bizarre setting you insist on. The fag stuff and the cards and the dice. The compound lights were switched off not because you were being caught out, but to aid your escape.'

'I was already on the plane, and about to go airborne.'

'Nobody knew that. Your first conclusion is the logical one, but not the only one. This Nuseibeh could have arranged for more than he told you. Unfortunately he was *hors de combat*. Once you got going you didn't hang about. So you could have been well ahead of schedule.'

Grant opened his eyes and said to the ceiling: 'Your thought about the searchlight carbon was the natural one, given your premise about the dowsing of the perimeter lights. If the alternative thesis is correct – and I'm merely advancing it, not pressing it – then it was exposed to serve exactly the purpose it did serve. To be the pilot's marker beacon. A gun is a terrible object, Captain Matson, as you well know, especially when it's being pointed at you by a man already high on killing, smeared with blood and half out of his cranium. Even so, there are plenty of Civil Airline captains – *and* combat fliers – who would have been too damned scared to roll that aircraft in the dark even if a madman *was* holding a howitzer in their ear. Part of me wishes you hadn't killed that Captain Anwar. It would be nice to have been able to coax him into admitting he was expecting that light to shine.'

8.

A minute intervened, a minute when nothing was said and nothing happened, so that the minute stretched a little and perhaps grew a second or two more. Perhaps it even cloned. Matson began to whistle. He whistled because he couldn't smile. Matson's whistle was never his strong point, even when it was fit and well. When it was fit and well, Matson never had any occasion to use it. He wasn't a bricky or a milkman. Now he filled his lengthening minute with it, and American people tiptoed out because of it then tiptoed in to reassure themselves it was still there.

Not Colonel Grant. Grant tiptoed out, truly, and Matson wished he could stop whistling and smile at Colonel Grant and at all the rest of them, because he and they were all of the same kind. They were Americans, it is true, and he was Camberwell Irish. But then most Americans are Irish, and the United States is just a cleaner Ireland that works properly and runs on time. The United States of America hasn't had a Camberwell since it landscaped the Bronx Zoo. Just the same, he wished he could smile instead of whistle.

No, Colonel Grant didn't tiptoe back. He strode back. 'We want you back in the shower-room,' he said curtly. 'That uniform of yours –'

'Gingivitis of the crotch, I'm afraid.'

'It's radioactive.'

'Aren't you going over the top a bit?'

'I'm not speaking of fume. I'm talking fall-out. Radioactive means becquerels, roentgens and mini-sieberts. We don't use metaphor where I come from. We prefer soap.'

Nurse Willoughby did it to him again, only this time it was in a shower not a tub, and the water-drops hurt.

It was also a humiliation, and one he could scarcely stand. Plastic Paul divested him of his clothes, but under running water, in a further delirium of pain and confusion. Then the man and the clothes had to wait in the shower with him, so there was nothing coy this time.

Nurse Willoughby, fully dressed as she was, knelt in the shower-spray as well, as if this was a fine hill rain that was falling, and as if her top wasn't transparent and her skirt seaweeded to her thighs, and Plastic Mack's hitherto reclusive dinkle growing recalcitrant at her ear.

Matson had been feeling a trifle doggy about the walrus for several days now, but his aspirations became no more than a lump in the throat as Nurse Willoughby siezed him in imperious fingers and began to shave his pubic hair with a discardable razor.

'And the armpits,' Grant enjoined her, nodding in on this convocation of naked cherries. 'Clippers'll do round the ears.'

They found Matson another suit.

'It wasn't much,' the Colonel said, when his blushes were zipped up tight. 'But you picked up some radioactive detritus somewhere – too much for your friends to let you pack it around your gonads. I must say it puts a few hairs on the chest of that story of yours.'

Nurse Willoughby had changed into an army blouse, slacks and wet hair. She looked alarmed at the Colonel's mention of chest hairs, but Grant said, 'Don't worry, Willow. You didn't miss anything. Ginger nuts means peachy skin, my mother always said.' He turned to consider Matson again. 'It's a bit soon, I know. But do you reckon you're up to getting on another airplane?'

'Providing I don't have to kill the pilot.'

9.

'Good. Then we'll jet you off to London.'

'There's no time for that.'

'If your story is correct – don't misunderstand me, I mean: assuming you weren't accidentally or deliberately misinformed – then we think the devices may take some time to instal. It's our best guess – five minutes' talking to the Pentagon, a couple more with London who had already spoken to Harwell – it's our best guess they'll have to build the things in there. The principles are simple, but they won't want the components falling apart – still less coming together – while they're on the International Airport in Tripoli or overflying Benghazi. The brains are all gathered in London and – as usual – they're deeply planted in their backsides. You're just a random intelligence factor, Matson, so we're jetting you home.

'Another wasted day?'

'Two and a half hours. We're going to beam you off to a fleet Fl-11 – say twenty minutes in a Huey from here to the floating flat-top. Two hours from there to RAF Northolt. I'll expect they'll manage to whirlifly you somewhere close to Whitehall. If they send a black cab or ask you to take the tube – *then* you'll know we don't believe you.'

10.

Some people enjoy killing. Matson did not. To shoot a partridge made him feel bad – not bad enough to leave it uneaten, but bad. Killing people left him ill. Never at once, but as soon as he came down from the high or lifted himself from the low that went with it.

Sometimes he killed with an exultation that was sexual. It was never good to remember, and when sex brought the same joy he regretted that as well. If he saw the woman in his arms as his victim, even for a second, then she activated his other victims. She became one of them. She became all of them.

There was a list, a number. He knew their facts if not

always their faces. They were all there to diminish him – those he had killed in fear, those he had killed in anger, those he had wrecked out of lust. Sometimes the fear, the anger and then the lust had come together – it made no difference. They were all the emotions of doubt, and doubt was what death always left him with.

He had been frightened on the Trident, angry for revenge against the people who had put him there, and when the bullet had punched home in the Tan with no balancing damage to himself he had gloated. He knew what the Bible meant when it spoke of saying 'Ha! Ha!' among the trumpets. It spoke of the madness of battle, the sinister glitter.

But he had no choice. He had bitten his way out of the box. It did no good to remember that Nuseibeh had provided him with the teeth, just the same.

And less good again to know his actions were even now being evaluated, and perhaps blamed as excessive. The doubts that torture induces were enough to bear. Now Grant had introduced another doubt – the idea that his story was all a fiction. It did no good to remind himself that he had been suspicious of everything that had happened in Libya. The fact was that he had killed Anwar and three innocent Arabs, and written off a Trident on the assumption that the story was true. Killing the Tan and Curly and perhaps the Düsseldorf Tart, not to mention the first guard, did not balance this out. He was chauvinistic enough to remind himself that three of the four were women. Neither his Old Mum nor the Holy Mother would forgive him that fact. The Big Fisherman would not let him home through the gates.

Grant had dealt him another doubt in the shower: 'I've been thinking about that woman. If she was half of what you said, she'd have come forward to blast you – or blast Anwar once the plane started up. I'm not even counting her hearing your shot.'

'Perhaps all she wanted was out. Just like me.'

'*Unless she was there to activate a bomb they were counting on you to deliver.*'

All this lasted him to London. They did send a black cab, but only to run him from the heliport across the river to Whitehall.

FIFTEEN

1.

The problem was too big or too small. Or there was no problem at all. Either the Sahara was wall to wall with thermo-nuclear devices, or one of Her Majesty's trusted and trustworthy employees was lying or hallucinating or preferably plain mad. The committee was impatient for Matson's arrival at its feet. It had a question to ask him: how far was he still in charge of his mind?

Hattie Dacres had been talking to Harwell. She was a scientist herself, but she had been instructed to ask the experts. As a result she had an impressive supply of fourth-form information.

She read aloud from her notes: ' "All that is required is to bring a slightly less than critical mass of fissionable material close to another almost critical mass of fissionable material, and the Bomb is an instantaneous and irredeemable event. Where better to achieve such a triggering of chain-reaction than inside the crumpling fuselage of a crashing aircraft?

' "Building nuclear devices is relatively simple. It is constructing a device compact enough for conventional delivery and sufficiently unvolatile to be safely handled and stored that presents the problems. The baggage holds of an aircraft, utilised together or even separately, would offer an excellent short-term solution to all the major hazards. The aircraft itself would provide an almost perfect delivery vehicle – it would have a substantial range, it would be impossible to detect, and – unlike an ICBM – it would not risk compromising the criticality of its fissionable material at the moment of launch." '

'Go back to the beginning of things,' Dixon interposed. 'The so-called hydrogen bomb was a pretty crude device. Yet it was a hundred times – or do I mean to-the-power-of-a hundred times? – more powerful than the Hiroshima bomb. We could be up against something quite frightful here. It's a brilliant concept.'

Mouths became a little more dry.

Ralph Dixon wasn't done yet. 'Suppose these people go for a "dirty bomb"? Why shouldn't they? We don't know what they're after. They probably can't formulate it themselves.'

Dixon had everyone's attention now.

'They could explode it over, say, Jerusalem. Or set it down at Ben Gurion – even though that's miles nearer the coast. With a little bit of cobalt they could render all of historical Palestine, and therefore all of Israel, all of Jordan and quite a lot of Lebanon uninhabitable for the next twelve hundred years.' He looked at Hattie Dacres. 'I think it's twelve hundred years. No-one'll lay claim to those places then, and not too many people'll be around to, either. The UN won't have to rehouse any Palestinians, that's for certain.' Again a glance at the Dacres. 'I'm speaking a bit off the top of my lid, as you know. I mean, it might be twelve thousand. Enough to see even your Government out, Minister.'

'Did someone say terrorism was street-theatre?' Barkworth asked. 'We're talking about a damn wide street.'

'It might be worth asking who the audience is meant to be,' Fisher put in. Everyone was going to put something in, as the voice took him. 'I don't see dropping a bomb where friend dies as well as foe!'

'Good point,' Pomeroy said.

It was like a Quaker meeting. The moment was so awesome that God would have his say all round the table, and not even Quinlan would stop Him.

'Group-captain Fisher is making the rational point,' Fossit said. 'I'd like to hear it developed. If we can define the spectator – the onlooker to whom all of this is addressed – then we can determine the scale of the outrage in terms of being precise about the target and the likely yield of the bomb. We can also cut some of our hysteria down to size.' Fossit put his reading glasses on, to blur Dixon's face a little. He didn't like being rude to a friend.

Dixon took the point. 'I thought there were fundamentalists who would welcome the chance to kill themselves and send a million friends to Heaven if only they could drop ten million foes in the other place. What is the population of Israel, by the way?'

'Three point seven million in nineteen seventy-eight,' Pomeroy said. 'Foes or imperfect believers,' he corrected. 'I must say that the Fisher-Fossit point is excellently taken, but probably irrelevant, Minister. There's more than one kind of Moslem who would be happy to kill other Moslems if only enough Jews – or Americans for that matter – were included in the option. Let us take some of Ralph's points again, *if* Ms Dacres has concluded her chemistry lesson?'

Miss Dacres had.

'You remember, for example, when the hydrogen bomb was first thought of, it was concluded that it could only be delivered in the hold of a ship? I bet Gadaffi has dreamt of delivering a bomb to Israel in the hold of a ship.'

'They'd intercept it.'

'Indeed they would. His problem would be how to get a bus-sized bomb – and a *crude* device would have to be that big – onto a ship innocent-looking enough to be allowed to sail to within a mile or fifty of Tel Aviv. Gadaffi's thought about it, just the same. We know, because he's asked questions about it. Everyone – wise man and fool alike, disinterested scientist and rogue boffin – has told him it can't be done.'

'So?'

'You could put a hydrogen bomb in an airliner, as we've just heard, and still leave room for the passengers.'

'You couldn't drop it, though.' Fisher argued.

'You wouldn't need to. You could land it.'

'The Israelis don't accept hijacks.'

'They don't stop hijacks overflying their airspace.'

'You mean –'

'The passengers were always expendable in this game. So were the hijackers. A hijacked plane is your perfect innocent vessel. While it is on the ground in the rogue country, and the rogue host is pretending to parley with the hijackers, he can prune around with the load to his heart's content. When it takes off, he can even play cush shots. He can land it in the Lebanon first, or among some other friendly or even neutral Arabs. It would depend on who the hijackers were alleged to be – to that extent I'll go along with the group-captain. The temporary host or hosts wouldn't need to know what load was being carried. Nor would the hijackers, or not necessarily. There could even be time for diplomacy. Embassy officials here, honest brokers there, a limited release of hostages, women and pewling babes go free, a volunteer change of crew – it all enhances the verisimilitude until it is over Israeli airspace. Then – *pow*!'

Pomeroys do not say '*pow*!' but this one did, *and* banged the table.

Quinlan had been summoned from the room by now. He left with Hattie Dacres and Lorna Benvenista to help him think.

'He steals their cigarettes,' Pomeroy stated. 'Night or Matson must come.'

2.

They were waiting by Reception, ready to pounce: two women in designer suits, one of heightened charcoal, one of lowered purple. Their ages were ranged around thirty-five in a nice tight straddle, if not quite a four-inch group. Matson had not seen them before. They must be recently eminent.

The older one, prim in her purple, said, 'Captain Matson, I'm Lorna Benvenista. This is Hattie Dacres.'

The younger said, 'CAC's already begun.' She spoke as if he ought to be ashamed of himself for arriving late. 'The minister wants you to go before full committee at once and deliver a verbal summary.'

'You're to wear this,' the purple one put in. 'It's from Terence's personal drawer.' She held out a paisley tie, and showed him all of her front teeth, which were designer as well. 'He says the Yanks'll never kit a fellow out in a decent tie.'

He took it obediently and knotted it round his neck. 'Their

taste is gentler,' he said, defending his recent hosts. The fluttering vulgarity of the pattern reminded him of the murdered woman's dress, blood-smeared beneath the Jumbo in Cyrenaica.

'Five minutes maximum,' Charcoal Hattie said. 'The verbal, I mean.'

'Don't you mean oral?'

'I mean verbal.'

'Not in semaphore then?'

3.

Matson was appalled at the number and variety of new faces CAC had co-opted. He felt especially bad about the people in uniform, as if he'd let them down somehow.

Ralph Dixon, halfway down the room and sitting next to some lout from Special Branch, rewarded him with a magnificently irreverent thumbs-up. Ralph would have done the same for Lazarus.

'Ssh!' Somebody said, to somebody. It was Lorna Benvenista and Hattie Dacres. A white light flickered from behind Matson's backside, as if the archangel had lost his way.

'Step aside, Captain Matson. Sorry to interrupt you.' Quinlan taking charge at last.

He stepped aside and saw he'd been warming his arse in front of the relay screen. A gruff voice was spouting in Arabic.

Matson was fed up with Arabic and gruff. Pomeroy translated for them. Apparently the Charcoal and Purple Principals were in charge of these tablets of stone. Pomeroy merely lugged them down the mountain.

'Philactery Pete isn't going to say this in English,' Pomeroy explained, 'in case ourselves and the U.S. achieve meltdown as a result. This news is restricted to Islam.'

Libya was not yet ready to commit itself to a declaration of war on an unspecified number of Western powers, Pomeroy explained. The damage caused by the infringement of its territorial integrity was not, of itself, sufficient cause for such an act of retribution.

Pomeroy also explained, for Matson's benefit, that the

armed incursion against Libyan bases had been Matson's doing, and no-one else's.

This was fine and dandy for the chucklers round the table, all of them friendly and welcoming, but it did nothing to return Matson to reality. It was bad enough to bear unbelievable tidings, and see them swept aside in committee procedure, then hidden behind a television screen. This further instalment of fantasy unhinged him completely. A sane man knows where truth comes in the pecking list. It comes last. Matson was no longer quite sane.

'Well, Captain Matson?' Quinlan was asking for his story. First he applauded. They all applauded. They applauded him as if he was an ice-dancer or an opera star. 'Your report, please.'

Matson told them. Feeling like this, and in full committee, it was surprising how trivial it all seemed.

Unless someone chose to believe it, of course.

CAC probably did believe it, but was uncomfortable that Matson did not believe himself. The Intelligence people would fork him later, no doubt. The Forces, particularly the Funny Forces, wanted to fork him now. Barkworth said, 'What's this Hollow Furnace?'

'I've no idea what you're talking about.'

'Hollow furnace, finnies, finis, fernies, Hullo Fur Knees – you've heard no silly stuff like that? The best we've come up with is Holofernes – and that was Mr Pomeroy's suggestion,' Barkworth said grudgingly.

'No.'

'Not from Nuseibeh or this Dragout fella?' Barkworth found no answering glint in Matson's eye, so he relinquished it. 'Damn. Bang goes half our thesis. The escape may have been a set-up, as you and Grant suggest. But it doesn't look as if you were fixed to bring a message back.'

'I think you underestimate the opposition,' Matson countered. 'Who brought you this fragment – what is it, anyway: a code-word?'

'Cyprus and Tel Aviv,' Pomeroy said.

' "Holofernes" suggests Dragout,' Matson muttered. 'Both in style and context. Presumably you didn't have "Dragout" till I arrived?'

'Of course!' Pomeroy clapped his bald spot delightedly.

'Both words come from the same poem,' Matson went on. 'Holofernes kills Dragout – isn't that the way of it? I'm sorry,' he said to Barkworth. 'I still think we're dealing in bluff.'

'I'm not sure you're in the best state of mind to judge that.'

'True. Cyprus. Myself. Tel Aviv. My old Irish mum used to say if you want to sell a lie to three people, tell them each a different one. But if they're friends with one another, feed them different bits of the same lie.'

' "Your old Irish mum"?' Quinlan was rebuking him.

'My old Irish grandmum actually,' he lied.

'Indeed. The fact is that the news you bring us fits all of the known components. And those components aren't usual for a hijack. Check them with Mr Dixon.'

Matson's desert doubt came tumbling in again. 'The fact I haven't yet offered – the moderately expert opinion, anyway' – he'd had plenty of time in the F1-11 to remind himself of this one – 'the fact is I wasn't interrogated out there, even though I was held by professionals who knew what I was. I was merely ill-used and softened up.'

Quinlan looked at him as if it was his brain that was softened. They all did.

Pomeroy, Fossit and Dixon led him very gently outside.

4.

They went up a floor, then crunched among renovations to Pomeroy's own room. An elegant young man was waiting.

Pomeroy sent this lily out to buy sandwiches, then dug in his cabinet for the visitors' bottle of Martell. He handed Matson the first glass and said, 'I hear you've been chief bride in the Black Sheikh's harem. I hope it was a mosquito did that to your neck, Paddy.'

Ralph Dixon smiled and said, 'It's no good your sitting there as silent as a South London H. Thump. Tell us the worst.'

Matson sniffed the brandy. His life was all brandy. He wanted those sandwiches, then he could start to suffer. 'You are not,' he said, 'going to waste valuable hours debriefing me.'

'No time,' Fossit agreed. 'We've got to get the picture, that's all. Even the frame would help.'

'Some little sod stuck one of those Idaho tyre-levers up my arse, if that's what you mean.'

'Let's hope you don't get diverticulitis, then.'

'Who was your interrogator? Sounds a bit of a rum cove,' Pomeroy said. 'Still there's a lot of that sort of thing in the south.'

Matson described him. 'He might as well have called himself Barbarossa or Suleiman the Red for all the difference it made.'

'Except, of course, he was black.' Pomeroy did his hyper-genius act with his eyebrows. 'Well, I've unearthed the fellow, I promise you. Salted away among the herring-boxes of my amazing intelligence I have discovered the very man. I shall cook him for you; then you shall eat him, Patrick.'

The sandwiches came in, and some polystyrene coffee.

Dixon sat forward, 'My interest is this end, Thump. The *modus operandi* of the actual hijack. We've taken evidence from Captain Lyall and from the bleeding Sergeant Mulhearn, of course.'

'I'll read the notes and let you know if anything strikes me.'

'Tell me about the hijackers.'

'Several of them had English – American really – perhaps as a first language. I've already stitched three of them – well, four – but all by bloody accident!'

'You were magnificent, Thump. Four would last me a life-time. They don't sound like people we know. Then they never do nowadays.'

'I wish you *had* perished, Paddy.' Pomeroy ruffled his hair, and he didn't like hands in his hair. 'We'd have had to re-invent you – and I'd certainly have done it much better.'

'I killed the bloody Tan for you. Shot the sod more by reflex,' Matson admitted. 'I lacked a decent design. Here's what I found in his pockets.' He gave Dixon the plastic pack of passes, notes and identity documents. 'Any good?'

'Why didn't the Americans take these?'

'They helped themselves to some samples, and simply photographed the rest.'

'The snaps'll look good in someone's official biography,

Thump.' Dixon took them just the same. 'Shirmin, the air-stewardess. She's our main conundrum.'

Matson dug his hand into his American suiting and took out her badge. 'There she is. Blood, bullet-mark and all.'

Fossit and Pomeroy looked at him very oddly.

Ralph was merely interested.

'His sodding little propelling pencil took this right through her,' Matson explained. 'It's a talisman.'

'It's Crown property,' Ralph Dixon said, but he handed it back. 'She had a sister who worked for the holding company.'

'I'm not just an incredibly pretty face,' Pomeroy said, inclining his head and flashing the bald patch.

'She's gone totally to earth.'

'I've seen the sister,' Matson said. 'She's a part of it. She's certainly worth following up. Did you start in Luton?'

'We started at the family home in Leeds. Family defunct. Sister decamped.'

'Look in Luton. I'll tell you how. Luton or thereabouts.' He'd dreamt of the Sally Shirmin look-alike for days. She had undoubtedly been the taxi-driver.

Pomeroy leapt up. 'We'll have to get back into CAC – I shall, anyway. Quinlan's trying to run it like a command post, instead of letting people get on with their jobs.' He indicated the Martell, the sandwiches and coffee, as if lesser men could stay for them but he had no time for such things. Just the same, he took a paper cup full of Martell and coffee with him.

Ralph said, 'You're quite right. We haven't got time to debrief you, Paddy. We can't even put you on hold or let Leonard send you back on leave. Obviously it's a worry for us – memory being as a stream, and all, full of slick and devious trout. But it'll be even more of a worry for you. You've just had a bashing, and we're sticking you back in the ring.' He took a sandwich to eat in the corridor.

He was back in a second, ostensibly for a second helping. 'Look, that sister. I take it you haven't got her actual phone number in your filofax?'

'No, it's just –'

'Thought not. I'll be in touch tomorrow. I'll happily pick people up at midnight, but I never look for them. Start poking about in the small hours and all the world knows you're on the make.'

5.

When it came to the point, CAC could do it, Fossit realised. It had been as a silted pond, blearing upwards and waiting for the first raindrop to fall. Matson was that raindrop and he had fallen. He had come crashing in with the illuminating news. So what could CAC do? CAC could dissolve itself.

'I've been talking to the Prime Minister,' Quinlan announced.

A lot had happened during Fossit's brief absence.

'The Prime Minister's view is –'

Fossit tried to clear his head. First Matson's miraculous escape with his rumour of mad atoms, and now this rumble of battle chariots, this flourish of exalted blades.

'So this committee will remain in place, but in executive abeyance,' Quinlan explained. 'I mean, Cabinet will undoubtedly have need of your counsel, but our finger will no longer be on the button. The decisions will spring jointly from Cabinet and Washington.'

'What about the Israeli dimension?' Pomeroy asked. 'It was urgent three days ago. It can hardly be less so now.'

'Washington will handle it.'

'That means the horse is already out of the stable and the Americans will pretend to whip it when and if it returns.'

'I'm briefing my meeting, if you please, Marcus.'

'Or whip its owners.'

'This committee – and I'm meeting Mr Pomeroy's point – is to be subsumed by another committee which will be co-chaired by a U.S. nominee and myself. The U.S. nominee is on the way here now. That committee will have Israeli representation, or an Israeli attendance; the status is not yet determined, and for the moment immaterial.'

'Not if it is to come to some swift conclusions,' Pomeroy insisted.

Fossit thought he was being foolhardy, but then Pomeroy was responsible for the Israeli desk.

'You're backing away from your own insistence on diplomacy, Marcus.'

'It's a bit late for diplomacy. If Matson's news is even partially correct, then now's the time for politics to make a bold incursion into event.'

There was a general howl of pleasure at this. Barkworth subsidised Pomeroy with the full weight of his grunt.

Quinlan chose to be patient. 'CAC's ideal – *my* ideal for CAC – was always to have the model plan at jiffy-quick readiness – that has been our thrust and achievement, gentlemen: a jiffy-quick plan at red plus. And then to have no need of it. If that's to be interpreted as procrastinating, so be it. I call it perfection.' He glared around the table, his eyes sore from other quarrels. 'At the minute we have this completely fresh intelligence, and therefore no plan that takes account of it.'

'Plans are a bit like soufflé,' Pomeroy mused. 'They go up. They come down. I mean, we *had* a plan. Why not use it – while those aircraft are still on the ground?'

Silence.

Fossit decided that however foolhardy Pomeroy might be, he was also magnificent.

'What's our new committee to be called, Minister?'

'TAC,' Hattie Dacres prompted.

'Tripartite Action Coordination,' Lorna Benvenista explained.

Quinlan was grateful for that. 'It, too, will be unexecutive, though it may well form the basis for our part of a tripartite command structure if Washington decides the Israelis are to play a central role.'

Fossit decided to take the heat off Pomeroy. 'What will that other tripartite body be known as, Minister?'

'TRIPE,' Pomeroy said. To Fossit he added, 'Quinny's not just dithering. He's fibbing. He's got custard all down his dicky, the old rogue.'

It was then the little American arrived. He was dressed as some kind of admiral with gold rings in abundance from under a buff raincoat. He looked jaded from his flight. He was in the business of introducing himself to the head of table, when he broke off angrily and was heard to say, 'Three days on this level of intelligence, and you've only got this far with it?'

Quinlan nodded to Hattie Dacres and she adjourned the meeting for fifteen minutes.

The little American was only beginning. As they went out, they heard him say, 'I know when to smell a rat in the Alliance drains.'

6.

Pomeroy led Fossit back to his office. He didn't lift his bottle, but his telephone. It took him ten minutes to get what he wanted.

'I thought I recognised him,' he told Fossit. 'Admiral Craw-Witts will be in what he thinks is the chair. Even though the Quimmy Quimboy will dispute with both teeth.'

Pomeroy yawned. 'He's a desk sailor, according to our transAtlantic friends and allies. The State Department don't know why we've got him and the Pentagon won't tell us. His appointment is either very good news for the future of Civilised Man, or very very dismal for the hostages. No-one wants to guess.'

'I think we can take it he'll get Terence moving?'

'I've met him,' Pomeroy went on. 'Last year. Duty trip for both of us, at the antlered home of some kilted nobleman. It wasn't a success. Shooting trip, which is not my scene, as Paddy could tell you. I missed everything, and the Craw found nothing to aim at. I must say, he impressed me. He didn't swear, and he didn't sulk. He didn't even sneer. He only spoke when it became nauseatingly necessary, like pass the salt, and it turned out he knew some very long words for a sailor. Unusual weight of meaning per syllable, too. I mean: Yankspeak is generally larded with all kinds of excess, because basically their good chaps don't believe in talking. They prefer to get on with the doing, so normally shuffle you their flatulence wallahs while they creep about at night getting the wallets frisked. The Craw is *not* a flatulence wallah, rest on it. Whether he's also a doer remains to be seen. You don't get a desk in the Pentagon without learning to creep about at night – that's for certain.'

'Who's this other U.S. admiral?' Fossit was combing

through the jottings on Pomeroy's telephone pad.

'Whose little fiche have you come up with?'

'Rear Admiral Walter G. Cravicz.'

'Dear child,' Pomeroy murmured. 'He means well. To be honest, Leonard, I greeted him in ethnic-speak myself. But the kilted nobleman assured me Craw-Witts was the norm. I thought it was a clear case of Churchillian chauvinism, or even mildew in the sporran; but our American friend really perked up when I hyphenated his handle. Besides, he is universally known as "the Craw", as I say. So our host *must* have been right.'

Leonard Fossit decided to proceed carefully namewise, just the same. 'What's his desk?' he asked.

'A Pentagon pal called it "the Nothing Office". That must mean Special Forces, mustn't it? Because none of us have any.'

The internal phone tinkled.

'Let's go and listen to some more of Terence's lies,' Pomeroy said. He detained Fossit a moment longer, just the same. 'I bet the PM's asked him not to wait for the Yanks, and that's why he's so uncomfortable with me.'

They hurried outside.

'Or the Chiefs of Staff have asked him not to wait for the Yanks. *Or*' – he was struck by sudden illumination – 'Or the Yanks have asked him not to wait for the Yanks.'

'Is that possible?'

'The Octopus has many hands, dear boy. Not all of them in its own pocket.'

7.

It wasn't so much that no-one took any notice of Matson. Far from it. It was just that no-one would tell him just what notice they took.

'You've laid your little egg. Let that be enough for you,' Pomeroy advised. 'Myself and Terence, not to mention Hattie and Lorna and all those big-bosomed land-girls in the Incubator Room, are going to hatch it for you. Birth is an ugly business for an invalid. Go home and powder your bottom.'

Fossit staggered from a meeting, held out his hand as if they were seeing each other for the first time, and said, 'You'd better get yourself some therapy and some rest, Matty. We'll muck around for another day or two perhaps. Then things'll either sort themselves out or the whole show'll move to Cyprus. The Yanks want Cyprus. So do the Israelis. I won't be wanted there. Nor will Ralph. Pomeroy's a foreigner, so he'll go. You'll be needed, if it gets down to Action Man and Lego, I daresay.'

'I'm hardly in the picture at the moment, am I?'

'Not as far as the politics go. Nor do you understand the Tripoli end. That Lorna Benvenista woman – the bag in the purple sack – she's done a marvellous digest. Quite as good as Pomeroy, but stripped of the Homeric metaphor. I'll send it round by messenger.'

8.

'Poor old Paddy.'

'Poor little sod.'

Pomeroy's office had become the local clearing house for inertia, and they watched him leave it.

'They treated him much as a chap in his position could expect to be treated.' Dixon said, only half unkindly. 'Oh, I know they threw in an extra refinement, but Arabs and expensively educated Englishmen do it all the time. Parents pay good money to have their little lads taught the trick in residential academies throughout the kingdom. I played with conkers myself till I was fourteen. I'd have been doing it now if a young house-matron hadn't turned me a friendly ear.'

'It must have been more than her ear, Dixon. You being a daddy, and all.'

Pomeroy's desk held a green telephone, among a jumble of others. But then Pomeroy's desk would, Fossit supposed. It did what it was not meant to do when people were present. It buzzed.

Pomeroy picked it up gravely, and yawned.

Barel unscrambled himself into his ear, the electronics making his voice seem shrill and alarmed.

The others crowded closer, as if Tel Aviv might hold answers to all of their questions.

Tel Aviv wanted to know about Matson's state of mind. Ministers in Jerusalem might be grateful for information received from government in London. Tel Aviv wanted an intelligence assessment Pomeroy could not give.

'Do *you* think Libya can build these bombs?' Pomeroy asked.

'Doubtless – but with what? It is a fossil-fuel economy.'

'That's our thinking. But I also have a terrible doubt, Major Barel. Call it a sceptic's fantasy. It is this. Fissionable material has already gone walk-about from several countries in Europe, and that includes war-grade plutonium. It's happened here in the UK –'

'I thought you merely suffered some temporary accounting faults.'

'You're being excessively delicate, old thing. No-one in his right mind thought that. You're simply remembering the public explanation. It's happened in West Germany. And we're countries who tell a percentage of the truth. Similarly, our painful neighbours – sweet little honestly dishonest France slimed up nuclear sites on your doorstep in Iraq –'

'We bombed them.'

'Did you count the bits?'

9.

He found himself unable to hail a taxi. They drove past him slowly, with their hire lights smiling, each one a terrible trap.

The young woman just ahead of him on the pavement was walking too slowly for both of them. Her legs were slim, pant-clad and close at the top. She was carrying a heavy case, and the weight of it glued her walk together.

He wouldn't help her with it. He felt as if his cuts would burst open or his trousers bleed if he even lifted an umbrella.

10.

The flat was as he left it, vast, underfurnished and in a tip. He daren't have a daily woman in, because of his armourer's smithy in the kitchen. If there was any chance of a nightly woman, he used to clean the place up a bit – dust the lounge, deodorise the bedroom and put Frish in the loo. In general he preferred women to invite him back with them. He needed to invade. Besides, he couldn't bear other people poking around his boxes of guns. Once a private man, always a private man. Brenda had invited herself here to live, and look what happened to her.

He muttered to himself – not a very good sign. He realised he was standing in the little hallway, exactly where Brenda had been killed. He wondered what had taken him there.

He retreated into the lounge, with its carefully patched-up Camden council parquet. This was where she had died. There killed. Here died. A smithereening blood-bursting split-second between one and the other.

He wasn't sobbing, just breathing emotionally. Leonard was right. He had to unburden himself on someone.

He had an exact picture of what he wanted. He wanted someone grave and senior and beautiful, but outside sex altogether. He wanted his mother when she was young.

He phoned Ginevra Kay. She was all of those things, nearly. At least, she despised sex, or with him she did. And she loved him just a little as well.

'I'm out,' her voice was saying into the phone even as she picked it up.

'It's Patrick Matson. I need to talk to you, please. Urgently, Ginevra.'

'Only if it's to do with Daddy. Otherwise I'm out for the next three months.'

Two drinks later, he phoned the Rape Crisis Centre.

11.

The place looked perky. There were institutional chairs, but with handmade cushions, aluminium windows fringed with undrawable curtains; their ledges softened by plants in pots, greeting cards, teddy-bears and fluffy rabbits. There were pictures and calendars and multicoloured pinboards from Habitat, but absolutely no posters. There was no crisis here. The crisis was all safely locked outside. It reminded Matson of the cells in women's prisons.

A girl in pebbled glasses sat at a desk, talking into a telephone. There were nearly as many telephones as flowers. 'You come in, love,' she kept saying to the telephone. 'Come in here and we're going to help you. Look, I've got your number. I'm going to call back in five minutes to see if you're on your way. You come in and we're going to help you. Come in, love. I'll phone in five minutes.' She put the phone down, and gazed at Matson in astonishment – he thought astonishment. Her lenses were so myopic that her irises were shrunk to pupils, to pinheads. They were feline, inpenetrable. 'Ah,' she said. 'You must be –' She sorted cards on the table, discovering him at last on a piece of paper beneath the phone. 'Ah,' she said. 'Yes, you are. With the daughter?'

'Patrick Matson.'

'Your daughter's called Paddy?'

'I'm Paddy.' He didn't say more. The interview would have seemed easier if he had been a Vizier and could have presented his cock and balls in a pickle bottle. Anyone's cock and balls, decently severed, and in a pickle bottle would have helped the atmosphere quite a lot in this place.

'They'll be down in a minute. Gina and Tessy, the girls who are giving you a –'

The phone rang. She took it and listened, then laid it down. 'Wrong number,' she said. 'We get them, would you believe? Even here. We like wrong numbers. We *prefer* them.' She dialled. 'Your five minutes are nearly up,' she said into the phone. 'Remember I said I'd call you in five minutes? Well, I'm going to and you'd better be on your way. You come in, love, and we're going to help you. You come right in here.'

She lowered the phone again and said to Matson, 'Your daughter's going to come in? You get her to come in and we'll help her.'

Two women entered the room from an inner door. One was neat and grave and wore an apple-green suit with an orange blouse. She gave Matson a level look and kept it there. The other was in a fawn cat overall and black, roll-neck sweater. On her, the black was strident. She kept her eyes on the suited one, and said nothing.

The suited one gave Matson her hand. 'Come on,' she said. 'I'm Tessy.' Her fingers were chunky with black stones.

'I'll stay here on the telephone,' Pin-eyes said. 'Someone's got to stay.'

'Gina'll be back,' Tessy said.

Gina still said nothing.

They went out. Gina smelled empty. Tessy smelled of soap.

12.

The wine tasted odd. That was a bad indication. Matson rinsed his mouth with it before swallowing. He felt it fur his teeth. It tasted like a mixture of potato-peelings and tea. 'Mellow,' he said carefully. 'Look, I'm paying. Please.'

'Of course,' Gina said. They were her first words.

Matson's tongue toyed with something wrapped in a lettuce leaf; he hoped a prawn and not a loose tooth.

'Your daughter,' Tessy began, after a salad-filled silence.

Matson shook a little, then said, 'Actually, it's not my daughter, it's –'

'Your girlfriend?'

'My son.'

They exchanged looks, then Tessy went on: 'Hasn't your wife been able to help? I mean, was it she who advised –'

'She's dead. I thought I told you that on the phone?'

'I believe you did. How old is he?'

'Pretty damned old.'

'Has a doctor seen him?'

'Of course.'

'He was damaged?'

'Yes, he was d–'

'We see quite a lot of women who've been abused in this way. And, of course, children. There's a sort of mother-with-child reinforcement which we can provide and which we think is helpful. In this case I'd really advise psychiatry, analysis, or at least counselling.'

Gina finished eating and was interested at last. 'Did he have any sense of sexual ambiguity before this happened?'

'I don't think so.'

'What about afterwards – is *that* the crisis you're worried about?'

'I don't think –'

'Surely he came to doubt himself a little?'

Matson couldn't answer.

Gina lost interest again.

A waitress came up and suggested sweets, coffee, liqueurs.

Tessy referred to Gina for a change, and Gina said no.

Maston asked for the bill. 'I live quite near,' he said. 'Can I invite you to –'

Gina's eyebrows went up like fever flags.

'I've got some brandy,' he said. 'And this – this really is being very useful to me. I'm most grateful.'

Gina looked at Tessy and said, 'Go and make Paddy some coffee for an hour.' Her tone was insolent. 'Go on. I'll be back at the centre.'

13.

Back at the maisonette Tessy didn't let him help her with her coat. 'You're being very civilised about it,' she said. 'When did you find us out?'

'You were deliberate enough with your signals,' he said.

'Perhaps we just didn't fancy you.'

He thought of Sally Sherman on the flight that had started it all. 'Perhaps,' he said. He was shivering again.

'I *could* fancy you,' she said. 'If I was in the way of fancying. I mean I don't like men, or their size, or their presence, or –'

'Let me find you that brandy.'

'And I've no intention of *ever* being penetrated. There's something vulnerable about you,' she said, coming closer to him. 'I'll whack you off if you like. I'll do that much for you.'

'Could you make us some coffee?' he said. 'That really is what I meant to invite you to. Or does that muddle the role-play? Only I've got to go to the bathroom.'

'You talk like an American.'

'I come from Ireland,' he said. He went to the bathroom and ran water for his face, bled into the loo, washed his hands, and took a long time drying them as if the fingers might come unstuck.

When he came out he smelled coffee and remembered Brenda. This wasn't Brenda: it was Tessy.

She came back in, with just the cup for him. She still sipped the brandy. 'Strange kitchen,' she said. 'you're in a hell of a state. I'll help you to bed. I'll go away,' she said. 'I promise to be a good girl. I'm a gay, we've both agreed that. And besides, I work at the Crisis Centre. It would be like the Fire Brigade starting fires.'

Some girls are natural nurses. So are some men. 'Don't you have any pyjamas?'

'Only when travelling.' Both pairs must still be in the Western Desert. 'I'll use some running kit.'

'Getting chilly in your old age? I'll make you a hot water bottle.'

'The place is centrally heated.'

'I'll make you a bottle, just the same.' She already had his shirt off. 'Jesus Christ,' she said. 'You've been whipped.'

He began to cry, a little boy with his mother.

She undid his shoes and socks, pulled down his trousers and slid him into bed. 'Jesus Christ – sorry, but if a *woman* comes in and starts talking about her sister ... Sorry, we should have known.'

He stopped crying.

'You don't look like gay,' she said. 'You're not, are you? And you're big enough to take care of yourself.'

'It happened in a prison,' he said. 'Not here. Somewhere else. Where it's a way of prison life.'

'Other prisoners or gaolers?'

'The state interrogators,' he said. 'Does Holofernes mean

anything to you? More than a character in Shakespeare, I mean?'

'Oh yes,' she said. 'A great deal.' Nonetheless she looked blank, her eyes watchful, as if she was talking to a madman.

'It's a sort of puzzle I need to solve,' he said. 'I met the word over there.'

'Holofernes is well known in feminist circles,' she explained. 'Read the Apocrypha. He is the general who tried to rape Judith.'

'Judith of Bethulia? Like the poem?'

'That's right. Only she got him drunk and chopped off his head with his own sword. We frequently advise it.'

She tucked in the blanket and was gone.

SIXTEEN

1.

Camden Council called it a 'higher rented maisonette' – suitable for someone like himself who was salaried and safe.

The maisonette was really a flat, up two flights of concrete stairs. It qualified as 'higher rented' because of this kitchen which was so huge the Council could only fill it with expensive surfaces.

They would have been appalled to see what the new tenant had done to them.

Burns, scratches, spillages and stains, and a lumber of machine-tools and motor-drives.

A swaging block, a mechanical crimping tool, a calibrated reamer, a hand-choking primer-reamer and a case-trimmer, all bolted or clamped to the rate-payers' ceramics. Some expensive optics and two or three humps of junk, bizarre enough to have been translated from *Halbritter's Armoury*.

Cartridge boxes, loose cartridges and spent cases, littered among a dozen pickling jars full of peppery granules, liquorice-like needles and plain black powder that might have been Indian condiments or snuff.

He stood with his issue singlet outside his running shorts and looked at an old copy of the *Sun*: monosodium prose. He dropped it into the pedal bin and concentrated on page three. Men do this all the time, when they feel fit enough.

This man's shoulders were fluffy with lint, like a sheep's back unfleeced by wire.

The *Sun* girl had fair hair, a body the print scale amputated exactly at her pubic interval, and a nice horizontal navel.

Her nipples were like bullets, just as the poet said. On the near side of the near nipple there were five little pin-size lumps. This observation introduced his Second Theory (or was it, like Avogadro's, a hypothesis?) concerning the ballistics of nipples in *homo* or rather *mulier sapiens*. Dum-dum nipples. Then he remembered how the poet had really put it.

Too early in the morning for a man who was losing blood.

He tossed the *Sun* girl onto the cooking shelf, where she draped herself across hardcover editions of the Oxford Standard Muses, and began to feel an old orange-juice carton between finger and thumb.

Too waxy and too thick.

It followed the newspaper into the bin.

He opened a floor cupboard and knelt before it, clattering copper, aluminium, iron. He stood up holding a frying-pan.

He put the pan on the hob among the swagers and cartridge boxes and sliced some butter into it. He peered at the spread of butter and didn't like what he saw. He took a lump of cold beef from the fridge and dissected it for fat. He dropped the solid white strips into the butter and watched them grow transparent, then fished out the mucilage with a teaspoon.

He whistled, rummaged in the drawer beneath the sink-unit and found a box of candles. He began to fry a candle. 'Melt,' he said. 'Don't sputter.' He mashed it with the spoon. It wouldn't break but it melted.

From time to time he wiped his hands on his shorts. One leg grew transparent with fat. The other already had windows of gun-oil. He dried his fingers on his singlet.

He reached up to the cooking shelf and took down the Oxford *Shelley*. The dustjacket was thinner than the juice carton. He tore it into two halves and dropped them into the frying pan.

They floated. Shelley refused to drink the fat. Shelley was coated in plastic. He should have known that poets don't drown twice. Shelley had drowned not too far from where he'd finished poor Anwar and rough little Curly.

He put the poet back and gently ruckled the *Sun* girl. He'd never used the *Sun* for anything so exalted.

In the bronze light of dawn he began to fry page three.

She took on oil at once: oily eyes, oily nipples, oily navel.

He switched off the heat and turned to the units behind him. Elegant boxes glowed with the facing sunrise.

Cases for handguns. Only the topmost pair were less than highly polished. Chipped embossed lettering announced a Colt Combat eleven-clip .45 and a Browning High Power.

He hated automatics, had only a business interest in his work guns. His passion was for revolvers – specials, superpacks, magnums and handpacks.

He unclipped brass on mahogany and took down a Ruger Blackhawk. He had three Blackhawks. This was the .44 Super with the overstrapping and the twelve-inch barrel. It had a home-made stock to keep his second finger under the recoil.

He went to the sink drawer again, and came back with a grey cardboard box of Remington magnums. He selected seven bullets and stood them in an upright row between two strips of softwood. He clenched this trough lightly in the jaws of a small vice.

He took a pair of pliers and pulled each bullet carefully from its cartridge, as tenderly as if drawing teeth. These he laid on one side.

He then picked up a jar of granules and made as if to top up the propellant, grinned to himself and thought better of it. His hand was still swollen from snapping people's heads.

He sealed the cartridges with tiny wodges of newsprint from the frying pan. There was just enough *Sun* girl to complete the spare cartridge.

He fitted little lengths of steel rod into the mouth of the cartridges, calibrated them, carried them one by one to his mechanical crimper and crimped them well in. He measured them for length and trimmed them, then filed them to a point to replace the usual Remington snub. He measured them again, then rechecked them by placing them inside a spare Ruger cylinder. This was a ritual. He knew the cylinder was 2.3 inches long, not counting the tube, but his religion was the worship of objects and took account of their cussedness.

The new slugs were slimmer than the magnums. He soldered a circlet of copper strip an eighth of an inch from the base of each, just like the driving band of a shell. The copper was too soft to foul the bore, but if it broke before the bullet was at maximum in the muzzle he would be wasting his time.

He whistled, mocking his pain. Life had to be lived like this. He loaded his spare seventh shell into the Ruger, rotated the cylinder, and swung the gun about looking for something to shoot at. He held it two-handed, but not in the daft way of police-films. He held it like a rifle with an imaginary stock, his right arm slightly crooked, his left hand forward on the barrel. His left hand was protected from cylinder burn by a long-wristed leather glove, a woman's glove snug on the wrist, not a gauntlet. The gun had been too well maintained for the cylinder to vent, even with a magnum special; but this was an adulterated hand-load with recrafted ballistics, and he saw no sense in skinning himself. Besides, the glove was a habit of mind. Any time he fired a whole cylinder the barrel would heat well beyond the boiling point of water.

His window faced south by east; hence the refracted dawn light. It was dirty and the sun would soon stoke it with dazzle. But it ran the length of the kitchen and turned one pane over the road on the western corner.

Here he took up his usual position, foiled as always for a new idea. There was a gap in the buildings opposite, and he looked through and across shaded gardens towards the unkempt glass-topped wall of the Chalk Farm Road.

Beyond the wall was a railway line, unseen but real on the map. Just visible at this angle, three hundred and twenty-seven yards away according to the 1:2500/twenty-five inch ordnance survey plan, was the hump of the reverse bank of the cutting.

The brick wall at its top was underpinned by wooden revetments: baulks of staging timber and old sleepers each a yard apart and backed by endless soil.

On the one in the middle of the gap there was a hard-edged dab of white paint just catching the rising sun.

He could see it because he knew it was there.

One night last month he had crept across and put it there.

It was his aiming mark. It called for calm guts and six-five vision. He couldn't see it after he had been drinking, and in those rarer dawns when there was a girl around he hadn't tried.

Somewhere through the rooms at his back a buzzer sounded

and idiot music switched itself on. His neighbours were waking up.

A Magnum in a Camden flat would make more noise than the cannon at Gettysburg.

On the worktop in front of him there was an old asbestos chimney pipe bolted horizontally on a hardboard base. It pointed towards his aiming point, and inside it was progressively slimmed by louvres and baffles with an underpacking of paper eggboxes. It was a silencer big enough for a field gun. A Boy Scout could have camped inside it in full equipment.

He pulled up a kitchen chair and sat behind it, pushing the Ruger inside it at the full length of his forearms.

He took slow aim and fired.

Next door there was a muffled gust from the lavatory. The Ruger made no more noise.

No-one complained. No-one altered the pitch of their wireless.

Beside the stove pipe there was a range optic, a fat and white-shelled Bushnell Spacescope from Beckelhymer. Its name was long enough for a poetry recital.

He turned his left eye to it and saw that his home-made projectile had struck just a long inch beneath the white flare on the plank.

Say one and a half inches' droop in just over three hundred yards as against the standard-barrel droop of two inches in the first hundred, followed by the immediate snub-nosed wobble.

More streamlining, of course, much more; but he also reckoned that the extra gas-seal of *Sun* girl's nipple and fried newsprint had given him another three hundred foot-seconds.

The cylinder showed no signs of anxiety. Tomorrow he would add a little black powder and go down in history. Or go up.

The Ruger's muzzle was still wisping unwanted smoke. The barrel was sooted with hydrocarbon and smelled awful. The cognoscenti advised kitchen foil or even tin can; but his Blackhawk was special. He had too much respect for the lands of its bore.

Three hundred yards with only minimal droop.

Then he noticed the window. He had forgotten to open it.

The homemade projectile had slipped through without a stress mark or splinter.

He examined the hole. Sweet as a mermaid's nut. He was full of remembered poetry this morning. There was a neat little copper rim in the glass where it had shed its driving band.

He stripped off the service vest he had been using as a towel, dropped pants that were now totally transparent with gun-oil; and set about a shower-bath and toast.

The shower-bath was impossible on his flayed skin. Toast was easier. Somewhere between the second and third slice he became Patrick Matson, civil servant, and wished he could look forward to a very dull day.

2.

It brightened into one of those mornings with a cloudbase so low he felt as if he was walking between the floorboards and the carpet.

Leonard had a new piece of equipment. His office had been issued with a carbon-and-cat-litter-filled columnar ashtray. Leonard didn't smoke. Matson knocked it over.

'I didn't have time to say it properly yesterday. I'm glad to have you back, Matty. You've mucked up the leave roster. I shan't be able to cross over to the wigwam country, and that's a relief. I never did want to see French River from a canoe.'

'You can't tell me the whole of Government's punctured its hernia just because of some little hijack – not before anyone's heard of the bomb bit.'

'Quinlan's in charge. That shows how it's rated. I don't mean in charge of us. I mean in charge. They're trying to bandage the Somme with a sanitary towel. So clearly they don't think it's the Somme.'

'So what's the fuss?'

'Interdepartmental friction resulting from departmental aggravation. I'm in it because Quinlan won't trust Pomeroy. You are in it even though you were absent, because you're already involved. The Department is in because we are. Ergo, all leave is up the spout. Don't ask the girls to make tea: they're all sulking.'

'What's Marcus done?'

'Sins of omission, our Pomeroy. Refuses the name of his intelligence snout, while insisting he's no good.'

'Nuseibeh *is* no good. I forgot to tell Marcus I've rendered him temporarily speechless by crunching his nose. How does he make contact?'

'Via Tel Aviv. You've got a friend there.'

'I'll kill the bugger.'

Leonard wrinkled his nose and refrained from asking which bugger he meant. Instead he summoned his Miss Dalrymple to make coffee. Miss Dalrymple sent young Mrs Hyem. 'They'll do coffee,' he said in her presence. 'Coffee is cooked by a machine wearing buttons.' None of his secretaries allowed themselves a first name.

The coffee was awful, made worse by the smell of fresh continental beans being ground in the typists' room.

Leonard said, 'I told you you'd probably be going to Cyprus.' He passed a sealed folder over. 'This came through this morning. Apparently, if you go, you'll be going Active.'

Matson was in no state for Active, and therefore no mood for it. He heard himself say, 'At least you'll be able to straighten out the leave roster. French River – that's active.'

Fossit tipped his coffee into his new columnar ashtray. 'I thought I'd tell you, because committee decisions look a bit different when you have to move up the wedge with them. Just a caution, that's all.'

'I've always been active, Leonard.'

'Not for me, you haven't. And never for this office. You've done some private deals, and I don't like it.'

'Like getting hijacked, you mean?'

It was Scotch time already, an ominous little sign so early in the forenoon. Leonard only served Scotch as a medicine or a punishment: he rarely took it himself. He handed Matson a sizable measure and said, 'You can't lead two lives – sorry, Paddy: I put that wrong. You can lead two hundred and twenty lives as far as the Department is concerned – you can have as many as you want, but they all belong here. Don't try to take one of them away from us on the sly.'

Matson didn't understand.

'You must have known we'd have you watched last night.

London's swarming with people from over there. I offered you help yesterday.'

'I live in a secure –'

'Don't go to Rape Crisis. Especially at a time like this. That's defection. We've got our own torture service.' He poured himself a Scotch on the strength of it.

3.

The Home Office clinic was in Hampstead – just down from where the plaque said Sigmund Freud used to live. It was a house similar to Freud's – huge, with a fluted cupola for a porch, and windows that were wide but expressionless, like the eyes of recent widows. Like Curly Ingram's when the buzz went out.

Matson ignored the eyes, and went briskly to the porch. Having been so bold, he spent an age before he could bring himself to touch the bell.

The woman was somewhere between forty and fifty, possibly fifty, certainly with the experience of fifty, but with the aging process kept carelessly at bay. Her clothes were too restful for Matson to notice.

Her face held all of his attention. 'I'm Helen Tesserer,' she said, with no contact of her hand. 'You're very exact about time, Captain Matson. That helps me. Please come in.'

She led him into the sort of office and consulting room that a big house provides, and said, 'We each act as our own receptionist. That means your visits here can be very private.'

She watched him remove his overcoat. 'We like to take our time here, but I'm told your life is in a hurry.'

Talking had been easier with Tessy and Gina.

'I'll need you to take some clothes off,' she said after filling in a card, and giving it a number. 'Your card is filed under twelve-oh-seven, Captain Matson. Will you remember that? I don't.'

'Another woman,' he said. 'I keep on having to deal with women.'

'There are a lot of us about,' she agreed. 'Just comfort

yourself with the thought that I'm young enough to be your mother.'

Smiling did not come easy.

She listened to his chest through his shirt. 'Well, you've got a heart,' she conceded. 'And it beats. Now you'll have to take some clothes off, I'm afraid.'

Still he hesitated.

She didn't. 'My employers are your employers,' she said. 'They're brutal people, and they've probably told me more than you'd like me to know.'

'I see.'

'You'd better get on the couch so I can take a proper look at you.'

'Not on the couch,' he persisted. 'Sorry, but –'

'You were tortured on a couch like this?'

'Yes.' His mouth would not close on the end of even so small an admission.

'We've got a bed here, with blankets. Is that better?'

He got onto it and undressed under the blankets, like an old lady under her towel on the beach.

'I ought to refer you,' she said. 'Don't worry – if that's worry you're trying to express. There's no time. We're coming to reckon it's a month's therapy for each hour's torture. How long were you interrogated?'

'I don't know. Several days.'

'And how heavily interrogated?'

'It was all heavy.'

'That's a lot of hours. I'm told they used an anal vibrator?'

He didn't answer.

'I'm going to need to look. There's a lot of blood on your pants.' She used an anaesthetic spray and she looked. 'You're torn,' she said. 'A damaged lower rectum heals quickly, thank goodness – I know: I damaged mine in childbirth – but it'll need stitches. I can do that now, while the spray's still effective.' She did it.

He was beginning to relate to the concern that showed through her matter-of-factness.

'Were you raped?'

'Probably,' he said. 'I mean he was –'

'So was I,' she said. 'You needn't explain.'

'He said I was better than his camel.'

'He would do, wouldn't he? Mine didn't speak. He was too busy chewing a hole in my shoulder. Would you like some Scotch? I'd like some Scotch. It's not easy to talk about things like this.'

He sat up and said he'd like some Scotch.

'Damn. Only sherry.'

It was Scotch – or Japanese – in a sherry bottle. Whatever it was, he drank some.

'You'll have to have a blood test – a pretty extensive one. Your records say you've been in the Army, so you'll know the score. Your bum will heal, but for the minute you've got a badly bruised prostate. That's one thing I can't share with you –'

He managed his first smile since returning to England.

'But the literature tells me it makes a man very depressed, manically so. You understand that's the point of the procedure in the first place.'

Matson nodded.

'There may be other problems. We can help you with those. You'd better come to dinner tonight if you can spare yourself the time.'

She passed over a card with her address on it. 'My family will be there. My son, that is.'

It was his second Scotch of the morning.

'Can you tell me what they did?'

He told her.

'They would, wouldn't they? There's not much you can do to a man, not much else to a woman. What there is, is what gets done, I'm afraid. It gets done to millions – but the plain fact is it wouldn't matter if it happened to everyone else in the world twice a week. It would still be traumatic when it happened to us.'

He liked the us. 'There was only the one torturer.'

'There always is. I've had women here abused by every guard in the prison, every soldier in the barracks; but it's always just the one they remember.'

'I'm hoping for a chance to kill the bastard – I mean, the chance is going to be there.'

'You should take it.'

He looked up from his glass in amazement.

'I may be a doctor, Patrick; but I'm retained by a single organisation. Besides, shrinks are like that. You talk, and they listen. You are outrageous and they refuse to be outraged. You want to eat your wife and they remind you to take some mustard.'

'I'm not married, by the way.'

'That's a blessing. You'd both be in for a rough few months.'

'And now?'

'Only you.' She discovered some more wisdom in the sherry bottle and said, 'I wish I could prescribe something except time. I mean: we can reinforce, but time is still your basic medication.'

'I'd like to play a nice languid game of village-green cricket.'

She watched him dribble liquid down the side of his glass. 'I'd love you to, but I can't let you. Almost anything you do is likely to be a total disaster. You'll funk with the bat, and you won't be able to catch the ball.'

'That bad?'

'Normally we'd say nothing and let you suffer it all through. Hope you encounter no trouble, but counsel you each time you do. But in your case, there's obviously no time. I must hope you're better in the cold outside than you are when you're baring your memories.'

'Perhaps I'll go home and play with my guns.'

'That frightens me rather.'

The office phone rang and she screwed up her lips in annoyance. She listened and said, 'It's for you.' She smiled.

4.

Dixon drank Fossit's coffee with salacious anticipation. He said, 'How about letting Matson do the job?'

Fossit said nothing. Pomeroy sipped the office iced water.

'Have you ever sweated a woman, Pomeroy?'

Pomeroy's nostrils became eminently fastidious.

'In fact, have you ever been around when *anyone's* getting a belting?' Dixon was beginning to nag.

'I've read the transcripts.'

'But not listened to the tapes? The transcripts don't squeak, Marcus. They don't wriggle and squirm. They don't *leak*. Matson's our man. He needs to serve it up to someone connected with all this. Anyway, she was his idea.'

'*My* inspiration. From the inception, through the conception to the spasm.'

'You'd better handle the delivery then.'

'I'm not a thug, Ralph. I'm like Leonard: silent and fastidious.'

'Only fastidious,' Fossit said.

'I've put everyone onto finding her,' Dixon said. 'The Branch'll help, if necessary. And, of course, the local police – if I can give them a safe story. It shouldn't take long.'

It took a couple of hours.

5.

Matson took the phone and heard Dixon say, 'We've got her.'

'Where?'

'Disused hospitality-suite near Luton nick. Was the sacred domain of the boys in blue. Now belongs to woodlice and spiders. We want you to see her, Paddy. You witnessed her loving up to those villains. You're obviously the man to twitch her little levers.'

He looked for approval from Helen Tesserer. 'I'll think about it.'

'No time to think. What do you need?'

'Standard preparation for a fast spill.'

'I thought so. We've got her in a room without lavatory facilities. A couple of very dykey operatives of mine ripped her jacket, scuffed her tights and tore her blouse buttons. She's cuffed to a dirty sink – you know: Heinz beans, sour oil, old plaster and any more shit the comedy team had time for.'

'Who needs thumbscrews?'

Matson was just about to put the phone down when Dixon said, 'By the way, we know the forger. The Tan's boarding pass. That's a Luton job too. It's happened before.'

'Tell me.'

'Ordinary civil racket. Those charters go to the British Sector – hardly a holiday home; Cyprus, where we've got ten thousand troops and some gents in blue; Hong Kong; and – once in a cheesy moon – the Rock. There are never any spare pricks at the wedding. Someone tips somebody off when there are going to be empty seats, and passes are forged.'

'It can't be worth anybody's while.'

'It isn't, not really. But it costs the airlines, and sometimes it costs HMG. Who, in general, prefer to grin and bear it.'

'Sloppy security.'

'First time it's happened on a German flight. *And* they spotted it. Ironically, they were going to arrest at the other end. Thought it was just a case of minor fraud, see. Hope you had a bona-fide ticket, Thump?'

'We'll never know.'

'One more point. It seems reasonable to assume the Shirmin sister was the link to all of this. Too much of a coincidence otherwise. It's the first time it's happened on a German flight, as I say; but your little air-hostess probably knew her killers – sister's friends – or recognised the forged boarding passes, anyway. The Yanks say the U.S. documentation was lousy. Then, of course, there was no need for any American to see it.'

Matson hung up and said to Helen Tesserer, 'I've got to go. I've got to be nasty to someone.'

'Will you still come to supper. You've got my number if not. If you come, can you bring some salad?'

'For your son?'

'Nothing stronger than table wine.' At the door she said, 'It may do you good to be nasty to someone. It's not a therapy we can usually prescribe.'

6.

From across the room she looked as attractive as he remembered. Nearer to, he noticed a coarseness in her features. Her eyelids were too thick. He realised she had been weeping – or refusing to weep. Pretty women mustn't suffer, any more than they must drink.

Two of Dixon's women were with her. 'Find her a shirt,' he snapped. 'I hate tits.'

They pretended to be suitably chastened. They found her an army shirt. It didn't look very clean.

He was holding a tape-deck and some cable. None of it was strictly necessary. Ralph had already wired the place up. He stood heavily to one side, while the women uncuffed her, pulled the shirt on as if she was an imbecile, and then let her go. She prowled about, flexing her hands, but too self-consciously to move far.

The women locked them in.

7.

Overnight CAC not only became TAC and without executive power, it became permanent. People left the conference only to beg lesser people to run the planet by proxy, or at least phone their wives. Heads of Department guided their offices by remote control. Soldiers, sailors and airmen of all the senior sexes sat in a limbo of self-contemplation. Quinlan expected to have America at his side, not an American admiral. He said so. He promoted himself Sun King while pretending merely to be Sunray One. The committee room became his Versailles and his courtiers' estates lay neglected. Such was the truth of things, and only its description was by Pomeroy.

Pomeroy shocked Fossit to absolute realisation of all this by leaping into his taxi before Fossit could alight, and ordering the cabbie to pull away from the kerb and park in the adjacent traffic jam. 'Have you cleaned your teeth?' he asked. 'And sweetened your breath for the Royal Bedchamber? You've been summoned, if not summonsed, to *La Petite Levée*.'

'Meaning?'

'You're to see my Political Master before he deigns to greet the world. Holofernes is too terrible for him. Matson's news is too hot.'

'Why?'

'No-one is over-disposed to place total reliance upon the word of an Irishman who dunks people's airliners in the Mediterranean with the same vacant abandon that other more institutionalised imbeciles display while breaking their baps into soup.'

'I believe Matson.'

'So do the Israelis. The Americans are not so certain. For the moment, he's clearly gaga.'

Pomeroy got out and paid the taxi for them. 'See how far we went while I interpreted the world to you? A mere five yards. The Yanks are like us. They dwell in a Whitehall of the mind in which no traffic moves, but above which the orderly little dicky-birds sing. In consequence, they reason as I do. They reason that Matson's story is unbelievable – and it is. I would not believe it even if I told it myself – and if it is unbelievable it is best not believed. This way. We're going above.'

Above was a spiritual not a spatial concept. Pomeroy found a door and led the way downstairs.

'Therefore the Yanks do not believe it.'

'And the Israelis?'

'Take the counterview merely because Holofernes is horrible and aimed at them. By, as it happens, an Arab. If I were to phone Shlomo Barel and tell him I'd overheard Arafat plotting to wire up his nation's teeth and starve it to death, my buzz would be taken without the least pinch of salt because the malice is known to be there.'

'Beware the Enemy who lusts after magic swords.'

'Beware friends who quote before breakfast.'

Terence Quinlan sat in what looked like his private office. Fossit had never been here. What he found odd was the tray in front of Quinlan on his desk. It held two boiled eggs, or at least two egg-cosies, and a rack of untasted toast. Quinlan poured coffee for the three of them. He poured as if to make himself feel capable.

He served Fossit first, and said, 'I've been sleeping on this thing of Matson's.' He didn't look as if he'd slept at all well.

'I believe him. I mean – I believe he was told what he remembers being told –'

'Ah!'

Pomeroy leant forward and took a cup. 'This Dragout, Minister. He's pretty certainly a chap called Khalil. Muhammed Ali Khalil. An Arab declension but for centuries a prominent Tibbu patronymic. The fellow was educated in

England. In the international intelligence community he's reckoned to be a bit fancy – you know: conjuring tricks with choirboys and cardamom seeds? Also – and this is significant – something of a wit.'

'So?'

'Holofernes is a joke word. It goes with the man. It has no esoteric significance in Arabic. If it's a cypher key it's a bad one, because it repeats its vowels. Anyway, a computer can crack a ten-column cypher rather fast, so we can forget the Jules Verne. Besides, what do we have that begs to be decyphered? As to its literary associations, I read you the Brewer. We get a general who loses his head, a send-up of a real orthoepist, and an imaginary grammarian who teaches a dimwitted giant to say the alphabet backwards before he is even potty-trained.'

'Do *you* believe Matson, Marcus?'

'It doesn't matter *what* I believe *if* Matson brings us the truth. Nor –'

'That's hardly helpful.'

'Nor if Israel believes something different.'

'Well, my options are dwindling. Have Matson come here, will you, Leonard? I'm going to kick his arse and listen to his brain rattle.'

How panic coarsens the cruder intellect.

'His father *was* a carpenter,' Fossit said on the way out.

'Stepfather,' Pomeroy said. 'His Dad was –'

Fossit was not given to blasphemy, so Fossit shut him up.

8.

CAC which was TAC was no longer a committee. It was a residency, Fossit decided. A residency for meat flies. Members buzzed in and out.

Quinlan had scarcely called the midday meeting to order when in swooped pretty Hattie Dacres to be urgent in his ear. Only herself and Lorna Benvenista ever got that close. Pomeroy, for example, merely bumbled under his nose.

'There's been a development,' Quinlan announced. Fossit would like to see one. 'There's been this – um – development, so I'm leaving Miss Dacres in the chair. I shall want Lorna with me, of course.'

Pomeroy rumbled and rose. He was senior to the Dacres by several, and he got ready to say so.

'You too, Marcus. And Leonard. Where's Ralph Dixon?'

'Catching terrorists at Luton,' Pomeroy ventured.

'A pity. This is an intelligence matter. Well, we'll have to make do with what little brains we've got.'

This left honours about even.

They left the room.

9.

Colonel Grant was waiting downstairs.

Quinlan sat them to some more of his breakfast coffee and said, 'You've cleared this with Admiral Cravicz, I take it?'

'No,' said Grant. 'I was asked for intelligence, not action. I need to get my hands on Matson's debriefing. It doesn't matter how flimsy the current material is, I'm here to ask for it. The White House is pressing the Agency for clarification.'

'I thought you interviewed Matson yourself?'

'We spoke some words. For what they're worth, I left Miss Dacres with my own conclusions.'

'And she gave me her pad.' Quinlan fell silent. Politicians dislike to bring bad news almost as much as they abhor action.

Fossit said it for him. 'Matson isn't being debriefed.'

The colonel's bleached eyebrows almost floated off his face. 'The White House insists he's debriefed, and with our people in attendance. We want him hung on a hook and drip-dried properly. You can't do less. He claims they're hijacking our civil aircraft to convert them into atomic bombs. Only what does he do with the one he brings out?'

'He puts it somewhere safe.'

'He buries it on the sea-bed.'

'You'll have to fish it up, if it worries you that much.'

'Not so easy. The Mediterranean is a shallow little ocean, but it's got these four big holes in it, these five mile deeps. One of them is south east of Sicily, right where he ditched. From inside the Matson skull, it might seem an obvious place, on the shortest straight line, and so on. From further off, to a bunch of sceptics bouncing it round a table in Washington, say, it seems altogether too damned convenient a hidyhole, much too handy to the purposes of the fellows who were programming him with the bright lights and the whips.'

'What can your satellites give you?'

'We can't *see* it, of course. But we can get heat-sources, even under water. We can detect something, several somethings.'

'It's broken up?'

'We don't think so. The fuselage must still be in one bit. But there are other wrecks on the sea-bed – small ships, a big-bodied World War Two plane, perhaps a flying boat. You see the difficulty? And the surface is intensely nuclear-positive.'

'So there *is* a bomb?'

'Or a sneaky little decoy of radioactivity. You *must* put some good people onto Matson.'

'If his story is true then there isn't time to debrief him,' Fossit insisted. 'Meanwhile, he's been invaluable over some loose ends to do with the hijack.'

'If his story's true we're looking at a themonuclear war,' Grant said.

'An incident, merely,' Pomeroy corrected. 'However nasty that may be. The minister has sent for Matson, just the same.'

'Let me tell you how Washington sees it,' Grant said. 'It won't necessarily tell the Craw, because he's charged with joining you and – more problematically – the Israelis in a plan of minimum containment. That may well be the plan we go on. Meanwhile there's the diplomatic dimension.'

Pomeroy favoured the Colonel's acne with a smile.

'Snag is we're dealing with Libya, where there is no diplomacy, only power politics. The reality is this. If Matson's story is correct, and if Tel Aviv is correct in asserting there is a massive plan afoot whose codename is Holofernes, then Libya *must* know about it. Towards hijackers its policy may be benign. But those hijackers can only assemble nuclear devices in an aeroplane with the host-country in total knowledge.'

'At Tripoli International and now Az Zawiyah, which is a military air station, yes,' Pomeroy agreed. 'At Sifr WaaHid, I'm not so certain.'

'Point taken. So Libya doesn't know after all, or doesn't know officially. Then they must be made to find out. Publicly and at once. Washington's view, *in the absence of fact*, is that we must share our suspicions with Tripoli.'

Pomeroy whistled.

'And with Moscow, of course. Then tell the Libyans that *if* those planes fly, and *if* their cargo is deadly, then the Sixth Fleet will retaliate in kind. If any American, European or Israeli city goes down, then so will Tripoli itself.'

'You'd be bluffing, of course?' Quinlan asked.

'Hardly.'

'They'll think you're bluffing,' Pomeroy said. 'They're an administration of zealots, world-revolutionaries, fundamentalists and madmen in a roughly equal mix. Personally, I wouldn't want to play poker with any of them, let alone all together.'

'Washington wants hard information,' Grant said. 'Failing the right stuff from Matson, it's going to squeeze Libya's tits.'

The phone rang. Lorna Benvenista took it, then fielded it to Quinlan with a slipperiness that suggested total awe.

'You're wrong,' Pomeroy said.

'I'm paid to do what I'm told,' Grant countered simply.

'That was the PM,' Quinlan said. 'Your embassy have just passed us a signal. We'll be conferring transatlantic later. Meanwhile, I'm to give Colonel Grant all I can, without reference to Admiral Cravicz, nor to the rest of CAC. Colonel, will you wait in the next office with Ms Benvenista for a few minutes? It's left hand and right hand, gentlemen, I'm afraid.'

10.

'Cosy.' She had one of those perky voices. 'What's the bed for?'

The bed was the only piece of furniture. Matson put the tape deck on it. 'In case anyone wants you,' he said.

'You, for instance?'

He didn't want anyone. He wished he could. He unfastened a circular bundle from the lid of the recorder and tossed it in her direction. It thudded beside her on the floor.

She looked at it. It was a coil of heavy-duty electric flex. 'Ooo!' she said.

'Ever seen any of this lead-sheathed stuff?'

The second loop was the same size as the first, and it landed partially on top of the first so its fall should have been muffled. It wasn't. It sounded like a body tumbling from a roof.

'Pick them up,' Matson suggested.

'Pick them up yourself.'

'Try them for weight – one at the time if you'll take my advice – then put them on the bed.'

He made a note in his pocket book.

She picked them up, tugging the rubber flex from beneath the lead flex with difficulty.

When she reached the bed with the second bundle she said, 'I could break your bloody tape-recorder with this.'

'It's for your protection, not mine.'

'It's not switched on.'

'Exactly.' He gave the idea time to sink in.

'The lighter cable bruises,' he said. 'About twenty whacks on the thighs, the pelvis, the ribs and you won't feel like wearing a bikini for months.'

'You're not allowed –'

'The *police* aren't allowed to,' he smiled. 'I'm different. I don't have any rights at all.' He let her ponder this paradox before adding, 'Anyone who finds herself with me has no rights either, by association.' He pulled a pair of gloves on, then picked up the lead cable and shook it out. It hung crooked, stiff with its own life, like a serpent in the cold. He folded it several times till he had a convenient shank. 'This won't just bruise you. Twenty with this and you'll decompose.'

'My family – someone will complain.'

'I don't have the vote.' He switched the tape on, but didn't say anything to it by way of signature.

'What's that bloody thing really for?'

'Music lovers. There's quite an audience for the sort of noises someone makes when she's being hurt.' He pressed the *stop* button, then squeaked it back on the rapid rewind. 'People who've been tortured, for instance. Some of those acquire most peculiar tastes. Not immediately, of course. But years after.'

She watched the tape with hypnotic fascination. It switched itself off.

'They're women's gloves,' she said.

'I know,' he said. 'I got them from a woman with very large hands.' They were his pistol-shooting gloves, but he didn't tell her that. They made an apologetic little flutter in the air, then took hold of her by the breasts and lifted.

After thirty seconds of acute self-disgust, he set her down again.

She gasped, unable to talk. She backed away, hunched forward on her pain, this time not noticing the tape at all.

His left glove caught her by the chin, his right hand tacked itself under the waistband of her skirt. His left hand tugged her from the floor. Her skirt button tore, but she didn't realise this with very much of her mind at all, her jaw hurt so much, not until he set her down again and she realised it was crumpled on her shoes and she was standing in her panty hose.

He watched her pull it up and try to fasten it. He did nothing to prevent her. Nor did he mention it. He simply retained this terrible advantage over her.

'Luton,' he said. 'Flight Number 303.'

11.

Fletcher could never be detached. He adhered to his own humanity. He perspired too much as a result of all that had been done to him. His torturers had reduced him to a state of permanent self-abasement, total embarrassment. If you think you will even recover from gross abuse just remember Fletcher. Fletcher had once been lean and fit. They had so impregnated him with universal disgust, so contaminated him with their sleek indifference, that his body had grown fatter by the year. He now weighed nineteen stones in summer and more in winter. And still he laboured to be delivered of something far more terrible than Blucher's elephant. He was pregnant with the Brontosaurus. They had mated him for ever with the primeval scream.

What Fletcher said was, 'Your aim is to reduce them to loathsomeness – in their own eyes only will be enough. As they descend into the contagious abyss, you must overlook them from a vantage point more lofty than mere disdain. You simply fail to notice them as they sink. They may curse you, plead with you, try to sell you their soul. You will not even notice. Then they will break and tell the world what you alone wish to know.'

12.

'What are you pigs doing to me?'

'Deploring your vocabulary.'

'You're bloody leaning on me.'

'Roughing you right up,' Matson agreed.

He was surprised he could be so genial. Fletcher would not advise it. He took hold of clothing and flesh, again near the top of her chest, and shook her. He shook her until he was out of breath. 'You're going to tell everyone we've harassed you,' he explained. 'So that's what we're going to do. We've decided to go along with you.'

'I'll bruise,' she said.

'You all do. You bump yourself on the sink.'

'What – bang my boobs on the sink?'

'It's about the right height for them.' He slapped her face. 'You tell us exactly where you want the scar tissue and we'll oblige.'

'This is a police dump.'

'It's a dump. I'll give you that.' He watched the doubt grow in her eyes, fine big girl that she was. 'You've got plenty of spunk for a little 'un – I'll give you that, too.' His backhand wiped indolently across her mouth. 'I don't mind doing this all night,' he said. He did mind, but he said it. He knew that once she had tasted the blood of her own face, she'd be through with prevaricating. She was brave but she was an amateur. She'd die for her cause, but not take a busted nose for it. A professional is forced to think these things through, and given a few unpleasant gobfuls of preparation for it as well.

Amateurism is its own motivation. She was attractive too. She couldn't help knowing she was that. A year or two back she would have been a pretty schoolgirl, and pretty schoolgirls know exactly what they are, however much they try to disguise themselves in later conventions.

'You enjoy doing this, you bastard.'

'Yes, I enjoy it.' He handed her his clean, extravagantly folded handkerchief so she could see more of her own blood. 'I like a winsome canvas to paint on. I'm like Old Father Time. A young woman can grow ancient with me overnight: I can kick arthritis into her bones, thicken her tissue – you'd be – no, well, in your case you won't be surprised.'

'All right,' she said. She was watching her own blood. 'All right, I'll tell you. I've been waiting for you to come and get me.'

No, he didn't enjoy it. He didn't enjoy it at all. There ought to be something with a pretty woman. He knew the priests said that man was more than his animal. He had lusted after this woman a few days ago. Now here she was, her clothing torn, and not only was there no stirring in the stump, there wasn't even the least ambiguity of role. He was detached all right. Dragout had seen to that. Fletcher would have been proud of both of them.

13.

'I'm political,' she said. 'I confess it. Sod it – no, I don't. I profess it.'

'You must like the taste of blood,' he smiled. 'Perhaps you want some teeth to go with it.'

He moved, and she shrank away from him. He was fetching a chair.

He set it down in front of her and let her look at it. He was still behind her, but she didn't turn round. She seemed too mesmerised to turn.

His hands fell lightly on her shoulders, and she trembled as if beneath an enormous weight. He had brought a seat for her and was forcing her to sit down.

From behind her he said, 'I don't care to hear the story of your life. Still less your silly protestations of faith.'

'What I want to make plain –'

'Two men. Two men in American Air Force uniform. You took them to Luton Airport in your taxi. You handed one of them a bag of plastic toys and a big kiss. He wore a bandage round his right hand – a bandage his hand had no need of.'

'It did. He –'

'The plastic toys included a pink tractor and a green water-pistol.'

She shuddered to hear so much. He smiled to himself. She was a novice, trembling at the altar of omniscience – in awe at the Security Services' accidental knowledge of her.

'He had white teeth and a black skin. We know him as Ahmed Younis,' he said, lying with genial aplomb.

'His name's Raymond,' she scoffed. 'Ray. I've known him – I've known him for some time.'

'And fucked with him. A man who does not bother you with his second name.'

'Younis,' she said quickly.

'I invented Younis. We've got plenty of people to fuck with you here, too. You won't know their names either. What's the other man's name – the putty-faced one?'

'That's racist.'

His hand found her shoulder, again gently, but again from behind. It was enough. 'There are no slogans here,' he said. 'The sooner I get some answers, the sooner you can start to enjoy it.'

'Pauli,' she said. 'Enjoy what?'

'The Afterlife. So it's Raymond and Pauli? You've known Raymond some time. When did you meet Pauli?'

'When Ray brought him to my flat – the night before. The night before –'

'The night before you did your bloody bit of business on that Trident. Where's your flat?'

'Here in Luton.'

He made a note of the address. She had given him the important thing.

14.

'Shabby little job, cabbing.'

'I used to be an air-stewardess. That's shabbier.'

'Did you now? Not with Avaroc by any chance?'

She was weeping again. God, he did love women to weep. 'That was my sister.'

'Your sister works with Avaroc?'

'And Avarel. Worked.'

'Until you delivered your two little friends to Luton? Then she got herself eviscerated, didn't she? Still, you'll have seen it all on telly, and read it in the tabloids. They even threw her body out for you.'

'It was meant to be a blow,' she mumbled. 'It *was* a blow. They've still got two hundred pongos out there, frying in the sand.'

'And all the rest of the Avaroc girls. All your sister's friends. And the women and little children. You've read what happened to the Avaroc ladies, haven't you?'

'I'd rather be fucked than finished.'

'I wonder. Still, there's no telling what someone like you would feel. Someone who could skid her own sister.'

'I didn't know she'd be on that flight. We neither of us live at home – I mean with my parents. Besides, if you believe in something –'

'Then you have to believe the world will forgive you,' Matson agreed. 'Your own sister, at least. You certainly mustn't believe in ghosts.'

'I don't,' she hissed, dry-eyed again.

'I'm a ghost,' Matson said. 'I was on that flight.' He hit her full in the mouth, the way he'd punch a man – when he was a man.

15.

Once Grant had gone, Quinlan said, 'Get me Matson. I know you've sent for him. I want him here at once, not by stages. I don't care if he's shell-shocked, hung-over, in a sedation-coma

kind of woman to win in the world – the right to be as witlessly coarse-tongued as the worst sort of man?

'You forget I was there,' he persisted. By telling her that much, he had certainly ensured she spent a long time inside; but he'd already sensed it was the only way. Coldly, but scarcely dispassionately, he told her everything that had happened on the entire flight.

Having completely destroyed her moral basis, he signalled for Dixon to come in.

17.

'I hope you played the gentleman, Thump.'

'I'm applying to join White's on the strength of it. Come on, Ralph. You've got your tape.'

'You didn't switch off at any point?' He spoke as if the Shirmin girl wasn't there. 'You know what the Old Constabulary Bill can be like about the wayward shoal of spermatozoa in the deceased's knickers.'

'Ask the tape.' Ralph was laying it on a bit thick, he thought. 'She's no next of kin. We can keep our compassion tidy.' How many days was it since both sisters had hung their smiles like miracles in his loins, each little face side by side like bullace on the bough? Four brief days ago when it was spring. Now it was winter. 'I've had all I want from her,' he said. 'She's got nothing else of interest to us.' His voice was much too histrionic, but she was in no condition to award an acting prize. 'Get rid of her for me.'

'I've got a place near Haslemere. There's a flooded gravel pit. Some good pike.'

Matson hoped he was joking. Just the same, he resolved to stay off the freshwater fish for a bit.

The Shirmin girl did not think anyone was joking. Even one truth in a hundred would seem the wrong odds to her.

'There's a room,' she said.

'Better still, we'll break that taxi-cab of hers,' Dixon said. 'Fix her a stomach syringe full of Bacardi and coke, and something awry in the front-end geometry. A bearing, say. So if you've been a bad boy, you don't have to worry, Thump. We'll arrange it so it burns.'

'Pauli had a room,' she said. 'With plans and – you'll see when you get there.'

'We know all about Pauli's room.' Dixon was dismissive. He noted the address, just the same.

'The aeroplanes are going to be turned into bombs,' she said.

'You're still romancing.' Matson decided to borrow one of Dragout's ploys. 'Tell us something original, Sweetheart.'

'Not an *explosive* bomb,' she blurted.

'You'll be telling us it's an atom-bomb next.'

They almost lost her again. She looked at him as if he was both ignorant and stupid; then she decided to confide in Ralph. 'It's a botulinus bomb,' she said proudly. 'That or nerve gas – whatever they could get.'

'That's two kinds of bombs,' he said carefully.

'They were going to pick up whatever Libya could provide for them. Libya had already promised it would be good.'

'Libya? Or someone in Libya?'

'What's the difference? They were going to take this plane and crash it in Tel Aviv.'

'Just Tel Aviv?'

'Anywhere they could reach. Anywhere pigs can die.'

'Anywhere pigs can fly,' Matson scoffed. Ralph was on his way to the door.

18.

'Holofernes mean anything to you.'

She shook her head.

'Solve the puzzle and stay alive.'

'Holofernes is in the Bible,' she remembered. 'He fucked with the wrong woman – like you.'

'She was a revolutionary, I suppose. But with a less confused vocabulary. You never heard Raymond mention Holofernes? Or Pauli?'

He believed her. He believed she didn't know. But only because he didn't believe anything she did know, either. He didn't believe anything about this whole affair.

Dr Tesserer's stitches were sore: he believed that much. He searched his pockets for another clean handkerchief for the Shirmin face. He couldn't bear what he had done to it.

'That's it,' she said. 'Blub.' She was quick to spot weakness. She fondled the torn skin on her arm, laying it back in place like a child with sunburn, or as if it was a sleeve that needed stitching. 'They're all the same,' she said to it, damping her finger with her tongue and soothing it down again, refusing his handkerchief. 'They grab us, insult us, bang us – every damn thing. Then they bloody crap themselves and blame it on their mums. I've seen it all happen.'

Matson's eyes were absolutely dry. He swore they were dry. He banged her on the cheek to keep the words in her mouth.

'Hold on, little lover.' Her voice was honeyed bile. 'Try not to sniff till I've found you a Kleenex.'

He hit her again.

The blow didn't affect her. She was searching for a question. She'd had relationships with bullies before.

'What'll happen to me?'

He didn't quite know.

'Prison?'

'If you're lucky.'

She wasn't scared any more. She ought to be.

'You'll be evaluated,' he explained at last. 'Normally, after that, and in circumstances like this' – seriously, *what* circumstances were there ever, like this? – 'in circumstances like this, we either decide to use you or lose you.'

'Let me go?'

'Lose you means making sure no-one else can use you.'

'Prison?'

'You should be so lucky. But, as I say, we'll evaluate you. And by "we" I also mean "they". There'll be a hell of a lot of people with a great need to look you over.'

'I could kill the bastards.'

'Perhaps you could. Now.' He gave her the handkerchief. 'We'll have some medics pickle that face of yours. In case your head's any use to anyone.'

He watched Ralph's butch ladies shackle her up and take her away. He wondered about their career prospects, working for Ralph. It was no kind of a job for a woman.

Botulinus toxin. Could they really make a bomb with it? Vitreous retorts in concrete cubes. Perhaps something even nastier than plutonium had been clamped on that trailer platform at Sifr WaaHid.

This thing the committee was calling Holofernes – they knew nothing about it, and he knew less than nothing. It was just that he was the one with all the clues.

SEVENTEEN

1.

'I'm afraid we overdid it, Khadduri. Who could believe those people would seek to guard *empty* aircraft so efficiently.'

'They put us to shame. I am ashamed.'

'Nonsense. And who could believe that my little Matson would be such a brute? Look at Nuseibeh, for example. He'll take days to repair, and his nose will never be quite the same again – I've a premonition about his nose, Khadduri. Still, his snout has served its purpose. He has snorted our messages to Tel Aviv. Matson's mouth has yet to do its work.'

'I don't think it ever will. He has killed many people and stolen an aeroplane. Now the plane, according to radio, is in a hole in the sea.'

'Matson put the plane in the sea because Nuseibeh told him there was a bomb on it. Matson is the kind of man who would do such a thing, and leave himself there with the bomb, if *that were his only option*. But he is a survivor, that Matson. You mark my words.'

'If he doesn't survive?'

'Ibrahim will have to straighten his nose and talk once more to Tel Aviv, that is all. I mean – why should this Matson put himself in the sea, they will ask. It is not a story for Israel to digest without taking a great deal of salt on the blade.'

'Sometimes I wonder what side you want Nuseibeh to be on. And sometimes I wonder –'

'What side I am on? That is because you do not understand our game, Colonel.' Dragout grew reflective, as if at last he was ready to confide in Khadduri. Instead he chuckled and fiddled for some coins. 'I'll wager you a lot of dinars – you may name your price – I'll wager as many Libyan dinars as you like that my sweet little Silken Bones is not buying supper for the fishes. He is telling my story to the CIA even now, or to all those people in London, perhaps even the Queen, telling my story and telling it wrong.'

'Or telling it right.'

'Right is wrong, Khadduri. Come on, how many dinars? Or do you want to wager in gold?'

2.

The Düsseldorf Tart tried not to look at her double.

The Düsseldorf Tart stood by the two keyhole-shaped graves the old man had dug in the sunlight, and first watched the stones going in on top of the brown-haired corpse. The mutilated face was only one foot under, and the graveside pinched in at the waist because the soil was so hard. The three ancient squatters would have buried both corpses on their side or in the same hole, or left them to the rats and perhaps Dragout's dog, if they'd been allowed to have their way; but Sergeant Modfai had put them to work. Sergeant Modfai knew about putting people to work. It was the first real work the old men had done, and they complained about it, but they did it. They had to. Digging holes is a woman's business, true enough; digging a grave is a man's; so there was the end of it. They dug the holes reluctantly and now they filled the first one in on an uncovered face.

They had lost one aircraft and Khadduri had refused to let them use blankets from the other aircraft, or give them any army blankets, because everything in his army was accountable and the aircraft was his responsibility.

Anyway, a revolutionary didn't need to decorate a comrade's corpse or give way to any such sentiment. A true believer did, and this young woman who was a Shia would have borne her own shroud of martyrdom into battle, if only she were not so inconveniently female. The aircraft held Jewish blankets, and that might have presented her with a difficulty. The Düsseldorf Tart was a Jew herself, if she bothered with anything; but her parents had run away from that fact when her grandparents had fled from Germany.

Soon the dark-haired face was gone, and now the Düsseldorf Tart stood looking down at her double. The hijackers had numbered two women with bleached and crisp-permed hair – there is something comforting about a blonde. That is why there had been two of them, one in each aircraft. You cannot credit blondes with stealing an aeroplane. Hijack is for curly-haired fanatics with dark skins.

This one was even plumper than the Düsseldorf Tart.

Her plumpness made for unattractive wreckage.

The Tart was angry. Three days ago she had had this Matson in her gunsight. Nuseibeh had intervened, and given him to the military and the military had let him out to do this. Three of the four women were accounted for as a result, and one of the men – all by Matson. She wondered how he could have commandeered an aircraft that had two of her companions on board and a further two guarding it.

3.

'I have lost the aircraft, Dragout.'

'On my orders, Khadduri.'

'Some of the Freedom Fighters are dead in consequence.'

'For them, death was a constant bedfellow.'

'Two squatters disappeared with the aircraft.'

'Such people do not exist.'

'Their women exist.' So did Khadduri's exasperation. 'Their women exist, and they will not stop their complaining.'

'You have an ear for women, Khadduri. My garden is free of its stones. So they need not exist any further. You may tell them this. Or shall I tell them?'

'I will tell them.'

'Let Modfai tell them. They will believe Modfai because he will make a joke about it. Is the widebody clean?'

'Yes.'

'Then give the squatters some food and send them away. Or have Modfai kill them. The main thing is for you to behave like a soldier again and take charge of the remaining aircraft.'

'What will you do for my shame?'

'I will write it a commendation, Colonel. But that Israeli aircraft is different.' They stepped to the window from which they could see its tailplane. 'The Israeli aircraft is very important to me, and most important to Holofernes. What you will do with it is this. You will see that there are always at least fifty people on board, fifty people made up of children and mothers. And they will be guarded by those we may now frankly call hijackers. They need not be the same children and mothers all the time, or the same hijackers. They all need a rest. But there will always be fifty on board.'

Khadduri made a note, as a good soldier should.

'The aircraft will be fully fuelled. Is its tyre replaced?'

'Yes, Dragout.'

'Good. Because if there is any attempt at a rescue, the aircraft will fly. If we can get more women and more children on board, well and good. If we can get everyone on board – better. But if we are attacked, then, as I say, the Jumbo will fly.'

'Is Tel Aviv to know this?'

'You mean – is Ibrahim to be encouraged to heal his face and tell them? No. Not until it flies. I have a written script for our spokesman in Tripoli. We are unfortunate that the loss of the Trident has kept the television cameras away from us, but that was a consequence I did not quite foresee. Or rather, I thought the cameras would be here before we became less attractive to them.'

4.

It was clear to Modfai that his commanding officer was only partially in charge. Colonel Khadduri gave his orders. The Tibbu gave his orders. They both said exactly the same thing about moving the passengers to and from the aircraft, and that was reassuring.

The problem was: whose orders were they? Where did they begin?

In the midst of such uncertainties a sergeant is as a rock. A man fit to become Sergeant-major is a cliff or a tower.

He must look to his status. He thought of his weeping stewardess again. What did the stories say? Suleiman had many wives, but they wept one at a time.

These thoughts had begun with him while he had supervised the white-headed woman reloading the passengers into the Jumbo. Her head was a silly colour, but her body was agreeably plump and he could see the enticing depth of her navel through the wet of her blouse just as she hitched at her slacks.

As a prelude to these considerations the palm of one of his hands had begun to explore her nearest breast. It was as cool as a watermelon and much more exciting.

He did not watch her as his hand allowed itself such a treat. He did exactly as she did and kept his eyes on the passengers.

Perhaps she glanced away from her task for a second. Perhaps there was no need. He did not notice. All that the sergeant felt was a great pain along the side of his head, from forehead to ear.

When he steadied himself and blinked in her direction, he saw she was smiling at him, grinning at least. It was a smile with a lot of teeth in it, and her lips were stretched tight along her gums. He never did decide what she had hit him with. If it was the top edge of her Ingram he was lucky not to have had his eye put out by the cocking nut.

He caused his face to smile back at her. They were, after all, allies and friends.

His pain made him think of his status even more. A man's pain and his status are what a man takes to his woman, or even his women, when a man has such things to take them to.

5.

Dr Tesserer did not actually live in her Sigmund Freud look-alike, but she still clung impressively to NW3. Her house was in the same red brick, but her pathway was uneven, her woodwork mellow, her paintwork distinctly middle-aged. She was situated in the seedier strip of North Hampstead, just before the trees have their perm, and the buildings wear pretty paint and call themselves Golders Green. It wouldn't cost her a fortune to live here: she just needed to be rich.

Matson tried her bell and her knocker and was impressed with both.

The door was opened by a young man in his mid-twenties. 'Mr Matson?'

'That's me.'

'I'm Lovell. Lovell Tesserer. I'm just on the way out.'

'Stay and help me with this bottle first?'

'I've tried Mum's cooking before. Your vintner cannot console me!'

Matson watched him jog down the front path, and wondered how voluntary his absence really was. Matson liked to think of himself as good company round a dinner table, even though his vintner was Safeway Stores.

The house was constructed from a comforting amount of darkness. A few carefully-spaced lights suggested volumes of midnight in reserve. It was a woman's house, a melancholy house, but not a mad house.

He could smell well-kept furniture, underused carpets. There wasn't the least trace of cigarettes or cooking, or cat, rat or dog.

There was Dr Tesserer, though, advancing carefully through a deep perfume.

6.

'You've only got one lettuce.'

'It was the only one I could fall properly in love with. The rest were either brown or limp.' He merely choked on his own witticism. 'The wine's stiff enough.'

'I know,' she agreed. 'It's the glass that does it.'

She pulled the cork, and poured two glasses long and fast. Clearly a party-goer, rather than a wine-freak. 'Would you like some music, Paddy?'

'I'd love to listen appreciatively to the silence, if you'll let me.'

'Shall we drink this before the steak?'

'I've got another colour for the steak,' he said.

Later she called from the kitchen: 'How do you want yours done?'

'Anyway so long as I don't hear you beating it.'

She came back to him and said, 'You can make jokes about it. That's good.'

'You think I'm recovering?'

'Let's wait until after the steak. You've changed your suit.'

'I had to go home to clean my knuckles.'

'Ah yes. Your nasty knuckles.' She examined his fists, curiously, as if they were sex on Mars. 'You're going to feel guilty,' she said. 'Each time you feel guilty, you must congratulate yourself for something. Like "I feel guilty, but at least I escaped".'

'I feel guilty for escaping.'

'Because you killed people?'

'Because I broke an aeroplane. Trident Threes cost money.'

'This one had a bomb on board. Allegedly an A-bomb.'

'There are those who want me to feel guilty for breaking that as well.'

Her knuckles held her attention. They kissed, knocked teeth together. He sucked the magic tingle in the nerve. He had been left with his upper tusks intact, but not with what she was unfastening.

'It might have exploded.' Perhaps she was being witty.

'Nowhere the Foreign Office would have worried about. It hardly ever thinks about Sicily.'

'The Americans will be grateful, you'll see.'

'The Americans in Sicily didn't believe me. Come to that, the State Department would pay hard money to have someone blow up western Sicily. It's where the drugs come from.'

Her hand was cooler than Dragout's. 'Permission?' she said.

'Go ahead.'

'The early evening is a slightly indecent time.'

'It doesn't interfere with the morning's hard thinking, the night's hard drinking.'

'Hard, hard,' she said. 'All the hards. E'en like thy chastity.'

'Aren't you being unfemininely forward?' he rejoiced. Nurse Willoughby was only twenty-four hours behind him.

'I'm old enough to feel unfeminine on occasions. And to be forward whenever the mood takes me. As for the rest, I never get involved with my young men I help. I'm a whore really.'

The phone rang before Hippocrates had a chance to dampen anything further.

7.

Matson might be deflated. Ralph Dixon wasn't. 'We found her sodding room. Her's. Not her boyfriend's. It's full of goodies. Plastic pistols, toy field-guns, genuine pocket wirelesses and cameras – they had more thoughts than one.'

'For the zip gun, you mean?' Zip was a painful word just now.

'Yes. Propelling pencils and ballpoints everywhere. God knows how many boxes of BICs there are.'

'They're glass or plastic.'

'They seemed to prefer that metal Papermate job. Strong metal, spacious tube, sharp – and you can unscrew the clip. There are some here made up with black powder, some with cordite, I think. It tastes like cordite. She was lying about botulinus.'

'She was telling us what she knew.'

'There's a lot of general stuff about the atom here. It all ties in with the big theory. You know, encyclopedic stuff as for fools.'

'Who're the fools, Ralph? Them – or us?'

'I never cook evidence, Thump.'

'That's what worries me. Somebody's cooked it for us.'

8.

They'd cooked it at Luton. They'd probably cooked it in the desert, too. Someone had certainly cooked him. You can only discuss this sort of conundrum with a Tesserer when she's being Doctor, though, not when she's playing Helen. He let her play Helen. Helen was Hell for him.

'The phone call was a pity,' she said.

'Let's have the steak.'

'We had it. Was she pretty?'

'I suppose so.'

'Sexy?'
'Perhaps.'
'So what did you do to her. Can you bear to say?'
'Not really.'
'Try.'
He began to talk to her again.
'Just lie still. I'm sure I can do something with this.'
She could. He couldn't.

9.

'Where, oh where, is this Matson?'
'He's been interrogating one of the hijackers' accomplices – who, incidentally, he led us towards.'
'Nine hours ago,' Quinlan muttered. 'Nine – no, ten hours ago I asked for him. Surely someone can contact him in that time? Or even recreate him for me?'
'Posting between Luton and the psychiatric unit.'
'God brought forth Adam and Eve with less effort. And God did not own shares in British Telecom. Psychiatric unit? Who?'
'Doctor Tesserer.'
'That one. The geriatric nymphomaniac. Better try her home address, then.'
Fossit allowed his distaste to show, before saying, 'She's good with torture victims. She knows how to straighten them out.'
'Accidental puns,' Pomeroy observed, 'are even more despicable than intentional ones.'
'Keep trying for him,' Quinlan said. 'And spare me the good taste.'
'Aren't you asking a bit much of him?' Fossit persisted.
'We're post the Holofernes theory now. And post the radioactive sea. The Americans want some more answers before they join us in a major commitment. The Foreign Office has been told to find those answers. Lorna has done a report. Marcus here has submitted his reappraisal. Masterly, Marcus. It's better than anyone could want. But it begs all of the original questions. So let's use what's left of Matson.'

'He's hardly the art of the possible, Minister.'

'I can't afford the luxury of that kind of politics. My kind is pretending to do what I can, even when I know damnwell I can't.'

10.

'Don't even try, not tonight. I'm flattered, but don't even try.' She massaged his belly with oil. He was glad she was too sensitive to ask him to lie on his stomach. 'I'm going to see if I can make you come,' she said. 'I should say "ejaculate", my sandy darling, because all things considered it looks as if I'll have to revert to the old intrusive clinical method. As in A.I.D.,' she went on. It was her voice that was hypnotic, not her vocabulary. 'It should ease the bruising quite a bit, but there's a fair chance it'll increase the depression for half an hour or so. Still, I actually remembered the brandy this time. It's really good Armagnac. At least, Oddbins said it was.'

She took a long time in his broken flesh. It was worth the depression.

'*Post coitum omn'animal* –' he began.

'In Ireland, I'm told the girls do this all the time. You are Irish, aren't you?'

'Yes. But I was brought up in Camberwell, where the girls stopped doing it when I was ten.'

11.

CAC did not want to see what was left of the Shirmin woman. She had bled and nobody liked that. But now they had her bloody little secret in a half-page digest on pure white paper they all had a question for her.

Quinlan decided it should be put by proxy. He arranged for one of the Ministry Eggs to come in and explain that the botulinus bomb could not work. The Shirmin girl was misleading them or had been misled. He reminded them of what they were all too young to know, that when it had become widely disseminated circa 1957 that a thumbnail of the stuff in the Staines reservoirs would obliterate Greater London in twenty-four hours, and that a coffee-spoon full of its untreated toxin would slaughter the inhabitants of all the cities in New York State and the State of New Jersey, and when it was believed that the KGB had sleepers all over the Western Alliance going around with samples of the poison in cigarette packets, matchboxes, condoms, insecticide sprays, and even packets of Aspros, the fear had been allayed by the discovery that the toxin oxidised in fresh air or tap-water. Its lethal lifespan was well under twenty-four hours.

'What happened to the idea then?' Barkworth asked.

'We lost interest,' the Egg said. Shortly afterwards the Egg gathered up his slides, his rat-film and his wall-charts and left.

Barkworth didn't lose interest. Nor did Hattie Dacres. It was a pretty simple biochemical problem after all. You just had to find a way to stop the toxin oxidising. 'Put that simply, anyone with time could crack it,' Barkworth said. 'There's been thirty-five years.'

Quinlan did not want to waste any more energy on botulinus bombs. True or false, they led to bifocal conclusions. 'Steady on, Brigadier,' he said.

'I mean: it's a simple idea, Minister. You can write it on a postcard.'

'It's like falling upwards.' Hattie Dacres decided to come to heel. 'Anyone can say it. No-one can do it. Let's stay with atoms.'

Quinlan continued to worry ahead.

12.

'Am I your first time with an older woman?'

'I love my grandmother.'

'That's not quite what I meant.'

'You're my first time with an understanding woman. You're not old, anyway.' Saying this made him tearful; but his eyes were full of Irish anyway, Irish and several other malts, and wine and Armagnac. He was remembering Brenda. She had been understanding enough, and lying about her memory made him weepy. He told Helen Tesserer about her.

'That's what happens after torture, I'm afraid. What you're feeling is quite normal. Not that knowing it is any consolation. Any more than it's any consolation to realise a bellyache's a shared experience.'

'It helps. You help.'

'Torture makes us feel broken into. All those memories we had stored tidily, or at least privately, at the bottom of the box, they're scattered everywhere. We can't stand our own past being thrown up in such a profusion.'

He tried to make love to her in return.

'Don't worry,' she said. 'There's lots of time. I'm suggesting you stay. I'm prescribing you stay.'

The phone rang again.

'At midnight? Then I prescribe you come back.'

He promised her most sincerely, but time would not let him.

EIGHTEEN

1.

Fossit began to see Judas Iscariot in a new light. Not quite as a tragic hero, perhaps, but as a nark deserving pity and a decent pension.

He huddled beside Matson – he'd refused the far side of the table – and gazed at Quinlan, Pomeroy, Barkworth, Fisher Benvenista and Dacres – the last two most of all – in total disbelief. Even killer sharks can be female. Numbing to see such an obedient pair of females become killer sharks.

Quinlan opened gently. 'Captain Matson, how many people will we need to mount a safe rescue at Sifr WaaHid?'

Fossit winced at Matson's moment of earnest reflection.

'You'll need a specialist squad to take out the hijackers – something like the SAS Pagoda Troop – and at least two battalions to deal with the reinforcing infantry. Perhaps even more. That Khadduri is a good officer. But the more you can blanket out the opposition, the less chance of bloodshed. God knows how you'll deliver so many men that far into the desert, Minister.'

Quinlan smiled his *I am pleased to offer you the job* smile, but still went off at a tangent. 'Suppose one were to arm and activate the trained servicemen on the British Forces' Charter?'

'They'd have an excellent chance of overcoming the hijackers – assuming our chaps aren't bound or blindfolded, or otherwise impeded. How would you propose to activate them, Minister?'

'Let me ask another question. Suppose *four* trained men – SAS or otherwise, but including a Jumbo pilot – were parachuted in somewhere near to that compound. They'd have extra weapons in leg valises – you know the form – and they'd liberate other fire-arms as their rescue progressed. Well, how high would you rate their chances of getting all the hostages away in that widebody?'

'Militarily, you mean? Assuming the widebody can fly and isn't totally taken up with trigger-mechanism? And not lethally radioactive?'

'All of that,' Quinlan purred.

'I'd say one in ten. That's only considering the military hazards. Ten percent would be about right.'

'Indeed? As high as that?' Fossit wasn't the only one who froze. 'Suppose – for intelligence reasons – it were just a question of lifting the airliner?'

'Sacrificing the hostages?'

'Leaving them to pursue alternative options.'

'A bit better. One of the rescuers would have to be qualified on 747s, of course.'

Quinlan nodded, but not to Matson.

Barkworth spoke from one of those huddles of stillness the military take so much trouble with. 'Suppose we ask you to go back?'

'Back?'

'To Gadaffyville.'

'I wouldn't exactly rate my survival chances.'

'How do you rate them here? Careerwise, I mean. You know the line of country. Corpses we can take. Even expensive corpses. But someone broke a Trident Three.' Quinlan smiled at the fun of it all. 'International terrorism is not accountable to the civil courts. Captain Patrick Matson is. What do you say?'

'I resigned my commission four years ago.'

2.

'Better go to the gym and stretch those bruises,' Barkworth said, 'Then take yourself up to Albany Street for some weapons. I'm a great believer in grenades for soldiers who kip in huts.' He spoke as if he was prescribing sleeping-pills or diuretics. 'Also all four of you'll need some stuns and smoke, I dare say.'

Matson licked his lips. They tasted of his doctor's kisses.

'I've found you a very good man,' Fisher said. 'RAF Intelligence. Has flown a lot of big kites, including the 747 as Second Officer, *and* done a dummy assessment of it at the Andover Military Test Fliers' course. His name's Collinson.'

'Almost as well qualified as you are,' Barkworth suggested.

'Get me three of him.'

A long silence, during which Barkworth's eyes did not like what they were looking at. Nor did Fisher's. Matson was alone with the two flatheads now.

'Get me three pilots.'

'Three plus four? Becoming a bit top-heavy, isn't it?'

'Three plus me. I can't afford to land up in the jebel without a flier to get me out again.'

'You'll do the fighting?'

'I'll do the killing.'

'Supposing you're the one to catch a cold out there, old chap?'

'I won't. A stunt like this is a bit like rock-climbing – assaulting a cliff, if you want the military analogy. The leader mustn't fall.'

No-one had quite thought Matson would be in charge. But that was where he put himself.

3.

Sam Kidgell was an ex-WO1 PTI. God knows what he looked like in his uniform. Out of it he was grotesque. He had a bald brown head on top of a physique of whitening body-hair that was like corn or coir and refused to stay inside his PE kit.

His gym was on the Euston Road, handy for the Albany Street Barracks, and Matson's flat. His gym was a bit like its owner, old and surprising.

Kidgell was short and thick-waisted, but his back was supple. He had loose shoulders like an ape and Popeye-style forearms. He believed in power-training in small doses only. He thought a man should be able to lift, pull up and press his own body-weight, but in private, without boasting about it. He used to encourage Matson to clench his knees to the high beam once in a while and show him he still had the technique and the coordination. He always said the same thing while he was watching him. 'I don't trust strength. When you were three you used to be able to bite your big toe. Since that time when have you been able to do anything so useful?' Sam Kidgell could still bite his big toe. Matson had seen him do it. If there was no-one in the gym, and there rarely was in the early morning, they used to wrestle a five-minute round together, but slowly, with lots of very deliberately applied wrist-whips, roll-throughs and somersault escapes like a circus limbering up. Matson would say, 'We ought to quicken this routine,' and Sam would always answer, 'I know. It feels a bit like Diogenes and his lover.' Matson presumed he was talking about Plato and consequently getting Diogenes wrong, but before he could correct him, Sam Kidgell would always say, 'The thing is – if we go any quicker you'll break something.'

Today he looked at Matson in his track-suit and said, 'You don't want to wrestle, then?'

'No, thanks.'

'What are you wearing those pyjamas for? Got acne?'

'Bruises.'

'You don't want to pull up with bruises. Go home and put your big toe in your mouth. What was it?'

'A motorbike.'

'A motorbike or a bloke on a motorbike?'

Matson didn't like that kind of talk, especially now.

'I know you're not gay. Don't be so sniffy with me. You don't take enough care of yourself to be gay.' He went into the little kitchen that was also his office and probably his bedroom, and came back holding a bottle full of clear liquid. 'I don't care if you've already got a rub. Try some of this. It's good for bruises. Only on the outside, mind. And not near any broken flesh.'

Matson was all broken flesh. He sniffed it. It smelled like paint-stripper.

'Not on your dick, neither. You'll levitate.'

Enough tea and sympathy for today, thank you. Tomorrow he would be dead.

4.

Barkworth's breath smelled of foot-rot. He leant it close to Matson's head so it wouldn't be diluted by the in-flight hum.

'Here's the Avaroc manifest. You're to regard the El Al people as civilians.'

Matson studied the paper. It was banded in transparent markers.

Barkworth breathed more uneasy conscience in his ear and said, 'Blue is adult males. Sixty-seven of them. They're all NATO servicemen. Red is active members of British combatant units. You've got three Airborne Artillery, seven 2nd Battalion Royal Greenjackets, eleven 1st Battalion Royal Anglian Regiment including three junior officers, two RAF Regiment. There are officers of field rank and staff rank, as you can see; but none of them come from active arms of the service. There are nine US personnel, seven of them Army. They will join in or not, as they see fit. General Randall Mackie used to fly V-bombers when he was in to that sort of thing, so he might be a good man on the flight deck in an emergency.'

'There's the El Al crew to consider.'

'They took injuries during the hijack. We don't know how badly.'

Nuseibeh's information seemed curiously selective. Was the doctor being shifty or merely coy?

Meanwhile the Transport Command Comet staged them to Cyprus. Brigadier Bad Mouth was hurrying them on.

Matson looked around at his companions on the one-way express. Collinson, Fison and Levett – all RAF, but sounding like a firm of solicitors, or did he mean sacks of manure? Some of them would be fertilising the desert soon.

Or they would if the jump-plane was ready.

5.

'I've found just the plane for you,' Fisher said. 'Fact is I nearly lapsed and said kite. It's a Broussard – do you know it?'

'Never heard of it.'

'Nor's Collinson. Means he'll fly it carefully. It's French.' He exercised his laugh. 'We'll give it some kind of jump-faring, but it'll still look as Frog as the old corrugated Deux CV. No-one in Libya will expect Brits in a plane like the Broussard.'

'Tell me some more.'

'Lovely ceiling. Not much range. We can take care of that with an extra gravity feed. Remind Collinson not to fly her for too long upside down, that's all.' Fisher was becoming a bit *Boy's Own Paper* (if that was what it was once called). Matson had noticed the syndrome in other hi-tech warriors once they were presented with something basic, like a rifle, bicycle or bullock-cart. 'Oh, and its speed is minimal, even in kilometres. Collinson'll have to come in low, under radar, then tactical fly inland.'

'You mean hug the valleys, crawl up the crests?'

'Moth round the topmost dunes. Absolutely. Somewhere about Zeltan – or on a collateral co-ordinate to Zeltan (you decide where, but somewhere in the appropriate grid) – he can pull the old control into his tum and take you as high as you like. I mean, I take it you'll jump high?'

'Free-falling with a valise I'll want a few angels, yes.'

'It's going to be a long flight, and exhausting for Collinson. Night-flying low over water is always a sod on manual. Then skipping round the jebel in the dark is calculated to bring the backside out in a few more freckles. I wish the boys had done a couple more jumps between them, too.'

Matson wasn't looking forward to jumping either. Or acting as despatcher. 'Ta!' he said, after a suitable pause.

NINETEEN

1.

The Broussard smelled of sick, a decent sick that strove to be eminently soluble in alcohol.

Matson didn't think anyone had actually thrown up. He was catching Levett's breath and Fison's breath. Their breath was just as uneasy as Barkworth's had been. But it tasted better. It was all Cyprus brandy, and they had enriched it on Matson's advice.

The Broussard flew slowly. Its starboard door had been removed, and the aperture caused a lot of drag, even with a jump faring to streamline it.

They had two hours to sober up, and then an hour to feel sorry for themselves.

Then they could dick themselves up with the oxygen bottle, gulp another cup of cognac and step through the hole.

Fisher's widebody nominee, Bob Collinson, was up front, and sober. He had to fly the thing. At one minute to zero he was going to set her straight and level, come back to the door and go straight out, free-fall.

Collinson had jumped a couple of times before, just enough to make him terrified. He was going to leave the controls and get out.

Levett and Fison were going to go out immediately afterwards, on a static line.

Levett hadn't jumped before, except off a number 37 bus.

Fison had, once. He had nearly killed himself by catching at the static line.

They were going to jump this time, at once, because no-one likes being left alone on a plane without a pilot.

They were both pilots, as it happened; but they were going to get themselves out before the tanks ran dry or they clapped into the imminent side of the hill.

Matson had explained all this, and they had turned green and nodded. Some people feel confident about aircraft, but pilots are never truly happy until they are out of them. They saw the logic and would go.

It would be a shade risky on a static line, especially straight through a light-aircraft door without using the jump strut. But if they used the jump strut, they would spin the Broussard; and he daren't ask them to free-fall. He wanted all three of them tight together.

Matson had to pull back the static lines, jump out fast and give himself a couple of thousand feet to scrub back to them.

If he lost them up there they would doubtless stay lost.

Each had a little red light on his arse. It was dull. A six-five eye could just pick it out at five hundred metres. That was if the eye didn't weep in the jump stream or catch a lonely aphid or some desert grit. Goggles sometimes steam up, and a vaselined lens wouldn't detect the little light at all. Sometimes, of course, the light didn't function. Sometimes it functioned insidiously and unseen. Not for nothing was it called the fart-fly.

Collinson and Levett and Fison were steady lads. They were all on the fringes of RAF Intelligence or covert operations, so they were used to assessing the risk-factor. They knew when they were being ordered to commit suicide. A little success and a lot of training develop an excellent nose for failure.

Matson was pretty sure that in the normal course of events he would abort the operation. He wouldn't abort before he'd got his little band of ruffians outside the door – it is an axiom of command not to run away until you've heard the guns actually fire, particularly when you're on a punishment mission.

But this was surely meant to be a forlorn hope? If it worked, fine. But it wouldn't work. Least said, soonest mended.

Matson dead at Sifr WaaHid, a couple of uniformed johnnies at his side – Quinlan would have Pomeroy tell Tripoli they had been there all the time, escaped from the Trident, and lying low up among the rocks and the thorn trees.

When Tripoli said they'd run away in the Trident, Pomeroy would say: how can this be? They cannot run away and still be there. You've abused poor Matson so much you have grown delirious. What – steal a Trident Three from under the guns of the entire Libyan Army? It was our Trident Three anyway. Besides, you've killed the poor chap.

Or you haven't killed the poor chap. Now you've got your thieving little mitts on him again you can ask him yourself. He'll tell you he's been up in the *maidan* living rough.

Yes, normally this was one that Matson of all people would abort. The other three would weigh it up and expect him to abort it.

But once outside the aircraft there was no going back.

The Broussard didn't have the range to return them anyway.

It had been a Kamikaze job from the beginning.

So Matson had drunk too much Cyprus brandy just like the rest of them. In other words, he had drunk just about enough.

The parachute harness hurt the cuts on his back. He wanted comfort, Helen Tesserer's or anyone's. The thought made him feel like a little boy. There were plenty of tears in a bottle of brandy.

2.

On both sides of the Atlantic the military arranged seminars for their political overlords. They were always well-subscribed, especially those that dealt with the ploys available to friend and foe in the case of a nuclear strike. Fossit had attended one in Warminster as an observer, and Pomeroy had been to Washington three times as a player – or that's what Fossit understood. Quinlan, of course, was one of the loud-mouthed keepers of the shoe.

These seminars were still available. The dummy war-rooms – once called simulation suites so that real friend and chummy foe could practise across the same world-table – waited beside their longstanding mainframe computers, old and not very rapid machines that no-one saw any need to enhance. This was in part because the first warhead, even when launched, would take a little time to arrive; more compellingly, because these war games weren't played as often as they used to be. In the age of constant modernisation and instant futurisation, they were considered counterproductive.

Smart young Americans, eager-eyed midAtlantic Brits, ageing statesmen on both sides of the ocean bedazzled by gadgetry to behave as if in their second youth, squeaking Principals from ministries, NATO allies and rivals, French- and Italian-speaking diplomats, hard-breathing communicators of mayhem and grunt who wore uniform only to fill the gaps between their medal-ribbons, all progressed rapidly beyond awe to embrace the infinite permutations of possibilities: first strike, second strike, nuclear-bluff, counter-bluff, counter-strike, proposed counter-strike, double-bluff, triple-bluff, wuf wuf wuf through dazzling programmes of ploys and plays, as if the whole thing was a game of ludo or at best chess. They deployed the world's rocketry like the pieces on an overstocked Halma board, to write off armies, cities, tribes, the Polar Ice-cap and an oceanful of deep-sea fish. If members of the Blue (which was the red white and blue) syndicate were successful in games that blew away a hemisphere, they erupted in cheers of ribald delight and yodels of derision to the Red's planning team. If their own half of humanity was judged by the computer to take first dip in the Colonel's finger-licking fry of atomised hydrocarbons, they expired to fake prepubertic screams. Fossit saw a Cabinet minister go down with pantomimic hands on pantomimic gonads – not, he remembered, a male Cabinet minister either. In short, the simulation suites were a place where grown men and women grew drunk on delusion. Clear-sighted action-men and highly intelligent and supposedly sophisticated staff-ranking women could be processed into tiresome global fools.

3.

Quinlan, Pomeroy, Fossit and Dixon were not global fools. They were thinking men.

In theory, thinking men should think quickly and variously – especially when thinking quickly and variously is what they are paid for.

Toss an atom-bomb into the equation and an awful lethargy steals across the brain. Ideas present themselves a terror at a time, and each terror has to be digested.

Men used to thinking variously and quickly also have to think correctly, and this is something they are not programmed for – or programmed to take responsibility for. If there's an atom-bomb to be anticipated, detected and deflected, you not only have to think at once and correctly, you only get the one chance.

An atom-bomb carries a penalty clause severe enough to make genius sleep and shock a committee of mensa-brains into eternal sputter.

Pomeroy had explained this all week behind his hand to Dixon, who didn't care, and Fossit who already knew. 'The last one I attended, we defrosted Greenland,' he confided. 'I used to think the cod-war was something that went on inside Quinny's jockstrap. Until I went on one of those – my *God*, Minister!'

Pomeroy's deliverances were rarely noisier than his asides. This one was a snake hiss of awe, so breathless that it sucked everyone in.

TAC had lost the Craw for a moment, so TAC was CAC.

CAC was on noisy chatter. CAC was on working. It fell into the black hole of Pomeroy's coffee-cup as he focused on its revelation.

'My God, minister – we're doing as they calculated. We're doing it for them. Either there's a bomb or there's a bluff, we thought. So let's go in and find out. How do we propose to find out? We bring one out to look at. Figuring *they* intend to fly it and detonate it themselves. What a suicidal proposition! They *always* must have reckoned that the Yanks, the Izzies, not to mention us were none of us the lads to sit around endlessly sucking our thumbs. We'd be *bound* to get it out. What were we going to do if a plane gave a little tick on a geiger? Believe there was a bomb on board? We didn't believe the radioactive debris from the Trident or radioactive Matson. We believed it was a bluff. No-one's going to write off all that real-estate because a joker smears a piece of low-grade radioactive waste along its belly.

'There's a bomb on that plane and Captain Matson's going to deliver it for them. When it explodes, as it probably will on touch-down, the hijackers will have achieved their aim, and Libya – still negotiating – will claim to have clean hands. It won't matter where in NATO he delivers it!'

4.

Collinson beckoned Matson forward.

He stepped across Fison's legs and smiled at him. It wasn't the Leader smiling to keep men's courage up. It was brandy grinning at a joke. Three of us end in *-son*, brandy thought. We're nothing but a pack of kids.

'Zero minus three,' Collinson said.

'It'll be splendid. Cut the engines when you're ready.'

The engines sputtered.

'Isn't that a bit previous?'

'That was the fuel gone. We'll glide far enough, and she'll stay up a good bit longer.'

The abort signal came on: NEGIT NEGIT NEGIT on the over-audible radio.

Levett gazed at the sound, grasping at instant hope.

There was no hope, just the propeller judder as the rotors dopplered back, the slam of coldness buffeting past the jump-faring at one hundred and twenty knots.

Collinson came back, whey-faced with tension, like a sick man rushing to get outside. He went straight out, his hands already on his D-handle.

Matson got Levett and Fison hooked up. Fison went. Levett didn't. Matson caught his backside with a full swing of his jump-valise – explosives, ammunition, machine-pistols, the lot. Levett went, and Matson went straight after, the Broussard already tipping off-course, Matson forgetting the two static lines and going through them like a waiter through a bead curtain.

5.

'What've we've got for the moment is the fog of war,' Quinlan mused. 'Static up to the eyeballs. The problem is – with what shall we seek to replace it? What is the realisable ideal?'

'The hope that Matson either breaks his neck or hears the recall on the ground. Cyprus can send a powerful signal.'

'I've already dispatched an overfly.' Fisher said. 'He'll be able to hear that, if he listens in. It has his frequency.'

'Is an overfly prudent?'

'It's not perfect, Minister. What is? You've got about twenty minutes to recall it.'

'Let it overfly. Let everything go. I ask you what we want and you offer me a choice between Matson and blind chance.'

'Matson *is* blind chance,' Pomeroy said. Less phatically he offered, 'We want a commando – not a big force, but a commando rather than a hit-team – that can hold and stabilise events on the ground long enough for experts to get into that cargo hold.'

'How long?'

'Say an hour,' Hattie Dacres said. 'They'd need to evaluate the potential of the postulated device.'

'If it's there they'll kill themselves,' Fossit said. 'I mean – they'll be exposed to such an intensity of radiation.'

The Dacres didn't deign to answer.

'They'll also be under substantial risk if the cargo hold is only bluffed up,' Lorna Benvenista said. 'Won't they?' Dacres was the nuclear expert; though this was only nuclear commonsense.

'It'll be a bomb,' Pomeroy insisted.

'Not again,' Quinlan moaned. 'If we look we're taking care of all eventualities.'

'Except what to do if you look and confirm the bomb's existence,' Dixon said, 'and confirm that it's unstable, or intended to detonate on landing.'

'Destroy the aircraft,' Quinlan said. 'That would be my order.'

'You'd almost certainly detonate the device,' Fossit said. 'Right, Miss Dacres? I mean, you can incapacitate a delivery vehicle that contains a *military* device and leave the device intact; but something that depends merely on critical mass –'

'Blow it up,' Quinlan said.

He left the room, but he couldn't quite turn his back on apocalypse. He came back to say, 'I mean, you set a charge, you get as many people away as you can, *if* you can; but you leave a force in place to ensure that the charge is not interfered with.'

'Suicide missions,' he muttered from the door. 'I hate 'em. They do us no good at all.'

Hattie Dacres was bright this evening, bright as cyanide anyway. Before following her minister out she said, 'That commando should be told to destroy the plane. Simple order. If it blows up a few hundred people, well – that's the equation. Best do it in the desert, where it's only hundreds and not millions.'

'In which case all it needs is an air-strike,' Fossit said.

'The man wants someone to look,' the Dacres said over her shoulder.

'It's a bomb. It's a bomb. It's a bomb,' Pomeroy said. 'I don't think there ever was a bluff – not in either aircraft. We've been dazzled by our belief that Libya can't make bombs and that terrorists can't steal them.

'Worse, we've been bondoozled by the sheer bloody Matsonness of Paddy, or the Paddyness of Matson. The hijackers – or their masters – planned on processing an action man from among passengers in that Forces' Charter. They couldn't necessarily guarantee the existence of one of high enough calibre to present the Trident to Daddy Neptune. Your average roughed-up officer might well have contented himself with getting the plane home. Full stop.'

'I think they intended the Trident to be detonated.'

'How?' The Benvenista was growing impatient. 'With a timing device? Or an impact trigger? It didn't detonate on the surface. Nor has it obliged us since.'

'Paddy's passenger woman was meant to activate it. Grant was right. They'll have something better in the Jumbo.'

'We're back and turning full circle,' Fossit groaned. 'All we've put a stop to is Matson.'

6.

He was scared, so the jump began wrong.

The wind tore into everything – his cut back most of all. The pain was so huge it destabilised him. He swung on it slowly, as if he had a rock on his shoulders. Not a rock, a concrete wall set with glass. He wrestled with the weight, and it fought him back. The updraught buzzed past his ears, updraught then controlled slipstream. He tore at the wind and heard Dragout laughing.

He got the moonscape level beneath him, and looked for others. Nothing. His eyes were streaked with pain, his goggles furred. Not a fart-light anywhere.

He turned through a hundred and eighty degrees, searching the reflections that blew off the sand. Moonlight lay on everything like poison gas. He was already lower than the jebel to his left, and there was the leg valise to consider.

He felt for his D-ring, dragged it and dragged it some more, then waited for the harness to crack his guts open.

The canopy came out clean and gentle. He felt nothing at shoulder and crotch, save this pain that had been with him since Dragout started laughing. He looked up, once, at a perfectly developed canopy.

No time for the usual prayer of gratitude. When the chute ran out and the ties crackled open it was tempting to exult, like a toddler beneath its granny's apron.

He had to unbuckle his valise and play it out. This one was extra heavy, full of too many of Barkworth's goodies. It was held with two straps. The second release jammed.

He began to rotate, coming down much too fast like a clown falling off a highwire with only an open umbrella to save him.

A clown? No: a suicide from a skyscraper. A clown has a safety-net.

If he couldn't spring the valise he was as good as dead. If he hit with the bag still along his leg, it would be like jumping in splints. There'd be the extra velocity as well. He'd telescope a thigh. Telescope his spine. Telescope something.

His fingers tore at the snaffle. He was inside the earthglow now, inside and corkscrewing in. A second or two more and he'd be jacked into the desert like a bottle-opener in its cork.

The clip parted, the valise tumbled away top-end first, giving him no time to seize the line and play it out. When it reached its fullest extent it obliged his shoulder and crotch straps in ways the canopy had not dreamt of: it cut him in half.

A military parachutist has two of everything. Two, then two twice.

He saw a lip of sand twisting beneath his valise and his foot. He tried to correct the rotation, kick his buttocks free from his arse-strap, stop the swing, stabilise the valise, get a decent anti-drift grip on the forward webbing; and probably managed at least one of these things before he struck and was rolling down a seawave of sand.

He seemed to fall for ever down the dark side of the world, little bits of which forced their way into his cuffs and up his trouser legs and entered all the broken parts of him like glass powdered into salt.

He stopped with a skull-trepanning jolt and two memories: the valise had hit first as intended, and released its weight just enough in the thin air for the canopy to flare and stop Icarus from breaking.

That was one memory. Oh yes. He'd heard and seen the Broussard go in. It crashed as he crashed. It made a red-hot scattering of fire, and a detonation much too demonstrative for the comfort of a covert operation.

Meanwhile, he was on the dark side of a dune, minus Collinson and Levett and the other bloody man, and he'd landed very badly.

7.

'Sir!'

Matson disliked noise. He had walked in places where noise is expressly forbidden. Such as the Valley of the Shadow of Death.

'Sir! Captain Matson, sir!'

The dune was huge. The dune – considered in detail on a recent aerial photograph – was no place for a parachutist, not even with a beach-buggy. Matson had collided with its lip. Its lip – at 20 ft per sec. – had teeth in it. He had then rolled in a tangle of valise-wire and deflated canopy all the way down its moonless side.

'Sir! Sir!'

He began to count his limbs and take account of his mind.

His mind and his limbs were largely encased in skin, skin which had been flayed by Dragout and Dragout's wind and now the laughing lip of Dragout's dune till they felt like recent second-degree sunburn.

He had tumbled down a prehistoric dune that was moving in the universal direction of all major calcine ridges of the Sahara at exactly one metre a year. Here it was, Rhondda-high, seeping north-west like an ancient slurry to arrive exactly at this second in time at the precise point on the undrawn map where it could interfere with his erratic trajectory.

Question: can a parachutist, properly speaking, be said to have a trajectory once his canopy is fully deployed?

Answer: not only recent second-degree sunburn but infected recent second-degree sunburn, bone deep.

'Thank God I saw you go in, sir. You've been lying here for the best part of a couple of hours.'

'Sir' as in shock. It was several years since Matson had been called 'sir', except by a tea-lady who had forgotten his name. He opened his eyes and saw Levett leaning over him by torch-light, as lovingly as Madonna with Child.

'Thank God I kicked you out,' he said.

'Thank God you did, sir.'

'Please not "sir".' 'Sir' was never used where Matson used to be. It marked a man out. No man likes to be marked out, not among men.

He struggled to sit upright, numbering his bones. His bones had the aforementioned sunburn, but were otherwise good. 'It was that sodding valise,' he explained.

Levett glistened with relief. Levett nodded at every word he said. Levett proffered him water. Did damn nearly every damn thing short of plug his mouth with a nipple.

'I'm all right. My hinges work.' He stood up and felt for the Browning on his hip. The rest was in the valise. The Browning would be full of sand, of course, jammed from muzzle to arse with schist and starlight.

'Let's get going,' he said. The dune would be impossible, but that's what he said.

He began to tug at the valise.

'Thank God you're alive,' Levett was saying. 'Collinson is broken, I'm afraid. And Fison pretty badly bent.'

8.

He thought of killing Collinson and Fison. He thought of everything. But they deserved their chance. They had no chance, but they deserved it.

Levett was the one he'd judged weakest in Cyprus and upstairs in the Broussard.

Now he seemed calm and strong. He had the two men secure in their survival foil and was looking for ways to splint them. 'Start on your antibiotics,' he told Collinson. 'We've all got some in our aid-pack.'

'What's the point?' Collinson spoke through the classical chatter of teeth. He'd broken his thigh, so his jaw reacted.

'You'll die in a lot less pain,' Levett said. 'And you'll smell better while you're doing it.'

Levett might just be on a post-jump high – it takes a lot of adrenalin to step out of a plane, especially at night, especially when you can't do it. Matson decided he was going to be all right. He watched him bandage Fison's gashed leg.

Collinson was their best-qualified widebody pilot, too.

Matson wondered why CAC had cancelled them. CAC might know something he didn't know. Or CAC might be resuming its normal existence as a centipede with cold feet.

Obedience was not necessarily going to be his way with this one.

'Snake,' Collinson said. It gave his teeth something to talk about.

'If it's not near enough to strike, scare it away,' Matson advised.

'Shit. I hate snakes.'

'I love 'em,' Matson lied. 'If we've got snakes then there are things here to eat – including the snakes, if need be. We'll move to better cover at dawn and try to find a less reptilian place, just the same.'

'What's the plan?' Fison was less pessimistic with his wound dressed.

'We'll lie up and wait for information. So we'll need a north or north-east facing lie-up, towards Cyprus. As sheltered from the sun as possible, and hopefully from Sifr WaaHid, which is north-west. When we're in our little laager we'll rig as much aerial as we can to enhance our radio.

'I'm in charge, as is clear. I intend to abandon no-one,' he lied. 'That does not mean that I will not leave the injured temporarily.

'Nor, for what it is worth, do I feel obliged to follow orders that contradict our own tactical appreciation. My authority is not Cyprus or London. It's my commonsense. Your authority is me. We may yet take the Jumbo out. We may even take it out empty, which will give us more chance and will not necessarily jeopardise anyone else. You all appreciate the importance of getting that aircraft out, irrespective of lives – our own or anyone else's.'

They grunted agreement.

'Levett. You've done a good job. You're in charge here. You chaps, try not to sleep until dawn. It's bloody cold, so stay inside your survival blankets. We can't post sentries or anything funny, but we must keep watch.

'I am now going to take a *very* distant look at Sifr WaaHid. I'll be back before sun-up, whether I reach it or not.'

9.

'There are those three trees in a slight hollow.' Matson had stalked his group without them hearing him. But he had worked round behind, and nearly sprawled over Levett's trip-thread. Levett was watching forward, and that was good.

He had not found Sifr WaaHid, but he had found Dragout's house, which meant he knew where Sifr WaaHid was.

Now he helped Levett lift Collinson and then Fison to the cover of the thorn trees. Collinson groaned, but he was soggy with dope.

Levett and Matson rigged an aerial.

'You chaps have all read your aircrew survival manuals, I guess? Well, you know that this sort of landscape is unlikely to have any nasties that conceal themselves in trees. Let's hope those things lend a bit of shade as well as cover.'

'We've got four quarts of water,' Levett said. 'Just our personal drinking bottles.'

'Your survival sheets are wet, though. We should be able to collect something tonight. Experience prompts me to believe we'll be lucky to manufacture more than a pint a catchment, though. And we've only two bits of spare foil.' He doubted if they'd get more than a pint in all. 'At nightfall we'll use some dry wood to make some tea.'

'There's no tea in a Zizzie pack – only chocolate and suckers.'

'I always keep a few teabags somewhere about my person,' Matson said. He didn't think he'd say where. They might have exploded in his boots and jockstrap. What he did say was, 'I know where there's water. But it'll be risky to get it, too risky more than once. So we'll deteriorate fast. Let's hope Cyprus comes in quick, or we're going to need to lift that Jumbo.'

They waited all day.

Cyprus didn't come on.

10.

Admiral Cravicz did not let himself grow angry. He tried really hard. He had heard of the Byzantine politics of Quinlan's little lot, and was ready for them. What he wasn't prepared to tolerate was the accompanying labyrinth of inertia. Quinlan himself seemed to carry his indecision around with him like a snail with its shell. If the man got his head stuck back in it this time, he knew he'd never get him out again.

The Craw let his jaw jut. 'We don't have to believe Marcus to act on what he says.' He let it jut some more: 'It follows naturally from our thinking about the bomb.' If they wanted ideas they could have ideas. 'We didn't believe that those planes had a bomb simply or even mainly because such a belief was believable. We chose to believe it as a *working* hypothesis.' He emphasised *working* to stop the slop-heads emphasising *hypothesis*: their brains grew fuzzy if you fed them abstract nouns. 'We've got to believe the bomb bit because it represents the worst case overall. Marcus has merely proposed a worse worst case. I won't say he's right. I don't say he's wrong. What we must do should have been done already. We must act decisively and within a very short time-scale to minimise the implications of every worst case. Those cases may change. The action is a constant.'

Quinlan smiled. He'd been busy with inaction all week. 'The risk has intensified,' he said. A disaster is always easier to bear than a decision.

Never help an idiot untangle his string. The Craw said simply, 'You British relieved Khartoum and Ladysmith and Mafeking, and consequently became victims of history. We were lucky enough to lose an entire command at Little Big Horn, and it's done us nothing but good. We don't reinforce failure. When it comes to reinforcing this one, the bottom line starts at zero. So, quickly, gentlemen, are we going to sacrifice aircraft, aircraft and passengers, or is there a lower zero?'

'There's another bottom line,' Quinlan said. 'That's why we put Matson back again.'

'I wondered just when we were going to come to that,' the Craw said.

'All that he's changed is my worst case,' Pomeroy said quickly.

'Let's stay where we're at, while we're at it.' The Craw still wasn't angry. 'So you've loosed this fellow off again. Why?'

'The Cabinet Office rather fancied the idea.'

'And just why would that be?'

'Washington encouraged the notion.'

'You didn't, by any chance, feel you might be doing something I should have been told about?'

'That's up to Washington, Admiral. Matson is information-gathering, that's all. I'm surprised you weren't consulted.'

'The consultation should have been from you, Mr Quinlan. A whisper from you would have saved a deal of subsequent hollering across the bay. So Captain Matson is on a reconnaissance merely?'

'Now aborted,' Quinlan said. 'We think aborted.'

The Craw smiled his contempt at that one. 'Perhaps he was aborted the way he was sent in, behind the back of someone's hand. I mean, I detect a certain lack of commitment here, an absence of brass. Where, for instance, is the excellent Barkworth? The estimable Fisher? My table looks empty. Are you sure this is the main feast?'

'*My* table,' Quinlan said.

'In Cyprus,' Pomeroy ventured. 'Seeing Paddy off.'

'He must be able to handle his own back buttons by now. It's a funny army that sends a pair of generals to wave a junior officer goodbye. A junior officer on a recce. A funny army on a funny operation. Well, I'm glad at least some of your people are over there, Terence. It's where they should have been a long time ago.' He stood up, sorrowfully. 'I'm grateful for the seat at your table, Terence. My own table is ordered elsewhere. You or your nominees can sit at it or not. But I want a command-structure, not a gossip-parlour.'

'Where, Admiral?' Pomeroy spoke for Quinlan, who disdained, or seemed incapable of, speech.

'Cyprus. It's all fixed with someone somewhere in London. We can make our own tea.' He smiled, amazingly gently in the circumstances. 'I've been playing the Washington game all my life, Terence. It's like any other act of leverage, a question of knowing where the force is. Washington is silted to its eyeballs on this one, just like Whitehall. But one thing was sure to happen if this thing dragged on – Marcus had the sense enough to see it and to say it.'

'The Israelis.' Quinlan was truly weary. 'I warned of it at the beginning.'

'The Indians were all around you, so you painted a pretty picture.' On the way to the door, he added, 'I wish it didn't have to be Cyprus, but I can't be seen trying to run Israel from the radio-room of a Sixth Fleet carrier.'

'Hateful man,' Fossit said.

'I told you he knew how to creep about at night.'

'So Israel is off the leash?'

'Not officially, Minister. And not the whole pack. I'd have

been told. You would have heard. It sounds like Zefat, or even Barel.'

'I want a firm hand on his collar, whoever he is. And I need to hear some barks from Matson. Tell Fisher. We pay enough money for the technology.'

11.

The man had come from due east. He came from a pinpoint drop on an exact bearing.

Cyprus had given him the source of Matson's carrier wave. Strange that Cyprus had given Matson nothing.

The man was tired. He had been dumped in the sand, six miles out, just where the dunes hinge up and make life difficult. He had jumped with a leg-valise, but there was no way he could lug all its contents here. He had buried it with his parachute. Others could help him with it later.

The people who'd dropped him knew what he might find and what he would need to bring. He had it in an eight-kilogramme backpack and he had been marching with it since midnight.

He had made good time, but the contents of the pack made a noise. He set it down quietly and checked his sketch map and his compass. To do this he sank his body between two broken flakes of stone and kept very still.

He noticed the three trees, the little hollow of dead ground just discernable in their shadow. He couldn't see the aerial or any kit, but he knew Matson must be there.

He stowed his map into his thigh-pocket and tucked his compass into his shirt where it wouldn't rattle. He cocked his Uzi machine-pistol, and latched it to safe.

He moved forward, feeling for silence with the sole of his foot.

Then he saw Matson or his sentry. The man was quite still, and facing away from him.

He sat about twenty metres to the right of the trees, with his head covered, a stone among dusky stones.

Matson was very thorough, or at least surrounded himself with thoroughgoing professionals.

The man began to stalk Matson or his sentry. As he got closer he brushed the soil with his heels, making sure there was nothing to crunch or snap beneath his planted bodyweight.

He noticed the trip thread about two paces before he reached it. As far as he could tell, it was meant to topple stones not detonate a grenade.

The gun muzzle against his neck was very cold. The temperature had been at zero for nearly half the night. The knife point that nudged his upper arm did not feel cold. It was hot with a little gush of his blood.

If the man turned to disarm his assailant, the gun might be detonated, and that would be a pity. The man knew of ways to surprise gun arms, but not when they were used in such crafty conjunction with a knife.

Still, he would prevail. His training would see to it. The knife and the gun were abruptly withdrawn. He had not sensed, had not smelled, had not seen the person behind him, yet that person had been there and now he stepped back.

The man lifted his arms, Uzi and all, and turned slowly. The knife and the gun were three yards off. They had touched him merely to warn him. Now they were where he could be killed by them, but where the hands that were holding them were out of harm's way.

'Shlomo Barel!'

The voice sounded surprised, but not towards affection. Barel heard the voice, and realised who it was for the first time. He did not love Matson either. He had once tried to have him killed, but the Matson he wanted killed had a different voice, a voice that belonged to Pomeroy. He was tired now, he must decide later whether his quarrel was with the real man or the imagined voice. He said, 'Captain Matson? I don't think you'll pull the trigger.'

'True, old dear. But I had to find out who you were. I can't say I'm pleased.'

'You will be when I've fetched my pack.' Barel did not seek leave of Matson's gun; he simply turned and retraced his steps towards the little cleft in the stone.

The gun was still pointing at him. 'Two gallons of water, Captain Matson. I suppose that even a desert bride grows thirsty.'

'Put your gun down beside the water.' Matson didn't sound as if he enjoyed the joke. 'What the fuck have they sent me you for? Superman would be more appropriate for this mess.'

Matson took water from Barel's pack and gave some to two of his companions who lay in survival foil, obviously badly injured. Then he offered the plastic container to his sentry, who drank deeply.

He returned the container to Barel. 'Walking's thirsty work,' he said, making the Israeli aware of his Irish accent for the first time. He didn't drink any of the water himself.

Nor did Barel. 'I'll save it for sun up.' He wasn't done with speaking. 'There will be an air-landing at midnight. An Entebbe-style operation, rather than a parachute commando.'

Matson grimaced his disapproval, but asked nothing.

'That being said, certain key personnel will parachute in earlier and rendezvous here. Those you will brief. I will lead, you understand; but we need your briefing. Have you recce'd?'

'I was at Sifr WaaHid tonight.'

The sun came up all at once, cancelling comfort. Barel did not see the sun. He was already asleep, away from the others, between deep stones.

Matson watched him for a long time. There were deaths between the two men, one above others. And the brain is full of strange thoughts once the sun is up.

Barel's voice came from the ground. It spoke slowly, as if in a trance: 'Within certain operational limits, I believe we should aim to eliminate this Ahmed Khalil, this Dragout of yours. Marcus Pomeroy also bids me say to you he sees very little commercial value in Ibrahim Nuseibeh. He has double-crossed us all.'

Perhaps Matson imagined Barel's tone. His words were clear enough.

Matson did not sleep. His wounds were full of hate.

TWENTY

1.

Lieutenant-colonel Khadduri's body was troubling him. The colonel's perception was growing out of hand. He was becoming ill at ease with his environment, and his environment was troubled with itself.

His spacious hut was just like its owner – cheerful on the outside and melancholy within. The whitewashed exterior was battered and faded – you have to live in a desert and try to decorate walls built of desert to appreciate that whiteness can be bleached to extinction, bleached almost black, not to put too crazy a point on it. Between hut and hut, the grey slabs of concrete and sand still shone with lime. In the shadow of the alleys, the murex footing had stood up very well. Limewash and murex gave way to mud-brown and mauve. Yes, his hut was an image of his mind.

Ridiculous to call it his home, but a soldier drops roots very quickly. Show him a tent and he sits in it. Sit him in a tent and he broods.

Particularly if there's a woman in the tent next door.

And if he himself is an officer, a captain acting lieutenant-colonel, and one of his men is enjoying the woman in the tent next door?

Such matters are galling in the extreme. They lead to envy and indiscipline.

Joyfulness among men breeds disquiet in an officer.

A contented officer is one whose men are not happy.

There was a rat in his hut. His men had not bothered to

catch it for him. There were signs that the rat was finding ways to breed. The rat had not arrived into the desert by itself.

Khadduri was the only solitary out here.

2.

All this only meant one thing. The desert was getting to Khadduri. It had been getting to him all week. He had it in his ears, his nose, his eyes, those little orifices of the brain. Now it was inside his head, and it was making him mad.

A soldier has his drills to hold on to. He told himself that. When a soldier speaks of 'living by the book' he means more than 'living by the *Qu'ran*, the *Reading*': he means living by *Army Book One* and *Army Book Two* and Army Books up to and beyond *Army Book One Hundred*, with their frequent revisions and deletions, their postage-stamp emendations which his sergeant, now his sergeant-major has lovingly pasted in for him, even here in the desert, most of all in the desert. Yes, a soldier has his drills, so the soldier keeps running like a well-oiled sand-proof timepiece. But a soldier can go mad. Khadduri had seen it happen. And when a soldier goes mad, he goes madder than a man. Clockwork is crazier than the untutored bone.

There were those, like Dragout, who pretended that a Libyan should be at ease in the desert. They argued that Arabs were at home in the sand. Dragout was a romancer, probably a liar. The fact is Arabs are never at home here. Libyans live always on the edge of the sand and hope to stay off that edge. They respect it and fear it. Their soldiers do not enter the Sahara. The Sahara defeats them before they set foot in it.

Of the Arabs, only the great tribes of nomads are at home here, and no town Arab trusts a nomad any more than one nomad trusts another. And no-one among the Beddu is as at home here as certain mad Englishmen and Germans and Americans are at home.

Or Irishmen. Sometimes Khadduri imagined Matson out there – waiting and deadly, somnolent perhaps as a snake without water, but digesting its own poison, brewing its rage and fermenting more. There was no real proof that Matson had gone with the plane. Or, if he had gone, got anywhere. Or if he had got anywhere, not come back. Nuseibeh's telephone told his cracked head nothing. Even a ghost can come back. Last night his men had spoken of a fireball in the sky, a fireball out of silence. He was coming to believe them. Yes: the desert had got him.

The desert gets a man in the brain and the balls. Take care of one and you take care of the other. So it was that his thoughts began to turn towards the Jewish aeroplane, and to its women who would soon be in the fire. What a waste that would be. He turned his thoughts towards them only by degrees, just the same, until he discovered that his thoughts had always been with them. He was the one who saw they had their ration of boiled water, their dried dates, their meal-bread and their semolina or rice. He had been the one from the beginning. He was the one they knew to be in charge and entirely frank and good.

Although he was the officer in command, he did not propose to have all of the women, or even any woman all at once. What his balls proposed to his brain was that his brain should have a talk with them one by one. He was, by inclination, an intelligence officer. He must search out the Israelis from among the rest, and find out what intelligence such women had on offer.

The women who sat on the plane, for example. The women who sat on the plane kept awake all night by their children. These women would not sleep sound like the ones in the huts. These women, last night's women, might have seen the flames in the sky. This would be one kind of intelligence. Or they might have seen no flames at all. That would be another.

3.

Once Khadduri had organised a procession of young women from the Israeli widebody to file through his command hut his sense of good order returned. It is not women's presence that drives a man to distraction, but their absence – particularly when, as all this week, their absence is no further off than the oasis of Modfai's breathing and grunting, somewhere in the sweaty Sahara of the next room.

Some of these warm-smelling fresh-eyed young females had indeed seen flames in the sky, flames like an aircraft exploding on a mountain or a house on fire. They had been the ones seated by the windows nearest the jebel, and several spoke to him with arrogant defiance, as if their burning God was at hand, or at the very least a rescue party.

The more Khadduri heard such certainty the calmer he crew. So many young women had a calming effect anyway. It was hard to worry about Matson while he was surrounded by all this. Especially hard to worry about a Matson who was probably a ghost. Besides, woman's talk is idle. These might come from cultures that pretended they were equal, but they were only equal in property, certainly not in the head. One of them had probably seen a circuit-breaker flare up among the ring of compound lights. This happened several times an evening. She had imagined a burning aircraft and spoken to her friends. Gossip had done the rest. The widebody windows were dusty. All glass was unclear in this land of oily sunshine.

There were other complications. None of them were dressed like his women; several of them were as incongruous in their brash American clothes as the ruined jukeboxes in the surrounding cantonment. Most of them spoke English, but it was not the English of the South London Polytechnic.

It took several hours and perhaps a dozen of these interminable interrogations before one of the young females said, 'Why are you grilling us women, anyway? Why not the men?'

He did explain that the men were in the huts, and that the huts overlooked relatively little; but he found himself walking her in order to show her all this, and finishing up not in his command hut, but in his other place, where he kept his disquiet and where he never was at this time of day.

4.

Modfai took a long time to find him, because he looked first in all the obvious places. A long time had obviously been quite long enough. The woman was crying and beating Khadduri with her fists, and the colonel looked embarrassed about something, probably about being caught out like this, but the sergeant-major had a message to bring.

'Women are a very great blessing,' Modfai said. He smiled, and soothed his hand palm-downwards across the pocket of his best shirt. 'I praise Allah for them.' Sergeant-majors are among the most tolerant of men.

'I praise Allah also.'

'Does this one perhaps come from the Jewish aeroplane?'

'She is American.' Khadduri regretted the speed of his reply. He knew a better one. 'Men belong to a million tribes and follow many faiths,' he said. 'Women are all of one kind.'

A man can click his tongue in delight or disapproval. Modfai's click suggested neither. He had perfected it as a sergeant.

'Being American, she will complain,' he said at last.

'Being American, she has done this she will complain of many times before,' Khadduri observed. 'This is because she is allowed to marry without bringing along her integrity. Even a president or a judge may marry a woman without integrity in America. So her complaint will be the less. Besides, I am going to release all of the passengers from the aircraft to the huts. If she complains, then no-one will notice her tears among the general rejoicing.'

'Is this what Lord Dragout commands?'

'It is what I command.'

Sergeant-major Modfai was glad that his colonel was no longer taking orders from a black man. It hurt him to see the Army degraded by a Tibbu, even a Tibbu who was ruler of his tribe. The sergeant-major was a farm Arab, the colonel a town Arab, and both of them were soldiers. They disliked nomads.

Sergeant-major Modfai was full of all these emotions when he remembered what the colonel's dishevelled woman had distracted him from. 'Sir,' he said, 'the Lord Dragout sent me with a message. He wants to see you at his house, sir.'

'His hut, surely?'

'He said his house. He was most insistent.'

'And he asked you to present his compliments?'

The sergeant-major sighed. The sergeant-major's sigh was not as perfect as his click. His sigh was not neutral.

5.

Barel slept for a long time. He was exhausted from his pack-march, and – like Matson – out of condition. Zefat had ordered him behind a desk; now this emergency had brought him out again. He had free-fallen without a refresher. He had hurried across rough terrain without practice. His body had done everything right, but now it was letting him down. Sleep was its only medicine; so his body took it.

He woke towards midday, when the sun got in deep between the stones. He didn't move at first. He could smell something unpleasant, like a dog that a snake has struck. It could only be a man, and near.

His hand was on his gun, so he lifted it towards the smell. Then he sat up quickly.

Matson crouched there, his nostrils flaring fastidiously. Matson didn't seem to like the smell either. He held his gun less alertly than Barel did, but he held it, just the same. He jerked his head towards Levett, who was burying some rags and the remnants of field-dressings. Levett could only cover them with stones. The smell grew better, but it wouldn't go away until the sun cooked it, and that was not yet. Barel remembered that he was visiting a disaster area, full of Matson's broken men.

'Well, Captain Matson –' Each time he woke, there would have to be some kind of negotiation.

Matson said nothing. No doubt he was trying to be superior, but he reminded Barel of nothing so much as a tongue-tied schoolchild at a party.

'It seems we have to work together.' Shyness is its own kind of arrogance, even in young girls. 'Perhaps you're thinking you'd like to give me the bullet, right between the eyes. Is that what you're thinking?'

Damn him for these protracted sulks, the European littleness of his emotions. Didn't he recognise that he, Barel, had suffered?

'No headshots,' Matson said. 'And certainly not a single round. When I come to get you it will be with the whole clip, somewhere between thorax and belly. That's the way I'm trained to do it. That's the way I've always done it.'

'Not in Barcelona,' Barel whispered. 'And certainly not in Yoffo. Nor, so far as I know, in Chislehurst.'

'I was responsible for none of those things.'

The accent was thick, as thick as Barel's own English. Perhaps it was because of the Irish in him. More likely it was because the stress of interrogation had robbed him of his proper tongue.

Matson stooped forward, causing Barel to tighten his grip on the Uzi. Only then did Barel realise how underweight the gun was.

Matson handed him a knotted handkerchief. Barel took it and tucked it into his tunic. 'So,' he said. 'You have light fingers.' He wondered, just the same, how anyone could have removed the magazine, emptied it of bullets and replaced it, without waking him.

'No,' Matson mused. 'You have heavy bullets.'

'I don't use mercury.'

Matson stood up and turned his back on him, signalling to Levett. The man came towards them, and handed an aluminium canteen to Matson and left them alone again, obviously by arrangement. Matson passed the container to Barel. It was full of tea, strong and stewed with powdered milk.

'I don't like Uzis,' Matson said. 'I mean, I don't like the submachine-gun. Other things they make I admire. You'd taken a lot of sand on board.'

'Ah – the heavy bullets. I'll clean my other magazines.'

'I've cleaned them already. I've got to trust my life to you.'

Barel sucked hot tea. 'Isn't the fire risky?'

'Not by day. Not here. You can smell tea for miles at night. You can smell Collinson, too.'

'Is his leg bad?'

'He'll need surgery, of course. They both will. But we've got antibiotics. It's the dressings that pong. When do you want to get that kit of yours?'

'Now, I suppose. They're coming in tonight.'

'I'll give you a hand. Levett will have to stay here.'

'It'll take more than two of us. There's about seventy kilos.'

'We *are* more than two of us.' He offered friendship like an infant, like John Wayne in a movie.

6.

Moving by daylight was easier than by night. They both agreed on that. You chafe more. You dehydrate more. Your head aches. You burn. But you walk faster. You don't trip so often. They both tripped frequently, but not so often. If they suffered, they suffered in silence. They had lived through similar courses of training, courses which encouraged the view that suffering is the universal norm. All flesh bruises equally. All bruises hurt. So write your fucking poems about something else. When men are in the shit together, there's plenty of stink for everyone, so sing us another song, not like the other one, do.

Barel stumbled badly and leapt back upright in a single dazed movement too quick for Matson's helping. Matson had turned to help, and Barel didn't show his irritation. Irritation was failure.

'I'm a professional,' Matson said. More John Wayne. 'Or I'm meant to be. Killing you can wait till I stop being one.'

'I come from a race of superior amateurs.'

'Yes, and you don't forgive. When I was a little boy in Ireland, I was taught that the inability to forgive was one of the great deficiencies of your religion. In Ireland I was schooled in the great deficiencies of every religion except my own particular brand of my own. In England they taught me nothing. England was right.'

'Are you trying to adopt a superior moral position, Matson?'

'Perhaps, Shlomo.' His use of a first name between them startled both men about equally. 'Moral only, and manifestly I'm no moralist. In my religion, God forgives me. In my religion he forgives you, too. It's just that I have to pay for forgiveness, so the system leaves you better off.' He was bitter now, bitter aloud in his sudden closeness to a man he'd tried so hard to hate. 'Yes, in my religion, God forgives, Shlomo. It's just the priests who hound you to death. They did for my mother, anyway.'

Barel held out his hand. 'I'm not going to forgive you, Matson. But I've got your face now. When I stick pins in it, I'll call it Patrick.' He smiled. Then he got busy with a prismatic compass. 'Last night I could grid on a star,' he said. 'By day we go mirage from mirage.'

Matson looked forward to being superior, but Barel led them to his overweight leg-valise with no trouble at all.

7.

In the heat of the day, a man lies down. And if he has a green place to lie, beneath old porous roof-slats encrusted with fungus and mould, he rests easy.

Modfai's hut was hardly a refrigerator, more a ruined oasis. His nostrils led him towards it. He had looked into its musty interior and chosen it for what it was, a dampness among drought, a cavern away from the noonday sun, a senior NCO's pleasure palace, an illusion.

He held his favourite Avaroc girl by the wrist, and in other ways as necessary. He had ordered her from the stewardess' hut, and of course she had obeyed. As they moved towards his own place she became more reluctant, never mind why. He was a big man, and patient. He changed his grip and put up with her ill-manners.

Such a woman in the market would be flattered if a sergeant of infantry spoke to her. Lowly though a soldier might be to some, she would know herself to be lower. As for a sergeant-major – it was beyond considering.

The girl dragged against his arm. Eventually she stopped walking.

He encouraged her.

She shouted. She did not scream. She shouted. She did not wail, unlike his own women; she could not keen through her nose. She shouted, and went on shouting, so he gave her a good slap that echoed round the alleys.

She shouted more words he could not understand. That too was unpleasant, and most unnecessary.

He slapped her again. Then he picked her up and carried her over his shoulder.

Modfai did not have a conscience in such matters. He left the conscience to Khadduri. Khadduri had promised them all sweets and set him free.

This one kicked her feet against his thighs, and hammered the small of his back. Modfai had good kidneys, and her kicks did not hurt once her shoes fell off. He plodded on.

If a conscripted man has one sweet, an enlisted man deserves two. As for junior NCOs then senior NCOs, not to mention the likes of sergeant-majors – well, the loins would burst to think about it, so best keep a tranquil head.

He pushed his senior stewardess into his little cave of a room, and closed the door. Then they stood gasping at each other while he unbuttoned the cloth of his tunic.

He had been with her before, of course. So had some of his men. Just the same, something of her had stayed with him and continued to nag at him. The memory did not tug him the way the Düsseldorf Tart tugged, because this one could not show as much reluctance as the Düsseldorf Tart. Still, she tugged, so she was here. It was easy to forget about his men. The woman was here, and his men were days and days ago.

She spoke some more words to him.

At first he could not understand. Then he recognised one word clearly. It was not said as he would say it, but it was in Arabic. She was telling him she was pregnant.

She waved the word in his teeth as if it was a kind of shield. An air-stewardess knows the word for pregnant in most languages in the world. It is a word like *sick* and *earache* that she has to listen out for.

Modfai did not know this. He heard her speak the word again, and pronounce it better. One might say she came to say it exactly, even though she did not get the case right.

He smiled at her, a smile of congratulation and sympathy. Then he pulled her on top of him. It is impossible to defile a pregnant woman, unless she is married. This woman wore no sign of marriage. No husband would allow her to do such a job.

He told her not to struggle, but her Arabic stopped at pregnant. He promised her substantial rewards and made lying protestations of love, but she struggled just the same. Modfai had strong arms and lots of breath, so he soon persuaded her not to struggle. He kept on talking in her ear, speaking words then phrases then whole poem cycles of adoration, reciting and crooning to such effect that they stayed with her for years afterwards; but however well she remembered his words, she never had the least desire to find out what they meant.

'You bastard,' she said. She couldn't match his eloquence.

8.

She supposed he thought he was done with her.

She was damn sure he wasn't.

She was a woman who had fought her way through many a tough negotiation with men. Standing up to the hijackers on behalf of her passengers was something she regarded as inevitable. Lashing back at Modfai was a similar reflex. 'You rotten bastard,' she kept on at him. 'You conceited, ill-tutored little sod. I'm going to teach you a lesson.'

Modfai understood *bastard*, but he grinned at it, and forgave himself. The rest he did not understand. He scratched himself contentedly, enjoying the wild disorder of her uniform. His sweat had larded it with medals, so much so that her blouse reminded him of the Düsseldorf Tart's, but the Tart was a pleasure he reserved for this evening.

He watched her gaze wildly around the squalid order of his room, searching for something to attack him with: a knife, some other cooking implement, a pair of scissors. Soldiers have scissors, she knew, because soldiers are their own wives in all of the important things.

She found nothing. 'We're going to kill you,' she said. *We* is a vague word, less satisfactory than *bastard*; but she knew what she meant by it: *we*, the agents and agencies of retribution. *We* were gathering in the desert out there, or on the islands to the north, and soon a kind of clinical dispassion would set free the enraged women and the sullen men in the huts, and their passion would overflow.

So she watched Modfai grin, and scratch, and put himself together again. 'I'll bloody see you dead,' she said, through stretched lips. She spoke her curse some more, this time really hissing at him.

He enjoyed her quieter sound. He liked women to smile.

9.

The aircraft arrived at dusk. Matson guessed it was a Hastings or perhaps a C130: the dead light furred its outline, and his eyes were gritty.

It passed over Barel's mauve flare and time-marker, took a long climbing loop towards the big mountains to the south then straight-and-levelled back again, a thousand feet above the rising dark.

The desert twilight lasts six minutes. The planning had been that tight.

Twenty-four parachutists came out, jumping two and by two, twin-stick from the plane's rear-exit. They were out in fifteen seconds.

The aircraft went north for about a minute, sinking lower and lower, burrowing under the dark, its engine-note restlessly loud.

'Cutting the phone-lines,' Barel explained. 'They're dropping six more, who'll close back on Sifr WaaHid. Just in case the politicians abort the airstrike.'

'Think they will?'

'Listen to my briefing.'

Matson and Barel had chosen a tiny triangle of sand and pebble between their own hill and the great dune. Time and distance forbade all the safer options. It was a pretty awful DZ, calculated to turn ankles and splay knee-joints, unless soldiers on parachutes were due for a change of luck round here. Those jumping with a leg-valise would need it.

They got it. Valises were unshackled in time, and the parachutes flared in consequence, so the valise-jumpers had the best of it. No-one folded a leg, though thuds, grunts and curses suggested the usual ration of scraped shoulder blades and sore coccyges.

There was no wind to disperse them, or drag them on landing.

Barel waited till they'd formed up, then led them close to Matson's H.Q. He didn't take them all the way there, Matson noticed. Casualties are an ill omen, and a good commander will do everything he can to avoid his men seeing any on the way in.

These seemed like a brisk lot. They adopted the usual position of all-round defence before squatting to check their kit. There wasn't much to see of them, what with the pre-moon dark and their greased-up faces. They didn't talk. They didn't need to. Their work with their guns, replacing rounds in magazines, easing actions, unfouling vents had a reassuring crispness about it.

Levett went round them with lukewarm tea, sweet as syrup. 'A chap needs his body-sugar,' he kept on explaining. Nobody answered. Perhaps nobody understood.

Matson reached down to feel at a weapon. His fingers took several seconds to learn what it was. It wasn't a standard Uzi. It was the twenty-two calibre smooth-bore machine-pistol beloved of Mossad and 101. Another bloody zip-gun, of course. But high-tech, with an extended external muzzle thread, waiting for its suppressor. Matson gave it back. The Izzies' execution weapon. Obviously these were a very special bunch of heavies.

According to Barel they might come looking out for him, one day.

10.

Barel said, 'Consider this the Assembly Area, and consider yourselves assembled. There are Enemy on the hill behind us – Captain Matson will show us where. Consequently, there is no Forming-up Place, no Start Line. Tonight is all Start Line. Once we take one step from here, the operation is on Go. We are not mounting an attack in the accepted sense. This is an extermination and rescue. Selective extermination. Comprehensive rescue.'

Men breathed their amusement. Matson hadn't followed anything Barel had said, but one word at least must have been good.

'There are four kinds of enemy up behind us and down in Sifr WaaHid. I am relying on Captain Matson's evaluation of them; we have no other.

'There are the hijackers – ten at most to start with. Captain Matson deleted three of them. We don't know if there were other terrorists waiting on the ground. Captain Matson saw no evidence. You've studied the photokits. All recognised hijackers are to be killed.

'There are the soldiers of Dragout's private army – to borrow a phrase. Captain Matson saw at least twenty of these. There may be more. These, like the hijackers, are probably well motivated to fight. If they get in the way, kill them. If they don't, applaud and press on.

'There was a platoon of very young conscripts – these *were* to be reinforced. From an intelligence source, not Captain Matson, I have "elements of two battalions". Captain Matson knows these "elements" amount to at least a company of infantry. We do not know whether these are the same poor quality.

'Lastly, there are some ack-ack people. These will probably be highly trained and well-motivated.'

Barel paused, and took in Matson again. 'I've briefed our air-landing people. I have spoken to them by radio again just now. They are already airborne. They'll be bringing in three transports, as you know, together with a snatch commando under the command of Dov Goradish. *They*'ll supervise the evacuation. *They*, if necessary, will provide the long-term cover. *They*, not us, will have to lock in to any extended fire-fight with the Libyan Army. *There is not to be one*. Certainly *we* are not to start one. I don't like giving this order, but we all operate under political restraints. We are here – Captain Goradish's party, yourselves, and Captain Matson – to rescue the passengers of the two aircraft down there. Both lots of passengers. If any limitations impose themselves, then the passengers from the Israeli flight will take priority, because they will be subject to reprisals. The women and children of the British flight come next. The remaining men are British and American servicemen, so they come last. But it is our intention to take them all. If that intention cannot be realised, then there is a senior British politician, a U.S. Air Force general, and two women who are too valuable as hostages to be left behind. Captain Matson will identify them. Captain Goradish has their names.'

'The politician has a girlfriend,' Matson remembered. 'I don't know her name. We'd better add her to our list.'

Barel translated this, then said, in English, 'About half of these chaps can understand you, Patrick. I'll arrange for you to be with some English speakers.'

He turned to his men and said, 'So much for the pep-talk. You've all studied the models and the sand table. Does anyone not know where he is? Right. You've had your orders days ago, and rehearsed till you're sick.'

More murmurs of agreement.

'That's why I'm throwing in a variant. We'll take the house first, eh? Smoke the wasps in their nest, and stop them getting their stings out.'

He translated this last bit for Matson, and made him feel much better indeed.

Only one thing bothered him. People were being given precedence over the Bomb, over Holofernes. How new was this thinking? Was it being shared with Washington and London? It seemed foggy with propaganda and sentiment. Was it wise?

11.

Khadduri was angry. The woman had made him angry for a start, angry with himself. Then he had done as Dragout had told Modfai to tell him; he had driven all the way up the hill in his jeep, only to arrive at his tormentor's house and find the omnipresent grin absent. Omnipresent, perhaps, yet not there. Dragout was apparently waiting for him down at the compound, with or without his grin.

Modfai had driven him here. Khadduri let Modfai drive him back again. He also let Modfai have a week's accumulated anger.

Modfai said nothing, not while he was driving. When officers swore at him he did not listen.

After he had parked the jeep the way soldiers do park jeeps, in a hurry, he offered a word or two. 'I prefer to deal with soldiers, myself, sir. Tribesmen and emperors I leave to the cinema.' Seeing that Khadduri was too angry to answer this sort of truth, he added, 'There are no genuinely black genuine Libyans. The blacks all come from Chad.'

Khadduri took his rage into Dragout's hut. Dragout's grin was waiting.

Dragout's grin was distorted. He was eating pancakes of bread. There was room in his cheek for a whole bag of bread, but the grin was not quite as it should be. He chewed as if eating was clever. Khadduri's father used to eat like this, and Khadduri had no use for it. Especially from the giant, who did everything as if he was instructing the Prophet in the articles of the Sharia.

Dragout was sitting on the floor, so Khadduri laid his rage out in a heap: 'First we drag passengers off the planes, then we put them on. We segregate flight crew. We segregate cabin crew. We segregate the women from the men. We mix them up again. Why? Why? Why?'

'Principally because I say so. Yunis Mohammed Khadduri. Principally because I say so. Also because anything we do here sends out ripples in the air. We have a Nuseibeh, we have an air-rippler, you see.

'Thirdly, because we are locked in a fight. And in a fight, my little colonel, you dodge behind your enemy, in order to keep him off-balance. You move, Khadduri, always you move. You are the one who attended Staff College, not me. You are the soldier.' He took another pancake. 'I am merely the strategist. It is because I am clever at this sort of business, I have been placed in overall command.'

Before Khadduri could think of an answer, Dragout leapt to his feet and said, 'I am keen to avoid unnecessary bloodshed, Khadduri. Why don't you move all of your men to the back of the encampment?'

'Unthinkable.'

'I must ask you to think about it, then. The aeroplane will fly off if anyone attacks us, so there is no need to have an expensive showdown.'

'The attacker would be violating Libyan soil.'

'The desert is very durable, Mohammed Yunis. It has been here for some time. What did they teach you at Staff College about choosing the ground you defend?'

' "The Commander must deny the Enemy all essential ground, including utilities, means of manufacture and supply, centres of communication and commerce." '

'Marvellous.' He clapped his hands. 'And which of these is Sifr WaaHid? Sifr WaaHid is the Nothing they gave me.'

'It is Libyan soil. It is Libya.'

'Khadduri, you still have a rat in your hut. A Libyan rat. Leave it to the English or the Israelis to kill it for you.'

'If the Israelis in particular move to attack, then it is my duty to be here.'

'And earn yourself a medal? Nonsense. There are officers who earn medals and officers who are alive to receive them. I do not think that any man who fights here will stay alive. I, for example, will go up to my house. I may even stroll about the hills.' He did his manic imitation of a chuckle. 'The enemy will not send ordinary troops against us. He will use Special Forces. No: I shall take a walk, or make love, Khadduri. I advise you to do the same.'

'Nonsense.' He had tried love. It was a sticky business out here.

'The English SAS, as an instance, they do not take prisoners. That Matson is such a one. I do not wish to wait here to meet my Matson again, even though I used him so kindly.'

Dragout seemed uncertain of Khadduri's commonsense. He caught hold of him by his uniform as if his buttons were door handles. 'When Her Majesty bears an unwanted child, it is this Matson who strangles it. I have studied his file. Look what he did to those women who guarded your planes. Look what he did to our own unwanted Nuseibeh.' He tugged a little, as if to adjust the Colonel's position in the air. 'When an English Prime Minister grows tired of a lover or a Cabinet Minister –' He shuddered.

'You make silly jokes.'

'I speak as I am guided. A man does not mistrust the truth of a poem, Khadduri.'

'There are poems, and there are the poems of the Bible.'

'Bibles, yes. But I speak of the Hadith. Now where is the real poetry?'

'Matson is too young, Ahmed.' A man had to be quick to catch the Dragout, and quicker still to catch a name to call him by without giving him offence. 'This Matson is too young to be enrolled in the traditional wisdom of Islam, I think?'

'He has another name there, Mohammed –' so crude, in the context, to remind the colonel of his own religious patronymic. 'In the Hadith, my Matson is known as the Angel of Death.'

Khadduri shuddered. He was a soldier, so he paid due respect to the Dark but Shining One.

12.

At some stage or other, Dragout had let go of his uniform. Having his tunic to himself again gave him a great surge of power. 'Dragout, I must ask you frankly as a man of conscience –'

' "A man of conscience"? Truthfully, Khadduri, you are the only person who could offer such a description of himself without making me snigger.' The giant sniggered, just the same.

'Are there any atomic devices on those aircraft?'

'Ah – you ask as a man of conscience and a soldier?'

Khadduri nodded glumly. He was sick at the thought of so many people, whose faces were known to him, flying off to die among so many more whose faces were unknown and whose numbers he could only guess at.

'You are a very oldfashioned soldier, Khadduri, but that's what comes of conscience. You would rather kill one man face to face than a thousand in the dark? Airmen had to solve this problem long ago. So did the Gods who sent towers of water and pillars of fire.' He put his thumbs into Khadduri's shoulder and lifted him as once he had lifted Nuseibeh. 'There are better questions for you to ask,' he whispered. 'Such as: did the Libyan People provide any bombs, or any money with which to furnish them? Ask me that question, Little One?'

'I ask you,' Khadduri croaked. 'I ask you.' He was already so high in the air and so dizzy with pain the answer was of no immediate interest to him. He was jolted down on his heels, and felt sicker than he would if he had tumbled from an assault-course wall.

'The answer to that question is *no*,' Dragout said. 'Libya gave me only these empty pots, and no money to buy oil. So I filled the pots with my dream, Khadduri. I used that Matson and this Nuseibeh to fill those aircraft with my dreams, and my dream is a vision of fear. In consequence the Israelis, the Americans and the Turks will shoot those planes down. For the fear of the Bomb is as terrible as the Bomb itself. Or it is among those who have built the Bomb – and rightly so!'

Khadduri found himself sitting, and at a table. Had he been thrown over it, dropped there, or simply groped there numb?

13.

'The best plots consist of nothing, Khadduri. Nothing has no requirements, involves no deceptions, because in Nothing there is no lie. You should be able to follow this very clearly because you are an Arab, and the Arab is, above all, a mathematician.' He shifted towards the window. 'My people are not Arabs nor mathematicians. They are goatboys. But if you herd goats, and you herd them on a mountain, then you also herd dreams. A dream is not quite a nothing, but it is nearly a nothing. You cannot weigh it. If a man gives you an empty pot, you may keep your dream in it. The State has given me plenty of empty pots in its time, and plenty of emptiness with no pots to keep it in.'

'I am afraid I do not follow you, Dragout.'

'The State let me steal four aircraft, Mohammed Yunis. On the understanding that I should give them back again – after extracting the maximum embarrassment from certain governments the State does not like. The Secretary of the Ruling Committee of the People's Central Congress loves to extract embarrassment.'

'There I can agree.'

'He sits all day in a tent, but he does not dream. He is not a prophet, he is a conjuror. He thinks up tricks.'

'I never comment upon such matters.'

'A pity. If I told him what I have just said, he would laugh. If I told him you had not seen fit to contradict me, he would cut your balls off.

'The State let me have those aircraft on the understanding also that the People should be free to dispose of those who stole the planes as the People think fit in the light of events. Not you, little Captain –'

How swift was Khadduri's demotion.

'Not me. But some of those riff-raff will kick their necks into a string, just the same.'

The colonel listened calmly, but the captain inside him felt sick. 'So there is no bomb,' he said.

'I did not say that,' Dragout purred. There were generators outside, and shoutings, and lights; for tonight was a night of generation in which jet-turbines turned and ignited, two, three or even four of the Jumbos. Pratt and Witneys thundered, not like the legendary roarings of the four thousand lions, but more the way the grains of sand howl in a storm, atom by gritty atom. They brought the sand to storm now, those turbines, and sent shreds and shards of desert drumming against the window glass.

For a time the giant and his officer shouted at each other; but Khadduri heard nothing.

The first thing he did hear was: 'As I say, I have been given Nothing, and soon I shall give it back again. Those aircraft must be ready to fly at dawn. At midnight I want you to embark all of the passengers, *and* the original pilots. First officers and all flight and cabin crew will fly as passengers.'

'And the bombs?'

'I wonder about the bombs, Khadduri. An aircraft is a pot in its way – how very quick you are. If you send a pot to your enemy, as the storyteller says, it may hold three things – a snake, his blood-child's head or –'

Khadduri was amazed the giant had not touched him in a fresh anger, hadn't breathed over him, hadn't even watched him as he talked. The Tibbu might not even be the pansy he pretended to be. Even that might be an act. 'A bomb?' he prompted quickly. '*The* Bomb?'

'The aircraft have their flight-paths,' Dragout mused. 'This Israeli to America. The American from Tripolitania to Israel. The silly little Greek to silly Turkey. Their captains will fly them there with someone in the first officer's seat holding a gun in their ear.'

'And we will explode the Bomb?'

'I was thinking of exploding the Dream, Khadduri. The

third thing to send an enemy is a Dream. It may be a bad dream, to frighten him. Or it may be a Vision that will change him into your friend.'

'What will this Dream do?'

'It will frighten him to death.'

'And what about the Bomb?'

'You are a literalist, Khadduri. An Arab mathematician. Even so you think in spirals. In my story the snake is as the bomb. The passengers are the blood-child's head. And with them both I send the Dream, the Dream that will leave tonight.'

The aircraft turbines were quieter now, or Khadduri was used to them. He had no control over the aircraft. It had become one of the giant's demons. He thought some more, then said, 'Why tonight?'

'Tripoli tells me the American fleet is very near. The Americans will probably attempt a rescue.

'Here?'

'No. I fancy the Israelis for here. Or the British. One or the other. Hardly both. Their nations get on, but their soldiers do not like one another very much.'

The noise had diminished but the window-glass continued to tremble.

'I did not say there was no Bomb,' Dragout explained at last, as if even the thunder of twenty thousand horse-power was too little to deflect the upsurge of his intelligence. 'I simply said that the Libyan People gave me no money to make one. The next question for you to ask is whether anyone else did.'

Perhaps Khadduri got this final question to the front of his face. Perhaps he only wished it there. Jetstream or simple desert wind had forced a rubble of black sand beneath the door, which now grated open.

Nuseibeh limped in, his broken face set in a leer of consternation. Nuseibeh was accompanied by Modfai, who seemed to have been searching for him.

The doctor's slippers scuffed on the floor. The crude on each grain of sand began to dry and stink.

'Ah, Nuseibeh. You are either much too early or much too late. I forget which quarter of the moon I ask you to be ready by. All that remains in my memory is that I commanded you to report to me at my modest little dwelling on the hill, not here. This, as you will remember, is merely my playpen and slaughterhouse.' He giggled, hysterically. Clearly it was the doctor's face that amused him.

'I will not have *this* lout bring me your orders, Dragout.'

'Pay no attention to Doctor Nuseibeh, country man,' Dragout told Modfai. He laughed more normally now.

'I will *not* be insulted,' Nuseibeh said.

'Pah! I'm insulting no-one. It's just that Modfai has a special place in the establishment here – eh, Modfai? Eh, Colonel Khadduri? Modfai knows where he belongs, and can be proud of it. Modfai is a Turk. He belongs on the toe of my boot.' Dragout contemplated the wreckage he made of their egos. 'It is not that *I* have any further need of you, Ibrahim Nuseibeh. Or of those who sent you here. But I think you all need me. You will be there. At my house. In a little while.' He opened the door. 'Or not. Entirely as your employers choose for you.'

14.

'That's Nuseibeh's Land-Rover.'

'So we have all the fancy dresses in the one place.'

Matson liked the way Barel's men got themselves into position. Two stayed back in the scrub with a l.m.g. Two others set themselves by the mud wall of the garden with a rocket-launcher in case the door gave any trouble.

A single telephone-wire ran in from a pole, and met a ceramic insulator under the roof. A soldier walking as nonchalantly as a milkman stepped down to sever the feed wire on the wall.

The door was a deep notch of shadow. The window was curtained light. Both were probably open, save for insect screens. They heard laughter, music – or at least, a kind of stereophonic drumming. A singer wailed aloud and was told to be silent. He couldn't be interrupted. His voice was on a cassette or a phonograph, or just high on the needle. It went on and up, in a fine puberphonic bleat, then came down into Arabic's lower, more guttural key – first ass, then camel, then donkey in pain.

'Party night!' Barel spoke normally. 'I don't see any sentries.'

A shape rose up at them, straight out of nowhere, the way a cobra stands up.

A shape with a glinting pun.

Matson had his Thug knife. He used it twice – once for silence, once for death. Barel caught the gun, and fingered home its safety catch, just as if they'd rehearsed it together.

Matson tried not to think about the death. It had been too good. He had reached round the man for the silence of the lower spine, then come back to the throat for the vascular system at the left angle of the jaw, but gone on driving upwards behind tooth and palate towards the final certainty.

One of Dragout's brownjobs. He wore scent. Everyone he killed wore scent nowadays, but it wasn't the perfume that brought the warm tingle. It was the beauty of killing well with his blade. He could hate himself tomorrow. Tonight was moonlit symmetry. He had even left the knife stuck home till the corpse had been lowered by himself and Barel ever so gently to the ground.

There was no gush of blood. The heart had stopped its beat on an immedate inhibition. The fellow would have died anyway when the hilt was withdrawn, but this way was neater. First the lumbar plexus, then the vagal nerve, then the brain. Death took only a second. Life remained with art.

Matson gazed down on his torture-house with renewed enthusiasm. Until a moment ago he had lost the zest for action. Action is always a hard place to get to. Each time you dredge up enough willpower to take you there, you exhaust a little of whatever remains.

Now it was different. Blood had not come in a rush, or in any way that was disgusting; but it was spreading its scent on the evening. There was a word for this in the warrior poems of ancient Ireland, a word that reached English as *reek*. It's a fine enough word in English. In Irish it is better: it speaks of the intoxication of men from the fume of blood freshly spilled in battle.

Matson only had a little learning. But his veins held a lot of Irish. Blood begets blood, they say.

The house held more.

15.

Dragout's face was suffused with contentment. His contentment grew fat on what it was drinking. He sat on a piece of upholstered carpet, and he sipped. He sipped sherbert from a dish, and sharpened his taste from time to time with a tiny glass of peppermint. It was what was in the peppermint that made his face glow.

He did not seem pleased to see Nuseibeh, even though he had demanded his presence.

'I must ask you –' the doctor began.

Dragout belched an interruption. 'Nauseous Nuseibeh! The disgusting predictability of your slyness!' He belched again, and gazed at the doctor as if grateful for the flavour. 'I never know what it is you will do, my naughty friend, merely that you will do it. Now here you come interrupting my evening hour.' Two belches mean a man is merely wise. The third makes him holy. He belched again, then several times more. 'The sun is scarcely down. I am still, as you see, at my prayers. As you should be at yours.' He took a little more of what was in the peppermint so that all the blood in him glowed. 'Is there no depth to your suspicion?' He became white hot, like that famous tower of bones that the Turks set on fire. 'Ask on, my little doctor of philosophy. Then I shall twist your neck.'

'I must know your plans, in detail.'

'Ah, my plans.' Dragout stood up, without uncrossing his legs, and went twisting away. 'Do you mean plans? Or do you speak of prophecy? If you mean what I think you mean, then you must kneel with me and ask Holofernes.'

'I have no time for kneeling.' The voice was harsh for a man with a broken nose. 'All I need is to know.'

'So you can warn Tel Aviv?'

'So my people may have value for their money.'

'By tomorrow they will have had their value. I always give value. It is going to be a very long night.'

'Tonight?' There was alarm in the doctor's voice, even if his face was beyond showing it. 'You mean the aircraft are –'

'Yes. And the phone lines to Zoltan and Benghazi are down. Isn't that a pity?' He squeezed Nuseibeh, but only briefly. 'You should tend your wounds, Ibrahim. Your face smells like an old man's slipper.'

'I do tend them.'

'But Matson's kindness continues with you? His passion suppurates? You must thank God you are not a woman, Ibrahim. He loves women more than men, I think. Look at the way he embraced those two on the runway out there.'

The doctor shuddered.

'They were quite broken up with lust, Ibrahim. Snapped right off.' Dragout trembled too, but with delight at the memory. 'Did you see their faces? They say a whore's smile is like a lizard's tail – attached to nothing.'

'Seventeen million dollars, Dragout. My people raised seventeen –'

'To buy cause or to buy effect, doctor? Cause is extremely expensive in this case. No, you must listen to me. How much Iraqi plutonium did they think I could acquire with seventeen million dollars? Acquire and ship? Or Dutch or German fissionable waste? Perhaps they expect me to buy four bombs from the Israelis, Ibrahim? Or simply steal them from the British, who cannot count? Or from the Americans who have too many to notice? Such things can be done – but they cost more than seventeen million dollars.'

'You promised –'

'I shall deliver my bomb. I shall deliver it tonight. Or in the middle of tomorrow morning while the sky is still clear. As I say, it will be a long evening –' He walked towards an inner door and threw it open. 'I did have a gift for you.'

The door swung open on a bed, but Nuseibeh scarcely noticed it. It was what was on the bed that made him gasp.

A youth sprawled there, dressed in diaphanous white like a western bride, drugged or swooning with drink and covered all over with plastic flowers.

The giant chuckled. 'When I bade Khadduri ask his Modfai to search the hutments for me I had an inkling he would find something special.' He indicated the lad. 'I am like the Archimagus, Ibrahim. I found a stone in the dust of the desert. I picked up the stone and rubbed it –' oh how he shivered. 'I *rubbed* it and found it was a lamp. So I *rubbed* the lamp to see if it would support my flame.' He lifted the young man and embraced him more gently than Nuseibeh had seen him embrace anyone before. 'Isn't he a beauty, even in such modest clothes? As I say, I intended him as a present for yourself – and as a gift through yourself to the entire Palestinian people. A youth who does not yet know whether he is going to grow into a man or a tree or simply wither like one of those beautiful lowland lilies in the souk.' He placed the adorable manikin back on its bed, where it sprawled in a languor of hash, overcome by rhetoric and soap and self-esteem, and the unexpected somnolence of Dragout's sheets.

The Tibbu began to close the door, with himself and the miraculous boy on one side of it and Nuseibeh on the other. 'I *had* intended this as a present for you, Ibrahim, as I already seem to have said. But he's too pretty for you to pet among the petrol cans in the back of that jeep of yours. And a man with a damaged knee is no good for this sort of thing.' He opened the door again. 'You can try if you like, but I think your nose will frighten him.'

With the door closed again, and bolted, he began to rummage around the lad in a most indecorous manner. He whispered, endearingly, and Nuseibeh struggled salaciously with himself to hear what he said. But Dragout whispered in English. The lad did not speak English; nor for the moment was Nuseibeh's ear tuned for it. 'Seventeen million dollars,' he was saying, fondling not the lad's leg but something beyond his leg. 'When a man comes into that sort of money the best thing he can do is sleep on it.' Dragout continued to smother, rearrange and cover by cushion and coverlet and rug the treasure which his dream was founded on long after his cleaned-up little squatter-boy grew bored and finally slept.

16.

Matson hadn't seen the living rooms before. Downstairs the torture house. Upstairs the harem.

He burst around the doorway, coming in from the darkness into a stage-set of cushions, silvered carpets, and little brackets set with carven ornaments of ivory and aragonite.

At one end of the first room there was one of those low couches that Westerners call divans and Arabs call no such thing, even though the word is Arabic.

The thing was as tastelessly ornate as the little slippers Nuseibeh habitually wore on his feet, and was wearing now. The old fox sat there, playing cards with himself, or preparing to play.

Or pretending to prepare. He wore a rug across his knees, a rug skirting the divan; and he shivered, as if against the evening chill.

It was too early for the evening to be chill. The doctor was sweating. 'Congratulations,' he said. 'Do you come from Mister Pomeroy?'

Matson had stripped some scab from his shoulder as he brushed round the doorpost. He stood for a moment, annoyed to be panting, trying to catch a marksman's breath as he watched the card-sharp's hands crab swiftly over the divan, soothing creases, settling under the wrapped-over rug, presumably searching for a pistol.

'No time to process a mail-order,' Matson observed. 'Marcus Pomeroy sends you this.' He shot the doctor's balls off. Revenge was all sexual tonight: it went with the ambience. That is, he emptied half a clip into the apex of the man's thighs, the base of his stomach. The switchfire did the rest, erasing the smirk, blotting out contempt.

The doctor went backwards, caught midway through a sales pitch, his bargain interrupted. He tried to lift a hand, but only spilled a gun; tried to speak, but could only whisper. His eyes looked dead, but the words came out.

They reached him in Arabic, by which time he was lying on his side, legs still folded in front of him, his wisdom drowning in froth. Then he stopped.

'Cut you off at last!' Matson changed a magazine on his Ingram 10. ' "From philosophers right down to doctors of philosophy",' he quoted. Wagner's little friend was appropriate to those who wrote in blood.

There was killing elsewhere in the house. The air became violent with silenced guns. Spaces trembled, each room-cube thumping with gas, the high velocity snub-dums splintering flesh and splashing it on stone.

'The old boy was fond of you.' Barel spoke from somewhere. 'Said you're a nice lad, but overhasty.'

Something intrigued them about the inner door. Matson stepped diagonally towards it, followed by one of Barel's sergeants.

17.

Torture is like rape: isn't that what Helen Tesserer had said? And when the torture *is* rape? The syndrome may be ugly and ultimate: it need not be terminal. Terminal is the lump inside the gun.

The sergeant tried the door from one side, then shot it in.

Matson elbowed him out of the way. He had seen Dragout.

Dragout was not wearing a rug. He wasn't wearing anything. He was dressed in a white-skinned lad. He smiled from the midst of his surprise.

The boy was not entirely white. It was just that Dragout's blackness was total. Together they looked like one of the plummier pictures on the wall of a curry-house.

The boy was about fourteen years old. Matson shot him. He was in the way.

The giant laid him tenderly aside, slowly and with profound sadness. He did not call him by one of his list of hot-lipped names. Matson was waiting for one of those – any one would tighten the trigger. Instead he began to croon. Matson tightened just the same. Matson had heard him croon.

All at once Dragout was levitating, rearing up and up like a distortion in a mirror to grip the sergeant with one hand and break Matson with the other.

No point in contesting the grip. Matson let the Ingram do it for him. It swatted the giant across the room, folding him back into a sitting position as it did so.

A sitting position in space, say all of halfway up the wall.

Dragout crashed down on his hams, emptying himself of blood, turning back to his roots in Ahmed Ali Khalil – or whatever Marcus had called him.

Even here there was illusion. As the body lifted across the coverlets and whipped its feet over the lad, Matson glimpsed among the uplifted rugs and cushions a bed built on bars of gold, and a neglected bejewelled pistol.

Barel was in the room now, interrupting his fantasy, taking in the scene: the dead boy, Dragout's pistol skidding, the nude body pumping blood and urine and afterbreath. 'Jealous?' He asked. He shot them each once through the head. 'Better set this lot on fire,' he advised. 'Put a match to the evidence.'

Matson liked it just as it was.

TWENTY-ONE

1.

Pomeroy often spoke of the White House at Athna. He spoke of it nostalgically. Ten, fifteen, even twenty years ago, he claimed to have run the Eastern Mediterranean from this slate-floored coolness in Cyprus.

When CAC became operational and rallied to the Craw's battle-flag, the White House seemed the natural place to go. It had the space. It had the facilities. It was just up the road from Famagusta. The Israelis liked it. The Americans could live with it. It was on the MOD open list.

Ten years ago – let alone fifteen or twenty – Pomeroy had been allowed to run very little, except his bank overdraft and his imagination. Even so, it surprised Fossit to discover that the White House looked pink and called itself Red. Nor was it at Athna, but Akhyritou. It was the Red House at Akhyritou.

'Jet-lag,' Pomeroy explained. 'That and the erstwhile discretion of my calling. Quaint little nest of vipers, ain't it?'

Akhyritou was even closer than Athna to Famagusta. It was just a field-combat link away from the much publicised Mossad Yacht. The 'Yacht' was a schooner-sized ketch concreted in on a fixed mooring. NATO winked at it, without smiling upon it. The Red House was more a string-bag of cables than a nest of vipers: and it was rumoured that some of its phone-loops fed or were fed by the yacht's communication system. The Red House was full of rumours like this.

Tonight it was packed with all the usual communications people, map-makers, model-builders, wire-runners and

WAAFs with prudent breasts who handed out soft drinks and teas, and headsets free of static. Barkworth and Fisher had set up mini HQs to watch over Matson from rooms they made look like depot hospitality messes or Home Counties golf-club bars. Fossit found a space with Pomeroy. Quinlan arrived from RAF Akrotiri in a procession of cars and disappeared upstairs for the duration. He was supposed to have commandeered everything above the first floor, and there was about ten thousand square feet of that. He had brought a lot of courtiers. Pomeroy wasn't clear whether he was one of them, but he chose to stay downstairs. There comes a time when a man can do anything he damnwell likes, providing he does it with taste and aplomb.

This was such a time.

Armaggedon might or might not be another.

At bunker-level, the Red House was full of orderly Americans with studious teeth and unnecessary spectacles ground to less diopterage than window glass. These were staff rank spectacles. Their owners 'hovered without swarming' (Fossit) or, more rarely, 'swarmed without buzzing' (Pomeroy) about the Craw who grew bigger, and more purposeful and quieter by the second as darkness wore on.

'The Sun King is sulking upstairs,' Pomeroy said. 'Behold the absolutely admirable Queen Bee.'

Fossit had no time to watch the Admiral any further. It was then that the Shogun arrived.

He refused the distractions of hospitality. He had been resting, or brooding, on his concrete-bottomed yacht. No-one saw him come in, so it must have been via the shadows of the lanes and the lawns. Now he called attention to himself by placing chairs in a circle.

'Too many people,' he said, when the Craw came up to him. 'Too many old men with glasses.' He was the oldest man in the room by at least ten years. 'I'll write my own notes. All my best people are in the field. Where we should all have been four days ago.'

The WAAFs did not make a crowd. Nor did the Americans. Now General Yigael Zefat had arrived, and the bunker rooms at the Red House were full to bursting.

2.

Fossit didn't quite know why he was here. He hadn't intended to be here. He didn't want to be here. His was an English job in England. England stopped at Surbiton, and became an unruly continent full of foreigners: his job was to keep them out of England.

He found, to his consternation, that if you have a man at the Front, then there has to be another man at the Back. If the Front is in Cyrenaica then the Back has to be further forward than Whitehall or Surbiton. It was his privilege as Matson's boss to be that man. He had little to do except worry, and shift chairs with Yigael Zefat. Soon he would be reduced to biting his fingerends and hurrying forward like any American general whose forces are under attack. Unlike any American general, he had nowhere to hurry to.

The Craw said to him, 'Don't you wish you were out in the sand getting your arse shot off?'

Fossit shifted another chair. 'My arse wasn't made for being shot at – but, yes, I do.'

He had last seen General Zefat at an Israeli Embassy garden-party in Kensington. The Man's hands had been big and restless. They had moved about from nose, to pocket, to knees, dragging his arms after him. His body was strong, well-dressed, too strong to be dressed as it was – his hair cropped short all over, as is the way with the modern soldier.

That was Zefat in a suit. Now he was in uniform. In uniform his body was in its home. He had made his magic gesture of equality with the chairs. Now he sat in one and waited. He did not practise calmness. He was calm.

The heat in Cyprus was too much for him. He was unfit and none too well. He was, if anything, overweight. A lesser man would have fidgeted. In uniform, he did not allow himself the luxury. He sat still and brooded. He looked like a man who was wondering when, just once and for maximum effect, he would lose his temper.

He lost it when the admiral said, reasonably enough, 'Item Number One: Structure.'

'Bugger Structure! Let's just synchronise our clocks!'

3.

It was Matson's second ride in Nuseibeh's Land-Rover. He sat up front this time, beside Barel. Barel's sergeant and three other men knelt behind on the passion couch. They tossed out the cushions, but the thing was still seedy with ancient buggery or camel's catarrh.

'Snuff,' Barel said, as he let in the clutch. 'Our friend took snuff. Did you get his tooth?'

'I don't loot.'

'Then you're not a soldier. A warrior dresses in his enemy.' He showed Matson his wrist. 'Your black and cuddly friend had two thousand pounds-worth of Rolex on him.'

Matson had never seen Dragout wear a watch. He obviously needed time on his wrist when he was naked. Now Barel was wearing the giant's last quick change.

'If any of your people find a Second Para tie,' he said.

The remainder of Barel's men were loping down the track in two files on either side of the Land-Rover. They weren't noticeably encumbered with loot.

'So you were with the Parachute Regiment.'

'Long enough to buy a tie.'

'They didn't teach you that business with the knife in the Parachute Regiment.'

'I wear another tie for that.'

It was about here that Nuseibeh had warned of snakes. Crouched in the back, Matson had thought they were passing under trees. There were no trees in this kind of jebel, he realised. No tall trees, anyway. He had crouched beneath his fear and the great towers of darkness.

He heard aircraft engines, the pulse of big turboprops throttling back, raucous on landing pitch. 'Lieutenant Goradish is on time,' Barel said.

'You're letting *that* be commanded by a lieutenant?'

'Dov is not a mere lieutenant. He is one of mine. Besides, what am I? Who are you? We belong to a silly part of our profession, Patrick. We come from where captains may be kings.'

Sifr WaaHid was below them at a sharp turn of the track. It

looked normal, at peace even – the hutments laid out in illuminated parallelograms.

'It's not Butlins,' Matson said.

'Your Levett.' Matson thought Barel spoke inconsequentially, to still his nerves. Barel had no nerves. 'Your Levett is an excellent man. I'm glad to know he's back there.'

'You're worried about protecting our rear?' Matson scoffed. 'On an operation like this?'

'Spiritually, yes. Especially in a matter like this. I've read my Wingate, you see. Perhaps you forget that the Israeli Army was trained by Orde Wingate before the Israeli Army even existed.'

Matson hadn't forgotten. He had never known. Nor had he read Wingate. He wanted to say so, but the Hastings' heavy wings were brushing in overhead; there were four of them, slatted with starlight through their splayed-back landing flaps.

The first one hit the landing-strip, its deadweight jolting the Land-Rover. Somebody began to shoot at someone with a heavy machine-gun.

But that was a long way off, in a dream. Matson had his own war now. The Land-Rover was down at the compound perimeter, and accelerating fast across the amalgam.

Matson's war wasn't Barel's war. It was private. It fitted his skin.

4.

Modfai sat back and spread his legs. He gazed once more at the Düsseldorf Tart, but in private as befitted the hour. His eye fell upon her nearer parts, her recently groped-for breast and its more or less identical twin.

The twins were ever so slightly in motion. The Tart was swallowing an alcoholic beverage a small sip at the time, and the drink made them wobble.

Modfai did not approve of her drinking, and would shortly teach her right and wrong in such matters. He approved of the wobble. He had spread his legs to encourage the blood to flow, and the coolness, into all his necessary places.

Drink made her smile. He did not like women to smile. The

Tart's smile was noisy. He could somehow hear her gums. It was also insolent. He thought insolent was the word.

Modfai had read all the great works of Arabic literature. He had read them because they were about lovemaking. They understood, as no other literature does, that loving a woman is a mechanical matter. To love a boy requires poetry and can be carried into the spiritual dimension. After all, a boy beloved can accompany one to Heaven. But to love a woman is like driving a car or, in the Tart's case, a lorry. Arabic literature understood this before cars and lorries were invented or even thought of.

The Tart was a difficult vehicle to get started. Perhaps this was his fault. He had already made love today, made love with poetry as it happened, because the flight-girl had been as skinny as a boy and only different in inessentials.

Arabic literature – the greatest books anyway – only allows a man the potency to make love once a month. Modfai had already used up a year's supply in the last week. He was growing short of flux. As a good follower of the Law, he only had about four hundred monthly connections remaining to him – minus the necessary forbearance during Ramadan. The thought made him sigh.

The Tart looked at him and laughed aloud.

Yes, insolent was the word. He sighed again.

She finished her little cup and wiped her lips and put it down. A woman who wiped her lips with the back of her wrist was perhaps signalling something.

He took hold of her with both hands.

5.

Matson hadn't agreed a role with Barel. Barel was in command – they saw eye to eye that far. Matson was not a part of Barel's command, just the same; so Barel wanted him off his elbow. He said, '*My* men are going to rescue the hostages, *all* of the hostages. That's a co-ordinated job. We've rehearsed it. Stay clear of the relevant huts until your people are out.'

'Right.'

'Don't start a war with the Libyan Army, if you can help it. Other targets in other huts may be of interest to you.'

'Right.' Matson jumped from the still moving Land-Rover, caught up with it as it slowed, to say, 'Good luck,' then felt foolish. Barel was already hissing orders in a tick-tack of Hebrew and action clack. He ran through the gate in the perimeter fence towards his first prison.

Khadduri's command hut was dark. It smelled empty. Matson passed on. He had a map-pocket full of stuns, three short-fuse fragmentations on his belt. He did not leave one behind him for luck. He was in no mood for prudence. He had his knife. He had a Browning holstered down his shirt and doubtless fouled up with sweat, grit and body hair. He had the Ingram 10 he had worked at all afternoon. He unscrewed its suppressor. To hell with silence. Grendel was coming in from the moor.

There was a light burning in the next hut. He lifted his eye to the window frame and owled in.

Modfai, the immortal sergeant, with his trousers fallen to his ankles, was trying to grope a woman who had a pistol in her hand – a standard issue Browning like his own – with which she was about to defend her honour or her something by blowing Modfai away. Or part of him away. A woman with yellow hair. Modfai knew about the woman. He knew about and was visibly regretting his fallen trousers. The gun was going to be a big surprise to him.

Time to interrupt the programme.

Matson bounced back to heel-and-toe the ground, did a full jack spring and heave on the window ledge, then dived into the television screen.

His scalp picked up glass as he rolled, and then he was inside the play.

Theatre is for Immortals and Indestructibles. The woman was an old acquaintance of his. He had killed her once before. This time she had her gun out and was tightening on him fast.

The Ingram beat her to it.

Finding the Düsseldorf Tart alive did nothing for Matson's contact with reality. Nor did sluicing her over the far wall with an overlong pressure on the trigger. She was, perhaps, Lord Dragout's final conjuring trick – big-breathing lard-breasted woman resurrected from the bottle only to be vaporised out in a rainbowing paint-spray of atoms: the picture drips on the wall, the frame sloshes to the floor.

What was Modfai doing while Matson was killing his hoped-for bedfellow in rapid-fire mind-spattering slow-motion? Modfai was feeling at five hundred frames a second for his trousers in order to feel for his gun. Modfai was a good man with or without trousers, and would be better still for a gun.

The trouble with shooting people in people's presence is that people grow angry.

What did not splash away from the Tart stayed with Modfai. Modfai kept most of her. He neither used her as a shield nor threw her aside. He remained in uncomplicated ignorance of the fact that she was about to kill him. He lifted a pistol from somewhere beneath her body and levelled it in a simple clean upward movement without haste or waver.

Matson had no quarrel with Modfai. As he shot him he tried to see the death behind his eyes. They were opaque and brown. There was no death there. He wanted to shoot at Modfai's arm or his leg, but you never do that. When a man levels at you, even your brother, if you want to stay alive you empty all you've got into his gut.

Matson only shot the one round off, and so did Modfai. Modfai's hit the wall behind Matson's head and became a hot whirr in the room. Matson's, intended to be the first of many and straight into the target square, smashed Modfai's upper right arm.

He was forgetting how to shoot, or holiness was taking over. He smashed the sergeant once on the head, he hoped just enough to stun. He had too much respect for him to turn his back on him otherwise.

The Ingram hadn't jammed. It was at first I.A. The sod was already empty.

6.

Zefat treated them to his ugly attractive smile and said, 'Gentlemen, I'll give you a text. It's from the Bible of General Patton. It is this, and I'll thank you to keep it before you: "A good plan today is better than a perfect plan tomorrow". Now if we were to wait for marines to break in spit-proof boots or special forces to be issued with clean tooth-picks, we may as well as go away and beat drums. The enemy is only in two places, in Tripolitania and Cyrenaica. I don't want a third enemy in this room, the enemy within. Let's keep it down to two, and let's got out there and hit the bastards.'

'Snooker them up the arse,' Pomeroy said with approval.

'I put it like that – you must forgive my English – I put it like that because we know the Americans have been left at the starting gate. We left them there because they dithered while our people were at risk. Candidly, we didn't consider the American hostages were in danger, or likely to be endangered by what we are now doing. I have no way of knowing what calculations the British made.'

'The same,' Pomeroy said. He glanced movingly heavenwards, towards the upper rooms and Quinlan. 'We only sent a reconnaissance force, so we weren't looking to endanger anyone.'

'If the hostages are safe – any of them,' the Craw said, 'it'll be to do with politics. I'm not allowed politics. I'm allowed, on my say-so, a strong brigade of marines. I put a brigade of marines ashore, I don't have to ask anyone. Not because I'm God out here, but because I already asked them. That brigade will be on the beach closest to Az Zawiyah at first light tomorrow. I'm not too interested in clocks, General. In Zefat-time, in British Cyprus-time, in Cravicz-time which is U.S. Sixth Fleet time. In none of them. I'm interested in sun-up and tank-light. I'm interested in the soonest practical hour.'

Zefat nodded his agreement.

'I've listened to a lot of talk, especially in London,' the Craw went on. 'In London, especially, the talk has been good. I'm a disciple of General Patton myself, General. I'm going to give you the perfect reason for a no-good plan now. And this *is* a no-good operation we have here. *None* of those aircraft must fly unless we fly them. *If* any of them fly, then the politicians have to decide who will shoot them down. Let's hope they agree in time, eh? Meanwhile, *if* we can bring even one of them out or prevent just one from flying with our people on board, then we are a third better off than we were at the start of all this.'

'Good,' said Zefat. 'He knows his maths. Now what about the Brits?'

What indeed? Fossit thought.

'We'll be sending more,' Pomeroy said. 'I'll be reporting at once, but we'll certainly be sending more.'

He left Zefat's group and moved himself purposefully upstairs. Fossit didn't accompany him. There was suicide. There was protocol. Suicide came first with Pomeroy.

7.

The Enemy was no longer in a fit frame of mind to put up a fight. Khadduri might be, but not his conscripts, and certainly not the hijackers. It was a week now since they'd first mounted their amateur guard-rosters, and strutted about high on adrenalin and self-importance. Now they were tired and disillusioned with waiting. The Lord was at hand.

Matson was so drunk with the certainty of revenge that he was surprised at the long burst of controlled gunfire that came from the rear of the cantonment. The infantry, always in error, called this sort of demonstration a 'stonk'. Khadduri's infantry seemed to be getting this one right. They might be firing at shadows – he couldn't tell – but they were making the darkness very difficult to cross.

Matson found himself near the hut where Dragout had first roughed him up. There was a light shining underneath the door.

Ghosts again.

To his right, a strange medly of cheers, shouts, screams – more screams than cheers. Barel was succeeding, or partly succeeding.

Dragout's little cave of limewash and lupins had no windows. Matson tried the door. It was fixed. He shot the lock in with the Ingram 10 – a dozen rounds of hard-nosed .45s in a brutish fretsaw.

Then he somersaulted in. This was a mistake. There might have been two dozen brownjobs in there, holding a whist-drive. There weren't, but there might have been.

What there was, was his scalpful of glass filings from his last elbow roll. There was also the black hijacker, astonishingly smart in the same American Air Force uniform. It, and his teeth, must have been dry-cleaned.

His hand lacked its bandage. It retained its Avaroc Browning just the same. The teeth glittered. The gun flashed.

Matson collided with Dragout's high altar, rocking the little table, spilling water from a white jug, draping himself in a wire of flowers.

He flipped up the table as the black fired. The black fired twice more. The table-top didn't stop bullets, nothing in the room would have stopped them. But the table-top was moving. Matson was moving. The black fired again. The walls sang with pain.

Matson rolled out into empty space, holding up a vase, holding the spilling vase. It didn't leave him free to use his gun, but his hands had other plans for the black. The black levelled again. The black was always level. Matson threw the vase and rolled, protecting his skull's pain. The vase seemed suspended in the air, took aeons of flight-time, like an aging planet. The bullet went like light. But the black flinched at the vase. He had already shot his fifth awry in the grinning expectation of a vase in the teeth. So when the vase missed him and Matson hit him it was much the same thing. Matson hit him and kneed him and bent back his arm at the wrist. He felt through a meccano of dropped guns for the comfort of his knife. The black fired again and killed himself.

8.

Quinlan came downstairs. He pattered down noisily, heavy with importance, like a Victorian water-closet releasing its night's work.

The image was Pomeroy's, already developing it at his elbow.

'Ah, gentlemen – at last!' Quinlan boomed. 'A committee. Well, we need a chairman.'

'I propose General Zefat,' General Zefat said. 'We don't need a committee or a chairman. What we need is an announcement from you, sir.'

'And the chairman will be the de facto Force Commander, surely?'

'If anything is to happen from boats then some Navy admiral has to be Force Commander,' Cravicz said.

'Admirable. An American multi-star admiral can be Force Commander. General Zefat can be Officer in Charge of Planning and of the Land Forces, in so far as they can be considered to represent a unified command. Only as O.C. Planning he'll be known as Chairman, and as Field Commander he'll be known as General Zefat. How's that?'

'And provided the American admiral is not blamed for the invariable flop!'

'The cock-up will be down to me, gentlemen.'

'General Zefat can have the cock-ups.'

'We don't want any inter-service bungling or any international sideswipes,' the Craw said. 'This is going to be a mess. We all know that. For the record, I'm simply here to get a better than plain awful result. I'll be commanded by a corporal if I can guarantee that.' He smiled at Zefat. 'No-one reckons there's any glory in this, so no-one's jealous.'

'No-one's jealous,' General Zefat said to Quinlan, 'but everyone's still waiting.'

Fossit liked Zefat, even against his will and instinct. Zefat was a soldier's soldier. You recognise them among friend and foe alike, and you always respect them. He had watched Yigael Zefat at work, calling his meeting into shape, even manhandling chairs and insisting who sat where. Yes, a soldier's soldier. That was Wellington's description of Blucher wasn't it? General Zefat didn't have any broken ribs yet, though Terence Quinlan was clearly trying to make him pregnant with a foetal elephant.

'We're going to put a marine commando on the beach,' Quinlan said grandly.

'With what exactly in mind?' Cravicz asked.

'In case there has to be a walk-out from Sifr WaaHid.'

'That *would* be a cock-up,' Zefat said gravely.

'If there's a cock-up – pardon my language, gentlemen; but I've had a long night – you're going to need your friends in beside you. HMG made its military pronouncements a week ago, as you all know.'

'Saying just what?'
'Mission impossible, Admiral. And General.'

9.

Matson had been in fire-fights before. They offended the soldier in him, quite as much as they did Barel. The discharge of weapons without purpose was an affront, even when it was an aimed discharge. When death resulted, and it did often, then it came as a ridiculous accident. Soldiers deserve to die as part of an equation, or at least as the end-result of a miscalculation. Not because – as in the Lebanon – untutored actors in the theatre of malice are jerking off noise at one another.

Just the same, this confrontation was like no other he had seen. Khadduri's men – or somebody's men – were spraying shot in an exactly calibrated latticework of crossfire. You wouldn't see better, or neater, at the School of Infantry, in a demonstration of a battalion protecting its front.

Fortunately for Barel's men, and for the airlanding people under Dov Goradish, Khadduri's battalion front was a long way away, somewhere beyond the back of the compound, in fact. It shouldn't be protecting anything, except its aircraft and its prisoners. To do this, it didn't need to lay down crossfire; it needed a whole lot of platoons in the advance, two companies encircling, the remainder of the battalion pushing forward its centre in the time-honoured ritual of advance-to-contact by platoons-in-section.

Dov Goradish was happy enough to join in this kind of firefight. He had the energy. He had the ammunition. He unpeeled a platoon with its three sections with their l.m.g. and assault-rifle groups apiece and let them cross tracer rounds ahead. The whole display was about as useful as setting a trio of small boys to piddle in a pond; but it kept Khadduri from infiltrating the intervening darkness and that was good enough.

Barel might not want fire fights in general. This one was particular. It was highly spectacular. Highly political.

You needed a trained eye and ear and a bloodstream rich in

vitamin B and anti-stress minerals to recognise all of this above the noise. Matson had the trained eye and ear. He doubted if any of Khadduri's recruits were as analytically endowed. This would be a good beginners' battle for them – magnificent noise and not much blood.

Meanwhile, the hostages were being brought out and made to lie down.

Israeli women do not lie down, are impervious to all orders, or perhaps just through with lying down.

Matson ran towards them. Some of Khadduri's men were in the way, but the Israeli commando was stalking them remorselessly, getting rid of the unwanted.

He ducked down himself. Down was safest. He was in danger of dying from the evil intentions of friends.

10.

Fireworks, perhaps. An infantry engagement, no. A litter of wasted brownjobs and machine-stitched hijackers. A kaleidoscope of blood and flesh blown abruptly bloodless. The normal brain either goes mad at the retinal photoprint of torn-open faces, skull-slates lifted by gas, the witless inability of a shot-through shirt to retain its contents in military good order. In which case it can't do the job. Or it files the images away in its memory album and goes mad tomorrow.

Matson could do the job. He saw another fancy uniform framed in its little eyeflash of darkness, and inflated it with a long burst of impact gas. They compress. They bloat. They fart at a dozen eyelet holes. They swell again, vacuumed full of sand and sighs and implanted memory seed. They vibrate in the air and empty themselves of bad language, a couple of jerked-off shots that might have even hit you. You are too high to notice. Then the extravagant current of switchfire – they use too much cordite, these modern guns – that has been moving them through the hang-up air switches off and drops them.

They tumble like an old punctured sack full of nothing. Full of farmyard. Full of offal.

What were the Dragout's funny boys doing here? Avenging

their lord and master? Guarding the hostages or the Jumbo? Guarding the Bomb? You can't ask the dead.

There is a third kind of brain, that neither files away images nor sickens instantly. This is the sort of brain that sits inside the skull of those who guard extermination camps. Matson prowled among the blood, thinking his thoughts.

He heard a roaring like a bullock under the pliers.

It was Modfai. An air-stewardess from the Trident was leading him by the shattered forearm, which she twisted.

'Kill the bastard,' she said to Matson.

He recognised the woman who had stood up to the hijackers during the flight.

'Kill the bastard,' she repeated. 'He raped me.'

'I just killed him.' He released Modfai's arm. Killing Dragout was one thing. Killing Modfai quite another.

'He raped me,' she insisted.

He soothed her away and kicked Modfai into the convenient darkness, gesturing with his Ingram for her benefit.

British servicemen the world over know the Arabic for 'Fuck off!' It is part of service lore. Matson didn't say it to Modfai. He kicked Modfai away, then aimed the Ingram carefully at the most empty piece of landscape he could find.

He fired a self-important burst and rejoined the stewardess.

'You murdering bastard,' she hissed.

'He raped you.'

'What's your name, then: Biggles, or Rudyard Fucking Kipling?'

'You've got me in one,' he said.

11.

Nothing continued real. When he came to write his report, this would be beneath reporting. Matson was past being surprised at the lack of opposition. As he had seen it, only the hijackers and Dragout's brownjobs had fought – the hijackers for their lives, the brownjobs perhaps because they weren't prepared to risk themselves to the Israelis' good intentions.

Far off, someone was still operating their fire-plan. It was a fire-plan with infantry weapons only, and small arms at that. It was beginning to sound so distant that it might well be in another desert. Matson wasn't blunted, or combat-stunned. A little warfare always renewed his disco-deafness, acquired from being too close to detonations rather than loudspeakers: but you sense incoming rounds in the soles of the feet, in the skull, with the skin. When the shit began to fly, Matson became a bleb of sensitised gristle. No shit was flying, not his way. Not towards the hostages, either.

Where were the Libyan troops? He didn't count Modfai. Modfai was here for lechery. One or two lads in an adjacent hut were obviously nursing similar ambitions – perhaps for the women hostages or the air-stewardesses. Otherwise there was no-one.

As he closed on Barel's rescue-operation, he noticed weapon-pits between the perimeter wire and the front row of huts; it takes determination to dig holes in the heat. There were any number of two-man slits, revetted, sandbagged and braced – some of them with mortar-shields.

He was relieved to find that Lieutenant Goradish had taken some prisoners. Six very frightened Libyans were standing with their faces blanched white and their hands moon-high. One vomited in fright.

'The crews from two ack-ack guns. One heavy machine-gun.' Matson's sergeant said. He sounded as surprised as Matson.

Were they here to sneak a shot at a departing airliner or an arriving rescue aircraft? Or just for appearance?

'Ask them,' Matson demanded.

Barel had fluent Arabic. He asked them.

They grinned sheepishly, even the man who was being sick.

12.

Matson had a task to perform yet.

He felt with foot and hand among the hostages, crouching on the edge of the airstrip.

They didn't look like staying down much longer. Some of them had an experienced ear for the improbable.

Matson grabbed Irenson first, and steered him towards an appropriate post in the chain-link fence. 'Stay here,' he said. A girl was clinging to him. She stank with fear and a week's lack of soap and water. Irenson was in better shape – less fear? More aftershave? Perhaps he had used her as a sunshade. Matson was glad to see him comfort her openly and with a hard grip on her shoulder. The night was cold.

Anne Chambers smelled too, but she and her sister had a richer pong. Less fear again, but their courage was pickled in ancient sunshine. Lady Chambers' breath was the sort of medley of Culpeper and bay-rum that used to flavour his Irish aunts' fox furs on party nights.

Her sister was in even better shape. Becky Potts was unbelievably, cheerfully, battered. Ravaged would be the word. She looked as if she had been had by every billygoat and stud camel in a large Beddu encampment.

'Tiddly-pomp again,' Anne Chambers said. 'Tiddly-pomp for ever. They gave us all the planes' medical supplies – know what I mean? Marvellous people, even though they're bandits.'

'Arse-bandits,' Becky Potts corrected.

'Not me,' Lady Chambers said. 'No-one above the rank of lance-corporal. Mine is made of sandpaper, didn't you know? Becky's made of blotting paper.'

The conversation was too surreal for Matson. He tried to find U.S. General Randall Mackie. He couldn't.

He rounded up a group of uniformed infantrymen – and there weren't many of them in uniform – and gave them to a Green Howard junior officer in civvies. He told them where to collect Modfai's pistol, and the Brownings discarded by the Tart and the black.

Other officers began to call in their men as well.

He was distracted by his little nun. She was one of a small circle of women gazing at a girl's body that lay face-down on the amalgam. Matson went over.

The corpse was multiply leaking. It had been very soundly stitched. It was odourless. It had been able to get somewhere to wash. One of the hijackers.

Matson turned the head with his foot. No-one he recognised.

People muttered behind him. They objected to his foot.

Her face lay on an Uzi sub. He scuffed it out from beneath

her. The vent had trapped some of her hair. He tore it free. The onlookers objected to that as well.

'Friend of yours?' He asked his little nun.

'She's a Jew,' she said charitably. 'That's halfway to being Christian. The rest are heathens.'

'Mohammedans.'

'Heathens. I despise them. I hated her.'

'I don't.'

'You kill them just the same.'

'Much worse to hate her. Read St Augustine.'

'He's a Roman,' she hissed. 'That's worse than anything. Also, he was black.'

'That's bad,' he agreed. 'Still, she was white.'

'Yes,' the little nun said. 'And some Jew killed her.'

He remembered how much she'd bored him before. He felt too weary to remind her that she owed her rescue to an army of Jews. He didn't want to confuse her.

13.

An hour before dawn the air is thickest, the mixtures in the turbines at their most compressed and powerful.

Dov Goradish was checking the guts of the widebody. With or without a bomb, they were near to take-off.

The long-range barrage had stopped. Time to be off before a patrol was sent out, or Khadduri enthused his men with enough courage to send some in with grenade and bayonet.

Or even moved them within range of their assault rifles. Bullets were definitely *not* an operational requirement.

Barel had ordered the hijackers' bodies to be carried up the ramp of his jump plane. Now he ordered them down again. That was a bad sign.

He came to Matson and said, 'Our Captain Stern says he'll never get the 747 off with its original loading – let alone extras. I'll have to spread some of the Israeli passengers through my military aircraft. Sorry! I'll have to take them all. Their lives won't be worth much if I don't. I can also – or so we calculate – just about take off your women, including the cabin crew.'

This piece of news was rendered starker by a peppering of

flash bulbs, as identity-pictures were taken of the dead hijackers and some of the fallen brownjobs.

'If you leave us we'll need weapons.'

'Special forces carry special guns.'

'Her Majesty pays over the odds.'

'So does Uncle Sam.' The presence was senior – presumably General Randall Mackie.

Matson would have been pleased to own one of the Hand of God's .22 rapid-fire assassination zips – so would Her Majesty and so would Uncle Sam.

'We've got ordinary infantry weapons in the transport. I'll give you a platoon's weapons. You're a big platoon, but there's a certain amount of junk on the carpet.'

There was an Ingram, an Uzi, an AK47, a pair of Brownings, the guns belonging to Dragout's private army – the usual detritus.

Barel held out his hand. Matson took it for the first and probably the last time.

Barel said, not without savouring the moment, 'Matson, you know how it is. It's a command decision. Not ours. Cyprus knows. I'll come back for you. Your Marine commando'll come back for you. Someone'll come back for you. No-one'll come back for you. You know what war's like. I'd say your chance is better than your two casualties back in the jebel. Better than Levett's, even.

'But not by much.'

14.

'The 747 is clean,' Dov said. 'The holds are empty.' He said nothing about the heroism involved in walking through them. 'All we've got are those brand-new loading sleds, obviously intended for something – you know, they're normally filled with freight and then stowed into the baggage holds. Those very suggestive sleds, and those even more suggestive cement blocks with their vitreous retorts.'

'The hoax was an elaborate one,' Matson said.

Nobody was paying much attention.

'So it was a hoax?' Matson demanded. 'I mean, we need to

know. Other people at other locations will need to know.'

Dov Goradish regarded him for a second of deep loathing, then said, 'I don't think so. The contents of one of those retorts was about to be winched up into the widebody. More to the point, rails have been laid in the load-compartments. It's an obvious way of running critical mass towards critical mass as the plane reverse-thrusts on landing. The retorts are Geiger-active, by the way.'

'Wire them up,' Barel ordered. 'Your party will have to move fast, Matson. When it blows, you'll need to be clear of the dust, because they're full of something fissionable, without a doubt. If it blows atomic – then heaven help you.'

'How long have we got?'

'We'll give you an hour,' Dov said. 'I'm not an expert, but what we've got inside those blocks looks as if it might be core rods. If they shatter and scatter – all well and good, except for the local microbes. If anything comes together, there's the possibility of a slow criticality. I wouldn't know how fast that is, but my guess is minutes not days.'

'We'll move fast,' Matson assured him.

'Unless someone stops you,' Barel agreed.

'I could stop him,' Dov muttered.

'We've made our peace.'

15.

Matson believed in slowly making haste rather than hurrying slowly. To be atomised would be a whole lot better than dying of a punctured peptic ulcer, especially an ulcer he hadn't got. He called out for the stay-behind party to gather round, but allowed himself to become chatty while they did so.

Several people were going to need cheering up. 'We're walking out,' he said. 'It's more dignified than running out.' He said this several times. In a moment they would all be collected in one place and he would tell them his plan.

For the moment, here was Captain Finch, the second officer of his own flight. It had to be Captain Finch. He wore a braid-peaked cap and no jacket. Matson had purloined his jacket.

'I owe you about fifty quid,' he said to Captain Finch.
Captain Finch was in shock.

'I frisked your wallet when I pinched the Trident the other night!' Matson never said 'quid' or 'pinched' so he must be feeling shaky himself.

'Any money I had I won from that fake Yank who held a pistol to my neck.'

'No wonder you couldn't fly.'

'*He* couldn't fly. He couldn't play cards, either. He said he didn't mind losing at cards. Cards was all he ever lost at. Losing to me was his luck.'

'You didn't bring him much this time.'

'I'm glad. He niffed.'

'So do we all out here.'

'Not of peppermint toothpaste, we don't.'

Barel put paid to the chat. He pushed in and said, 'Are you qualified to sit starboard in a 747?'

'I'm not qualified. But I can do it. Where are we heading?' Finch's teeth chattered.

Barel controlled his impatience and said, 'Akrotiri, Ben Gurion or somewhere military – we don't know. Let's get it up.'

You need a long time to bridge-load a widebody. To fill it by getting old people up improvised ladders takes an eternity. A burst of machine-gun fire, a few threatening shots even, could have made the whole operation impossible. Matson blessed Khadduri. Blessed? No: wondered at him.

'The runway could be mined,' he blurted. 'Have you checked it?'

'Our lot got their flight on, without mishap,' Barel observed. 'We must assume we can get the widebody off.'

16.

The amalgam behaved strangely in the pre-dawn cool. Fisher said it would. Fisher was right. It was harder but brittle, brisker once the aircraft was under way but much more bumpy.

The multicart undercarriage of the 747 had broken through

the surface during its several days of standing. Its damaged wheels were supposedly replaced or repaired. Khadduri had spoken of new tyres at their first encounter. Who could tell? They were all sunk in, like prunes in piecrust.

So the widebody revved but couldn't move. Or perhaps its surrogate aviator had the brake on.

Its turbines piled up the decibels, Middle C on a forest of bassoons. Then it moved.

It moved easily and boldly forward in a multitrack axle-deep trough. The double octets of hinged wheels splintered the crust by inch then by yard and by furlong with a horrible ongoing crackle like bone splitting. If this didn't fracture the undercart, repuncture the tyres, nothing would.

The huge double tracks, double then double again, lost themselves in darkness. The plane was moving quickly now in the pre-dawn glim, much too swiftly to be still silted in.

For a second it seemed to stand absolutely still, at the furthest blur of Matson's straining eyesight. Then it grew smaller as his focus relaxed, tilted nose-high and lifted. It glowed upwards, then shone brightly in the above-the-desert sunlight.

The military aircraft didn't break the landing strip. They manoeuvred to avoid the huge ruts of the Jumbo. They lined up, stuck their noses due north, and one by one were away. The last one, Barel's headquarters aircraft, took off in a full daylight.

Matson was alone with his command.

TWENTY-TWO

1.

The Craw was a civilised man. Restraint was his power. As Pomeroy said of him, 'He's one of the few members of the American officer corps who doesn't think he was written by Norman Mailer'.

So when the Craw said, 'I have to report there's been a Grade A drop-arsed fuck-up', the moment had force.

They followed him to the split map-table as if to draw strength.

He peered at its western end, and ran his finger through the start lines of the U.S. battle-plan. 'Yes,' he repeated, 'a top-class screw.'

'Everyone knew the Sixth Fleet had to chew the tough apples.' Zefat's sympathy bristled with unasked questions.

'We took the beach. We crossed the coast road. We occupied Az Zawiyah. We put two battalions of Marines on the airfield perimeter. Casualties – nil. They wait for the visual, red over green over red, from the snatch group.

' "Snatch",' he said morosely, 'is the word. It is on time; it is going fast for that airfield vedette, the penants on its jeeps can be seen by both battalion commanders. So it stops dead. It stops for a British picnic,' he raged at Pomeroy. 'For all I've got and for all we know it's still brewing tea.'

'Didn't those Marine battalions go in anyway?' Zefat asked. 'You must be able to salvage something.'

'They're probably brewing too.' Admiral Cravicz spoke quietly, bitterly. 'Something unforeseen has happened.

Something that's going to hit you at Sifr WaaHid too, unless I'm very much mistaken and you're a jump ahead of schedule. Meanwhile the fog of war descends. If the absolute worst case has happened we won't know till the fleet AWACs beam in, or your people on Troodos have something to tell us.'

As if on cue, the two relevant signallers on the communications console began to write on their message carbons; the one on the radio telephone repeating back three words at a time in a nasal sing-song.

The Troodos link was lucky. He wrote, because that was the procedure, but he was getting a print-out anyway, on a relay-machine that looked like a small roller-towel. Or, in this case, lavatory paper.

2.

Lieutenant Norris Lamberty was in the lead jeep. When the shooting started, it would be on his say-so.

Captain Reinhardt was in overall command of the rescue group, but he was six trucks back – not because it was reckoned to be an ideal place for an officer of Marines to be, but because if the head of the column took a lot of incoming then someone would need to redeploy the centre.

Lieutenant Vaugn was in the jeep behind Reinhardt, and his six vehicles were the ones that were going to dash for the Greek aircraft, unless Lamberty's men took casualties or Reinhardt told him something different. Lamberty was going to handle the TWA 747.

Reinhardt was reckoned the best company officer, Lamberty and Vaugn the best junior officers, in the regiment. They had all done a lot of 'cutting-out' and confined assault training. They had practised aircrew/ and aircraft/seize-and-rescue ad nauseam. They were good at thinking on their feet.

Lamberty sat beside his driver and watched the vedette and the drop-gate in the perimeter wire come towards him along the road at a relentless five and thirty miles in the hour. This mileage had been calculated by a lot of careful planners to be the optimum speed, combining the maximum rate of closure with the minimum amount of alarm. They had shared their thoughts with others such as Zefat and Barkworth who had no official rights in the matter but had pronounced their opinions good.

There was a sentry box beside the gate, a sentry box and a flag-pole with flag. Lamberty took one turn on his suppressor-cylinder: it was too tight to twist, but he rotated the sweat of his hand. Then he pulled back the cocking-nut.

If the sentry in that sentry box was a good lad, the two Marines behind Lamberty were going to dive out and secure his wrists in his garters.

If, on the other hand, he was ambitious or officious, Lamberty was going to spray him round the paintwork with an instant throughput of silence.

It was going to be silence and suppressors till they hit those aircraft, the sheds and the fucking hijackers; then it was going to be noise noise noise.

The feed road was already wet with mirage. At six hundred yards the post-dawn heat-haze above the bubble-gumming tarmac stretched the sentry box till it looked like a spindle that whirred itself in half.

Lamberty's eye did its best with the liquid air. At four hundred yards it recorded several truths with instant clarity. There was no sentry. Instead, beneath the lowest fracture of air beside the sentry box, there was a hole full of heads and sandbags. The heads were lidded up in steel helmets.

'Go!' He shouted to his driver, 'Go! Go! Go!' As the needle jumped to sixty and the jeep put on a hysterical whine, he pressiled his head-set and said to Reinhardt and everyone else who'd watched his vehicle accelerate forward, 'Heavy machine-gun. Twelve o'clock. Left hand side of the gate!' He heard the other vehicles pick up behind him. He was leading a battle charge. He added, again for Reinhardt's benefit, and because he had to say something with his death so imminent, 'It looks like a point five, if not a twenty millimeter.'

Sixty miles an hour seemed much more languorous than thirty-five. Lamberty noticed his driver hunch over the wheel, felt someone's nose burrow between his shoulderblades. It could only be Sergeant Buerk's, and Buerk was a tall man. The Marine beside Buerk was hanging half out of the jeep.

Meanwhile the machine-gun nest and its three – no, four –

infantrymen came on only slowly, as if the jeep's tyres were spinning in sand, as if its wheels were doing sixty but the rest of it was static in tarmac, embedded in mirage.

Lamberty alone sat up straight. He did so from training, duty and philosophy. He used to dream of this moment, dream 'the taller a man makes himself the less of him the bullet will hit at any one time'.

Sergeant Buerk felt differently. Sergeant Buerk knew that being hit by a heavy machine-gun would be like having a concrete mixer drive right through you. No man could make himself big enough.

The jeep began to skid. The driver was down on the footbrake. The gate was on top of them. No-one had opened the gate. The gate was a solid steel drop-bar. This is what drivers notice.

The driver saw no such thing. He braked like hell just the same. He stopped out of military etiquette. What he saw was that the four men in the machine-gun nest were waist-high out of the ground with their hands thrust up in the air. One of them waved an off-white flag.

Then the gate lifted open. A Libyan-green Citroën filled its entirety.

Three officers in flat caps stepped out, two air-force blue, one khaki. They were of exalted rank, even for foreigners. Especially for Lieutenant Norris Lamberty.

Lamberty had never been surrendered to before. He'd certainly never had a military airfield surrendered to him before.

Surrendered or placed temporarily in balk under white flag or feathers pending negotiation.

He supposed that was what was happening, all of it or some of it, and one of them seemingly a general.

He heard another jeep beside him and saw Reinhardt's penant. His own driver was swearing quietly. Buerk was being sick.

Lamberty stepped down. He saluted. He embraced Libyan hands.

It was then the shooting started.

3.

The sea-link was unequivocal: *Pigeon pancake ... Pigeon pancake ... Eagle out of the bag ...*

'Cassandra,' moaned Pomeroy, 'versus the poetry of technosqueak!'

They had to secure three birds: *Eagle* and *Pigeon* in Tripolitania; *Dove* in the desert. Fossit was skilled in such matters. He made death clear.

An aircraft destroyed by Libyans or hijackers would be *Eagle* or *Pigeon* or *Dove choppered*. An aircraft destroyed, for whatever reason, by the attackers, would be *Eagle* or *Pigeon* or *Dove arrowed*. An aircraft rescued but still on the ground would be *pancake* – a good old Air Force expression – and an aircraft rescued and flying would be, quite simply, *flying*. *Eagle out of the bag* spelled that the U.S. Jumbo was indeed flying, but with the hijackers still in charge. *Eagle out of the bag*. Did it have a bomb in its claws?

Pigeon pancake was half way to being good news, at least.

'Your boys had the hard apples,' Zefat kept saying. 'They've done a good job. They've got the bloody duck and all its Greek stuffing.'

'They've also secured some hundred U.S. citizens,' the Craw confirmed. 'But that leaves a couple of hundred more.'

It also left the Israelis and the British at Sifr WaaHid. There was no news of *Dove*.

Quinlan came in, with the U.S. consul from Larnaca.

'The Libyans bugged us up,' the Craw explained. 'They bugged us up by cooperating. They white-flagged our attack, and simultaneously assaulted both aircraft themselves. They said they had been preparing the ground for days. We say they responded to our demonstration of force.

'In the event, their preparation wasn't good enough to stop our widebody being scrambled. So, at the very least, the hijack continues.'

'The hijack, yes. But what becomes of Holofernes?'

'I said "at the very least". Our people are looking at the Greek aircraft now. The Libyans are very reluctant to let them. Does that smell of Holofernes?'

The Troodos operator passed a print-out to Barkworth in an unnecessary flurry of protocol. Barkworth handed it straight on to Cravicz who read: '*Speedbird believe Eagle 0613 hrs 32°25'N 17°W heading 091° radar spot geometric 0615 still 091° radar spot geometric.*'

'Egypt or Israel, not yet Lebanon,' Zefat muttered.

'091° is Israel, about two hours' flight time.'

At 7.15 local time, Troodos told them: *Speedbird 0700 hrs 32°36'N 21°40'W radio spot geometric.*

AWACs via the sea-link fed them: *Eagle still angels 32 variable 090° airspeed 320 knots.*

'We're shadowing with a flight of 1-11s,' Cravicz said. 'I don't think there are any logistics against staying with them. Can you help?'

'I've got six Tornado 3Fs standing by at Akrotiri. Two ought to go now if they're to assume a meaningful position.'

'Please. It might help our status. We'll stay with it, but we'll have to relay.'

'I'll alert my people,' Zefat said.

'No need, yet, surely?'

They knew why he was growing fretful. It wasn't just the lack of news from *Dove* and Sifr WaaHid.

Sea-link confirmed everyone's worst fears, the Craw's and Zefat's most of all. The signaller took the message on Charlie William then clear; then gave them a flimsy from his note-pad without waiting for the print-out.

It read *0700 hrs Pigeon still pancake Pigeon pancake with chilli repeat with chilli.*

'*Con* bloody *carne*,' Pomeroy hissed to Fossit, both well in the background.

'Tel Aviv,' Zefat said. 'They're going to hit Tel Aviv. Holofernes was always right. So was your Mister Matson.'

'I'll have to call Washington,' the Craw said. 'I expect somebody already has, but I'd certainly better make sure.'

' "A grade-A drop-arsed fuck up",' Pomeroy quoted as he went to talk to Quinlan. ' "With chilli"!'

With chilli meant that the Greek airliner had been fitted with an atomic device. God knows what degree of courage had been involved in prying into it.

They could only assume that the 747 closing on the Eastern

Mediterranean was similarly armed.

So what would Zefat do now?

4.

'The White House is leaving it to me,' the Craw said. 'That is – the timing is being left to our best judgement in this room. My clear instruction is that if or *when* I think the sands have run out, an interceptor from the Sixth Fleet must use a missile on that 747. The President is emphatic, for political reasons, that a U.S. aircraft can only be sacrificed as a result of U.S. intervention.'

'I've got somewhat different instructions,' Yigael Zefat said. 'They're not incompatible,' he added softly. 'Mine are these. There are two forward strips in Sinai. They are not good, especially for a civil widebody. Nonetheless, my people will try to force a pancake out of harm's way in the desert.'

'No.'

'First, yes. If we fail, we'll let you do your own dirty work.' He put his arm round the Craw's shoulders. 'We'll try not to tip Eagle into the jebel by mistake. Unless you'd prefer us to, of course. Sometimes accidents make the best politics.'

'Need anyone know?' Quinlan came forward to ask. It wasn't, after all, his problem.

'The American public has a need to know,' the Craw said simply.

5.

'Information,' Matson said. 'I'm in command here. You'll have heard my good news. I've already disseminated it by gossip while you've been rubbing the sleep from your eyes. My good news is we're walking out.

'Behind me you'll notice some baggage sleds, some of them full of your kit. Leave them alone. Claim it on insurance. They're fused to detonate. You'll also see four blocks of concrete compress. Leave them alone. Booby-trapped ditto.

'You've got, what with loot and Israeli left-overs, about one firearm between two of you. I want all officers armed. All NCOs armed. All members of the four fighting arms of the Army armed. Small-arms-proficient members of the Navy and RAF armed, RAF Regiment especially. Officers will arbitrate.

'Otherwise I want men to group themselves so that each unarmed man is with an armed one. One gun looks after two people. If the chap with the gun gets sunstroke or catches a cold, his pal inherits his hardware. Understood?

'Over there, being prudent, are several detachments of the Libyan Army. They have left us alone so far, but they may only have been frightened of the dark. If they put in an appearance, we shall discourage them. You will fire *only* on my orders. You will not fire all groups, or by group at all. I shall nominate individuals. Our aim will be to keep their heads down, not shoot their tits off.'

By now everyone was relaxed and laughing. Matson well knew there's nothing like a bit of national or sexual chauvinism to set your average pongo chomping.

'It is now oh-four-oh-seven hours. At oh-five-hundred precisely, the aforementioned charges will blow. The concrete blocks are probably full of fissionable material. They may even contain weapons-grade plutonium. That gives us fifty-three minutes.'

'We can run a long way in fifty-two minutes thirty seconds, even running in files and in good order. We can also run a long way in forty minutes and save ten minutes' puff.

'The Libyan Army wears rotten boots, so it must have some vehicles. They seem to have bugged out in a hurry last night. We've got five minutes to make ready anything they left at this end of the compound.'

Matson hoped they'd left something that moved with wheels.

If Dov Goradish's charge triggered a chain reaction, then the dynamics of fusion or fission would begin. Whether the result was instant criticality or whether it was meltdown, he didn't think forty-two or even fifty-two minutes would get them far enough.

While his command bustled itself into action, he permitted himself a stroll to the concrete blocks. They were off-loaded now, but their size was much as he'd estimated them a few nights' ago in the dark.

They each bore the same stencilled sign in red letters. The inscription was in Arabic. It would be, wouldn't it? A long word followed by a short word. He knew the short word. It was Al. Arab speakers put it in front of, therefore behind, everything. He couldn't decipher the long word. It might say danger, or record the name of a shipper or a destination.

Or it might say Holofernes. It was long enough.

6.

The catch was three jeeps, Nuseibeh's passion-Rover, and a platoon lorry. This last was the best find. It wasn't armoured. It was canvas-topped and tin-sided, a bit like an old-fashioned British Army TCV; but it would hold forty men in four front-to-back files. Khadduri had probably used it to bring his first body of men into the desert.

He now had about half of the transport he needed – assuming it all worked.

After six minutes, two of the Royal Greenjacket officers came back with a fourth jeep, from the far end of the strip. It was smeared with blood and full of bolted-in searchlight. Someone had put up a struggle for that one.

'Piles,' one of the Greenjackets said.

'He had an embarrassing nosebleed,' his friend contradicted.

'See if you can dump the searchlight,' Matson insisted. 'There must be some A-braces or somesuch in one of the tool-kits.'

Libyan vehicles did not have tool-kits.

The searchlight drum was mounted on the usual needle-roller hub and platform. The whole thing was bolted to a reinforcement plate on the jeep's rear chassis by means of half a dozen hexagonal countersunk plugs. Like the nuts on a lorry's bell-housing, they were beyond being loosened with fingers.

'Strong teeth, anyone?' Matson set the joke pattern. His morale was still patchy. He needed jokes. He was going to develop and rupture and die of a peptic ulcer after all – all in forty-odd minutes.

7.

'Right', said Matson. 'Here are my orders. Half of this column – you on my left – are going to ride out now. You will be under the command of *this* officer here.' He tagged one of his Royal Greenjackets. 'You will keep yourselves in a distinct group from this time forward. You will be known as Blue Force. Red Force, under the command of this officer here' – he indicated the other Royal Greenjacket – 'is going to come with me at a very fast walk. *Don't* embus yet!'

He made sure he had absolute control and complete attention, then said, 'Blue Force have the harder task. Or their drivers and escorts have. They are to move in convoy for five miles or ten minutes down that track there – the one that runs away north – five miles or ten minutes, *whichever is sooner*. They will *debus*' – how Pomeroy would have enjoyed the majesty of the language – 'and come back, under the command of an officer to be nominated by O.C. Blue Force, and pick up Red Force. A swift removal of all fingers from the works will mean we can each do two staggers before these charges blow. Any questions?'

The silence was compressed rather than pregnant.

'Blue Force – mount up!'

The drivers had already chosen themselves.

Blue Force drove away in style, Nuseibeh's passion-Rover jeep, the TCV which held the bulk of them, jeep, jeep, jeep.

For some inexplicable reason they cheered, as if they were off on leave or going to rape Constantinople.

'Armed to the teeth,' someone said beside Matson. It was the store-clerk – or was it the company cook? – who'd kept his little nun company on the flight out. 'Armed to the fucking teeth.' He spoke with admiration, longing, approval. He hadn't qualified for a weapon himself.

O.C. Red Force had arranged three squads in two files of ten each. He reported to Matson. He turned them to the right in file. They set off at a purposeful, dehydrating muscle-drying double march in the full blare of the sun.

Khadduri did nothing to stop them, nothing at all. He hadn't sent them any fruit-juice either. Why fight a battle when the Sahara's on your side?

Matson was in no state to double, but he was in overall command. To command is to lead is to be an example. He doubled.

8.

If this had been an exercise it would have been a snarl-up. If these had been a handpicked group of specialists, and they'd practised the manoeuvre for a week, every seasoned NCO among them would have placed a tenner on at least something going wrong when they did it for real. War and Chance are like that. Fate has rusty shears.

Matson was a twenty-minute deep-fried sunball when the Land-Rover stopped beside him. Behind it was a jeep, then the TCV, then three more jeeps.

Beside each driver was an armed escort. The TCV had its first hoop of canvas lashed back and an Uzi medium machine-gun strapped onto the top of the metal frame.

His Green Howard officer was the come-back commander. He reported, briefly, then watched Red Force's Royal Greenjacket get his men loaded up. They hopped on quickly, considering the condition they were already in.

The Green Howard was clearly appalled by them. He sat in the back of Nuseibeh's Land-Rover, and eyed Matson. 'How was it, sir?'

'Awful. You'll find out in a few moment's time, I'm afraid. Awful. There's water at Zoltan. But we'll have to get there.'

'That truck's going to be the problem,' their driver said. He gestured with his thumb towards the TCV. 'Its radiator was dry.'

'Leaky.'

'Neglect,' the Green Howard said. 'So it was basic remedies, I'm afraid.'

'Half of Blue Force got up on the bonnet and pissed in it.' Drivers are less fastidious than Green Howard officers. 'Half of them got blistered knees. The other half got scalded dinkles.' He said it well. He'd said it before and he was going to say it again. He said it several times more with evident approval till it was Blue Force's turn to double march.

The Green Howard waited until he and Matson were alone in the Land-Rover, then said curtly, 'Why didn't we bring water, sir? Command oversight?'

'I looked around a good few huts,' Matson said evenly, 'and I only saw open-topped vessels: jugs, washing-bowls, lavatory buckets – that sort of thing.'

The Green Howard nodded, thoughtful but satisfied. You can't carry water over rough country in a lidless container.

Even in the desert, you won't find an Irishman who's slow with an explanation, either.

9.

They'd been lucky once. Matson ordered both second legs of the stagger to be short ones. He doubted if Red Force could double in the sun for another twenty minutes. Blue Force looked terrible when it was their turn to use the transport.

A week ago they'd been on leave, boozing. They'd had another week out here, cooped up in idleness. They'd been fed, after a fashion. They'd been given water. Thirty minutes ago, Matson's command had been lard-faced and puffy. It was now a rattle-bag of flame-cheeked skeletons.

Matson's second run didn't last long. The Green Howard in the Land-Rover came back even sooner than anticipated. 'There's an oil-donkey and a water-tower in that little frieze of jebel,' he said. 'O.C. Blue Force doesn't know if the water-tower's functional, but he's stopped our stag there.'

'Good man.' Matson climbed aboard.

'I'm senior to young Black-buttons and Bugle, by the way.'

'I'm probably junior to both of you. But that's the way it is while we're in transit.'

10.

O.C. Blue Force was a clever man. He'd made it very unlikely that Matson would set his fellows running again, not until they'd explored the contents of that water-tower, nor until the charges fired at Sifr WaaHid. Once the charges fired, they could hope to move more slowly. Or move not at all.

'I make it we've got nine minutes,' the Royal Greenjacket said.

Sifr WaaHid looked very near from here. They could oversee it well from among the boulders of this tiny fringe of jebel.

'Everyone take cover,' Matson advised. 'Time fuses are never one hundred percent reliable. I don't want anyone up the tower until the charges detonate.'

He looked south, towards Sifr WaaHid in its hot bowl of sand. One minute everything was clear, then the mirage shimmered and blurred its details to fog.

He felt inside his shirt for his monocular. It gave him everything binoculars gave him at half the weight. It gave him 12 × 50. It gave him range-finding graticules. It gave him four concrete blocks at Sifr WaaHid as near to his fist as bathcubes.

Then someone switched the light on, someone sluiced the steam. His lensful of Sifr WaaHid shuddered and melted and boiled itself apart.

11.

Pomeroy was weeping. Not his brain, not his heart, but his eyes, leaking fatigue and frustration in droplets that ran down his cheek and probably tasted of pure alcohol.

'So there's a bomb at Az Zawiyah, and another bomb flying,' Fossit said.

'And my Matson has done nothing, and my Quinlan has revolutionised mathematics by doing even less.'

They were watching a small group of kitted-up Marine Commandos file up the ramp of a Hastings. If Pomeroy wept for anything it was this brutal end of diplomacy.

In an hour's time this miniscule airborne force would step out into the early morning light one thousand feet above Quaminis, cut the coastal link telephone lines, blow the junction boxes at Zoltan and seal off the main road from Benghazi.

At the same time, the beach-landing party, long afloat, and hoping not to wet its ankles, would secure the beach at Quaminis and push forward to join them.

According to Pomeroy, this was about fifty miles up the coast from where they needed to be.

The ramp closed on grinning faces, catcalls. It wasn't pre-jump bravado, nor the result of a pump-up of adrenalin. It was all too relaxed. Good troops get this way when they think they're going in against a soft target.

All targets are soft till you get there.

12.

They walked back to join Barkworth in his car.

Fossit said, 'By the time we reach Athna, that U.S. widebody will be landing at Lod. Or blowing up Tel Aviv.'

'Hardly. It'll be in the drink with its two hundred passengers. Or the Israelis will have forced it down on Sinai.'

'You're being bloody calm about it.'

'Anyone can be calm, provided they teach themselves to think in big enough numbers. Or if they're prepared to get themselves drunk enough.'

'God, I hate Cyprus.'

They slipped into Barkworth's presence, old red cheeks sniffing suspiciously.

Pomeroy eyed Barkworth's ears and his driver's neck. 'What Cyprus has for me,' he said loftily, 'is the cheapest brandy outside South America. There's Spain, of course; but I loathe grocers' shops. I must get myself a couple of dozen cases before the bloody English finish spoiling things.'

'I think of you as the quintessential Englishman, Marcus.'

The brigadier snorted.

'I loathe us, dear boy. Look at the people God puts us with.'

Fossit searched his mind for a cliché.

Pomeroy obliged him. 'I'm not English, British, mid-Atlantic, cosmopolitan, polyglot, nor mere man of the world. The brigadier's a man of the world, and he won't let me join. I'm a member of the Foreign Office, dear thing. So I belong almost nowhere. There may be a planet that will take me in.'

'I hope, for your sake, it's not a dry one.' The brigadier spoke round his ears, without moving his head. He was glaring down the road, getting an early look at the future.

'Let's take our good news to the Zefat.' Fossit thought Pomeroy was supposed to be the diplomat. 'He'll perk up when he hears about the brigadier's Marines.'

'Not when he discovers where he's sent them.'

'God – I wish I could post you after them.'

'You were born in the wrong century for the brigadier, Marcus.'

'I should have been born in Mecca, or even Jeddah or Medina, at about the time the Prophet was marrying all those women and slitting all those throats while founding a world religion on the basis of abstinence and mercy. I do enjoy an epoque-shattering fibber above almost everything else. That's what excites me so much about Communism and microwave ovens.'

'What would you have been in Medina, Marcus – a camelboy or a Grand Vizier?'

'The Eunuch. I'd choose to be the Eunuch every time.'

'Always the profundity, Marcus!'

'There's nothing profound about an absence of bollocks. Ask the brigadier.'

'No – you and the epoque-shattering fibber. A clutch of aeroplanes that are going to set the world on fire. Holofernes could only have been thought up by people who believe in the Jihad – the Holy War that starts without anyone lifting a finger.'

'Holofernes was invented by some little pimp in London or New York, rest on it. Or some big ponce who was educated at Harrow.'

'I was educated at Harrow,' Barkworth said. 'So was Winston Churchill.'

The sky might shortly be burning. The driver chose now to laugh.

13.

Never watch an explosion through an optic. Matson had once used his Spacescope to monitor a phosporous grenade. He thought the earth had erupted and set his brain on fire.

Sifr WaaHid was undoubtedly involved in a very big explosion. There had been the detonation of the charges followed by something larger and longer, much more brutish and sullen.

Matson lowered his day-glass and saw that a huge mass of molten smoulder still pulsed and enlarged, spreading a groundswell of white fume then tarry black smoke.

A burning mushroom, brandishing its own canopy of flame, went vorticing skyward.

The men around Matson gasped, muttered briefly in awe. But it was not atomic burst. If it had been, it would have blinded him. He'd been a fool to use his monocular. It was some kind of complex lesser explosion, a savage linkage of agrochemical and the amalgam of the landing strip, which continued to melt and spread and burn.

The atomic risk was still there, of course. There was a deep glow at the fire's centre, a kind of dragon's eye which whitened and brightened. This was what Goradish had set out to disperse and destroy. At the very least, his charges had scattered dozens, perhaps hundreds, of core-rod elements like so many burning spears. At the worst, the melt was still on, the Bomb still baking.

14.

Matson stopped looking at the fire, and tried to think. Thinking was difficult; he forced himself to realise his loss of capacity.

The sun was ripening overhead, tightening and shrinking. He was growing witless with dehydration. So, without doubt, were the rest of them.

Yells of dismay from the water-tower. 'Nothing,' one of the climbers reported. 'No water. It's all cooked out.'

Matson examined the tower, noticing a fixed pipe running down one of its supports, then underground.

'The water will be underneath, if it's anywhere. This thing must have been designed as a siphon, not a cistern. You can't store water above ground in this kind of heat.'

The cries were croaks now. His men were like sick crows, thirsty for grain. They grubbed at a shale of rock, pecking and petulant. They cleared away a rough paving of stones and uncovered an inspection hatch.

The tube of darkness beneath it smelled moist, mushroomy as a sleeper's breath. Someone kicked in a stone. The splash was immediate.

They broke the bottom from a petrol-can and lowered it on a tow-rope, backside up. They drank.

Matson drank last, after the other officers. He let people drink and drink. He had to reckon they weren't so long dehydrated that water would harm them.

This water tasted like poison, anyway.

'It'll be full of amoebas,' the Green Howard said.

'They'll take a few hours to work through,' Matson encouraged.

His sunburnt flock of albinos became less crow-like, much more like men. He got them to juggle jerrycans of petrol, topping up vehicle reservoirs. That way they freed four jerrycans, enough for eight gallons or, more likely, forty litres of polluted water.

'Right,' he called. 'Move in five minutes. We're doing twenty-mile staggers this time. No more double marching – just a nice brisk walk. If the vehicles are up to yoyo-ing up and down, we'll all manage to ride a fair amount of the way.

'My aim is to reach Zoltan as a compact unit, all of a piece. Zoltan is Libyan, of course, but psychologically well-disposed to us. There are lots of Europeans there. It's an oil-field, a kind of Sifr WaaHid where the cola fountains work.'

Some of them had enough spit to laugh.

He gave this intelligence time to sink in, then said, 'Perhaps Zoltan will be less helpful than we anticipate. Perhaps the powers-that-be will want to shilly-shally. That's why we are going to arrive in good order and with our side-arms in evidence. No-one is going to stop us. Our Marines are waiting for us on the beach. The beach is just a little bit further, that's all.'

He didn't tell them how much further, nor that Barel's radio-link had said Qaminis – a damn silly rendezvous altogether. He thought it was time to have a little laugh himself.

They took a little laugh with him. Some of them had enough laugh to spit.

15.

An unnatural euphoria had settled over his party. He noticed this, as he checked they had carried out his order concerning the appropriate distribution of weapons.

Their women had got away. They had got away from their women. They could look forward to reading about themselves in the *Sun*. They were fit and free, with an interesting assortment of guns and ammunition.

They radiated a healthy air of splash and pillage, enhanced by the fact that most of them were out of uniform. Matson encouraged those to improvise their ranks on shoulder or sleeve. A few of them were in military number ones. Most were dressed in casuals, their feet shod in bumpers or trainers not much good for up-country walking.

Soil, sweat, crude and sand had blighted whatever they wore. They didn't look smart enough for buccaneers. They were more like an Indian raiding party sporting last year's loot. They seemed a good enough random bunch to lead into a fight, just the same.

He didn't intend to get into a fight, did he? He wondered whether to follow the Green Howard's advice and give rank precedence, combat-rank anyway, in case they did run into trouble.

It was Red Force's turn to ride. Men getting on a vehicle are always too happy.

16.

Thank God he had no Yanks, no politicians and no VIPs. He had nothing against any of them, but he didn't want the responsibility. They were Barel's concern.

Thank God.

When you're falling in beside three squads to join them in a sweaty run through the post-dawn light you do not check who they are, and how well you know them.

Especially when you're running from an atomic explosion.

And when it is your turn to ride, and you're breathless and burning and bushed, it is numbers you check as they board the TCV one by one, not faces.

He had only met Irenson once, in the dark. Irenson had been draped in a weeping girl.

He had not met Randall Mackie at all.

This time he was fresh. They were boarding after a ten-minute rest.

Mackie wasn't in uniform, but his creased, older face with its lacklustre hair was very noticeable beside the younger men around him, now a long drink of water had restored them to their youth.

Irenson was with him, cheeks much more fleshy, hair dyed to please his constituents and his muffins; but Irenson was there, and Irenson had also evaded the arrangements that had been made for him.

'I could have done without this, gentlemen.'

Old soldiers always call people 'gentlemen' when they're displeased with them.

They didn't try to look sheepish. Men of influence brazen things out.

'It looks bad when generals avoid the action.'

'It looks good for ministers to be around this sort of thing.'

'Terence Quinlan will eat me for breakfast,' Matson said.

'We're already late for breakfast,' Irenson grinned. 'If he's feeling hungry, he'd better eat me.'

'I'm giving you this sergeant as bodyguard,' Matson said, indicating a man with three smudges on his sleeve. 'You're in charge, so you'll do exactly as he tells you.' He turned to

General Randall Mackie. 'I know you're a flying man, sir. So I'd like you to command the flying column.'

'You're not a soldier, young man. You're a politician.'

'He's better than that,' Irenson said. 'He ought to sell second-hand cars.'

Even if he'd noticed the delinquent pair, the first time round, it would have been much too late. Barel had already left by the time he'd gathered everyone together.

Matson sent Red Force ahead without him. With a man like Mackie in command, the transport should work. Any difficulties would be expertly rationalised. He kept Irenson back, just the same.

'Dump in twenty miles and double back,' Matson instructed. 'See the men take up all-round defensive positions before you leave them.'

He intended them to live as far as Zoltan.

17.

They never got there.

Mackie was back in twenty minutes. Matson saw the vehicles ahead, and knew there was trouble. If things had gone according to plan, Mackie would have taken well over an hour. The road was good; but running in convoy, even without breakdown, thirty miles in the hour would be more than satisfactory.

The vehicles were empty, just the same.

'There's a road-block,' Mackie said. 'About five miles ahead. I'm afraid I committed you. But in view of the situation at Sifr WaaHid –'

'Better forward than back,' Matson said. 'I agree.'

The Green Howard had come back with the general. 'About a company of them,' he said. 'A lot more than us, anyway. They've got an armoured vehicle and a heavy mortar.

'The armoured vehicle is blocking the actual road. The mortar is already deployed, and surrounded by a little laager of rock. The infantry are either dug in or in good cover – it's a bit hard to tell.'

'We'll pull the rest of these chaps forward, then we'll bluff it through,' Matson said.

'I doubt it,' Mackie advised. 'The armoured vehicle – it's only an itty-bitty tin-side, a kind of scout-car – the damned gunner opened fire on us.'

'Machine-gun,' the Green Howard filled in. 'Not, I think, for effect.'

'It was just a little smoke-signal,' Mackie agreed. 'So we've got ourselves a face-off.'

'Then it's down to the politicians,' Irenson said happily.

'The general's dropped us well,' the Green Howard said. 'We're in another little run-out of rock from the main jebel, just like the one we've left. You know, a kind of outcrop. Plenty of cover.

'The opposition is on the open road, a bit lower down, but in a big scatter of stone.'

'So we've got the commanding position?' Matson said.

'It commands,' Mackie agreed. 'I picked it well for a mere flier. We've got the better ground, all right. Trouble is they've got the water.'

'We'd better get there before we're caught from behind and forced into action here,' Matson said. 'Orders, everybody.'

As the men gathered quickly, Sifr WaaHid was a tower of smoky darkness, as wide as a map-square and heaven high.

18.

All men want to play the ultimate chess game. They yearn to control one side of a battle, however miniscule the combat, no matter how unevenly matched are the forces.

A punch-up is never the same: the stakes are too low. Nor is a one-to-one encounter. The board is over-simple.

A battle sets the cosmic kaleidoscope a-shimmer. Or it does until the bright lights are swallowed up in the fog of war.

Matson had been in a number of shoot-outs. His leg-injury had been acquired in what might just qualify, in the new terminology, as a fire-fight; even though the fire had been on one side and the fighting on the other. He'd been scared like hell after each event, more than scared after he'd taken the rip in the leg. Panic had stepped right out of the future then. It was with him today, a tremor much nearer than memory.

Except that today he was in charge, even of generals and the ministers of queens. He could marshal one side of the board. If he kept faith with the challenge, his fear and himself need not join hands until the actual second of his death.

He placed his men carefully. He set them at due interval, mindful of the mortar. He set them two by two, knowing how a pal inside the weapon-pit helps keep men's courage up. Unfortunately, they dug no weapon-pits. He made each man without a gun hoard the ammunition, pile up stones for throwing, choose a rock-lump for a club. He placed each pair for all-round attack. He deployed them in depth.

He still had his grenades: three fragmentation and two stuns. Barel had left him none. But he distributed what he had to five of the men without arms, at selected points on his front.

19.

Matson kept his vehicles behind the outcrop. The Libyans at the road-block knew he had them: they'd seen Mackie progress in them and halted them with a whiff of grape. Just the same, there was no point in flaunting them under the enemy's battlements.

Matson was beginning to evolve a plan.

Meanwhile he crept about his position and kept his eye on the mortar and the armoured car.

The armoured car's machine-gun was probably a .300 – heavy only insofar as its cooling system would allow it to fire long bursts.

At two thousand yards it would probably be near its extreme range. It would not be accurate against a nominated target, but it would have a pretty adequate and totally lethal beaten zone to fusillade a group of men if they left cover and tried to run for it.

The mortar-tube needed attention from his monocular. The heat made observation difficult, but he was willing to bet it was a standard old-style artillery mortar, such as a British or

American 4.2 inch or 100 millimetre – probably one or other of them.

Forty years ago the Western Desert had been full of discarded mortar-tubes. All that the Libyans ever needed to do was take them in and grease them. Not much can happen to a mortar-tube. It needs a sight to make it happy. Sights weren't so often thrown away, but this one had its sight just the same. It was the one thing his monocular could pick out clearly from the mirage. It squatted against the swirling post of the mortar-tube like a buzzard on a stick. No: like an owl, a malevolent calculus-headed owl.

If this was an English or American mortar they were well within range. In conditions like these, the English 4.2 can manage about 4400 yards.

'Hot bang, but thin compression,' he explained to someone. Gunners know this sort of thing, so do historians. Ordinary soldiers can't give a shit.

The mortar would make dogs' meat of them all on their stone outcrop. It would make it difficult to run across the stony ground to their left and shelter up in the main jebel. They would remain in range for at least two kilometres.

On rock or the ground to their left, it would be very dangerous indeed.

They couldn't run away to their left: the mortar would catch them.

They couldn't try to cross the high dune to their distant right: the machine-gun would cut them off.

They could neither run from their enemy nor outflank him. All they could do was return to Sifr WaaHid, which was still close enough to ignite totally and kill them.

20.

Matson stood beside his little storeman or cook, the one who had shown some character at Sifr WaaHid. 'Stay down,' he advised. 'I'm the commander on his horse. I can be as tall as I like.'

His naked eye showed a jelly-tremble of blobs round the mortar-tube. He put up his peeper to take a look.

Two loading numbers. An NCO in charge: a Number One. Another little group at a distance. The command post? With or without a ranging board.

'Stay down, everyone. They're going to mortar us. You know the form: bloody long time in the air. The shorter the range, the longer the time of flight.' To his little man he said, 'You're a bit out of condition.' Hark who was talking!

'It goes with the job, sir. I do the regimental fry-ups.'

Matson continued to watch the mortar.

'I'm not fat. It's wind mostly. A really good fart'd make a fit man of me.'

The mortar fired five rounds rapid, without rechecking elevation or azimuth.

They hadn't ranged. Their fire for effect was extraordinarily rapid, just tube-time: five rounds in twelve seconds, all without levelling a bubble.

'They'll spread themselves as the base kicks in,' Matson called. 'Time of flight a very long minute.'

He made a present to the cook of his Ingram 10, together with two clips. He had a Browning on his necklace. When the going got tough he'd keep himself calm by cleaning it.

'Wogs,' the cook said to his Ingram 10, 'are here to be flogged. I am here to flog them.'

'They've got themselves into a very business-like formation and posture – for "wogs", I mean.'

'I've always been a football supporter, sir. What I'm volunteering to be here is a man. In football, the other side is always filth. I never believe it. I just act on it.'

The mortar rounds dropped faster than sound, too fast to hear them whistle. Shock waves first, then the barrier bang. Five flashes, five jolts in the spine. Landscape siling through the air in white-hot unfriendly meteors.

A nice little rattle of instant fire-for-effect. What a pity it had all fallen to their right, in the sand. The *hammada* would gobble up mortar rounds like Deep Throat.

'Everyone all right?'

They lay under deep dust, like workers in a flour-mill or plaster saints in the morgue.

For the moment, the Libyans did not repeat.

21.

Action is like this, not so much dull as ordinary. You notice the weather. It is hot. You watch the scenery. It is hot. Unless there's an attack, people keep low. The dust turns into flies and maggots which pasture your neck. You imagine the sea, seventeen-year-old schoolgirls in cerulean underpants. It's not much like Napier at all. Suddenly a dozen guys are dead.

'The lavatory,' Matson called, 'is over there. Remember your friends.'

'I think we should shoot only to kill,' Mackie said. 'I'm being political,' he explained to Irenson. 'But we can do nothing at this range. Not with small arms. So don't let's shoot.'

'Agreed.' Matson nodded.

'Let's only fuel international misunderstanding if they press us really hard!'

'I like that.' Irenson was in a liking mood. 'I mean, if they come rar-raring up here, then we can be expected to protect ourselves.'

'Exactly.'

'Otherwise.'

'Otherwise.'

The agreement was total.

'They can keep their desert,' Matson said.

They were keeping it very well.

22.

'I'm in trouble here, Patrick.'

He had Conrad Irenson all to himself.

'I don't think you're going to die the death, sir.'

'I had young Bettina with me.'

'I gather she's what's expected of you.'

'If Lady Irenson finds out ...'

'Whitehall is being very coy about the passenger lists. The papers can't get into a Forces' Flight the way they would with a normal charter. Besides, Miss Whatsit's in Cyprus by now. I take it your muffins mind their tongues?'

'Where'd you get "muffins"?'

The mortar-tube had never been far from Matson's attention. Like anything else of its size at a distance of two thousand yards, it was there only because he knew about it. His mind saw a loading number stand and muzzle a bomb and crouch again: his eye glimpsed movement in one of those brief miracles of focus it can have once the afternoon turns silver and the mirage has stilled.

'You've got yourself shot at, Conrad. A woman'll forgive a man anything once he gets himself shot at.'

'Yes. Then hate him for forgiving him.'

'I don't know any of these new women, Conrad.'

'I wasn't thinking of Bettina. I was thinking of Lady –'

'Time of flight about sixty seconds.' Matson pulled Irenson down to shelter from his own rhetoric. 'Stony ground here, sir,' he explained. 'They can do nasty things on stony ground.

In fact the mortar landed in soft sand again and dug in before exploding. Mortars don't behave like that, sand or not, but this one did, with an angry wuf like Dragout's dog clearing its throat, before the sound shock leapt out of its hole and really bit them.

'Anyone hurt?' Matson called. 'O.K., sir?' he said to Irenson, before he realised he was behaving as if he was back in the Army, like any prune of a subaltern smoothing up to a visiting dignitary.

Irenson was a dignitary, all right. And his scalp and forehead were bleeding. That made him a hero as well.

'Impacted sand,' Matson said. 'Lady Irenson will love and forgive you, and Bettina will adore you, in some such order.'

The mortar fired again.

'I don't think they mean to hit us.'

'They don't need to,' Irenson said. 'They're frightening us to death.'

'Nothing I've seen suggests the Libyan Army is incompetent enough to take ten ranging rounds.'

'They should have found us by now,' Randall Mackie agreed.

'They've not even applied a correction,' Matson went on. 'I

mean – allowing for the zone of the gun and the slight waning of temperature, that tube must have been laid on the same point of aim all day.'

The mortar fired.

'Just the same,' Irenson said.

'That's why the infantry hates them so much. They have an incredibly long time of flight, especially at short ranges. A heavy mortar-bomb is always up there plus of forty seconds, and you know how long a four- or seven-second grenade fuse seems to take. Forty seconds is a prescription for slow madness.'

'In films, people always talk bold then duck at the last minute,' the warrior cook said. 'Whatever the weapon. I mean they hear the whistle.'

'Only in films. The thing is always travelling faster than sound. Though, in the case of field artillery, not by much. You can duck when it fires, though. With a mortar, once it's got your range, you know its time of flight. So you count. You have someone on the position count aloud. It helps.'

Irenson queried something. Chit-chat helps as well.

'Light,' Matson said. 'You see the flash. The projectile may come faster than sound, but – unless it's ultra high velocity – its trajectory is so curved that straight-line sound still beats it.'

'Thanks,' said Irenson. 'I can be highly knowledgeable in committee as a –'

The bomb interrupted him.

The detonation was tinny and tasted fierce in the teeth.

This time the bomb fell on stone. There must have been a deliberate right switch of some seventy-five yards. They were being squeezed in a lateral bracket, and the air was full of sharp and menacing shards.

A mortar-bomb on stone again turned the sky to glass. Several men bled. They wouldn't enjoy too much more of this.

If the gun-position officer halved his switch, Matson would take immediate and major casualties.

'He's forcing us to attack him,' Irenson said.

'It'll be dark in an hour,' Matson cautioned. He wondered if Irenson was trying to commit suicide. Or not quite that – more leave his fate to chance.

'I shall be bold. Let God strike as He will.' Matson had seen this many times before.

Or Irenson was high on action, tingling with event? He had an attractive personality, but – unlike Mackie – he had no experience of being shot at. It requires patience.

'Our main problem is our lack of WT,' Matson said. 'Barel will have told Cyprus of our overall intention, but without an overfly the world does not know our exact situation.'

'Depends on how good the mortarman's radio-discipline is,' Mackie said.

'There's a point.'

'If he drops any clues, AWACs'll pick it up. Your spy-dishes in the Troodos mountains can probably do even better.'

'We can't sit here all night while they cut us slowly to pieces,' Matson said. 'We've got two options. The chicken one is that we bug out when it is dark, abandon the vehicles and walk a couple of kilometres up into the main jebel. He won't be able to chase us with his mortar in the dark.'

'Water?' Mackie asked.

'We've got about half a pint a man. Tomorrow will be rough.'

'And the day after?'

'We'll be dead of thirst. It's a good death. You dream of iced drinks and pretty women.'

'I don't sleep well,' Mackie said. 'What's your other option?'

'Blue Force walks down the road and skirts round the enemy.'

'Red Force?'

'With those six vehicles we're a mechanised unit. We put a gun in each. We take the handbrakes off and we roll downhill. We frighten the life out of them with our stuns, and if they're slow to frighten we use the real thing. We break through. We pick up our friends. We motor like hell to the coast.'

'Until we hit the next roadblock,' Mackie said. 'Still, I'm getting bored with this one.'

'Right,' said Matson. 'I'll put it to the combat officers, and take their observations. Some of us are going to get hurt, so it needs forking over.'

He had just honed his plan, and called in his orders-group

when his little cook came up and tugged him by the sleeve. Little cooks are like that.

A Libyan officer and two NCOs were coming up under a flag of truce to parley.

He thought parley. He doubted if it was a flag of surrender.

23.

The truce party halted ten yards off. The officer spoke execrable English. In fact, he probably spoke no English at all, but he spoke a message by rote. It had probably taken all day for someone to coach him.

'Mat*son*,' he said. 'You all come no harm. Cap*tain* the Mat*son* will come with me.'

'No way,' Irenson said.

'Mat*son*. You all come no harm. Cap*tain* the Mat*son* will come with me.'

He couldn't refuse and let good men be shot to pieces.

'Mat*son*. You all come no harm. Cap*tain* the –'

'We've heard your poem before,' Matson said. He walked tiredly towards the truce party. He knew he was doing the heroic thing. What a pity he was in no mood to do it heroically. 'They'll eat my balls,' he muttered.

'They'd better have mine too,' Irenson was walking with him. 'I'd be better of without them.'

'Four whitebreads, gentlemen?' Cooks are knowledgeable about such things. 'Not enough for a banquet, but if they're going to eat them, then I'd better be there to ensure they're cooked properly.'

'Silly arse,' Irenson said. 'I'll do the politics here.'

'Do you want yours marinaded or deep-fried, sir?' Never give sauce its tongue.

'I'm grateful,' Matson said to Irenson. He was talking to the cook really. If he was to die the death, he needed the jester with him, like a heroic martyr of old.

'We won't let them feed you any dirt.' Mackie was walking too.

The truce party had come without vehicles. Two thousand yards seemed impossibly far to go.

24.

It was Khadduri. Khadduri looked cleaner, neater and more military than ever. He was sporting more brass than a week ago. He had grown up with rank. He hadn't stayed to fight at Sifr WaaHid. He had driven down the road last night to cut them off.

Matson saluted. He was in combat kit. It was the appropriate courtesy.

Khadduri did not salute him back. He relished the whiteness of his own teeth, the rigour of his tunic, before saying, 'Ah, Captain Matson. You look better as a soldier than dressed as a gentleman, I think.'

'We have a number of points to make, Khadduri.'

'Demands? But there – a man does not change his attitude in a few days. Still less his nature. I am afraid there is no time to consider them. I can hear the helicopter now. Your people will be given water, if that is what you are after. Water and some rations.'

There was indeed a helicopter, racketing fast and low from the north: a four-seater scout, the one with the wasp-bubble nose and meccano fuselage.

It hovered, and made a cautious, half-rotated landing, to let the pilot pick out the snags in the dying light.

'Hurry, Captain Matson. We are taking you to Tripoli. Everything is ready and waiting for you.'

A noose in the souk seemed the most reasonable expectation, with a televised appeal for clemency to the crowd, in a language it couldn't understand, from a ruffian it wouldn't bother itself with. He was a foreigner. He was from the secret world. He had killed on Libyan soil. The Administration at last had someone to blame for Sifr WaaHid.

Matson gestured his agreement, then eyed the helicopter. He couldn't fly the thing, but he might just hijack it. It was time the Empire struck back. The Browning was still bruising his sunburn.

'Your pistol, Captain Matson. There are times when a gun is not permissible. And your knife, please. You see, I have read about you all. I know there is always a blade somewhere.'

Matson unfastened the sheath on his right calf, and wondered how many other ways there were to kill an armed guard in the cramped seats of a helicopter bubble.

Khadduri received his surrender with distaste. The weapons were caked in skin and salt. The knife smelled of work.

Irenson said, 'We insist on accompanying Captain Matson to your capital city. I am a member of Her Majesty's Government.'

Khadduri considered Irenson's dilapidated suiting at some length. 'Indeed? I, too, am who I am. You did not tell me about Her Majesty's friend a week ago, Captain Matson. I could have arranged something for him. Tomorrow, perhaps.'

Mackie knew better than to demand a seat on a helicopter no bigger that a cheese-trolley. Instead, he stated, 'If we can't go, Matson stays. I'm General Randall Mackie of the USAF.'

Khadduri saluted for the first time. 'I am Lieutenant-colonel Khadduri of the Army of the Libyan People's Revolution. You have many more generals than we have colonels, I think. Captain Matson must leave at once. May I be tactful and simply say I insist?'

Matson walked towards the helicopter. Khadduri insisted, so he went. Khadduri insisted proudly. Khadduri insisted in the language of the Polytechnic of the South Bank. He spoke quietly and simply, but he had a couple of hundred men with carbines more or less at his back. The heat was making them impatient, even them.

TWENTY-THREE

1.

'I oughtn't to be here on this island. I ought to be on that carrier where the fleet admiral flies his flag.'

'You're better off here, Cravicz. No-one can sink Cyprus,' Yigael Zefat said.

The Craw moaned in despair.

Troodos came on. The print-out said: *Eagle pancake ... Eagle pancake.*

They were greedy for copies. Paper can wound, of course. Paper has sharp edges. Paper can cut to the bone. Their copies said: *Casualties ... Casualties reported.*

'God,' said the Craw. 'Why did I listen to you?'

'We did not shoot. I am assured we did not use cannon or missiles,' Zefat said. 'We did as our planners offered. We went for a force-down on that first airstrip.'

'It was a widebody. I've just been shown the dimensions of the landing-area. It's not even a ball-park. New it wasn't big enough for a 747 to stand still in. Airstrip! It's a fucking prayer-mat without the tassels. What are they going to do to me?'

'Eat your own oil and malt,' Zefat said. 'Stick to your own decisions. You're a boy in long pants now. The White House told you to air-to-air that speedbird. They like to burn their own people. They wanted a flame-out over some Mediterranean deep hole. So you didn't have time to touch it. The pilot altered for Sinai and went for a let-down.'

'Everyone's hands are clean,' Quinlan was full of interesting phrases.

Chilli, Troodos relayed. Or somebody relayed from somewhere. As always when nothing new was happening, there were enough print-outs for a tickertape storm. *Chilli ... no bonfire.*

'We've got radioactivity, but so far no explosion,' Zefat commented.

'This flimsy says "bonefire",' Pomeroy reported. ' "*No bonefire*". "Bonefire" is better.'

'Still no news of Paddiforce,' Barkworth said glumly. His "Paddiforce" had caught on, like a new pickle.

'Send your Marines down the road for them,' Zefat suggested.

'They're not mobile,' Barkworth said. 'They had extremely precise objectives, with which they were entirely successful.'

'Quaminis was a lovely place to send them,' Zefat agreed. 'It's got a beautiful name.'

'It's been a good day for Marines,' the Craw said drily. 'Marines have done exactly as they've been told, and they've achieved absolutely nothing. All I can say is the people in this room must have told them wrong. I certainly told them wrong.'

'The truth is,' Barkworth said wretchedly, 'the truth is ours have already been withdrawn.'

'I arranged it with the Libyans,' Pomeroy said grandly. 'The Libyans were very helpful and said it would be very helpful if we were very helpful. So we were.'

'That's a lot of very helpful,' Zefat said.

'You've got men out there in the desert,' the Craw scolded.

'I've got men all over the place. I've got men not fifty miles from Paddiforce working in oil. Two thousand men.'

'Slippery Brits.'

'It's American oil they're working on, Admiral. Old Mad Eyes nationalised it, of course. But he pays a bigger royalty than you ever got profit. He can't afford to let go of your *slippery* American technology.'

Quinlan had heard enough of all this. People were speaking as if he wasn't the man around here. He said, 'Marcus did the deal because I told him to do the deal. The brigadier pulled back his Marines because I told him to pull them back.' He smirked like the child whose mother always stocks her larder with a second pot of raspberry jam.

NATO's AWACs had news or the Fleet's AWACs had news

or the Fleet had news or Troodos had more news. There was a lot of news just now.

Eagle pancake, the news said. *Chilli ... casualties indicated ... casualties reported ... Chilli but no bonfire*.

'There's members of a House of Representatives Fact-finding Committee on that flight,' the Craw said. 'I haven't thought to tell anyone, but there it is.'

'And that's the paradox.' Pomeroy agreed. 'They've got the facts, but we've got the news.'

Casualties ...

2.

AWACs gave them more. AWACs was bringing the essential details now. As Pomeroy said often, it is surprising how essential details are.

Eagle Pancake ... three zero ... zero three ... zero two North ... zero three two ... three two ... zero zero East

'Jesus – who wants to know?'

'Your signaller mislaid a preliminary zero,' Pomeroy told Fisher. 'He should be pulled up about that.'

'They used the other landing strip,' Zefat said suddenly. 'The one near Mitla. It's much bigger. Your widebody pancaked on the big strip.'

'It still overshot.'

Pancake, Troodos said. *Eagle pancake ... survivors ...*

They waited in silence for half an hour.

'Like the inmates of the Grand Seraglio,' Pomeroy whispered, 'waiting for the Sultan to grow tired of his racing camels.'

Fossit hoped he wasn't whispering to him.

Lorna Benvenista came downstairs. She was thirty-six years old, and they paid her more than anyone else in the room, including the U.S. admiral. She was very confident of her function.

She located and positioned and switched on a relay-screen.

No-one had seen the Libyan Queen for days, or for hours that seemed like days. He was extraordinarily close to Cyprus, and popular with the people who lived on the island. He was near and clear and he came in exactly the right number of lines.

To these people who did not live on the island, Troodos relayed an excellent picture with a depth of focus that made him appear almost three-dimensional. It also made him pink. He did not appear to be African or Arabic or even lightly suntanned. He was more like a cuddly doll in its polythene box.

Lorna Benvenista had switched him on, so they watched him.

He was wearing a brand-new uniform from the property cupboard, and there was obviously some deep significance in the fact that he had awarded himself row upon row of U.S. gallantry ribbons in a cluster so huge it would have put Audie Murphy to shame.

He was also the only man living to have won three Victoria Crosses. He wore these honours not as a single ribbon with double bar but as three separate blocks of purple, out of respect for his audience and reverence towards himself. He was whining in Arabic, but to a background of ethereal music. The absence of military sound was perhaps meant to suggest some more elevated conquest among the Gods and the angels, and the spirits in their spheres.

'Dreadful,' Pomeroy said. 'Like a West Coast poetry recital.' He began to translate for them. He began just in time.

A large raiding party of irregulars, led by disaffected members of the ancient ruling cast of Tibesti and other clan chiefs from among the Tibbu, had crossed over from Chad and penetrated deeply into the Libyan heartland. Its advance had been so ruthlessly abrupt that it ranged as far north as the valuable petro-chemical exploration centre at Sifr WaaHid, which it had wantonly destroyed. At this point it had been routed by forces stationed nearby under the command of Lieutenant-colonel, now Brigadier Yunis Mohammed Khadduri. Brigadier Khadduri's units had sustained only minor casualties. Among the wounded, special mention must be made of Company Sergeant-major now Regimental Sergeant-major Abu Modfai, who had been resolute in defence and exemplary in attack before falling at the head of his men, weakened by loss of blood and the cumulative toll of his numerous injuries. These and many other names who eluded Pomeroy's boggling inattention were to be awarded the Gold and Silver Star of the Libyan People's Army and the Grand Medallion of the Revolution at the appropriate grade, et cetera, et cetera.

'The very crooks who were holding your people and ours, General.'

Only last evening, Regimental Sergeant-major Modfai had led a successful storming party to rescue the passengers of two aircraft illegally hijacked to Sifr WaaHid. In this, he had been helped by certain military personnel on the British airliner. The operation had been planned in secret between Brigadier Yunis Khadduri and the officer in charge of the British hostages. The hijackers were all dead. They had turned out to be a heavily-armed group of international gangsters posing as pan-Arab sympathisers and friends of the Libyan Revolution. There were no casualties among the hostages. The operation would be seen as a monument to the indomitable spirit of the undefeated Libyan People's Army and a symbol of the cooperation that exists between friendly nations.

'I'm afraid your lot don't get a mention, General. Then you wouldn't expect otherwise.'

'I've had Barel's report.'

'We still don't know about Matson, and Paddiforce, Conrad Irenson or the admiral's General Mackie,' Fisher said.

'We're getting the scenario,' Pomeroy said, still listening. 'I really do expect quite a big quid for our quo with old Barkworth's dozy Marines.' He continued to watch the screen. 'Oh! what a wily lot! The commander of the invasion force has just been executed by firing-squad. He was a traitor to the Libyan People and their Revolution. Ahmed Ali Khalil, sometimes known as Dragout, formerly of Tibesti and a major in the pre-Revolutionary Army of Libya. So I'm afraid your Captain Barel and our Captain Matson can't have done the job on him. A bit of a fibber, your Shlomo Barel, according to the Old Queen here.

'Ah, the medal-ribbons are at last explained. We now know why he's wearing all that American tat on his tit. It's tit for tat, Admiral. The Marines Lamberty and Vaugn and about forty-seven of their bleeding sergeants are to be awarded the

Gold and Silver Star, did you know that? It seemed you planned the rescue at Az Zawiyah with old Mad Eyes himself. The Libyans were responsible for the finesse, the flair and the bright flame of courage. Your lads from special forces were able to supply certain items of equipment and the necessary expertise. Freely translated, that means Lamberty in a jeep.'

'The State Department won't let our men accept those silly honours,' the Craw said.

'They have just accepted them.' Once more Quinlan was the little boy with the jam. 'Special instructions from the White House.' He liked to rub the salt in. He turned from the phone. Admirals and generals only do things. Politicians know. They know things that admirals and generals never know, and he wanted them to know it.

'At last we get to Matson. They've mentioned Paddiforce at last. It'll be another Barkworth cock-up, I fear.'

3.

'Only you lesser mortals could be honoured,' Marcus Pomeroy said later. 'It really wasn't on for admirals from the Americas or for generals from among the Untouchables. As for those of us who did the actual work ...' His yawn was more graceless than he intended.

'Right up to the last I thought they were going to hang me,' Matson confessed. 'Khadduri always was. Dragout always was. It was there written large in the cards. I'm a spook, after all. I'm also a disgusting thug. I've broken necks on their sovereign soil.

'I even came back for more. I was the lonely captured particle of an Israeli Snatch Squad.'

'Well, I patched matters up.'

'Nobody translated. Once I'd left Khadurri, nobody could translate. They stuck me in a robe, just like they do the condemned. They propped me up on a platform with red all over it. I couldn't spot the gallows, but it could easily have been hidden up there in the canopy, or they could have dangled me from the scaffolding. Then these two grinnies came up to me, and everyone cheered. I thought it was the

High Executioner and his mate. One was carrying the noose and the other the blindfold. They both got stuck round my ears.'

He fingered his woven silk sash and tassel, barred in Libyan green; then adjusted his ridiculous gold lanyard. He had to join some American Marines for a photocall. They all looked like twits, and they all felt equally sheepish; but certain people in London and Washington had insisted, and there was an end to it.

Pomeroy waited till Matson had gone, then said, 'The Libyans aren't allowed to honour me. I mean, Quinny won't hear of it. But they've promised me a damned nice holiday. All those Roman stones they've got over there. I shan't go, though. You can't get a decent drink. Only figs and marrow-juice and sherbert. No good for me. You can have my ticket, if you like.'

'What's the final count on that 747?'

'Six dead, I think. Quite a lot burned. You know how it is. Some more are going to die. Some of the rest are going to grow fat and awful and wish they had.'

'Where are they?'

'Tel Aviv, for the minute. They've got a good burns unit.'

'So what about Holofernes? Did we call it right?'

'I certainly never called it wrong. At the simple least, we couldn't allow that Jumbo to let down at any international airport with all that stuff on board, whether it was rigged to blow, or had the potential or not. We'll know a lot better when Barel arrives to give his bit of the report.'

Fossit lacked Pomeroy's stamina for all this. He didn't have the stomach, and he couldn't stand the fuel. He stood up and walked outside, to stretch and breathe and get rid of forty-eight hours of prattle-laden fatigue.

It was much too hot for him in Cyprus. He preferred Surbiton. In Surbiton he got more sleep.

4.

'I try to see things in the round, Patrick. God knows I get no Libyan medals for it, but I try to see things as they are.'

'So you went to Sinai?'

'It was the general's idea that we pancaked that widebody at Mitla. An Israeli plan going less than well, so I had to take a look. They were still picking up the bits. It was worse than a tank battle. I've seen tanks brew, and I've seen what comes out of them. This was worse.'

'It was done the only way, Shlomo. The best way. There are survivors. There was radioactive garbage in the Greek airliner at Az Zawiyah. Radioactive junk in the hole I made in the sea. Some pretty sophisticated material had been assembled at Sifr WaaHid. There were tramlines in that Jumbo's belly. It all pointed towards a simple trigger device, as your Goradish fellow predicted.'

'There were tramlines in this one. They were obviously after something more definite in the case of the two widebodies. More definite or more persuasive. But the fact is it didn't trigger.'

'Perhaps it wouldn't on an ordinary deceleration, even a crash-landing. I gather it skidded over the surface?'

'For about three kilometres.'

'There was a surrogate pilot. One of the hijackers. Perhaps he was meant to kamikaze it in at Tel Aviv, or Ben Gurion or Jerusalem.'

'Or perhaps someone had to go down into the cargo and release a coupling. Or even set a charge to blow one truck against the other. Thank you, Matson. You'll make us all feel better. It's a pity we can't ask anyone. But they're all dead. The flight crew are dead because the nacelle eggshelled. The hijackers are dead, because hijackers always die in a crash. They're the ones on their feet. The ones who fetch up against the bulkheads. We may get something if Uncle Sam lets us debrief some passengers. Or if the Pentagon tells us what it uncovers with its own debriefing.'

He yawned. The Red House boasted a kind of conservatory that ran along its north wall. A row of flowering trees tussled against its roof; many panes of glass had been removed to let the high branches poke through, but it was still hot here, hot and clammy from the water hoses.

Matson yawned too. This was the only private place they could find. He rather liked the steam after the impossible dryness of the desert. He shared some more of the celebration wine. It wasn't local, or even Israeli. It was an expensive claret flown out specially from the UK, and it was awful.

Shlomo Barel was saying, 'Fissionable material everywhere when that 747 ripped its guts out – a whole map-square of Sinai buzzing with bequerels. Man'll have to keep off for generations, and so will lizards and grasshoppers. But a bomb? An A-bomb? I wish someone could say. I think it's all part of the same bluff.'

'So what's your plot?'

'We were meant to bring one another's flights down. That's the first component. Two thousand dead. A modest outlay of *actual* funds, and millions of embarrassing international repercussions. With a brain like this Dragout-cum-Khalil's, who can tell? But he must have arranged to let you out, and letting out someone like you could only have had the one purpose.'

'I still believe Nuseibeh thought he was telling the truth.'

'So do I. But Nuseibeh was a double, and doubles are often lied to.'

'You said "actual outlay" or "actual funds" – something like that.'

'We know there are some real funds somewhere, huge ones. The Palestinian movement has some excellent bankers worldwide, and they've been shifting millions of late. That's why we took Holofernes so seriously. We were bound to. I think we were wrong. I think your Pomeroy was wrong. I think this Cravicz, who is admirable, was too straightforward for words. It needs someone slippery like your Quinlan. And the fact that he couldn't operate should have given us thinking men our clue. The crooks never got to talk, let alone negotiate.'

The wine was losing Matson.

'We thought Dragout was either going to bomb us, or bluff us. There was excellent evidence that he was bluffing. The best evidence of all was the fact that he let us find him out. He fed us all of the components of Holofernes bit by bit, like a jigsaw. It was no longer a military operation, nor the work of a fanatic. It bore all of the hallmarks of the crook. But if a crook was letting us know, there could only be one motive:

extortion. There was no extortion. He let us know because he believed we would be forced to take those airliners out of circulation. His best hope was that we shoot them down. He wanted us to destroy the evidence or disperse it: an aircraft here, say, and an intriguing stock of radioactive material left out there in the desert, where no-one could examine it properly, and where it would tick with roentgens and set buzzing the rumours. He wanted to deceive us, but he was never bluffing us. He was bluffing his paymasters into thinking he had spent their loot as they wished it. A thousand Westerners dead in a shoot-down, five hundred Israelis especially, might be an acceptable though reduced bottom line.' The wine had got to Barel now. He sweated against Matson and shouted, 'His bastard employers were meant to believe in the bombs. We were meant to find out just enough to shoot them down.'

'And Mad Eyes – sorry, I mean the Libyans?'

'They're always good lads when it comes to a hijack of Western aircraft. They would be especially splendid to him if he bagged one of ours, and he did. He told them in advance, and they liked him for it. He was one of their intelligence people, and here he was bringing them some of the best 'Eye' they'd ever had.'

Matson had a drunken desire to strip off and dance naked along one of the streaming hosepipes. Somehow, though, because of this man Dragout, he fancied he would never go naked again.

Barel had no such inhibitions. When he was walking the water wearing only his shoes and his socks and his identity disc, he turned and yelled, 'I wish we'd had the time to search that house. I wonder where he stored all the loot?'

The wine was gone. Matson did not answer. Barel climbed into the leaky twinings of a giant magnolia tree and tried to fall asleep.

Matson had an image of bars of gold, a criss-cross of gold forming the basis of a bed built on bullion, the boy's blood jumping across it, then the giant's leaping, too, all on the fabric of that selfsame bed. He remembered the sound the two bloods made, scampering on the damask. It was like lizards on a cardboard box. No: it was heavier than lizards. It was like rats.

He could remember the sound. Perhaps the dripping hosepipes helped him. The sound stayed clear, but his memory lost the picture. The brain pretends it can recall the colour of blood; but the colour of gold is always a fiction. An oldfashioned pirate might have noticed the loot. So might a Tartar horseman. Barel and Matson were warriors from a different time.

Barel was a conviction assassin. He had no nose for gold. Matson had gone for revenge. He wanted Dragout's balls, not his bullion. And if he could draw the Queen's shilling for having such sweet recompense? Well, that was what kept him better than the animals. That was what made him pure.

5.

When they shook hands they were sober.

Matson said, 'You were right about Levett. I wish it were otherwise.'

'Levett? Remind me.'

'And Collinson and the other chum. The desert swallowed them up. The Libyans let us look for them. They let us stage a chopper via Zoltan. Not a sign.'

'Your searchers went to the wrong place.'

'They found my little mascot.' He showed him Sally Shirmin's badge, and explained its significance.

Barel shuddered. 'We're light years apart, Matson. We should live on separate planets, you and I.'

TWENTY-FOUR

1.

Contagious death. You toy with it. It bites you. It poisons the bloodstream with loneliness.

His flat was sour with gun-oil, and lard, and pickled newsprint.

He dropped his duffel-bag and opened his phonebook. He didn't loot. Unlike Barel he felt no compulsion to wear his enemy about his person. He was recovered enough to suffer another need.

He phoned Hampstead.

'You didn't come back.'

'I had to go away.'

'Night's a cruel time.'

'Cruel for me, too. I had to go to –'

'It's in the papers,' she said. 'I can read. My eyes and ears are good too. I know how to operate TV. And my little bedside radio.'

He remembered her bed. Not her bedside. Not her radio.

'I wondered –'

'It won't be possible. I'm just off on holiday.'

'Where?'

'My vacations are a part of my privacy,' Dr Tesserer said. 'I must insist on keeping my life that way.'

'When will you be coming back?'

'Can you remember your case number – I gave you a personal file-code. Do you remember?'

'Not really. I think I'm recovered.'

'I can only see you again if your departmental head –'

2.

Dixon drove him there. Dixon wished he hadn't told him, but he had. He owed Matson for her. He owed Matson for all sorts of things.

Poor old Paddy. He was off his bloody loaf.

Matson watched her come through the door. She looked dejected. She had been through a gritty time. She was lucky to be alive.

He pushed through the little knot of onlookers and placed himself in front of her.

She was still attractive in spite of it all. He had desired the other sister, but she was the sexy one.

She had to listen to him. He represented authority. He had the power to do all this to her.

Unfinished business, the psychologists call it.

'Can I give you dinner sometime?'

'Why would that be?'

'There are some things to say. I was going to give your sister dinner.'

'Did she say yes? I expect that was because you hadn't pulled her tits for her.' She looked at him and beyond him, neither meeting nor refusing his eye. 'I'm not under arrest, am I?'

'No, you're –'

'I'm not wanted for anything? See that bloke over there? He's my solicitor.' She went round Matson and then she was walking.

He did not turn at once. That would be weakness, with the other man watching. With Dixon watching. When he did turn, she wasn't with the other man. He wasn't her solicitor. She was walking alone.

TRIPLE

Ken Follett

'Sizzling narrative . . . One of the liveliest thrillers of the year.' *Time Magazine*

A Jew, a Russian and an Egyptian meet briefly in Oxford in 1947. Twenty years later a shipment of uranium disappears between Antwerp and Genoa. And the man who returned from death takes on a mission that will lead him back into its gaping jaws.

'Ingenious, sentimental, violent . . . ' *New York Times*

'Highly imaginative . . . fascinating.' *Washington Post*

'A compulsive page turner.' *Associated Press*

FUTURA PUBLICATIONS
FICTION/THRILLER
0 7088 1804 8

A shattering, electric thriller debut

EXIT WOUNDS

Michael Baldwin

The strike. Charles Kay: eminent expert on snakes, a respected man with a fully documented past and an attractive daughter, Ginevra. Mossad snatched Kay and killed the girl – but they hit the *wrong* girl and kicked over a diplomatic hornet's nest.

The venom. In Tel Aviv Kay was charged as Ernst Halder, a major in the SS and a war criminal. Mossad claimed him as their due.

The kill. Patrick Matson, British counter-intelligence ace, forced Mossad's hand. And they in turn pushed Kay too far – for nothing. He was just a tired old man. Dead.

The cover-up. Perhaps Kay was Halder. Perhaps not. Who really cared? It was time to close the file. It was time to call off Matson. But who could stop him? Matson had the scent of blood . . .

EXIT WOUNDS – a viperous web of mistaken and multiple identities in the cynical world of national expedience.

FUTURA PUBLICATIONS
FICTION
0 7088 3782 4

BLOOD TEST

Jonathan Kellerman

'A relentlessly intelligent thriller' *Newsweek*

'Family disputes are a cop's most dreaded calls, for they are the most likely to erupt in violence that is murderously sudden, stunningly intense . . .'

Little Woody Swope was gravely ill. Treatment was possible, if painful. But his parents, members of a bizarre sect called the Touchers, threatened to take him out of hospital.

Then Woody was gone. So were the Swopes, leaving their motel suite heavily bloodstained.

Enter Alex Delaware, child psychologist, young, burned out and semi-retired. He and his LA cop friend Milo find a heap of suspects – an ageing ex-hippy doctor; a back-country police chief; a male stripper; even Nona, Woody's sister, a flame-haired Lolita with hate in her eyes and larceny in her soul.

But the truth was more bizarre than even Alex could have imagined . . .

BLOOD TEST

the new Alex Delaware thriller, brilliant successor to WHEN THE BOUGH BREAKS – 'an ingenious and horrifying first novel' *Sunday Times*

FUTURA PUBLICATIONS
FICTION
0 7088 3032 3

WHEN THE BOUGH BREAKS

Jonathan Kellerman

It began with a double murder: particularly vicious, particularly gruesome. There was only one witness: but little Melody Quinn can't or won't say a word. Which is where child psychologist Alex Delaware comes in – and takes the first step into a maelstrom of atrocities . . .

WHEN THE BOUGH BREAKS

A stunning debut, a breathtaking novel of the sewer of perversion and corruption lying below the glittering surface of California cool.
'A gruesome psychodrama of depravity and organised vice . . . assured skill and horripilating effect' *Observer*

'Exceptionally exciting' *New York Times*

Winner of the EDGAR AWARD

FUTURA PUBLICATIONS
FICTION/THRILLER
0 7088 3141 9

OVER THE EDGE EDGE

Jonathan Kellerman

A deeply troubled young man . . . a series of vicious crimes . . . and a trail that leads to shattering revelations and murderous passions . . .

OVER THE EDGE

The case against Jamey Cadmus is open and shut. Found clutching a bloody knife at the scene of a horrifying double murder, he's prime suspect in a series of killings that have rocked Los Angeles. Even his lawyer won't do more than plead diminished responsibility. No-one – not the police, not the family, not the lawyers – wants Alex Delaware lifting up stones. But under those stones lies something unspeakable . . .

'OVER THE EDGE is a compulsive page-turner . . . filled with insight, charged with suspense, and laced with just enough humour to make the whole thing sparkle. This one is simply too good too miss' *Stephen King*

'As sleek and high-powered a performance as its predecessors' *New York Times*

'The first two Alex Delaware books were very good indeed. This one, more complexly plotted, more richly psychological . . . is the best yet' *Publishers Weekly*

'He writes with the sharpness of Chandler and the compassion of Macdonald' *Sunday Tribune*

'Impales the reader . . . worth a four-star rating' *Guardian*

Don't miss from Futura
WHEN THE BOUGH BREAKS
BLOOD TEST

FUTURA PUBLICATIONS
FICTION
0 7088 3585 6

THE BUTCHER'S THEATRE

Jonathan Kellerman

'Kellerman is a thrilling writer . . . brilliant' *Independent*

In the late 60s Jerusalem was dubbed 'The Butcher's Theatre'. Now, twenty years later, the City of Peace is a butcher's theatre once more . . .

The first victim is a young Arab girl. Her obscenely mutilated corpse is found in some bushes on the slopes of Mount Scopus. She has been drugged with heroin, carved up with chilling care and skill. The mixture of calculation and frenzy in the killing sends a shockwave through a society where warfare and terrorism are everyday facts of life – but where sex murders and serial killers are virtually unknown.

Chief Inspector Daniel Shalom Sharavi, himself a Yemenite Jew, takes charge of the case, bringing together a team as exotic and disparate as Jerusalem itself. Methodically and desperately slowly, they uncover a complex trail that leads to a point where private psychosis and public politics threaten to explode. The question is: will they be too late?

THE BUTCHER'S THEATRE

Shattering . . . shocking . . . Kellerman at his spellbinding best.

FUTURA PUBLICATIONS
FICTION/THRILLER
0 7088 4231 3

EYE OF THE NEEDLE

Ken Follett

First published in the UK as STORM ISLAND

'An absolutely terrific thriller, so pulse pounding, so ingenious in its plotting and so frighteningly realistic that you simply cannot stop reading'
Barbara Bannon, Publishers Weekly

His weapon is the stiletto, his codename: THE NEEDLE. He is Henry Faber, coldly professional, a killer, Germany's most feared deep-cover agent in Britain. His task: to get the true facts about the Allies' invasion plans to Germany. His master: The Führer – in person.

EYE OF THE NEEDLE: a dazzling and totally gripping adventure thriller of World War II, that ranks with THE EAGLE HAS LANDED.

'Top notch thriller, as gripping and persuasive as THE DAY OF THE JACKAL'
Ira Levin, author of THE BOYS FROM BRAZIL

'A tense, marvellously detailed suspense thriller built on a solid foundation of fact' *Sunday Times*

FUTURA PUBLICATIONS
FICTION/THRILLER
0 7088 1470 0